WORLD WAR 3.1

A NOVEL OF THE AXIS OF TIME

THE AXIS OF TIME

JOHN BIRMINGHAM

AUTHOR'S NOTE

World War 3.1

This book continues the series that began with *Weapons of Choice*. Including novellas and ebooks, it is the seventh title in that series, but you can safely start here if you want. Just take a deep breath, close your eyes, and imagine a multinational battle group from the twenty-first century, falling backasswards through a wormhole and popping out into the Pacific on the eve of the Battle of Midway. That would mess up your high school history texts, wouldn't it?

Or, you could just go read *Weapons of Choice*. There's certain to be a dog-eared copy lying around your local library. Either way, I wrote this book, and the two to follow, because I loved this series, the premise and the characters. It was written at the turn of the century when things were, let's face it, simpler. Returning to this alternate history has been a little like escaping a timeline that went badly wrong. I suspect that's why so many readers have asked me to get back to it for so many years.

Well, here it is my friends. Come and get it.

PROLOGUE

On 15 January 2021, the Twentieth Century turned inside out. At 9:42 AM that day, a large multinational force lay at anchor ten nautical miles off the coast of Timor Leste at the southern end of the Malay Archipelago. Under Admiral Phillip Kolhammer's command, the fleet prepared to move north and challenge an invading Chinese armada. By 9:42:31 AM, the force gathered around Kolhammer's flagship, the super-carrier the USS *Hillary Clinton*, was gone, pulled through a wormhole created by Professor Manning Pope.

The professor did not survive his creation.

The ships and one submarine that survived the Transition, as it became known, arrived mainly in the South Pacific in early June 1942 - on the eve of the Battle of Midway. Some, however, fell into the hands of the Axis powers, gifting the dictators Stalin and Hitler nearly eighty years of technological and scientific progress, but also the foreknowledge of their demise.

The history of the Second World War was suddenly and massively disrupted. The history of that disruption was first told in *Weapons of Choice - the Axis of Time.*

At the war's end, after nuclear attacks on Japan and Germany, the world again divided into monolithic blocs, East and West.

In 1954, after a decade of fragile peace, the Soviet Union launched a pre-emptive strike on NATO, using orbital bombardment technologies, based on research by a German scientist turned peace campaigner, Professor Ernst Bremmer. The definitive history of the war's genesis can be found in *Stalin's Hammer*.

This is the story of what happened next.

1

The email arrived on the President's old iPhone early on the evening of 21 June 1955. A pleasant chime sounded to alert Dwight Eisenhower that he had received an encrypted personal message from his Vice President, Phillip Kolhammer, who was at that moment somewhere in Paris. Eisenhower did not hear the chime or even notice the phone buzzing in his pocket. He was busy hurrying down a corridor in the West Wing, all but running towards the South Lawn to where Marine One thundered in the warm summer twilight, waiting to evacuate him. A phalanx of Secret Service men surrounded him, almost carrying the former general forward in their grip, so insistent were they that he move at their speed.

And they were moving quickly.

Everything was moving quickly.

America's thirty-fourth president had been enjoying a light supper with the golfers Sam Snead and Peter Thomson. The Australian, Thomson, had been in fine form, regaling them all with the story of his win at the Open, when Bobby Cutler, Eisenhower's National Security Advisor, had barged into the Old Family Dining Room, closely followed by a flying wedge of Secret Service agents. One of the agents pulled away from the leading group to usher Snead and Thomson away through a side door. He was courteous but insistent. The team leader of Eisenhower's security detail, a blocky, shaven-headed Hoosier called Mike Curtain, took Eisenhower's coffee cup right out of his hand, uttered a softly spoken apology, and lifted the president by the elbow from the chair in which he'd been seated, enjoying Thomson's gentle teasing of Snead's double bogey on the final nine at St Andrew's.

"My apologies, Mister President, but we have to go. The First Lady is en route and will meet us at the checkpoint. If you wouldn't mind, sir?"

It hardly mattered whether Eisenhower minded. He was already moving across the room, propelled by the half dozen hard-faced men with headsets and handguns who surrounded him. The President tried to apologise to Snead and Thomson, but this human shield wall already enclosed him, and the last he saw of his guests were a couple of very confused-looking golfers; Snead still holding a half-eaten cookie, as they were bustled out of the dining room under the stern gaze of John Quincy Adams' portrait.

"Mister President, I'm sorry, sir," Bobby Cutler said, as he jogged to keep up with the bodyguards, "The Soviets have launched a massive attack out of the frontline Eastern Bloc states. Red Army tanks and mechanised infantry are pouring into Western Europe. They used some sort of space-based weapon to destroy most of our forces in Germany."

"Wait, they used atomics?" Eisenhower asked, finding his feet, and increasing his pace to keep up. He looked around for Captain Chandler, the USAF officer who carried the Football.

Chandler, a young black man, was keeping up with the detail. He looked like he could run for hours.

"No sir," Cutler said as they turned a corner. "Something almost as powerful, but no atomic or hydrogen warheads. First intelligence suggests satellite-launched kinetic impactors, sir. Very hard to defend against once they're launched. And very powerful, very destructive when they hit. Like a nuke, but without the radiation and fallout."

They moved quickly through the White House, which had been quiet as the long summer day wound down into a pleasant evening.

Now it heaved with frenetic activity. Staffers, military personnel, and people he'd never seen before hurried and hastened and sometimes even ran through the hallways, but Ike, the former military commander, could see that it was purposeful, directed chaos. They all had jobs to do and no time to waste in dawdling. And they all deferred to the dark arrowhead of Secret Service agents flying down the hallways with the president at its centre.

"Where are the Joint Chiefs?" Eisenhower asked, his casual demeanour sloughing away in the rush of the moment.

"Admiral Tisevich and General Taylor are en route from the Pentagon, sir. General Twining was in California for the F-15 ceremony with Secretary Otton. They are inflight to Colorado. Secretary Dulles is in London, of course."

"Probably the best place for him," Ike puffed. It had been many years since he'd been required to pass the Army physical, and nine holes of golf every couple of weekends had not kept him in martial trim. Even so, they were running now, actually running out of a pair of French doors held wide open by two marines and across the South Lawn to where the helicopter waited, ready for take-off. Ike felt the whipping blast of the rotor wash at the same time as Agent Curtain firmly placed a calloused hand on his neck to keep him moving forward but bent over. All nine men advanced in such a fashion, at a run, under the blades of the big, augmented Davidson Aerospace chopper.

There was no ceremony to the departure. Just haste and confusion.

Where did they say Mamie was?

What about John and Barbara and their kids?

The Cabinet?

Congress?

Ike knew better than to slow everything down by asking. There were emergency protocols. Procedures for all this. There were no missiles inbound. He was sure of that. It was the first thing Bobby Cutler would have told him, and they'd be headed deep underground, not up into the sky where hundreds of Russian nukes would surely find them.

The Russians and their allies in the far east had not enjoyed the free world's giant leaps in computers and electronic technology since the war's end, but as old Joe Stalin liked to say, quantity still had a quality all its own. If your crude but powerful ICBM was likely to miss a whole city by fifty miles or get plucked out of the stratosphere by satellite beam weapons or an anti-missile rocket...why not shoot off a hundred of them? Some were bound to get through.

Agent Curtain almost lifted the president up the folding metal staircase into the main passenger cabin of the DA2 Condor before strapping Ike into his seat. The urge to slap his hands away and tell him to stop fussing was strong, but Ike resisted. Instead, he spoke around the agent and over the uproar of the big, twin-engine bird.

"Bobby, tell me about this space weapon they used. What do we know?"

"Not much, sir," Cutler shouted back as he strapped himself in, and the security detail took to their seats. The main door slid shut automatically, cutting the outside noise dramatically. "The Brits sent Langley and DoD a big data packet. They'd had their own people on it, they say."

"They could have said earlier," Ike groused.

Cutler gestured helplessly.

"They raised it with our station chief in Rome a few weeks back, but this took them by surprise too."

Eisenhower waved away the excuse.

"It's too late for what-ifs, Bobby. Just tell me what I'm dealing with."

The National Security Advisor took a deep breath and started his briefing as the pilot fed power into the blades and the big, heavy-lift transporter climbed free of the South Lawn. Ike felt himself pushed into the plush leather cushion of his seat. Cutler took a piece of paper from his suit pocket, scanning the closely printed blocks of text on it.

"The communist first strike punched a hole in NATO ground and air defenses in the Frankfurt Main Fulda Wurzburg Triangle," he said. "US 5th army has been annihilated. Pentagon estimates that it has been reduced to well below ten percent of its combat strength, with just a few survivors, all of them rear echelon, scrambling to retreat to the Rhine. Estimated casualties are 240 000 US troops, 300 000 dependents and half a million German civilians."

He paused to let the carnage sink in.

"Good God," Ike said quietly. So quietly, nobody heard him over the noise of the flight.

The chopper banked over sharply, and he braced in his seat.

The Washington Monument shone with spectral beauty in the window to his left.

Cutler resumed.

"The Eastern Bloc air forces have scrambled. Squadrons from the Polish, East German, Czech, and Hungarian air forces swept in immediately after the strike. Red Army Air Force wings staging out of forward bases in the east followed them five minutes later."

"Did we get anything up?"

Cutler nodded, but it was a grim expression.

"NATO quick-reaction forces scrambled just over 50 aircraft, including two AWACS, to intercept. They shot down 209 Pact fighters and fighter bombers. Confirmed kills by hard data. But Moscow still has a 5:1 advantage in aircraft."

President Eisenhower felt dizzy. His vision was blurring at the edges, and he wasn't sure it was from the quick take-off.

"And on the ground?" he asked.

Cutler consulted his notes again, but he never answered.

He died while he was reading the brief.

Three Type 93 surface-to-air missiles, two of them shoulder-launched from the roof of a hotel on 15th Street and the third from the back of a flat-bed pick up on Constitution Avenue, streaked up through the deepening twilight, homing on in the Condor's image profile, written to the silicon in their image-seeking guidance chips. The Type 93, an uptime Japanese-designed weapons system, ignored the Condor's automated defences, cutting through chaff, smoke, and electronic countermeasures. All three warheads intercepted the president's flight.

One failed to detonate.

Two did not.

THE ORBITAL STATIONS, like much Soviet technology, even a decade after the Transition, were bulky and crude. The Russkiy Mir constellation of satellites had long worried Western defence planners. The ultimate high ground weapon, Curtis Le May called them, demanding they be shot down before they could be armed.

Nyet, the Kremlin replied. They were merely the first fruits of a peaceful program to carry socialism to the stars. Nothing more than scaffolding in space to support the fraternal effort of the world's workers to claim their rightful place on the high frontier before Western oligarchs and warlords could annex it.

USAF spy satellites kept a close watch on the expanding orbital installations. Still, although the scaffolding grew more extensive and more complex, the Soviet space agency Roskosmos never built out the structures with crew quarters or engineering spaces.

As Dwight Eisenhower sat down to drinks with his two guests, the reason why revealed itself.

The stations were not designed to carry weapons.

The stations were the weapons.

At a signal from the Red Army Rocket Force Headquarters in Baikanoor, unfinished sections of the Soviet platforms explosively detached themselves from the main structures and accelerated down Earth's gravity well. Dozens of titanium girders, each about the size of a terrestrial telegraph pole, picked up speed and heat as they speared down through the atmosphere. The orbital math was as complex as the mechanics were simple. More than a hundred white hot spears of superdense metal shot down through the atmosphere to simulate, in a very modest way, the Late Heavy Bombardment of the planet nearly four billion years earlier—at least across a twenty-two-mile-wide swathe of West Germany that was home to the US Fifth Army, the sword and shield of NATO.

The first sign that something was wrong was an almost occult vision of crimson, amber, and violet hues painting the high heavens in the dark of night. Observers outside the blast zone later recalled a distant rumble resonating through the air. A priest from Munich compared it to the deep body vibration he felt in his chest the first time he had stood near the ringing cathedral bells as an altar boy. Commercial airline pilots a thousand miles away reported trails of bright incandescent light carving arcs of brilliance through the night.

And then the impact.

For all the high science and accelerated technology required to place these weapons in space, they were not as advanced as some of the small guided anti-tank or anti-aircraft missiles that had recently entered service with NATO's forces. The accuracy of any single projectile was measured in miles, not inches. But it hardly mattered when so many were fired at a relatively small area.

The first kinetic rod struck a hillside two miles south of a Canadian light armoured cavalry regiment. For the two men standing guard at the gate to the regiment's headquarters, the blast turned inky darkness into a blinding whiteout, freeze-framing the atomisation of millions of tons of rock, soil, and forest into a surrealist image of a whole world suddenly disassembling itself. However, they had no time to reckon with the bizarre change as another rod punched into the earth a few hundred yards away, turning the men into superheated plasma.

As hail arrives with the first fall of two or three isolated stones before quickly escalating into a frenzied storm of impacts, the balance of the Soviet bombardment swept across Germany in just a few seconds, obliterating thirteen small towns and ninety-eight per cent of US Fifth Army.

VICE PRESIDENT PHILIP KOLHAMMER was sworn in as the 35th President of the United States high over the English Channel by the co-pilot of the small passenger jet carrying him from a darkened airfield in France to an RAF base in Sussex. Turbulence buffeted the Davidson Aerospace Lear Jet analogue, forcing Kolhammer to brace himself against the headrest of his seat while he took the oath. Outside, high above the clouds, which had dropped soft rain all over northern France as the Red Army Rocket

Force poured orbital kinetics down on NATO bases in West Germany, two F-5 strike fighters escorted the new President's plane to safety.

Or relative safety, Kolhammer thought.

There was no guarantee that Stalin wouldn't unload a second orbital bombardment on the United Kingdom.

"Repeat after me," Lieutenant Gloria Meller instructed him.

And he did.

"I do solemnly swear that I will faithfully execute the Office of President of the United States," he said, "and will to the best of my ability, preserve, protect, and defend the Constitution of the United States."

Lieutenant Meller, a temp, stepped back awkwardly and saluted, nearly tripping in the turbulence.

President Kolhammer returned the salute, flexing his knees and lowering his centre of gravity against the buffeting of the aircraft. He'd spent almost as many years on the pitching decks of warships as he had on dry land, but even so, he was glad to resume his seat.

He took up the folder he'd abandoned when Meller returned from the cockpit, ashen faced, to inform him of the attack on President Eisenhower's chopper. Kolhammer had been reading everything the military and civilian intelligence agencies had on the Soviet preemptive strike. Some of the details surprised him, but not the simple fact of it. He had been warning against this since the end of the war.

He tried to take up reading the file where he had left off.

The simple, buff-coloured folder was stamped TOP SECRET: 5E.

For Five Eyes, the alliance of five English-speaking democracies. Australia, Canada, New Zealand, the United Kingdom, and the United States.

The contents were brief. Three typed pages, some photographs, and schematics.

In the first photograph, a jowly, middle-aged man in a tweed suit smoked a pipe and stared at the camera with watery eyes.

Herr Professor Ernst Bremmer, a German rocket scientist whose theoretical work underlay much of the Soviet space program. However, Bremmer was an avowed pacifist, and as far as the Five Eyes intelligence services could tell, he had given the USSR no solace or support.

Which was probably why Stalin had sent the KGB's top operator, Alexei Skarov, to kidnap him in Cairo.

There was no photograph of Skarov, but the CIA had put together artists' sketches of the man based on the testimony of those few Western agents who had met him and survived.

Kolhammer examined the photographs of two such men. One, Major Pavel Ivanov, he knew from the Multinational Fleet. A former Spetsnaz officer, Ivanov was a committed anti-communist and private military contractor on retainer with the Davidson corporation. He was, in not so many words, a ghost. The other man was famous.

Harry Windsor, a former prince of the realm and SAS captain. After the Transition, a private citizen, or as private as he could be, but also a part-timer for Britain's Secret Intelligence Service, which found his continued celebrity helpful in gaining entry to those exclusive environs where more commonplace agents might seem out of place.

Harry had been in Cairo working on Bremmer's disappearance when everything had gone sideways.

According to the latest from Langley, he was still chasing Bremmer, thought to be somewhere in the Mediterranean now.

Kolhammer rubbed his tired eyes.

Even though Stalin had already launched his orbital strike, they didn't want Bremmer falling into his hands. The man's family was missing too, and Kolhammer did not doubt for a second that Stalin would have them tortured or killed, probably in front of Bremmer, if he refused to cooperate.

What damage could he do now?

"Too fucking much," the President muttered to himself.

If he improved the Soviet's missile forces by even a few percent, it could make all the difference.

They needed Bremmer back, or they needed him neutralised.

Kolhammer closed the file and noted on the cover that he was to be briefed daily on Windsor and Ivanov's progress.

He turned to a report on Eisenhower's assassination but had to put the file down again to get his head around the surreal moment.

President Eisenhower was dead, and the assassins, too, killed in a shootout with DC police and the Secret Service. The TV networks back home were running non-stop coverage. The big papers had rushed out emergency editions. Nothing in the ten years since Manning Pope's wormhole experiment had cast him, and thousands more from the 21st century, back into the Pacific war of the 1940s could match this moment for its bizarre sense of dislocation. So much happened that shouldn't have. And some things that should have been by now were not. Kolhammer had long since stopped losing sleep over the seemingly infinite number of branching possibilities the Transition had created. But this...this he had seen coming.

He had tried to get Ike to take the danger of a Soviet sneak attack as a clear and present danger to national survival.

And he had failed.

"Mister President, are you all right, sir? Would you like a glass of water? Or something stronger?"

It took Kolhammer a moment to realise the Secret Service agent was talking to him. When he heard the words "Mister President," part of him reflexively expected to hear Eisenhower respond.

"I'm fine," he said. "But yeah, maybe some cold water. With an antacid if you got it. How long until we land? I'm gonna need to put out a statement. Assure people back home we've got this under control."

"Sir, we would prefer you said nothing to alert anybody to your whereabouts until we can get you safely home."

"Then you better get me back to the ranch five minutes ago, son. I can't fight this war from a suitcase."

Agent Byers checked his watch, a chunky steel analogue timepiece. It looked like an original model, not one of the weird, hybrid technologies which had grown like Topsy since a little piece of 15 January 2021 had folded back into 2 June 1942.

"Understood, Mister President. We're working on a transit plan to get you stateside ASAP. Wheels down in fifteen minutes, sir. They've cleared the runway for us, and ground transport is waiting. You're to meet the Prime Minister first up."

. . .

He meant Sir Winston Churchill. Older, observably frail, but back in power, and still in better shape than he would have been at this point, were it not for the advanced drugs and therapies that had come back with the fleet under Kolhammer's command.

The President thanked Agent Byers for the paper cup of chilled water and tried to throw off his uncertainty. He had gone from the largely powerless occupant of 'a bucket of warm piss' to the leader of the free world.

And the free world was currently getting its ass handed to it.

2

Senior Lieutenant Ilya Egorov endured the bumpy ride aboard his ferry to war, an Antonov rigged for paratroopers like him. The thin metal tube reeked of av-gas and stale sweat. A proud member of the Guards Airborne, he wore the blue-and-white T-shirt and distinctive beret of the VDV. Of course, he'd jammed his beret into a cargo pocket for the moment, and the famous tee, which had been so popular with the young ladies of Moscow, was hidden behind a thick combat blouse and body armour. A Kah-Shlem, the Kevlar helmet specially fitted for paratroopers, perched heavily upon his head.

The weight meant nothing to Ilya. He was hard and fit, an experienced veteran of harsh training and combat in Afghanistan, China, and the Kuriles. He knew himself, down in his meat and bone, to be the best, and he knew for damned sure he served with the best. The Vanguard of the Soviet Airborne.

His target tonight was Naples Airport, specifically the control tower.

He did not doubt he and his troopers would seize the objective. This was not his first combat jump; that had been a HALO drop into a rocky field outside of Kabul, and Ilya remembered it well. The shock of landing, the confusion, the very first war shot he had fired from his Kalashnikov. All of it.

This time would be different, he thought. Ilya closed his eyes and went over the plan as somebody nearby vomited onto the steel plates, adding to the stink inside the aircraft. They weren't fighting jihadi savages tonight. Here they would face Italian Armed Carabinieri and a grab bag of Italian, French, and US forces later in the day.

Ilya might not be alive by then, of course. But it did not help to dwell on such things. Instead, he concentrated on his breathing and the feeling of the tightly slung and taped-up assault rifle pressing against his chest. An AKSU-52, the latest and the best from the massive arsenal in Tula. Much more accurate than the old AK-47, and the wicked 5.45 rounds made the most ghastly wounds. He smiled faintly. He would use it on the fat capitalists very soon.

For Comrade Stalin, he thought. And the thought helped banish some of his anxieties until a loud bang kicked the aircraft sideways in the sky.

More dull, percussive thumps soon followed. Triple-A zeroing in on them. Egorov nodded to himself, tasting salt on his lips. He tried to lick them, but his mouth was dry. The briefing officers at Sarajevo had warned them of the enemy's anti-aircraft artillery. They did not know whether the batteries at Naples were radar-guided, but even if not, there would be enough density of fire to decimate the regiment before they hooked up static lines. This was known.

Such were the sacrifices demanded by history.

This was also why they were flying as low as the pilots dared. No more than two hundred meters from the nap of the earth. Some planes would crash. Others would be hit. But Ilya shrugged. If he died, he died, like his friend Vanya.

Poor Vanya was a *kulturny* boy, an accomplished violinist, and there was an argument, perhaps, that the state might have been better served by not pressing a machine gun into those long, delicate hands. But that was not an argument for Ilya Egorov to make. He was no theoretician. He was a soldier and servant of the people. And the people's commissars had decided that Vanya was, too.

The captain called out a one-minute warning over the roar of the engines.

Vanya was not well suited to war. That, at least, everyone could admit. But history had sent him to Afghanistan anyway. Sitting on the hard wooden bench in the back of the Antonov, his ass cheeks numb, his stomach fluttering, Ilya remembered how his friend had struggled to do his best. Day after day, amid the mud huts and slaughter, Vanya seemed to harden and dissolve simultaneously. His fingers had yellowed with *makhorka* tobacco, and his fingernails grew dark with gun oil and blood.

The plane jumped again at another explosion, like a horse bitten by a giant black fly. But the tough little Antonov droned on.

Ilya grunted and laboured fiercely to keep the pucker in his asshole. Somebody, he could smell, had not.

He had found Vanya in a latrine with a service pistol in his hand and the back of his head missing. Well, not missing. It was all there on the wall.

The captain called out a thirty-second warning, and the aircraft pitched wildly upwards to reach the minimum jump height. He hoped they would drop at about 130 knots, but he feared the speed would be higher, and he knew this would be painful no matter what.

"Twenty seconds! Stand up."

He stood and watched as the jump master peered out the door. The man swore loud enough for Ilya to hear. "Bozhemoi!"

What was he seeing?

No matter; it was time. Ilya stared at the red drop light. It was all that mattered now. He would push his stack forward when the light turned green. Ten seconds later, it did. Ilya shouted and slapped the back of the man ahead of him; his ass tingled with pins and needles. His balls too. He ignored the distraction and clipped on to the static line that would open his parachute when he fell from the aircraft. All they had to do was jump.

His first trooper stood in the doorway, and the jump master shoved him out. The line moved forward, and Ilya pushed hard from behind.

An odd sound punched through the uproar of engine noise and

the crump of Triple-A. It sounded like a rock hitting a tin can, and a man a few places before him screamed and dropped, writhing on the deck. His static line stretched taut, and the trooper behind him almost tripped.

Fuck your mother, Ilya thought as he roared.

"Keep moving! Move! Move!"

He pushed harder on the back of the man in front of him. They had to get out now. Someone else tripped over the wounded man's static line, yanking out the keepers that kept the line in place. Ilya cursed, fearful the chute might even pop inside the aircraft. The jump master flung another trooper from the door, his stack shortened, and he slipped in blood as the stricken man's static line threatened to tangle him. *Enough of this foolishness*, he thought. Ilya shoved and swore at the man before him while pulling out his bayonet.

Cutting the line would cost him two seconds he didn't have, but if he didn't cut it, someone, maybe him, would get wholly entangled, and bad things would happen. He grabbed the tough nylon webbing and sawed for all he was worth. It separated, and Ilya hastened forward, his hand on his static line and his bayonet back in its sheath. The wounded man screamed; Ilya shuffled by him without a glance down.

He secretly feared if he looked, he might see Vanya.

It was a stupid thought. Unworthy of a VDV officer.

Perhaps five seconds had passed since the first man went out the door. Maybe more. He didn't know; he didn't care. He jammed his forward-slung rucksack against the man in front of him and yelled.

"Move, you fucking pussies! Get out!"

Another screaming trooper exited the plane. Then the man in front of Ilya stood before the door as if by some magic trick, and the jumpmaster forced him out with a boot to his ass.

It was Ilya's turn.

He stood in the doorway for a split second and saw what the co-pilot had seen. It was another Antonov, so close by the wings were nearly touching. He knew that to maximise jumpers on the DZ the planes would fly in upward staggered waves, five abreast. But seeing it for real was something else. He accepted his surprise as the wind rushed and roared in his ears. He squinted into the dark abyss below where a sea of parachutes dropped towards the earth, and thousands of red tracers zipped back towards them.

As Ilya gaped in a split second of awe, the jump master's hard shove hit him like a sledgehammer, and he flew out the door, spreading his arms wide to steady himself. He imagined his commander was right behind him. The prop blast and buffeting were so strong that Ilya knew immediately this would fucking hurt. For the briefest second, he saw the airport beneath him, shrouded in smoke.

It seemed impossibly close and getting closer, faster.

One hundred and thirty knots, my ass, he thought.

His chute snapped open, wrenching his body back into the sky, and his rucksack struck his face with great violence. He saw stars as he automatically looked up to check his chute; it was fine. Then he looked down quickly. The ground was coming up so fast it would be a wonder if he didn't break a leg. A body shot past him, screaming. With sick fascination, he watched as the man bounced upon impact.

Then it was his turn.

Ilya hit every bit as hard as he'd imagined he might, and then some; he wasn't too proud to scream, although more in shock than pain. His training paid off as he collapsed and rolled through the impact. Ilya kept low and released his parachute harness. Then, staying flat, fucking the earth, he unfastened his weapon and started pulling off the tape that covered the muzzle, charging handle, and sights. Bullets zipped through the air overhead.

From above, he heard a distinctive *whoop-whoop-whoop* sound. Someone had lost a helmet, and he prayed it wouldn't land on him. What ignominy, to die like that. The helmet landed with a loud crack nearby, and Ilya watched it bounce from the ground – nearly six feet. He also saw a rifle sticking from the ground like a spear. A boot nearby. A single human leg a little further away. Shit was falling all over the damn place, and he had yet to see a single Italian.

So far, he would admit, he was not enjoying this particular march of the proletariat. It seemed even worse than that stupid field outside of Kabul if such a thing were possible.

Green tracers flashed through the night, skimming over the

ground close by. His own assholes were shooting at him. He unfolded the stock on his carbine, slammed the long safety lever downwards, and charged his weapon.

Ilya fired a burst back at the fuckers. He didn't care who they were. Maybe they would keep their heads down for a while as he crawled off the enormous billiard table of a taxiway or whatever the hell it was.

Was he even at the airport? He thought so, but this was a mess. Where was the control tower, and where could he find some troopers to help him take it? There was more shooting, followed by an odd silence. Then red tracers from the right flank, NATO red.

Finally! Ilya swung his weapon in that direction and squeezed off a few more shots. Someone ran by, screaming gibberish. Ilya didn't think it was Russian, so he shot the running man, who toppled like a sack. To make sure, he shot him again.

That felt good. Like he was in charge at last.

Senior Lieutenant Ilya Egorov moved to the sound of the guns.

3

Harry was dozing fitfully when a man from the Embassy arrived well after midnight to tell him the war had begun. Julia was deeply asleep in her hospital bed, becalmed by heavy sedation and pain relief. Still sore and aching from the damage he'd taken in the fight on the Russian ship *Mikhail Bulgakov*, Harry tried to rest in the deep leather tub chair the orderlies had dragged into Julia's room for him, but he never really slept. While not severe, his injuries throbbed constantly and flared into real pain whenever he moved in the armchair. No matter how much the doctors implored him to have a care for his own recovery, however, Harry would not leave his fiancée.

Julia had nearly died on that ship, and he blamed himself for that.

He had asked her to accompany him to Cairo, knowing even though it was supposed to be a milk run, that didn't mean things couldn't go sideways.

And they had, of course. Hard.

The head of MI6 had asked of him a simple request to speak to Professor Ernst Bremmer, a German rocket scientist turned peace campaigner, and to determine whether he might be under some form of coercion from the Soviets. Harry had made an absolute arse casserole of the whole thing, with lashings of extra arse. People were dead all over Cairo, including Viv, his oldest mate from the uptime years. Bremmer was gone, almost certainly a captive of the NKVD. And half the bloody city was shooting at the other half.

"For what it's worth, Your Highness, the whole world is shooting at each other now."

Harry bit down on his annoyance at being addressed by his old, redundant title. It hardly fucking mattered that Harry Windsor wasn't in the line of succession anymore. Part of his usefulness to MI6 was the way people were forever tripping over themselves to afford him the deference and privileges that would have been his by right of birth had he not chucked the whole thing in.

And McGregor, the fellow from the Embassy, looked every bit as strung out as Harry himself.

"I got that. Yes, thanks, Mitch," Harry said, rubbing the grit of poor sleep from his eyes. "But I can't go anywhere without Duff, and as you can see, she's a bit under the bloody weather."

Mitchell McGregor, a lantern-jawed Scot, was almost certainly not a mere third secretary responsible for commercial affairs. The shoulder holster and the steel-capped boots he wore gave the lie to that, as discreetly fashionable as they were.

"I'll sort you an ambulance then," he said. "But I have my orders, sir. From the Circus."

That got Harry's attention.

"I see," he said. After all, McGregor was not a humble toiler in Her Majesty's Diplomatic Service. "Go on."

"The boss wants you on a flight to Gib before close of business today, sir."

"And what about Julia."

"She can be safe handed to London. All the family members of embassy personnel are evacuating too."

Harry looked at his fiancée, and his stomach clenched tightly. Dark circles stood out under her eyes, and three separate IV lines ran into her arms. The blade had not cut any organs or major arteries. But it had still cut and deep. She had been almost grey with blood loss.

Outside the well-appointed hospital room, he could hear the

uproar of a city in chaos. Cairo was filthy with spies and mercenaries of every stripe. The regime here was riven with factional, sectarian, and even familial schisms, and he did not doubt that every bloody operator in the Egyptian capital had lit up their networks even before the business with Bremmer and Skarov had gone bad.

"An ambulance and a doctor," Harry said. "Promise them whatever bribes or inducements you have to. I'll make good on it."

McGregor looked as though he was about to argue, but Harry's expression told him everything he needed to know about how fucking pointless that would be.

The Scotsman cursed under his breath and turned on his heel, stalking out of the room with every appearance of a man who was about to kidnap an Egyptian doctor and an ambulance driver.

Harry perched on the edge of the bed next to Julia. She did not stir.

The surgeon had told him that she was past the worst of it. The little Russian monsters who'd tried to shiv her on the *Bulgakov* had buggered up their chance, and Jules had done to them what they intended for her.

What a gruesome bloody shit show, he thought. Using children like that.

The rattle of gunfire, distant and meaningless, sounded somewhere to the north. A few moments later, a deeper rumble, the report of an explosion, rolled in from some faraway quarter of the city. Harry did not doubt that things would get pretty bloody sporty in Cairo and in short order. None of the strategic imperatives that had drawn the Afrika Korps and the British Eighth Army into contention here a decade ago were any less imperative now that the Americans and the Soviets had replaced the earlier combatants as paramount rivals. Perhaps the Free French might drop a parachute division from Beirut, but they would do so at Washington's bidding. And it was just as likely that the Marines would lob an Expeditionary Unit over from Naples.

Harry settled back into his tub chair, readying himself for a long wait. He had spoken true to McGregor. He would not leave this room, let alone Cairo, without Julia Duffy.

The Scot surprised him less than five minutes later, returning with a doctor, a nurse, and a set of keys he claimed hand-on-heart to have "borrowed" from an ambulance driver in the Emergency Room.

So early in the morning, the drive to a private airfield on the city's western edge should have taken an hour. Four and a half hours after pulling out of the hospital, with dawn breaking over the desert, McGregor turned off the unsealed road and drove through a gate guarded by a platoon of Royal Fusiliers. Riding in the back of the ambulance with Julia and her medical attendants, Harry only saw them through the small, dusty window of the rear doors. He didn't bother asking McGregor why they were guarding an Egyptian aerodrome. Along with all the undercover operators, Cairo also played host to thousands of troops from the Soviet and Allied sides, a function of King Farouk's hugely profitable policy of strategic ambiguity.

A filthy Arab cock-tease, Viv had called it.

Of course, it was an open question just how profitable it would be now that those friendly visiting forces were shooting the shit out of each other.

Julia had drifted in and out of consciousness as they crawled through the massive snarl of traffic, and while Harry held onto her hand for most of the trip, he did not pester the doctor or the nurse with questions or, even worse, instructions. The American University Hospital did not hire amateurs. They knew their job. They also knew Harry, or at least they knew who he was, and were only too happy to ingratiate themselves with such an eminence in any way they could.

The two hundred pounds sterling he'd paid them for their time was also an encouragement.

"Right then," McGregor barked from the driver's seat. "Everyone out. Dinnae buggerise around about it neither."

His accent, Harry thought, *grew more Celtic the further they got from the city.*

The doctor and nurse climbed out first and called over to a couple of passing squaddies to come help carry their patient. When the men demurred, McGregor blasted them with a stream of profanity that would have made a Highland rugby coach proud.

They hopped to pretty bloody smartly after that.

Blinking as he emerged from the rear of the ambulance into the harsh Egyptian sunlight, Harry tried to fix his location but found it impossible. They had arrived at some anonymous and utterly nondescript way station. Quonset huts and shipping containers. A helipad somewhere nearby. Dust. Diesel fumes. And the tightly orchestrated chaos of a military facility suddenly crashing into high gear.

"Camp Burnley," McGregor said as if reading Harry's mind. "Logistics hub for the Allied Joint Force Mission in Cairo. Let's not linger for happy snaps. It's an arse of a place, and I wouldn't be surprised if Ivan decides to drop a shitload of fucking BM 21s on it before the day is done."

Harry grimaced as the soldiers hauled Julia's stretcher from the rear of the ambulance.

McGregor was almost certainly right. The 21 was an uptime design, a truck-mounted rocket system, forty tubes of crude and not incredibly accurate whizzbangs that were nonetheless perfect for hammering down sprawling targets like Camp Burnley.

"Where to then?" Harry asked.

McGregor led them to a demountable hut already roaring with AC units. Two dozen civilians, all Westerners, stood under the thin strip of shade provided by a narrow veranda. More of them had crammed inside.

There was no way Harry was letting anyone drop Julia onto the back of that queue, but before he could say anything, McGregor stomped past the corner of the building, roaring at the two Fusiliers to keep up 'and mind the young lady'. The doctor and his nurse hurried alongside the stretcher, and Harry double-timed to keep up with them, ignoring the sullen and resentful glares of the stranded and the left behind outside the small admin office.

They crossed a tarmac, busy with light aircraft and military vehicles. The further into the camp they proceeded, the more it took on the aspect of an RAF base, with uniformed personnel outnumbering and finally replacing all civilians. McGregor strode into the shade of a large hangar where a Hercules, painted white and daubed with the red cross of a medical mission, was already turning props. The airplane was augmented tech, of course. What the temps called 'augie'. Nothing like a C-130 had come through the Transition, but he felt much better anyway, especially when he saw Royal Air Force medics waiting to receive them.

Harry followed the stretcher towards the loading ramp and relaxed even further when he saw the fit-out inside. It was a virtual flying ER.

But he never made it on board.

McGregor took him by the elbow and steered him away from the mercy flight.

"I'm afraid you'll be flying coach on the express service," he said.

"You what, mate...?" Harry started, but words failed him when he saw who was waiting at the rear of the Herc.

Pavel Ivanov and Charlotte François.

4

General J. Lonesome Jones seethed with quiet rage. Just over the Bay of Naples, marines made daily preparations for war while he was marooned behind a cheap plywood desk in a cramped and windowless office at a vast remove from any prospect of action. The office, on the ground floor of a two-storey prefab, half an hour from the airport, was a good twelve klicks across the bay from Camp Jordan, the giant Marine Corps base in the shadow of Mount Vesuvius. Jones wrestled with the urge to sweep all the files from his desk to the floor. He wanted nothing more than to grab a rifle and charge out into the night. He would meet the enemy there soon enough, he was sure of it, and he could hardly be less useful than he was here, reviewing chickenshit administrivia. The files, bundles of buff-coloured folders thick with original paper documents and flimsy carbon copies, were all tied together with fraying lengths of faded red filing tape.

Seriously.

Motherfucking red tape, for real.

Still, it was fitting, in a grim sort of way. General J. Lonesome Jones had been consigned to the command of the 571st Joint Sustainment Brigade, and specifically to the oh-so crucial role of the Marine Corps representative to NATO's Joint Committee on Military Nutrition Research with a specific tasking to review and advise on 'Overcoming Underconsumption of Military Operational Rations.'

Motherfuckers wanted him to explain why the grunts wouldn't eat their fucking rat packs.

Because that shit was flavourless fucking ass meat, that's why.

But of course, they already knew that. That's why Cronauer had sent him here. To banish his black ass to the outer fucking darkness in the vain hope Jones might never come back. He hunched over his desk and crouched down behind the file wall, grinding his teeth as he wrestled with his anger. His mood was as dark as the sky outside. He should be commanding a fucking corps or at least a division. Instead, he had to wet nurse three thousand odds-n-sods who didn't even think of themselves as warriors when he'd turned up.

For damn sure, they would before he left.

General J. Lonesome Jones had been about as popular as tofu in Texas when he'd first taken charge of his brigade of supply troops from all the services. Not because he was their first African American commander, although that was part of it for some. Or it had been. Those assholes were mostly gone now. No, his people chafed because he reminded them they were fighters, not a bunch of fucking pogues and remmies.

The first day on the job, he'd forced everyone from battalion COs to assistant clerk-typists to train to standard on basic rifleman's skills, starting with their service weapon, the venerable M-4 carbine. The 571st might be a backwater, and logistics had to come first, but by God, they would demonstrate competency on a basic tactical level while he was in command.

Even here, far across the bay from Camp Jordan, if the wind was right, he could hear the occasional snarl of the great beast. Rotors sometimes thudded overhead, that old familiar dull-sharp sound recalling battlefields from another time, in another world. To Jones, the rumble of heavy metal and the distant clatter of tracked armour was as sweet an evensong as any man could hope to hear but bitter with it because General Anderson Cronauer had made it abundantly clear that no uptime negro could ever expect to command men in combat whilst Cronauer sat the throne of SACEUR.

Jones was forever to serve in the rear.

A bitter irony, given that Lonesome Jones' wars, uptime in the twenty-first, had known of no rear echelon. For this, he made every limp dick, sad ass troop, squid, and flying fairy in the Five Seven One write out and commit to blessed memory the story of Lance Corporal Elana Mitchell, the fightin' file clerk, who had died at a 240 in the Siege of Taipei. He'd be fucked if anyone under his command couldn't do what she had done, and on the first day of his posting here, he let everyone know.

Frustration finally drove Jones to his feet and out of the office. He was, he knew, likely to be the only soul in this building. The day shift had left hours earlier, and the budget of the Marine Corps representative to the Joint Committee on Military Nutrition Research did not stretch to overtime. The fall of his boot heels echoed around him as he marched down the passageway, heading for the small window at the end where he could at least catch a glimpse of Camp Jordan from across the waters. It would be quiet over there now, both divisions being out on deployment, the Third to Egypt, and the Fifth on the float somewhere in the Med. Still, it soothed his temper to watch the moonlight on the bay. Professor Vanderveen's doubtless fucking fascinating paper on 'Antioxidants and Oxidative Stress in Female Personnel' would have to wait.

"General Jones? Sir?"

Jones turned around quickly, surprised that anyone but him would still be at work.

A nervous-looking Army corporal had come up the stairs and stood about as far away from Jones as he could while still in earshot. His eyes were frog fat under a pair of bushy eyebrows, giving him an air of comic absurdity. Nonetheless, his uniform was pressed crisp and sharp, and that salute was worthy of the Ranger Handbook.

Lonesome guessed he was the Charge of Quarter's noncom, having pulled the short straw for the graveyard shift.

"Spill it, Corporal."

He looked like he might spill his guts instead.

"Shit, uh..."

Lonesome stared at the boy; he didn't like this. The kid was sweating. He still had pimples, but his skin looked dry and mottled, as though his heart was racing and slowing erratically. He was holding his helmet under one arm like a life preserver.

"Whatever it is, son, I'm sure it ain't your fault, so the hammer ain't coming down on you. Take a breath and cough up whatever you got for me in one big fuckin' hairball. All at once."

The corporal gulped.

"Sir. I just received a recorded message from SHAEF on the secure line. We have been alerted. The brigade is to move to one hour's readiness."

Lordy, Lonesome thought. *What fresh hell is this?* Aloud, he said, "All right, son. Is this an exercise?"

The corporal shook his head.

"No, sir. The message said this was real-world and to stand by for further comms."

Jones knitted his eyebrows together.

"You better tell me someone is sitting on that phone right now, Corporal."

"Yes, sir," he gulped. "Private Fisher and a runner, sir."

Lonesome nodded, satisfied. "Good job. Go now and get my battalion commanders out of the rack, or the O Club, or wherever you gotta drag them out from. You are my personal emissary, son, and you go with my sword and shield. Do not take any shit. I will be in headquarters in five mikes."

"Yes, sir." The young NCO barked, snapping out a salute. He turned and hurried away, looking much happier now that he had orders to follow.

LONESOME HASTENED BACK to his office and started gathering his shit. He took care to put on his pistol belt and check the load. He eyed his body armour on its stand in the corner. It was ready, just like every motherfucker in the glorious Five Seven One would be in less than one hour unless, of course, they wanted the wrath of God and

General J. Lonesome Jones descending upon them like holy hell and thunder.

He strode into his brightly lit headquarters as promised precisely five minutes later.

The air smelled strongly of instant coffee and tobacco. The walls of the unremarkable room were painted pale green, and the wooden floors were waxed to a shine.

Jones looked at his watch. All his commanders had yet to arrive. The phone rang, and Private Fisher, a young woman cursed with red hair, picked up the heavy black Bakelite handset. None of those nice new walk-around phones in the Five Seven One.

"571st Sustainment Brigade Headquarters. This is a secure line. How may I help you, sir or ma'am?"

The private regarded Lonesome anxiously as she spoke.

"Yes, sir. No, sir. Right away, sir."

She held out the phone to him, and he took it.

"It's a Colonel Grieve, sir, from Camp Jordan."

"This is General Jones."

The voice on the other end spoke. Jones' expression hardened as his first BC rolled in the door.

"Acknowledged," Jones said and hung up.

He said nothing while he waited two minutes for his last battalion commander to arrive. It was Colonel Perkins, and time had just run out for him. For all of them.

Jones looked the commanders over while the silence stretched out.

He stood in the centre of the warm and stuffy room, filled with the humming of fans. The 571st didn't rate air-conditioning.

At last, he spoke.

"Each of you. Alert your subordinate staff and open the armoury. Within two hours, every sailor, soldier, airman, and marine will be assembled and under arms with a full combat load. Within three hours, we will be in close-quarter battle; I am developing a plan of attack now."

The assembled officers stared at him. Mary O'Connell, the lone female officer, let her jaw fall open.

Jones held up one hand.

"No questions. We have received a general alert from SHAEF, and I just received confirmation of an incoming Soviet aerial assault, probable target Naples International, size unknown. The Marines are not here, and our heavy units are at the DMZ, so in the game of tag, we're it, people."

"Holy shit!" That was Perkins.

Jones smiled. "You can clean your britches later, Colonel. Now, you move. Two hours to mass and arm, half an hour to brief, half an hour to move to the airfield, then we assault immediately, repel the enemy, and defend the airfield against follow-on attacks." He paused and looked each commander in the eye. "Do you understand? We are the only large unit close by."

Four voices replied with varying certainty.

"Yes, sir!"

"Outstanding. A rough plan executed immediately with maximum violence and intent wins over an elegant design hatched sometime next week." He clapped his hands. They came together with a sound like a rifle shot. "Move!"

The battalion commanders scattered. All the hard and frustrating work in this assignment from hell was about to be put to the test. It would be a goddamned miracle if his brigade stepped off from their assault positions on time.

Jones smacked his fist into his palm. No. They would fucking do it because he would make them.

An explosion rumbled in the distance, followed by the scream of jets and belated anti-aircraft fire. Lonesome strode out of the room, heading toward the armoury.

He felt better than he had in ages.

5

A humble Veep might get away with a small travelling entourage, but when the President of the United States of America got his ass rolling, it could seem like the whole damn world got rolling with him. Dozens of dignitaries, roughly split between local notables and his embassy staffers, waited for Kolhammer's jet to touch down at an RAF field in Sussex. The Secret Service had minimal assets in the UK, but HM Government had seen to his immediate security by re-deploying a half-squadron of the Special Air Service from a nearby training facility. Their six-wheeled patrol vehicles formed a half circle outside a hangar, where a receiving party stood in the light of their headlamps.

Kolhammer could see from the final approach just how rudimentary the facilities were. Burning pots of pitch marked out the limits of the second runway. The main strip was busy. He counted at least eight fighters roaring down the tarmac as his jet came in from the south.

The voice of Lieutenant Meller, the woman who'd sworn him in as they raced across the channel, came through on the intercom.

"They've cleared the deck for us, Mister President," the co-pilot said. “But we’re going in hard and fast. You’ll need your belt on securely, sir.”

He was safely strapped in, but he heard a couple of his Secret Service guys click-clacking in the back of the cabin. The head of his detail came forward to check on him, but Kolhammer waved him back down and quickly jammed all the files he’d been reading into a sports bag, which he placed under his seat.

“Not my first rough landing, son,” he said, keeping his tone light. “Strap in like the good lieutenant says.”

The descent was steep, and they touched down hard. The improvised landing lights blurred into a fiery, yellow streak outside the tiny windows of the Lear Jet analogue. A single fire engine and an ambulance raced through the network of runways to keep pace with them as the pilot deployed spoilers and reverse thrust to slow them down. Kolhammer rocked forward in his seat.

It was nothing like a landing on a carrier, but it was a hell of a lot rougher than he was used to on Air Force Two. As soon as the aircraft stopped, his protection detail was up and swarming through the fuselage. Kolhammer insisted on carrying his bag. He thanked the aircrew as he passed the cockpit, and they saluted in return. A Secret Service agent opened the cabin door and dropped the steps. He exited without ceremony.

The night air in southern England was warm but redolent of jet fuel and diesel. Turbines whined, and a couple of F-5s screamed in to land on the main runway as he hurried down the three steps to the tarmac. A grim-faced Ambassador Tim Kelly stepped forward and saluted. Kolhammer responded, then shook his hand.

“Mister Ambassador, hell of a way to meet again.”

“Mister President,” Kelly said, turning slightly to introduce another man. “This is Deputy Foreign Secretary Charles Farru-Hill. Sir Anthony Eden sends his apologies but—”

Kolhammer cut off the formalities with a stiff hand chop.

“No need. We all got caught with our asses hanging out. Mister Farru-Hill, it is my pleasure, sir. Or it would be, were the circumstances different.”

“Her Majesty’s Government extends her condolences on the loss of President Eisenhower, sir. And for the casualties in Germany. We understand the losses are heavy. Our own were considerable."

Kolhammer shook hands with the 2IC at the British Foreign Office and said, "Thank you, sir. It's appreciated. But unless we want to add our names to the butcher's bill, I suggest we haul ass out of here."

Farru-Hill leaned in and raised his voice over the roar of the engines.

"If it would please you, Mister President, the PM would meet with you in London at your earliest convenience. He suggests a working breakfast in the war rooms. Five AM."

A little under two hours from now.

"Sure," Kolhammer said, "Let's get moving."

He started to walk toward the line of vehicles that waited nearby. The SAS troopers all began to move as he approached, turning over engines and climbing into the open trays of their vehicles. Kolhammer ignored the buzz and dizziness of exhaustion. He knew he would need to sleep at some point today, but he was used to going without rest. He would be fine if he got a few hours before his judgment started to fray.

"One thing, Mister President," Ambassador Kelly said, hurrying to keep up. "You need to release a statement."

"A what?" Kolhammer said, genuinely confused.

He'd been thinking about releasing thousands of fucking missiles in the general direction of Joseph fucking Stalin.

"A statement, sir. You're the president now. You need to talk to the country, to the folks back home."

Kolhammer almost stumbled to a halt.

"Shit, you're right," he said. "I'm thinking like a task force commander, not a president. Can you put something together for me, Kelly? Something short. Don't tell people I'm here. The Sovs don't need to know that. Let them think I'm still in Paris if you want."

"Better not," a gruff voice said. "That'll freak out the bedwetters back home too."

Kolhammer turned to the new voice.

Ambassador Kelly raised a hand toward the man, an Air Force General.

"Mister President, this is Andy Porter. He's the military liaison at the Embassy. He can get you up to speed and plug you into the Combatant Commands worldwide."

A wiry, bullet-headed man in a Marine Corps uniform snapped out a machine-tooled salute.

"Mister President. Lieutenant General Andrew Porter. Call sign Havoc, sir."

As Kolhammer dropped his salute, he gave Porter a closer look.

"What did you fly, General?"

Porter grinned.

"A Cobra, Mister President. Off the *Kandahar* back in the upwhen. Buffs at the end of the last show."

It shouldn't have made a difference, but it did. Porter, like him, had started this long, strange trip back up in the twenty-first century. Kolhammer felt himself relax ever so slightly. It wasn't purely a matter of trust. He would trust any man or woman who wore the uniform. But he also knew that Havoc and he would likely share an understanding that was not possible with somebody who had not come back through the wormhole.

"Okay. Good to know. And you're right about Paris. Kelly, just let people know I'm fine, I've been sworn in, and I'm taking names and kicking ass. Tell 'em I'll address the country in the next day or so. After we've declared war."

"Congress is meeting in a few hours, sir," Kelly said. "We'll be at war with Russia by the time you meet Mister Churchill."

"Son, we're at war with the assholes right now. General Porter, you can catch me up on what I missed on the way to London," Kolhammer said, raising the sports bag full of briefing papers. "These are all a few hours out of date by now."

"Let me get that for you, sir," Havoc said, taking the bag from him.

The four men—Kolhammer, Porter, and the two diplomats—hurried into the rear of a Rolls-Royce. The phalanx of anonymous hangers-on trailed along behind them.

He had no idea what the hell they were doing there. Surely there was more important work for them somewhere else?

The commander of the SAS troop, who did have a real job, spoke briefly to the Secret Service agents and pointed them toward a jeep they could use. Three agents piled into that while the fourth, his detail chief, followed Kolhammer to his ride. The whole thing was a patchwork of improv' and making-do, but Kolhammer was determined to clear that airfield as quickly as possible. The Reds had already carried out a decapitation strike on American soil. It made sense that they'd try the same thing here. It's what he would do.

"How is Mister Churchill doing?" He asked Farru-Hill as they got to the car. "Have you guys increased security for him? Because you need to."

The Deputy Foreign Secretary gestured in frustration.

"Sir Winston has started carrying his old Tommy gun around again. Says it kept him safe from Hitler's goons during the last show, and he doesn't want a lot of fuss and bother just because Uncle Joe has decided to have a go now."

Kolhammer overrode his reflex response to stop dead in surprise.

A fucking Tommy gun? Seriously?

"Stalin just assassinated President Eisenhower," he said. "At the White House. He's not screwing around."

Farru-Hill nodded.

"I know, I know, but he is travelling with a company of Horse Guards everywhere he goes, on her Majesty's insistence. And we're keeping his schedule Top Secret Ultra, of course. But he is who he is, Mister President."

The Secret Service agent let the driver of the Rolls know he'd have a friend sitting up front with him, whether he wanted one or not. Kolhammer climbed into the rear cabin, which reminded him of a London taxicab. The seats had been arranged so the four men could face each other. After settling in and buckling up, the chauffeur started the engine. A minute later, they rolled through the airfield gates and into the dark of the British countryside, accompanied by the military convoy.

The convoy ran with hooded lamps. They turned onto a major

motorway without stopping or even slowing down appreciably. Kohlammer was glad to be on the move, but he knew well the capabilities of the Soviets' missile guidance systems. They were much better than they should have been at this point in history, even if they still lagged severely behind the Allies' more advanced satellites and silicon. It wouldn't make much difference if they launched a bunch of kinetic impactors from orbit.

“Havoc," he said, turning to his military liaison, "Can you talk to the... relevant authorities—”

He almost said ‘temps’, the shorthand term all of the uptimers used for the locals, even a decade after the Transition. It wasn't an insult, exactly. But it wasn't entirely friendly either.

“—Ah, can you get onto them about maintaining EMCON and movement security?” Kolhammer said. “No need to make it easy for those assholes in Moscow.”

Farru-Hill blinked at the mild obscenity, but Lieutenant General Porter nodded brusquely. “I'll fire a goddamn rocket up their asses and keep the fire coming until they see the fucking light," he promised.

"Good," Kolhammer said. "Mister Farru-Hill, on this, I'm afraid I must insist. Until we degrade the Soviet's long-range surveillance and interdiction capabilities, it is simply not prudent to concentrate our national command assets at predictable locations such as the war rooms under Downing Street. If I were Stalin, I'd have eyes on Number 10, and the minute this convoy rolled up, I'd call down holy hellfire. Old Joe doesn't need to thread the eye of a needle. If he atomised half the city trying to get to us and Mister Churchill, he would not consider that collateral damage. He'd think of it as a bonus."

The Englishman did not look entirely happy with that news.

"Well, I can talk to the PM," he said. "But he can be very set in his ways, and the bunkers resisted all German attempts at..."

"Hey, Pal," Havoc said. "You even listening? These guys are throwing rods from God down on your fuckin' heads. It's not the same thing as the dainty German doodlebugs that fat fuck Goering dropped on you. Until we put out their eyes and take out those orbital platforms, we all gotta keep our heads down."

Both diplomats looked more than a little put out by the military officer's crudity, and Kolhammer offered up a small olive branch to smooth the awkward moment.

"Stalin's orbital platforms have been taken care of," he said. "At least all of the ones we know about. It will be another twenty-four hours before that's confirmed, but I can say with a high degree of certainty that, for now, we can move orbital bombardment down our list of things to worry about. Conventional bombing and missile strikes, however, are a certainty. They're coming."

They all looked surprised, Porter most of all.

"We took out their platforms? How? I thought anti-satellite weapons were banned."

"They were," Charles Farru-Hill confirmed.

There was no sense holding back. This was going to come out and quickly. Better to get ahead of things now.

"Sovereign states agreed not to develop anti-satellite capabilities and space-based offensive systems at the Brussels conference in 1948," Kolhammer said. "Of course, Stalin's word wasn't worth the love of a two-dollar whore, as we've just seen. But the treaty's wording was such that private entities could develop dual-use technologies to protect themselves from, er, what was the phrase, Tim? Substantial hazards?"

"Substantive functional hazards," Ambassador Kelly supplied.

"What's that when it's at home then?" Farru-Hill asked.

The military attaché answered.

"Space junk," Porter said. "Busted ass satellites. Flying garbage. Inconvenient meteors and shit like that. It was a real problem back where we came from. Goddamn sky was full of junk, especially after the Chinese lit off a bunch of anti-sat rockets just before they tried to grab up Taiwan. Scattered thousands of bits and pieces of crap all over the thermosphere and exosphere. Made a hell of a mess."

As they motored down a six-lane motorway, the sodium wash of overhead lighting pulsed through the cabin of the Rolls-Royce. Kolhammer wondered how far out from London the freeway lighting would run and why the hell it was still burning bright now.

It wouldn't be by tomorrow night, that was for damn sure.

"So what are you saying, Mister President? The United States developed a satellite killer? Illegally? Because I can tell you now the only thing the PM will care about is getting one for himself."

"Not the US, no," Kolhammer said. "A US company. Davidson Aerospace. And we are going to need their help again."

6

Jack Edmonston had been dead for ten years when a new war brought him back to life. Of course, he didn't know it yet. He fumbled at the pack of Luckies on his workbench and tapped out another smoke. The fluorescent light in his garage hummed away as he fired up the coffin nail. A dirty blue cloud of smoke spread slowly under the white tube light, turning and twisting like a snake slowly waking from winter. Every time Jack lifted his hand to take a drag, he saw the tattoo on his left arm and wished he hadn't.

The tattoo was crude. The ink a fading blackish-blue and slightly blurred with age now. Lady Luck, naked and wrapped around a dagger. Above her head, a scroll, and in the scroll, the motto 'GARRYOWEN'.

Jack was a quick, thoughtless smoker. He soon stubbed out the butt on his workbench and looked around. His white V-neck undershirt stuck to his sweating torso, pinching under the arms. Evening in June, and it was hot as Hades. His excuse for being in the garage, the family's newish '53 Chevy, was parked in front of him with the hood open. He idly recalled that Brits called the hood a bonnet. Once that would've been enough to make him laugh, the idea of a flowery bonnet on a couple of tons of American steel like that. But Jack Edmonston wasn't much for laughter these days.

Turning from the car to his toolbox, he saw the pistol in the top drawer. Jack found himself staring at it. The .45 auto was a dull greenish-grey with a brown Bakelite grip. He could read the stamping on the side without a problem; there was nothing wrong with his eyes.

ITHACA GUN CO. INC.

He knew the weapon was loaded, the hammer was cocked, and the safety was engaged.

Jack remembered.

The kraut was saying something, but Jack didn't know what. The prostrate soldier was lying in a pool of blood in the corner of the shattered stone farmhouse, and his legs were twitching. Jack could see the German eagle with the swastika in its claws on the other man's left sleeve. Just like he was lying there in Jack's goddamned garage. He stared again at the German's rifle with its long, curved magazine. The weapon had fallen out of the wounded man's reach. He was no longer a threat.

Jack Edmonston, thirty-three years old, thicker through the middle, slower all around, wrenched himself back to the present. It took some will. He was still looking at the .45, but at least he was back in his garage again. Thousands of miles from that farmhouse. No wounded man was lying in front of him. Just the pistol. If he were to taste that weapon somehow, he knew the gun oil would be bitter on his tongue, the metal cold on his lips.

He stepped away from the toolbox, leaned against his workbench and shakily grabbed for the pack of smokes. He was almost out. He'd have to ask Alice to grab another carton when she was next at the stores. Jack lit up and tried to focus on the car again. It was only two years old and running fine, but he liked to do his own tune-ups. Even if the car didn't need maintenance, a man could lose himself in that sort of work.

Laughter drifted out to him from inside the house. Probably his six-year-old, Louise. Jack's family was young and growing like everyone else in this neighbourhood. Things seemed fine. America was racing into the future with the gift of foresight. That was a helluva thing, knowing your mistakes ahead of time.

That was why he'd voted for Ike and the Hammer. They knew what to do now and, more importantly, what not to do later.

He sucked in a deep lungful of smoke, held it. Let go. Of course, he knew what the cigarette was doing to him. He understood his mistake there, even though he'd been told beforehand.

But that was one thing he couldn't seem to change.

There was nobody happier than Jack Edmonston when the war ended. He'd known he was going to die. Had felt it for months. When they nuked Berlin, and the Germans folded, Charlie Troop had been back in England. Floods of replacements pouring in every day, and they'd made Jack feel like an old man at twenty-two. Those kids were so young, and there were so many of them. He'd known like all the old hands knew, that when the Seventh Cav was up to strength, they'd be riding back into the shit.

And he'd felt himself a dead man in that camp outside of Gislingham, England. A dead man walking, the uptimers called it, and Jack couldn't imagine a more fitting description. Then the nukes had finished off the krauts, and all the dumbass kids were bitching about never seeing combat, and Jack just laughed at them because he knew he was saved. That A-bomb had saved his life.

So why did he feel like he was still waiting for a bullet? A real slow bullet, inching towards him from the ruins of that farmhouse. Jack took a last drag of his smoke and rubbed it out. He lifted his sixth beer. The can of Blatz had gone a little warm, and the beer tasted flat and tinny. He didn't care; he chugged it down anyway and pitched the can in the trash.

His hands found the box from the auto shop. His excuse for being in the garage, away from his family. Jack turned the blue cardboard box over in his oil-smeared hands. A new distributor cap for the Chevy. The car didn't need it, but good or bad, old habits died hard. When he was a kid, cars needed a new cap every couple of thousand miles. So he'd bought a new cap just like his father had. There was a circular logo on the box with the letters AC. That logo guaranteed that Jack Edmonston had bought a genuine General Motors part.

Beneath the logo in the fine print was a list of patents. The top one read DAVIDSON AUTOMOTIVE ENTERPRIZES MAY 21, 1946, PATENT NO. 2403417.

He opened the box. The shiny black plastic cap sat on a bed of foam peanuts, which he'd heard you could eat, but he wasn't that dumb. The cap wasn't one of those cruddy Bakelite jobs he'd grown up with; they said this one should be good for a hundred thousand miles. It was one of the new electronic units Chevy had come out with a couple of years ago. Time was when he'd have enjoyed all this, marvelling at the ingenuity of it. Now, it just felt heavy and dumb in his hands. Meaningless. And his fingers felt alien, almost numb.

Jack set down the distributor cap and reached into the wire milk crate for another beer. He worked the new-style opener and heard the can fizz. He'd been in high school when the uptime folks appeared, and it seemed they'd changed everything, right down to the humble beer can. He couldn't remember the last time he'd seen a church key can. The new lift tab just worked better.

Jack swigged from the sweating beer can and closed his eyes, but the darkness let his memories come creeping back like fast shadows, hungry to swallow everything.

His AT M-4 leapt to his shoulder. The kraut was gibbering. "*Bitte! Bitte nicht schiessen, kamerad!*" As soon as his sights lined up, Jack pulled the trigger. As always, he heard the spring in the stock go *twang*. He felt the slight recoil against his shoulder and nose. Funny thing was, he didn't hear the report of his weapon, but he heard the dull clang of the bullet on the kraut's helmet.

Jack took another long swig of beer. Sometimes the booze helped dull his thoughts, but this looked like it was gonna be one of those nights when the ghosts would chase him, demanding their due.

Jack looked back over at the toolbox, where the pistol waited. Sweat trickled down his neck.

During the day, it wasn't so bad. He would get up at six, and Alice would be waiting on him with a hot breakfast and coffee. Sometimes there were bags under her pretty, bloodshot eyes. The couple had taken to sleeping in separate beds because Jack would thrash about at times, and once, he'd even woken up with his hand around his wife's throat.

He'd eat breakfast, drink a few cups of joe, and smoke one damn Lucky after another. Even though Alice begged him not to. Even though she was right about it, too. Jack left before the kids got up. Alice would kiss him when he went out the door in his steel mill greens. He worked as a millwright in the new continuous caster, another technological leap forward from their uptime friends. He kept busy all day long doing his bit for American industry. It was important to stay busy, but he loved it, too. The shattering noise and heat of the mill, and even the danger of the place. The eight hours of his shift would pass like magic. He didn't think about anything else while wrestling with machines in the moly-grease pits. It was only in the quiet hours that the war bubbled back to the surface like gas bubbles in a dark swamp. Especially at night after the kids were down.

Jack threw beer number seven away and picked up the distributor cap. He made uneven progress towards the car. His legs weren't as steady as they could be. He looked down at the engine. The Stovebolt Six's basic design was almost twenty years old. On casual examination, it had changed little since the thirties. However, there were some big differences if you knew to look. The intake manifold on the left side of the engine sported one of Chevy's new throttle body injectors. It gave the 'Thriftmaster' unbelievable fuel mileage. And sticking out of the side of the motor was the object of Jack's attention, the distributor. He needed a screwdriver to get the old cap off. He fished out another smoke from his dwindling supply, lit up, and turned to go to the toolbox.

He glanced at the pistol, shook his head, and opened a drawer. He got the tool. Went back to the car and got to work.

Jack allowed himself to be impressed again by the stuff these twenty-first people had brought with them; the new automotive electronics made it so his car started first time, every time. There was even talk of cars coming off the line in a year or two that'd be all electronic. No pollution or anything. And if you plugged them into the new-fangled solar roofs like they had in California, you wouldn't even have to pay the electric company for the juice.

What a goddamned time to be alive.

Jack unplugged the module from the top of the distributor cap, laid it to one side, and removed the cap and wires. He reached over to the car's fender, grabbed the brand-new unit, settled it into place, carefully replaced the wires in firing order, and plugged the ignition module back in. He tightened the two screws on the side of the cap, and presto, he was done.

There was nothing else that needed his attention. No points to file or adjust, nothing. The car was good to go. Jack walked around the side, opened the door, and climbed behind the wheel. He briefly admired the busy chrome and steel interior before hitting the ignition. The motor purred to life. He was feeling his buzz now and decided to listen to something. He turned on the radio, and music started playing. There was no slow increase in volume as there had been with the old tube units. In '49, Chevy started using transistor models.

He switched off the engine but left the radio on. Elvis Presley. Good stuff. Jack wanted some music with his beer. He walked with exaggerated care back to the workbench and grabbed himself beer number eight. He popped it open and took a long pull. He sat the can down and shook out a smoke. The one last in the packet. His hand trembled slightly as he lit the sweet-smelling Lucky. The cap change had gone too quickly. Jack was alone again. He took another swig, and the garage started to rotate slightly. Maybe tonight, he'd sleep like a stone and dream no dreams of war and murder. Jack burped, lifted his cigarette and took a drag. He glanced at Lady Luck and thought about everything that'd come into the world. His M-4 had been one of those things. He remembered the first time he had hefted it in basic. Felt like he was holding a Buck Rogers death-ray gun.

He came to know that rifle as if it were his right arm. And he had killed with it.

The German's body slumped, and a new pool of blood started spreading behind his head. It spread across the flagstone floor of the ruined farmhouse. Jack lowered his rifle. He heard a voice behind him. "Friendlies coming in!" Automatically, Jack answered with "Clear!" Bezak, a corporal from his squad, came up behind Jack, glanced at the dead kraut, and spoke. "Hey Jack, hold tight here for a while. We're getting held up by those fuckers with the gun on the other side of the street." Jack heard the roar of an MG-42. Bezak turned and left, leaving Jack with the man he had killed.

A man he didn't have to kill. Not really.

Back in his garage, Jack Edmonston remembered every detail of the German's face. The dead man had sandy brown hair, freckles, delicate lips, and a black hole above his right eyebrow.

He couldn't do this anymore.

Elvis sang "Suspicious Minds" as Jack dream-walked towards his toolbox. He reached in and lifted out the heavy chunk of steel waiting there for him. It had been waiting for so long. For Jack to accept, he had to make good what he'd done.

Outside of the garage, the insects sang their peaceful chant. Elvis finished singing.

Jack's right thumb flicked off the safety. He looked down the barrel. The bore loomed as large as a sewer pipe. A single tear rolled down his cheek.

Bitte nicht schiessen.

7

How strange it was, thought Josef Stalin, that the miracles and conveniences of the so-called future should be so damned inconvenient. He did not hate staying at the dacha on the lake outside of Moscow. It was just that he hated the necessity of it. The trouble and bother of even getting here in such a fashion that the Americans would not know his location. The aggravation of being so far from the Kremlin when all his plans were finally coming to fruition. The creeping sense that perhaps Lavrentiy Pavlovich had connived with his enemies to exile him here at this crucial moment.

Josef Stalin had many enemies everywhere, and the more he piled up into mountains of corpses, the more who seemed to emerge from spider holes and secret fissures to turn their hands against him.

He tried to turn his hands over in the soft woollen blanket on his lap, but only one would move. His right hand lay as dead as a rotting fish on the shore of the lake so far below. Why would it not move? He could not imagine.

Whole peoples had once moved on his say so. Millions of them, into the grave if it be his will that they should die. The Chechens. Ukrainians. Those stupid Meskhetian Turks from the Caucasus. They had all disappeared into the great Siberian wastes at a stroke of

Joseph Vissarionovich's pen, yet now he could not even lift the hand that had signed those papers. The supreme leader of the Union of Soviet Socialist Republics grunted, and his grunt turned into a snarl as he tried by sheer force of will to make that ancient, liver-spotted claw move just an inch or so.

Move, it did not.

Yagi, Stalin started to shout, meaning to call his bodyguard into the room.

But although his jaw worked and his mouth fell open, no sound emerged. It all felt so wrong, as though he was only half there, in his wheelchair, looking out over the pine forests and the striking, deep blue waters of Lake...

Of Lake...

Gah! He could not even remember the name of the damned lake down there.

Y-a-g-i-i-i...

The man's name was not lost to him. But he seemed to have forgotten how to say it.

Joseph Vissarionovich Stalin rocked back and forth in his accursed wheeled chair, his mouth gaping open and closed, wordlessly but not soundlessly. Small grunts and guttural retching noises crawled out of his throat, but so quietly that Yagi Osipov did not hear his master's voice, and the stroke which should have carried off the maximum dictator in 1953, finally tore through the flimsy skein of blood vessels and neuronal webbing like the fangs of a timber wolf two years later.

THE CHIEF of the People's Commissariat for Internal Affairs and the lead engineer of the Functional Projects Bureau stumbled from the armoured black limousine and nearly fell to the gravel driveway which looped past the main entrance to the lakefront dacha. Lavrentiy Beria was terrified, and that terror had robbed him of any semblance of control over his limbs. His legs were numb and impossible to command. He seemed to have lost any sense of where his hands might be and how to use them. He dropped his briefcase and struggled to regain his feet until one of his bodyguards bent down to help him.

Pah! They would soon be stuffing his body into the trunk of the reverse-engineered Packard.

Beria allowed the guard to haul him upright but quickly shook off the man's grip. It was intolerable to him. For a certainty, these men, or more just like them, would seize him on the orders of the Vozdh at some point in the next few minutes, and if they did not simply murder him in front of Stalin, they would deliver him to his executioners with all despatch. He tried to suck in a deep breath of the clean, warm country air, to have something to appreciate in these last few minutes. But instead, he took in a face full of pollen from the lilac and hawthorn trees that lined the white stone driveway, and he fell to sneezing and weeping from his hay fever.

At least it gave him some excuse for blubbering like a giant baby.

He had maintained his composure on the drive from the city, even as his heart seemed to slow in his chest and the darkness of mortal fear stole over him as he contemplated the dire news he must deliver.

The hammer fall had failed. Not entirely, however. The orbital strike on the US Fifth Army had annihilated the entire formation. A stunning demonstration of the technology's power and effect. But the reactionaries had...reacted, as they were wont to do, and some secret orbital weapons system of their own had neutralised the balance of the Red Army Space Force's pre-emptive strike. They had deployed some illegal, prohibited anti-satellite defense according to the best estimates of his scientists and spies. It had raked five of the six orbital platforms from the sky before any had loosed a single spear in anger.

Beria stumbled up the wooden steps of Stalin's dacha, his thoughts a thousand miles away. He could only shake his head in grim acknowledgment of the Allies' maskirovka, of their fiendish act of deception.

No, he told himself as he robotically removed his coat and hat and handed them to an unsmiling orderly. Not the Allies, as such.

This would be the work of the *Vodyanoy* Kolhammer and his imps. As the NKVD boss, Beria knew well of the shadow state that answered only to the American Vice President, utterly independent of any oversight by the supposedly democratic leadership of the United States. He already had reports of satellites missing from the Davidson Aerospace fleet – satellites the Red Army had not yet targeted for destruction.

Ah, but none of it mattered. Did it?

He was a dead man on the walk, as the uptimers would have it.

Two military officers awaited his arrival in the antechamber of the Vozdh's executive suite. A colonel of the Army and Admiral Zhdanov of the Military Maritime Fleet. Neither smiled at him in greeting nor moved to approach or offer their hands. So, word of his failure had preceded Beria, and they would no more reach out to a condemned man than he would stick his hand into a pig iron smelter.

But even now, with everything about to fall in on him, Beria's mind raced from one point to the next, seeking some escape route. The hammer fall had not missed entirely. The much-vaunted US Fifth Army was no more; with it had gone much of the 4th Allied Tactical Air Force. The sword and shield of NATO lay shattered before them. And there could be no denying the stunning advances made by fraternal forces, deep into Germany from the east and France from the south. And...and...

And Stalin would hear none of it.

He would care only for the failure of the attack, which Beria had personally guaranteed.

There was no escape.

Lavrentiy Beria tried to at least go with some dignity. He straightened his back and lifted his chin. He ignored the mordant glares of the military officers who fell in beside him without a word.

Osipov, the bodyguard, patted him down in the corridor while Beria took a moment to admire the painting on the oak panel walls outside of Stalin's personal suite. It would likely be the last piece of art he would ever have a chance to admire; a portrait of the poet Alexander Pushkin by Orest Kiprensky. Pushkin wore a black coat, and his arms were folded over a red plaid scarf, apparently referencing the English poet, Byron. The Russian writer's fingers appeared like talons, and he had posed as though for a Roman bust. Beria did not wonder what message their leader was sending with such imagery. There was none, beyond his unquestioned power, to simply have the damned thing and show it off. It had previously hung in the State Hermitage.

Beria started shaking as he waited for Osipov to finish his search.

This foolishness was a new symptom of the Vozdh's increasing paranoia. He was so old and frail now one would not require any instrument to put him down. Nothing as gross as the ice pick Stalin put into Trotsky's brain from afar, for instance. No, you could pinch off his nose and cover his mouth and he...

"You are clear to go in, Comrade Beria," Osipov said. "Comrade Admiral, Comrade Colonel."

Beria almost jumped in surprise. He had become lost in his reveries.

Osipov opened the heavy wooden door and held it for them.

Beria led the way through a short corridor that opened onto a large, furnished room with floor-to-ceiling windows that afforded a grand view of Lake Imandra. Bright red Turkish rugs covered the floor, and stuffed animal heads lined the walls. A great stone hearth dominated one end of the room, but the warm summer's day allowed of no need for a fire, and it lay cold and empty.

Beria saw Stalin was perched in his wheeled pushchair at a spot with the most excellent view, down a gently sloping hill alive with wildflowers. The lake's deep blue waters blazed with sunlight, and only a few fat clouds broke up the far horizon. Beria's mouth went dry.

This was it. It was happening.

He cleared his throat.

He could hear Admiral Zhdanov breathing heavily to his right, and he almost smiled to realise the navy man was just as scared as he. As well he should be. The Vozdh was known to be intemperate and arbitrary in his rages. There was a slight chance Beria might even leave this room alive and redeemed, while Zhdanov and the nameless Colonel somehow took upon themselves the burden of his failures.

Not much of a fucking chance, though.

"Vozdh?" Beria said, clearing his throat.

Stalin did not reply or even move.

Lavrentiy Beria did not dare hope because hope was a greater killer than the cold of the tundra, but...but...

"Move. Now!"

He felt himself shoved aside as the bodyguard elbowed his way through the small phalanx of supplicants and visitors. Beria glanced at Zhdanov and found the man's face a caricature of slack-jawed stupidity. He had no better idea of what was going on than did Beria.

The NKVD chief faltered further into the room as Yagi Osilov reached his boss.

"Call the doctors. Call them now," Osilov barked.

As the most junior of the other men, the colonel did not hesitate. He spun on his boot heel and ran from the room, calling for a medic.

Beria and Zhdanov exchanged a wary glance. They each took another step in.

"Is he all right?" Beria asked.

Osilov looked panicked and angry, and confused all at once.

"What do you fucking think? He's dead. That's what. He's dead."

A veteran of decades in the Kremlin, a survivor of more purges than he could remember, Lavrentiy Pavlovich Beria arranged his features behind the stern, unforgiving mask of accusation.

"What have you done, Yagi Osilov? How has this come to pass?" Beria demanded.

The bodyguard stared at him. Stunned. And slowly, as it dawned on him what was happening, mortified.

He stepped back from Stalin's body as though it might be contagious – because it was. Death was always catching in the Soviet Union.

Admiral Zhdanov remained grounded on the shoals of stunned passivity.

Beria took one step towards the corpse and, finding that his footing was now secure, another.

"I am the Director of the People's Commissariat for Internal Affairs," he barked. "And I am in charge here. Admiral, summon the house guard. Place this man under arrest and join me afterwards. We have much to do. A war to win."

8

Ilya didn't know where this giant *raspizdyai* had come from, but he was strong as an ox and slippery with it. The two men rolled on the tarmac in a deathmatch, each trying to find some leverage over the other.

Ilya tried to knee him in the crotch, but the man turned and took the kneecap to his thigh—a hard, painful blow, but nothing like getting your eggs crushed. In his turn, the big Italian tried to deliver a vicious elbow to the face. Ilya ducked, and the blow rode off the crown of his helmet. They rolled again, with Ilya struggling to get a mount, but this shit-eel reversed the momentum, and Ilya ended up on his side, trying to crab away. He was breathing hard, sweating freely, and dark blossoms were creeping at the edge of his vision.

The enemy kept getting inside Ilya's fighting arc. He didn't have a weapon, or Ilya would be dead already. His fists and elbows were bad enough. The fascist tried to wrap his legs around Ilya, but that gave him a chance to rake out a nice painful shin scrape with his boot. He saw the man's face contorted with the flaring pain and felt great satisfaction. It gave Ilya a split-second to crank a poorly executed neck lock on the man with one arm while he drew his bayonet with the other. Groping for his knife, he sawed his forearm across the other man's carotid, and as he'd hoped, the shock of that violation paid off. His opponent lifted both arms to try and break the choke. "Borrowed reaction," his unarmed combat instructor had called it.

Ilya borrowed it now.

There was no time to get fancy. With an underhand grip, he punched the knife into the man's back again and again, driving the steel to its hilt with a bunch of hard, messy thrusts under his ribs into the kidney. The giant let out a hoarse roar as he began to convulse, and Ilya clamped down on his neck even harder in case there might be any fight left in him. His reward was a spiralling scream and his attacker's face contorting into a rictus of agony. His body went rigid, and his bowels let go.

Ilya had already pissed himself, so it was no great inconvenience to get shat on.

Nothing like suddenly finding eight inches of Russian steel in his guts.

Ilya heaved the body away. He was panting and exhausted, and he could do nothing for a moment. He just lay there, too drained even to move. His heart seemed to pound louder inside his ears than the nearby gunfire. Ilya didn't even have strength enough to hold onto his bloody knife. It fell from his fingers, which he stared at, mesmerized. They looked like broken claws. Finally, he rolled to his side and puked so hard he thought his ass would fall out of his mouth. He heaved and sucked in air. If another one of these fucking goons found him like this, he was dead.

But they didn't. The forces of history aligned behind him on this evil night.

After a moment that lasted forever and not nearly long enough, Ilya Egorov forced himself to sit up.

A tracer cracked and burned past his head, a streak of red and orange light that seemed to slow down and almost stop as it flew past Ilya's face. And then it was gone, leaving a bright afterimage on the back of his eyeballs. He tasted bile and a faint metallic flavour at the back of his throat.

He dropped again and rolled to his stomach.

When would this fucking shit end?

Had he shouted that?

He didn't know and cared even less.

Casting his head from side to side in search of his fallen carbine, he felt like he'd cracked a disc at the top of his spine. He hadn't of course. He could still move. Could still feel all of the thousand storms of pain raging through his body. His vision swam, blurring the world around him, but only for a second.

First things first.

He recovered his bayonet and used the cooling wrestler's coveralls to wipe it down. He placed it back in its sheath and crawled over to his weapon. A quick check. All good.

Ilya propped the assault rifle on his forearms as he crawled away from the dead man as fast as possible. He needed to find the tower. He needed to get his men in order. And he no longer doubted that this was Naples airport; a large transport plane burned brightly a couple of hundred meters away. Ammunition cooked off and shot hundreds of feet into the night sky. Ilya gagged on the caustic fumes. It also killed his night vision and obscured the structures on the other side of the wreckage.

He crawled on, praying to a God that didn't exist to show him something, anything he could take as a sign. For now, though, there was nothing but smoke, fire, and occasional figures running hard. As he watched, a Soviet soldier jerked and fell.

It was hell in this place. If only he could just stand and run. More tracers, bright red ones, skimmed across the tarmac, throwing off golden showers of sparks. One round hit something and bounced wildly, like a firefly in a bottle. He shook his head. *Fuck that*, he thought and continued to crawl in the direction of a cement barrier.

At last, he reached it and crawled behind the solid chunk of cover. It was pockmarked and fire scorched. A woman lay curled up there. She held her arms over her head, wailing and crying, begging for everything to stop. Ilya could see blood on her hands, and he heard sirens wailing in the distance. She screamed when she noticed him and scurried away like a frightened bird flushed from cover. He hauled himself to his knees and watched her go. He'd thought she was a hundred years old but saw now that she was running in a dress and high heels. She was young and probably quite pretty. She had long dark hair with curls the colour of rich chocolate.

Ilya wished her luck. She'd need it. A pair of comrade soldiers ran by.

"You! Stop and come over here!"

"Fuck you!"

"That's 'fuck you, Comrade Senior Lieutenant.'"

"Shit."

The soldiers hustled over to his cement berm and dived behind it, looking guilty and worried. More worried about him than the enemy, which was how it should be.

"Have you seen the control tower?"

"Da."

He stared at this fool.

"So where the fuck is it?"

One of the two gestured to the southwest. "There, about four hundred meters."

"You will come with me. We will find others and seize the tower."

"But we have orders."

"Fuck your orders. I am here now, and you have new orders. Do not disobey them."

Ilya turned his rifle ever so slightly. It wasn't quite a threat. The other soldier looked at his companion and spoke.

"We serve the Soviet Union, of course, Comrade Senior Lieutenant."

Ilya nodded. "Of course you do. Now...." He gestured along a series of concrete barriers. "These barriers, we use them. We bound forward toward the tower. Any of our guys we find along the way, we bring with us. When we reach the tower, we assault immediately. Any questions?"

Silence answered him. The only answer he cared for.

"Good." He paused. "You two advance to the next barrier, and I will cover you. Then it's my turn. We do that until we reach the last one. Clear?"

"Yes, Comrade."

"Then go!" Ilya popped his rifle over the barrier, and the two soldiers ran for all they were worth. It could have been that Ilya had his rifle at their backs. Of course, their sights would soon be on him, so fair was fair. They reached the next barrier and started laying down fire. The Soviet bullets stank of copper and charred fish. The air tasted like a lake of ink, turned to acid. Ilya stood and sprinted towards them. He slid behind the barrier as bullets snapped and whistled by.

He let everyone catch their breath, and then it was his turn. Impressive, given how exhausted he'd been just a minute or two ago. He ran for all he was worth and hoped the two men at his back weren't done following orders from him. When nobody shot him in the ass, he jumped behind the next concrete barrier and sent fire into the night to cover their movement. The three men repeated the move until they cleared the burning aeroplane.

And there it was.

The tower. A thick cylinder of concrete and metal spewing tracer fire everywhere. It seemed bizarrely medieval just then, like a dark castle turret in a land cursed by dragons.

Another runner came by. Ilya gathered him up. He was less than pleased, but Senior Lieutenant Egorov didn't give one wet shit about that. They continued, leapfrogging forward, shooting occasionally. When they were one hundred meters from the Tower, Ilya had seven paratroopers under his command.

It would have to do, but how exactly? Machine-gun fire raked at them from the tower, and whoever that was didn't seem to be short of ammo.

Ilya looked around, taking a quick and dirty sight picture. He judged the shooter in the building couldn't see them because of the little cement walls, but there was no cover for the last fifty meters.

A soldier tugged at his tunic.

"Comrade, look. A supply bundle."

Ilya looked. A small pallet had landed haphazardly on a tow vehicle and flipped on its side, its parachute stirring in the breeze. He recognized it immediately, a munitions pallet.

The forces of history.

Ilya pointed at three men. "You, you, and you. Bust that thing open and see what's in it. Find something we can use. We will cover you." As Ilya and the other men poured fire at the tower, the three troopers hustled away. All the time, he chewed at his lip, thinking through the problem. It was his duty to take that tower, but how?

He heard a soldier whooping behind him. He didn't look. *They had probably found vodka*, he thought sourly. He heard a scraping noise and looked over.

For the first time since boarding the plane, he smiled.

His rotten little shits had recovered an automatic grenade launcher and three boxes of ammo.

Ilya laughed.

"Get to work, comrades."

THE ADVANCE along the highway was as bad as Lonesome had expected. The moon hung low in the night sky, casting a soft silver glow over the rocky landscape. The hills here were dry and barren, covered in sparse clumps of withered shrubs. Rocks the size of human heads dotted the terrain, while a few twisted trees clung to life here and there. The Sovs had pushed some assholes onto the road to the airport, and First Battalion had to clear them out. The 571st lost nine of her number for that first taste of the old wine, but they punched through, and Jones pushed them on. The hot night air was still heavy with the acrid scent of battle. The new grenade launchers slung under their carbines chewed up the enemy, but his scratch force of clerks and cooks fired off so many of the 20mm bomblets he worried they'd run dry before they got anywhere near the Sovs' main force effort.

"Fire discipline," he roared at his officers. He didn't expect a bunch of rear-echelon gimps to fight like seasoned marines, but he could and would demand more of his leadership cadre.

The six-lane road to Naples airport, a centrepiece of post-war construction, lay strewn with debris and bodies. Moonlight glinted off twisted metal, casting eerie shadows across the asphalt. He summoned his comms guy. The staging area for 2 Batt was a parking lot filled with cars, and he could hear the firefight raging to the northeast, not three hundred meters away.

"Gimme that mic, soldier," he said.

His RTO was a scared-looking kid with an Adam's Apple bobbing all the way out to Wednesday.

"S-s-ir," he stuttered.

Lonesome took the handset but clasped the kid's shoulder before he opened the call.

"Son, all you gotta do is haul that heavy-ass box around after me tonight. Breathe deep and keep your head down. You'll be fine."

The kid started to say thanks, but Jones was already talking to Colonel Perkins.

"One Six. This is Hammer Six. How's it looking, Colonel?"

Perkins came back. "Some bullshit with the perimeter fence, but we dealt with that, One Six."

That would make for a good story one day, Jones thought. Maybe he'd hear it later, maybe never.

"All right. Carry on. Hammer Six out." He paused, recalling which jobs he'd given to which of his senior officers. He keyed the handset again. "Three Six. This is Hammer Six. What is your status?"

He heard static and the roar of small arms fire. Shadows danced around in threes and fours, playing games between the stones and boulders off the main road.

A woman's voice replied. Struggling for air.

"Six, this is O'Connell. We are engaged with Russians by the main terminal."

"How many of your companies are in contact, Three Six?"

"I think... two, sir. I held HQ and Bravo Company in reserve."

Some handholding was gonna be needed, Jones thought. O'Connell was a hell of a supply officer, but this was her first real fight. Beefing with supply chain remfs to score those grenade launchers they'd just used didn't really count.

"All right, Three Six. You making progress?"

O'Connell's voice came back crackly and muted by gunfire.

"We took the departures area, but the Russians made a stand

further in. Fucking RPGs and a heavy machine gun. We're trying to deal with it now."

"Don't try, Mary. Just do. Look at where things are shittiest and commit your reserves there. Pour on the fire, push past the Russians. Plough those motherfuckers under. You are gonna lose people, but Ivan is gonna lose everything."

"They keep popping out of nowhere, sir."

Her voice had a serrated edge to it.

Jones dropped his voice an octave and spoke slowly.

"The enemy is stretched thin and disorganized, Three Six. Scattered to hell and back by a bad drop. They're sprawled out on the ground. Kick their fucking teeth in before they stand up again."

He paused.

"Do you have assets out on the tarmac?"

"Yes."

"Have you linked up with elements of the First?"

"I don't know."

"Find out, Three Six. You and Perkins need to be in constant contact. Don't tap him on the shoulder and wait politely for an answer. You need to be rub-fucking him. Hard. He assaults now. So do you. Hammer Six out." He paused again. "One Six. You copy that last transmission?"

"This is One Six. Yes, sir."

"Launch your assault and maintain contact with Three. She's up against the shit, but we cannot have a gap in our line. We're organized, and they're not. Don't piss that away."

"Roger that. My guys will move right the fuck now."

"Get it done. Hammer Six out."

Lonesome handed the mic back to his RTO.

In the distance, the dark silhouette of a damaged airport tower stood like a sentinel, its shattered windows reflecting flames and tracer fire. Beyond that, way off on the horizon, the flashes of an electrical storm silhouetted the peak of Mount Vesuvius in a rich palate of purples and blues. Maybe there was thunder, but he couldn't hear any.

He knew O'Connell and her guys would be having a hell of a

time. But he needed her fully committed before he decided on 2 Batt and his HQ. He was almost sure he'd have to send Prezwalski in to backstop her, but who knew what Perkins was about to step into?

Jesus fuck, this was easier to do when he'd had eyes in the sky, drones out the fucking wazoo, and Combat AIs programmed into the fucking kill chain down from sensor to shooter.

As if on cue, firing erupted due north of Lonesome's position in the car park. Perkins had launched his assault on the northern side of the field. Of that, at least, Jones was sure. His RTO held out the handset, "It's Colonel Perkins, sir."

Jones nodded and took it.

"Go for Six."

"This is One Six. My assault is rolling, and we're taking heavy grenade fire from a platoon-sized element with a fucking auto launcher."

Jones grunted as though gut punched. The Soviet AGS was bad news. A belt-fed, air-cooled, fully-auto bomb thrower, it spat 40 mm grenades at a cyclic rate of up to 60 rounds per minute. The Sovs had straight up stolen the design from the 'old' Mk19. 'Old' because the 19 would've entered service with the US Army in 1968. Now there was a knock-off version auto-shitting high explosives at his people a couple of hundred yards away and fourteen years ahead of time.

Jones made his decision quickly.

"Go around them at speed and have your follow-on forces fuck 'em up when they run dry."

"Can't, sir. They are tearing up my lead elements."

Jones rubbed his face. Stubble was starting to come through. He wasn't up there, so he didn't know. Maybe the Sovs had taken a position where they could dominate all the approaches. That's what he'd do. Uptime, he'd have called in an airstrike or smart drones, but he didn't have any of that happy shit to hand here.

As fucked up as it was, he was gonna have to smother the Russians with bodies. He keyed the mic.

"They don't have unlimited ammo. Take that position and push past them, Perkins."

There was a pause.

"Roger, Six. One Six out."

The man's voice sounded like it came from the bottom of a well. Lonesome nodded. He knew he'd just killed at least a company's worth of men and women. All to take out maybe twenty-plus Russians. But the clock was ticking. With every moment that went by, the Sovs would harden their positions. He needed to hit them now with everything he had.

Simply waiting, exercising tactical patience while standing next to a brown Fiat and listening to the battle, was one of the hardest things he'd ever done. Way harder than jumping into the TSMC complex on Taiwan, back in the upwhen. Due north, he could hear the crump, crump, crump of the automatic grenade launcher. So Perkin's people were catching it bad.

The sky behind Vesuvius flared with lightning, zigzagging in jagged bursts of pure white. The rocky landscape was a grey-brown abyss stretching endlessly off to Mordor.

Then he heard the action immediately to the northeast.

A sudden, roaring firefight with multiple explosions.

Jones fancied he could even hear the occasional scream when the gathering breeze was just right. So now First and Third Battalions were fully committed and had closed with the enemy. The Sovs might even be staging a counterattack. If he were the Soviet commander, where would he hit back? What would he do?

Jones thought, and he thought hard. If he were a Russian, he'd tell his people to sit tight in the terminal and hold. Then...

He called up a mental map of the airport.

Then he would attack along the north side of the runway.

For fucking sure! He'd want to get behind Jones's Brigade because he would know the main effort of the assault would be the terminal and tower.

Jones tapped his RTO. The kid handed him the mic.

"Two Six, this is Hammer Six."

Prezwalski answered. "Go, Six."

"I need your people to move now and backstop First Battalion. I think the Soviets are up to some sneaky fucking shit."

There was a pause. "Roger, Six. What are you thinking?"

"It's a counterattack. Get moving now and help First Battalion refuse the flank."

"Yes, sir."

"Hammer Six out. One Six, you copy that?"

Static and gunfire. "Roger, Six. Things are far from fucking ideal around here."

"It's about to get worse. Continue your advance, but be advised I anticipate a Russian attack in your AO."

"One Six copies."

Jones handed the mic back to his RTO. His face, lit by firelight, was drawn and tight. Jones knew he was up against the witching hour. The outcome would be settled in the next sixty minutes.

He hooked his thumbs in his body armour and listened. There was a constant, industrial frenzy of small-arms fire, but the grenade launcher had gone silent. He could see it in his mind's eye. A company of Americans, falling on the Russians who would receive them with teeth bared and guns hot. Close-quarter battle in the dark, each soul locked into their own personal hell.

At that moment, he heard a crescendo of explosions and gunfire on the other side of the runway, drowning out the clash immediately to his front.

Jones smiled and held out his hand to the RTO.

Perkins would be calling.

9

"Oh my God, Jack, no!"

Jack Edmonston jerked up when he heard his wife's voice. His thumb automatically released the trigger of the forty-five. With one guilty, furtive movement, he lowered the pistol. The sight tapped against his front teeth with an unpleasant click. His mouth tasted of metal and oil. He felt ashamed and somehow soiled by the contact with the gunmetal.

Alice spoke with shock and anger trembling in her voice.

"Put that thing away. Right now." She stood in her flowered apron, moving her hands onto her broad hips, dropping them, and putting them back again. She was shaking.

Very slowly, Jack lowered the pistol and pointed it in a safe direction. He caught one last sight of the cavernous muzzle as he clicked the safety back on. He didn't trust his own hands to lower the hammer. They were shaking too.

He couldn't look at Alice. He placed the Colt back in the toolbox and let out a breath he didn't realize he'd been holding. It took a conscious effort to breathe in again, but he made it. Alice rushed over to him, throwing her arms wide and crushing him in her embrace. He smelled his own stink, a cold, rank sweat, and inhaled the smell of her instead. The smell of Alice and cooking. The scent of love. They trembled in each other's arms. Not with passion but with relief. This was not his first time at the edge of darkness.

She wept, and tears flowed down his graven face as well. They stood close together for what seemed a very long time.

His daughter Louise called from the house. "Mom, when are we eating?"

The spell was broken, and they separated. Alice mopped at her face with the apron and called back, her voice thick. "In a minute, darling. I'm talking with your father."

Louise called back. "Oh, alright. I'm watching TV then."

No surprise there. Both children had been nailed to the floor in front of that television since Jack had brought it home from the store. A colour model, too, with one of the new remotes that didn't even need to be plugged in.

He tried to speak, but words were still beyond him. He looked at his wife and back toward the house.

She understood, calling back to Lousie, "Okay then, but none of that uptime stuff. You can watch Disney for a few minutes."

"Disney is uptime, too," Jack said weakly.

"Hardly the issue," Alice scolded, but gently.

Jack rubbed at his face with one hand. His palm glistened with tears. He reached for a cigarette and fumbled with the pack until he got one out. He jammed it in his mouth and lit it with his Zippo while Alice watched him. She shook her head and spoke in a low whisper.

"Jack, don't you ever do that again. You promise me you will get rid of that...that thing," she gestured at the pistol in the toolbox. "You do it, or I will. There is no sense at all in having a gun in the house. None. I'm done with it."

Jack dragged hard on his cigarette and nodded. His voice remained weak, almost brittle. "I know. I know," he said. "Something has to change, Alice. But I don't know what."

Her lips pressed into a thin line, and she gestured toward the empty beers on the workbench. "You could start by laying off the bottle. It's not doing you any good. Jack, you get so down when you're taking a drink these days. It doesn't make you happy. It's like it's not even you anymore."

"Yeah. I know."

He sagged, leaning his ass back against the bench. He drew on the smoke again. They said these things would kill you, but he figured something else would surely get him first. The buzz of the fluorescents was loud in his ears. Alice said nothing. Her silence was reproach enough. She watched him as he finished up his smoke with a shaking hand. He ground out the butt, squeezed her arm, and moved past her toward the house. She followed on click-clacking heels.

Jack pushed through the screen door into the kitchen, his gaze scanning the black-and-white checkered linoleum floor, the new Kelvinator range, and the Kit-Cat electric clock on the wall. Everything seemed brighter, the colours deeper. It was hard to believe he had been so close to turning out the lights on all this forever. What the hell had he been thinking?

But he hadn't been thinking at all.

Certainly not about what would happen after he pulled that trigger.

Jack hobbled through the kitchen and into the small dining room, where his kids sat watching TV. He could tell instantly that the show was something from the future. *The one about the family whose flying saucer got lost in outer space*, he thought. But the older version. There was another scarier one with better effects, but the kids had chosen the simpler, less...sophisticated version.

That's what smart folks called all the stuff from the future that Jack didn't much like and didn't always understand. Sophisticated.

Horrible was another word for it.

His toes felt numb, and he tripped and stumbled a little on the old brown rug. The food stood on the table in the big blue enamel pot. Pork chops, it smelled like.

"Turn that off and come get your dinner," Alice said.

"Oh, but M-o-m," both children wailed.

"You can watch it later," she said. "It's dinner time now."

"But it won't be on later, and we don't have a recorder," Henry complained. "Like Eddie's family."

Jack nearly teared up again as he took his seat at the head of the table. He could have been dead, and he would have missed his son's constant complaints about how much better life was at Eddie Monaghan's house. He carefully sat down and did his best to conceal his distress.

Louise noticed his red eyes, though.

"Are you okay, Dad?" she asked.

"Just got some sparks in them from the mini welder," he lied. "Wasn't taking care is all, darlin'. Now sit down like your mom said."

Alice stood at the opposite end of the table and lifted the lid on the casserole.

It was his favourite, pork spare ribs and stuffed peppers.

"Let me have your plate, Jack."

As always, she served him first. The children followed in order of age. Louise, the oldest first, then Henry. Finally, Alice helped herself, but she cut up little Henry's portion before she sat down.

The family ate. Or, at least, they tried to. Jack put a bit of meat into his mouth, and instantly his throat clamped shut, and he jumped up, hurrying for the bathroom. He just made it, put his head in the toilet and heaved repeatedly, sending a hot spray of beer and peanuts into the bowl.

Somewhere in the background, he could hear voices.

"Is Daddy sick?"

"What's he doing in there?"

"He's fine," Alice insisted. "Just eat your dinner."

Jack heaved again. Bile burned at the back of his nose. He felt hot and cold all at once, clammy and dizzy. Whatever it was, it finally stopped, and he shivered once. He clung to the toilet. He looked up and saw Alice's legs. She brushed a black lock from her face, turned her head and pitched her voice to carry.

"Your dad's alright. He's not feeling well. Keep eating. I'll be back in a minute."

She turned back to him and spoke in a tired murmur. "Get yourself cleaned up, Jack. If you feel like eating later, I'll save some food for you."

He looked into her blue eyes and nodded. "Okay. Thanks."

She returned to the dining room. Jack closed the door to the bathroom, stripped off his clothes, and showered. His mind cleared as the hot stream played over him, and he thought about what he had almost done. It was too much. He pushed the thought away. He finished, shaved, and changed into fresh clothes in the bedroom.

He felt a little better, probably from getting all the beer out of his system.

Alice was right. He was losing himself in the bottle.

When he returned to their small living room, the children were gone. The dinner plates tidied away. Jack lowered himself into his favourer recliner and flicked on the radio. He wasn't hungry and didn't want to listen to anything. He just needed something in the background to fill his thoughts.

He dozed off, and Alice was sitting on the couch beside him when he woke up. She was snoozing, too. A sock was on her lap; her darning needles were still in her slack grip. She snored lightly. He sat up; the springs creaked.

Alice's eyelids cracked open, and she peered groggily at Jack. He yawned and leaned toward the coffee table to grab his pack of Luckies. He held the pack out for her, and she took the last of his coffin nails. He lit the smoke with his Zippo, and they shared it.

About halfway down the cigarette, he spoke. The kids were in bed, and Kitty Wells was singing softly. They had some privacy for a moment.

"I'm sorry, Alice. I don't know what came over me. It was like I wasn't here. It wasn't me."

She nodded and took the cigarette. Inhaled. After a moment, smoke trickled out of her nose. Her voice was quiet, shaky. "I don't know what we'd do if we lost you, Jack." Tears welled in her eyes, and she dabbed them away. "Think of us, would you?"

He glanced down at the tattoo on his arm; she looked at it too. She spoke again. "The war is over, honey. I wish you could forget."

"Yeah. Me too."

Alice sat back and took another draw on the cigarette. A deep one. Had it pulled forward the moment of her death by any measurable amount? It seemed unlikely. He'd smoked so many of the damned things, and he was still here, despite his best efforts. Were they supposed to give up this small pleasure too? What the hell would be left to a man?

Kitty Wells sang on.

"Open up your heart and let the sunshine..."

Her voice cut off abruptly. Alice and Jack turned to the radio, one of Truetone's bright red plastic models. *What the hell*, Jack thought, wondering if a tube had blown. But no. A man's voice crackled over the air; his words edged by real fear. Jack was familiar with the sound of it.

"We interrupt this broadcast for a news flash. This just in over the AP wire, and I quote. President Eisenhower is dead. Communist assassins are suspected. Allied Forces Europe have been subjected to a massive surprise attack by the Soviet Union. Casualties are unknown but expected to be heavy. The whereabouts of Vice President Kolhammer are unknown. End quote. We'll return to our regular broadcast for now, but this station will provide updates as they come in."

The music started back up. "Smilers never lose, and frowners never win..." Kitty assured them. Alice and Jack stared at the radio, then at each other.

10

The face of the tower disappeared in black explosions, brick dust and flashes of light. Ilya Egorov yelled at his men.

"Let's go!"

He assaulted forward with five random paratroopers, their bodies crouched low and weapons in hand.

Ilya hoped the guys on the AGS would do as he said: stop firing when his group reached the halfway point of the dead space in front of the tower. If they didn't, half-a-dozen brave sons of Mother Russia were about to get shredded. He plunged on, trying to think only of the door to the tower that lay straight ahead, blasted off its hinges.

The explosive storm of grenades suddenly stopped, and Ilya's crew plunged through the smoke and dust and falling chunks of brick and steel. They didn't stop by the door. They charged in pell-mell. A trooper in front of Ilya was first through the breach, and he shot at something with Ilya hot on his heels.

Ilya broke right in the dark space and trusted that the next soldier would break left, as he had been trained. Sweeping the area with his rifle, he could see directly ahead to a closed elevator and a staircase on his side. *Fuck your mother*, he thought. *I fucking hate staircases.*

A quick look around.

No shooting. The only people in the entryway were his men and the dead. He kicked a woman's legs aside and gestured at two troopers.

"You and you. Come with me. We're going to clear that machine gun nest upstairs."

The two men looked grim. He pointed at the other three. "You stay here and secure this entry. When I call down, signal the AGS crew to come in and tell them to come upstairs. But not before then. Clear?"

"Yes, comrade."

"Good."

Ilya paused and looked at his two helpers. "We will clear the stairs, then kill everybody in this tower. We don't have time or the men for prisoners. Here's how we do it. Unless they are fools, they will have security on the steps. So we roll up two across and one back to cover the rear. The man who pulls rear security holds on to my belt so we stay together. Understood?"

They nodded. One soldier's Adam's apple bobbed. The other sweated profusely. Ilya grabbed the sweaty bastard. "You come with me. We stay together up the steps. Rifle up! Always looking up."

He pointed at the other man. "Grab my fucking belt and stay with us. Watch our asses."

"Da."

Ilya tested the heavy steel door to the stairwell. It was unlocked. He pulled a grenade from his battle harness and called back to the others.

"Grenade!"

He yanked the pin and let the spoon fly. One-one thousand. Two-one thousand. It was enough. He pulled the door open and tossed the grenade up the stairs. Then he closed the door and quickly stood behind the brick wall. The others pressed themselves against the walls as well.

THUMP.

The grenade detonated. Ilya heard the muffled thud of the blast, a dull reverberation that felt like it punched up through his boots and his back to go off inside of his ears and chest.

"Now!"

He pulled the slightly buckled door open and grabbed his wingman. As ordered, their rear guardsman grabbed Ilya's belt. Side by side, with weapons aimed high, Ilya and his flanker ascended the stairs, making damn sure to cover as high as they could see.

He saw movement. He fired, the short burst echoing against the concrete walls of the stairwell, ringing in Ilya's ears and making his heart pound in his chest.

They kept moving upwards in step, just as they had trained. Ilya felt a steady tug on his belt as he moved along the stairs, his breath hard and sour through his dry mouth as his heart pounded and the reek of ordnance choked him.

Something rolled down the steps. Something round. Ilya didn't hesitate. He yelled, "Grenade," kicked it behind him and rushed up around the corner. The hand on his belt slipped, and Ilya didn't have time to collect the man behind.

As soon as he cleared the corner, he saw a soldier. At the very same moment, the grenade detonated. The man looked comically surprised, and Ilya cut him down with a burst from his carbine. *Speed*, he thought, racing up the stairs with his wingman on his heels. Ilya paused only to grab another grenade and pull the pin. He lobbed it through the waiting door and stood aside, hoping the thick brick wall would hold.

THUMP.

The wall held. Shrapnel whizzed through the open door and, through some evil ricochet, sliced into the other paratrooper. He grabbed his neck, folded over, and fell back down the steps.

Shit, Ilya thought.

Alone now, he swept onto the level housing the machine gun nest. It was up to him. Someone moved. Ilya shot him. Another one tried to swing his weapon around. He died, too.

A silence descended upon the dark, blood-splattered chamber.

To his amazement, Ilya found that he had taken out the nest.

But now to finish the job.

He called down the stairs.

"Get the AGS crew over here, now! You fuckers come up here when they arrive!

They shouted back with the only answer he wanted to hear.

"Yes, comrade Lieutenant."

Ilya pointed his weapon up the stairs, mindful of yet more falling grenades. Within a minute, three paratroopers ascended the stairs. They manhandled the AGS and a few boxes of ammo. Ilya directed them into their new position by a window, placing them to cover the most likely direction of attack. Then he grabbed two more guys and continued his murderous ascent.

However, there was no more opposition. Floor-by-floor, they searched and found nobody. At last, there were no more steps to climb. They stood at the top of the tower, only the control room ahead of them.

Ilya and three men burst into the control room, ready for anything.

There was nobody left alive there. Just two corpses, beeping machines, and a lot of broken glass. The smoke and fire spoke of a grenade explosion. Yet a single cup of expresso rested unscathed upon a small table. Ilya made a face. He would rather have had tea, but the Italian mud water would do. He was thirsty. Ilya dropped ass into a chair and stared out the window, tiny coffee cup in hand. The view, at least, was magnificent if you had a taste for hellish panorama. The vast open space of the airfield seethed with tracer fire, explosions, and dark swarms of men hacking at each other.

A soldier came up the stairs, a radioman.

Ilya looked at him and spoke softly; he was exhausted.

"Can you speak with Regiment?"

"Da, comrade."

"Good. Call them and say the control tower is in Soviet hands. For Stalin!"

The man answered with the standard, "We serve the Soviet Union!"

Then he placed the call.

Ilya sat back in the luxurious seat and sipped his lukewarm coffee. The first hints of dawn lightened the sky.

He smiled to be alive.

And then all hell broke loose to the South.

"HELP IS ON THE WAY, One Six."

Perkins keyed his mic. Jones could barely hear him above the staccato uproar of machine-gun fire and the crunching thumps of grenades.

He craned his head slightly, turning away from the parking lot and trying to will his hearing to sort out the mad clamour of battle in the distance. The airport was illuminated by bursts of orange flame and glowing plumes of smoke that faded into darkness. Flares streaked into the sky like shooting stars, leaving trails of fluttering sparks in their wake. Jones thought he might even be hearing light mortar fire somewhere.

Colonel Perkins' voice crackled from the radio handset.

"These assholes are all over us," he reported. "Charlie Company's HQ's been overrun."

Scratch one, Captain Dowler, Jones thought. He saw the man's face in his mind's eye and the picture of the twin baby girls Dowler had shown him just last week.

"Support on the way, One Six," Jones said flatly.

Perkins' reply was strained and bracketed by explosions.

"They can't get here soon enough."

"Understood. Two-Six is rolling on you right now."

Prezwalski broke into the conversation. He was struggling for breath as he addressed Perkins.

"One Six...my lead elements...just contacted your Alpha Company...leadership. Where do you...need us most, Colonel?"

Lonesome tuned them out and focused on what was happening to his front. O'Connell also needed support at the terminal, and Jones could all too easily picture the shitfight she was in. Corpses, or pieces of them, hanging from the rafters, a carpet of gore underfoot, most of the dead...civilian.

He'd seen this type of thing too often. In Damascus, Taipei, Jakarta.

The Lord does work in mysterious ways, he thought. Perkins' fight to the north would be decided soon; he'd done what he could. Now it was time to help out O'Connell.

He had four hundred troops in his command element, all just standing around scratching their asses in this goddamned parking lot. It was time to commit them.

"Three-Six. This is Hammer Six."

Echoing gunfire. A scream, but not O'Connell's.

"Fucking send it, Six," she shouted.

Tsk, tsk, thought Lonesome. *Swearing over my net*. He grinned like a stone gargoyle.

"I'm moving up to your position with my element. Tell your rear security not to light us up. Contact in five."

"Thank fucking God, Six."

"When I get to your perimeter, shout out and let me know where you are. Good work, O'Connell, and know that help is coming."

O'Connell came back at him, "From the Halls of Montezuma, sir."

Lonesome keyed the mic.

"To the fucking shores of Tripoli via your terminal building. Hold tight, Six out."

Jones felt the old rush, the sweetest high. The long, broken years all fell away. *Thank you, General Cronauer, you fucking asshole*, he thought. *Thank you for banishing me to this fucking backwater command.*

He looked around for his RTO. The radio kid was nervously smoking a cigarette.

"Those things are terrible for your health, son. Give me the HQ push."

The RT sucked the last of the butt down as he passed Jones the handset.

"Done, sir. Going wide."

Lonesome hit the button on the mic. "Listen up, HQ. Be ready to roll in three minutes. We are headed into the terminal, so there is no need for maps. Headquarters leads and the other elements to fall in on the standard order of march, just like a weekend fun run. But more fun. We will relieve Third's most fucked-up units. We will kill every one of these Russian motherfuckers. And combat commands through all of Europe will fucking curse themselves that they weren't here to kiss the ass of the mighty 571st Joint Sustainment Brigade. Stand by for changes. Sound off in sequence."

His HQ commanders answered, their voices hard and loud. Their warrior spirits on fire, Jones hoped. He nodded, satisfied. He looked at his RTO.

"You ready to step off, Lance Corporal?"

Every line in that kid's face was drawn too long and too deep. "Semper Fi, sir," he said, coughing.

"Outstanding. I hope you get to regret that Chesterfield one day a long time from now, son. Tell 'em to fall in behind me. We lead the way."

The young man, a boy no longer, made the call. Jones pumped a fist at his staff.

"Follow me, ladies and gentlemen. Guns hot."

His headquarters staff fell into a file, with Jones in the lead. They double-timed out of the car lot, surging across the highway towards the airfield. Yellow lighting gleamed off their weapons and equipment, casting thin shadows on the pavement as they moved.

"Sound off," he called out. The file behind him called back.

"One. Two. Three..."

Jones waited until his staff were done. Then he bellowed.

"Odd numbers advance, leapfrog in turn." He paused. "Now."

Jones ran forward and didn't look back. A strong smell of jet fuel and exhaust filled the air as they ran, the scent of metal and oil mixed with sour sweat and fear.

Behind him, a line of staff officers from all service branches performed the basic fire and movement exercise. The even numbers covered down, and the odd numbers ran forward. Boots crunching on asphalt echoed as men and women rushed across the highway. Jones was hyper-aware of clinking gear and the muffled shouts of sergeants keeping their flocks together.

You're up, you're seen, you're down, Jones thought. A cadence he'd learned a long time ago, many decades from now.

He dove behind a massive terracotta flowerpot. Its surface was rough textured with an orange and yellow hue and smelled of damp earth and clay, with a faint hint of some herbs he recognized but couldn't quite name.

Footsteps crunched up behind him, and he saw his RTO bolt past. He needed to stay close, but hanging around with a commo in the open was a proven way to get your ticket punched.

Jones didn't feel like getting Swiss-cheesed just now, so he'd go without comms for a while. As long as he kept track of the RTO. He watched the kid go to ground, a surpassingly athletic slide into cover behind an abandoned, bullet-scarred taxi. The gift of youth. It was his turn again. He bolted forward, zigzagging through cars and buses. Jumping over discarded luggage and occasionally around a fallen body. *Bounding fucking overwatch*, he thought. Not for the old or faint of fucking heart. And certainly not for generals in the usual run of events. But at least he didn't have a heavy radio bolted to his ass. He made a mental note to write his RT a commendation, maybe with a 'V'.

The main terminal drew closer.

Three hundred metres was a long way to move like this, but Jones had made a point of physical fitness among his troops, pissing them off mightily. As he bounded forward again, he thought that anyone who survived this wouldn't go bitching about PT anytime soon. Might even have made a few converts.

He heard the dreaded call of a panicked sentry.

"Halt! Who g-goes there?"

Jones froze. If he flinched, the kid would nail him, and he didn't feel like turning in his old body armour for a new set—if he was lucky.

"It's your fucking Brigade Commander, pencil dick."

"Oh. What's the password?"

Thanks for sharing that one, O'Connell, Lonesome thought.

"I don't fucking know."

"Advance one and be recognized."

Jones stepped forward. A stray tracer caromed off a nearby delivery van. The sentry never took his rifle from Jones's face.

"Holy shit, it is you!"

"No lie, son. Now can we reinforce your boss?"

"Yes, sir!"

The sentry was dressed in Air Force fatigues. His eyes were bugging all the way out.

"Airman," Jones said, "This is called a passage of lines. Didn't they teach you that at Lackland?"

The young man shook his head. "Hell no."

"Hell no, sir."

"Yes, sir."

Jones shook his head and waved his crew forward, collecting his RTO as they entered the battered terminal. Even with half the lights out, he could see the walls were scorched and blackened from gunfire. Every window was shattered, and the floor was covered in glass and debris.

"Patch me through to Three Six."

"Done, sir."

Jones took the handset. The noise was much worse in here, just as he'd expected. He keyed the mic.

"Three Six. I'm in your AO. What's your location?"

"By the baggage claim, sir."

"Alright. I'm heading to you with my people. We'll figure out who goes where when I get there. Are you in contact with either Two or One Six?"

"Yes. Both are holding off the counterattack by the runway."

"All right. You'll see me soon."

Jones crouched and headed along the ruined thoroughfare. The baggage claim was ahead by the escalators. He wondered for a weird, dissociated moment whether the baggage carousel was native to this time or had travelled back down from the twenty-first century.

A PK rattled with its distinctive tack-tack-tack.

A 240 answered it, and Jones stopped wondering about technology exchanges between the upwhen and the present day.

Outside, the popcorn-like rattle of small-arms fire scaled up fast. A grenade boomed. Jones turned to his exec.

"Anderson."

"Sir."

"Send Records down to the runway to beef up Third's people. I think they'll need it."

The man turned and shouted to someone. Jones moved forward again, crouched low. The luggage carousel drew near. He looked around and spotted her, shaking his head. It was a miracle she hadn't been hit. O'Connell was standing tall, ripping somebody a new one. Yelling at this guy like a fucking drill instructor. For his part, the man stood with hands on hips, shaking his head and jutting his chin defiantly. Jones recognized the grin on his face. It was the sneer of a man who'd rear-ended a woman driver and got out to explain it was all her fault.

"You useless piece of shit, you'll do as I say or—"

"Can I be of help, Colonel O'Donnell?"

Jones's voice was low but powerful enough to cut in over her shouting and the backing roar of battle.

The two of them—an Army Captain, Jones could see now, and O'Connell, his diminutive Supply Colonel—looked over at him. The Captain suddenly backed away one step. He looked like he wanted to run.

"No, sir," O'Connell said. "The situation is under control, but Captain Sykes here needs to get his people unfucked and resume the advance."

Lonesome glowered at the man.

"What part of do as you're fucking told, don't you understand, Captain?"

"But General Jones, sir, I—"

"Resume the advance, or I will have you arrested and charged with cowardice in the face of the enemy."

The man froze.

Jones was about to call for a couple of men to take him into custody when he gulped and started to salute.

"Don't you fucking dare," Jones said.

Sykes froze, his eyes wide.

"What?"

"Don't sniper check him," Captain O'Connell suggested. "Even a supply reef knows not to do that."

"Just go," Jones barked. The terrified officer stumbled away. "Colonel," Jones said as quietly as he could in the uproar. "Remind me later to transfer Captain Sykes to the Antarctic command. He can salute the fucking penguins all day long down there."

"Yes, sir."

"Right. I sent a platoon-sized element to reinforce Perkins out on the runway." Jones paused. "What do you need here?"

Somewhere close by, an RPG boomed out from a launcher. Jones pulled O'Connell down, and his RTO flattened out. The round struck an Arrivals board, exploding with a roar and spraying shrapnel everywhere.

Automatic fire answered the rocket-propelled grenade.

"Honestly, General, I'd give up my silver birds for five minutes of quiet time with a frappa-fucking-cino and an old Reader's Digest."

Jones snorted.

"I feel it, O'Connell, but this is Italy. Frappuccino's illegal here."

11

There was some guy from the future, one of those super-rich computer guys, who said people were always wrong about how much they could get done in one year. They always overestimated. But they were even more wrong about how much could change in ten. Dumb bastards always went low on that.

But not Slim Jim Davidson.

Nope. Slim Jim always bet the over.

That was why he got to fly out of Paris in his business jet while most people were trapped in the city with the Red Army rolling on them. And he should have been happy, or at least satisfied with that, leaning back in his comfy leather recliner, nursing his beer, and enjoying the short skirts of his personal flight attendants.

Except that O'Brien was making him drink coffee, not beer. And she wouldn't let him recline his chair in case he fell asleep again. And the smokin' hot trolley dollies who typically attended to his every fuckin' whim on these flights had been replaced by a platoon of grim-faced bodyguards in tactical coveralls and combat goggles.

Those goggles were nightmare fuel.

You see the dudes' eyes, but it wasn't really their eyes. They were like little movies of their eyes behind the goggles. It was deeply unsettling, and he wondered why his boffins had invented the goddamned things. Or rather, why they'd ripped off the design and the tech from the future.

Because there was a buck to be made, you fucking idiot, he thought, answering his own question.

Slim Jim waited for the seatbelt sign to go off, but it never did. He waited for someone to ask if he wanted a drink, but that somebody never came. The twin-engine corporate jet banked to the right shortly after they took off, affording him a view of Paris at night until the pilot put the pedal to the metal, or whatever the hell it was that pilots did, and they accelerated away to the north.

Maria O'Brien, his personal assistant, company secretary, and Fixer-in-Chief, ignored him while she plugged her computer into the plane's on-board systems.

She was swamped. With what? He couldn't say. But he didn't dare interrupt her. She ripped out short, fast bursts of typing, sending messages or emails or some shit across his empire. She made terse calls on the headset she plugged into that laptop. And occasionally, she spoke with the pilot and co-pilot, asking brief questions and issuing even briefer instructions.

Meanwhile, Slim Jim was left to look after himself. Beyond the most obvious and basic information—the commies had attacked, and he was getting the hell out of their way—he had no fucking idea what was happening.

Twenty minutes into the flight, and O'Brien finally slowed down. She checked her watch, closed the laptop lid, and breathed out.

"I think I'll have that drink now," she said.

"Would you like me to get that for you?" Davidson asked, not bothering to buff the edges of his sarcasm.

"Yeah," she said. "I'm sure you know where the beer fridge is. But I'll take a bourbon, single shot, on the rocks."

Jesus Christ, she wasn't joking. Slim Jim shrugged and got up anyway, figuring, "What the hell."

He fetched a couple of drinks from the galley behind the cockpit and carefully returned to their seats, stopping several times to check his balance against the mild turbulence. He didn't bother asking if any of the heavily armed goons wanted anything. They were on the job and would act like killer robots until he was delivered to...

He stopped.

He wasn't sure.

"Hey, where the hell are we going anyway?" Davidson asked as he dropped back into the soft, hand-stitched leather of his flight seat.

"One of your properties about a hundred miles north of London," O'Brien said. "There's an airfield nearby with a big enough runway. When we can grab one of our long-haul jets, and when it's reasonably safe to get across the pond, we'll fly back to the States. For now, though, Hamilton Manor is secure and has all the data links you'll need to run operations."

Slim Jim passed the drink across to her.

He knocked the top off the beer he'd grabbed for himself.

"Why don't we cut the shit and stop pretending I'll be running anything, Maria," he said.

"You're the boss," she replied a little cryptically.

"No, I'm just the guy whose name is on the shingle. I haven't made one damn decision worth a pinch of shit for a long time now."

Maria O'Brien took a sip from her bourbon. The ice cubes tinkled against the cut crystal. With her tailored suit, mannish haircut, and the subdued LED lighting throwing sharp-edged shadows from her cheekbones, she looked like she had just stepped through a portal from the far future. She was almost entirely alien to the 1950s as they would have been.

She tilted her head slightly, and those shadows moved, giving her an even more sculpted, intimidating air.

"You're the richest man in the world," she said. "Do you have a problem with how things worked out?"

It almost sounded like a threat.

He didn't answer immediately. Instead, he looked out of the window into the darkness, but all he could see was his reflection. He looked tired, but it was coming up on three in the morning, and he'd had a hell of a day. A hell of a life, honestly. The image of the man reflected at him in the glass wasn't a stranger, but Slim Jim wasn't entirely sure who that guy was either. Late thirties, a little jowly from all the fine living, but not fat. The bags under his eyes would fade. He always partied hard when he travelled for work. He partied pretty hard when he was at home, too. But he was still young. He'd been 27 when the Transition had folded the future back in on itself and speared that cruiser from the twenty-first century deep into the heart of the USS *Astoria*.

Jesus fuck, what a thing that'd been. Those two ships fused together. Hundreds of men (and women, it turned out) killed when the *Astoria* and the *Leyte Gulf* crossed over in time and space. And somehow, from that horror and madness, he had walked a path that led him here to fortune and glory and all the private jets and five-star Hollywood pussy a man could possibly want.

"No, Maria, I got no problem with that," Slim Jim sighed. "And I got no problem letting other people make decisions that I got no business making myself. I made my choices back in '42. And they were some pretty fuckin' good choices, I reckon."

He gestured about him with this beer as though the aircraft in which they flew illustrated his point, which it totally fucking did. He used to be scared of flying. Or at least he'd thought he was. Turned out he was just afraid of flying around in creaky fucking tin plate shit-boxes like the Navy's Dakotas and Conestogas. Give him the option of a Davidson Aerospace Lear Jet knock-off with Italian leather love seats and a full-service bar, and your boy Slim Jim could show that fascist-loving cocksucker Charlie fucking Lindbergh a thing or two about how a man was meant to fly.

The judge who sent him to that fucking Alabama chain gang didn't have a personal jet.

Chief Mohr, who busted his balls so hard back on the old *Astoria*, didn't own the biggest fucking company in the world.

Commander Evans, who'd had him on punishment detail so many fucking times Slim Jim could still peel a goddamned spud in his sleep, hadn't even survived the war to see what'd become of not-so-able Seaman Jim Davidson.

"It's just that I..."

He trailed off. He had no idea what he was trying to get to. O'Brien looked directly into his eyes. There was nothing romantic in her expression. It was more like she was reading him. Translating him.

"It's just that you have come to feel that you don't really understand what you have done, and because you don't understand it, you can't control it. Because you can't control it, you worry that you might lose everything one day," she said. "Does that sound right?"

His jaw dropped open a little, but he snapped it shut again.

He raised his beer to her when he got his shit back together.

"That's why I pay you the big bucks, O'Brien," he said. "You know stuff."

She nodded.

"You can stop worrying," she said. "It's like you said. Your name is on the shingle. As far as the world is concerned, you are Davidson Enterprises. Nobody will take that away from you unless Uncle Joe's barbarian hordes come charging up Wall Street, and we're doing our best to ensure that doesn't happen."

The plane banked to the left, and Maria reached out to secure the laptop resting on her knees. It wasn't one of the old uptime models that had come through the wormhole nearly a decade ago. Most of them had failed by now. Some egghead told him why once. It was another one of a thousand details that Slim Jim might have been across eight or nine years ago. But he had people like Maria for that now. She was rocking one of the latest models from his own electronics division. Bulkier than anything that had come through the Transition, for sure. You couldn't just magic up seven decades of science and progress and shit in less than ten years. But like that future computer guy said, you'd be surprised what you could get away with in that time.

"What am I supposed to do, then?" Davidson asked. "This was a hell of a lot easier when I was just stealing flexipads and laying insider bets with the Hawaiian mob."

O'Brien cocked one eyebrow at him.

"I don't imagine you're developing a conscience at this late stage in your personal story arc," she said. "So, what is it that you're after? Surely not a sense of purpose in life?"

She was smiling but sort of lopsided, taking the edge off the mocking tone hiding in the back of that question.

"I guess I just...I dunno..."

He struggled to find the words because he didn't know what was suddenly bothering him in a way that had never bothered him. She was right. He was the richest man in the world. There was him, and there was daylight back to the next guy. Probably one of the Rockefellers or that Getty asshole.

He'd met the guy once. Jesus, what a prick.

Getty had dissed Slim Jim as a fucking grifter, which was fair enough because he was. But that just meant he recognized his kind; all those rich assholes were the worst grifters. The sort who believed their own bullshit about earning their money instead of straight up stealing it off the working stiff.

The day that Getty had sneered at him in that snooty Manhattan club, Slim Jim had ordered Maria to triple their investments in renewable energy technologies and to start making some quiet buys at critical points in Getty Oil's supply chains. He told everyone he was gonna save the world from the fucked-up weather in the future. The money press said Slim Jim was cornering another market. The truth of it was, he just liked fuckin' with J. Paul Getty.

Another fact, now that he thought about it, was that getting into clean energy was the last really big decision he'd made for Davidson Enterprises.

He'd done it out of spite, but it had paid off, too.

"Maria," he said, coming to a decision. "I know I been an almost perfect boss for you. And I don't intend to change any of that. I know you and your people got all your little schemes and shit you get up to when you think I'm not looking. I don't care about any of that. I recognized that everything changed as soon as, you know, everything changed. Way back when you assholes turned up."

The quiet, augmented-tech engines of the Davidson Aerospace jet grew even quieter as they reached some crucial point in the flight where they needed to start slowing down for their descent.

"You already had my attention, Jimbo. Now you have my interest," O'Brien said.

"I want you to tell me everything," he said. "Everything I'm into. Everything we've done. I knew about those satellites we turned into weapons. You told me about them. But you don't tell me everything, and I been cool with that. But now I want to know."

She didn't speak for a long time.

An uncomfortably long time.

12

Senior Lieutenant Ilya Egorov pushed a body aside and looked over the sights of the stubby grenade launcher. The cooling corpse had that terrible, almost dark-magical deadweight, but Ilya had the strength of a man operating at the edge of his limits. The AGS launcher had a good field of fire back toward the terminal, where he imagined the main counterattack would originate. His men had done well here. A smaller force was assaulting the airfield from the south, and his RTO said all the chatter was that they were probably American Marines.

Ilya sneered. Of course, the capitalists would send their fiercest dog soldiers to try and maul the Soviet Airborne. But they would fail, and he would put them down like the dogs they were. He had some twenty men under his control now, and he meant to hold his tower against all comers until he was relieved.

The Regimental radio net was a mess, and so was battalion. The company net wasn't even there anymore. He understood many of his fellow officers had been lost. Some captain he didn't know from 3rd Company was in command of the whole battalion, but Ilya was on his own as a battle within the battle raged to the south. So, he grabbed every man he could find and obeyed his straightforward orders from that 3rd Company *pizda*.

"Shut your fucking mouth and hold that fucking tower."

To do that, Ilya had twenty troopers, half of them wounded, the grenade launcher with three boxes of linked ammo, and a captured FN MAG with about seven hundred rounds. Not great, to say the least. Also, he hated sitting tight when it was clear to him that Americans, or someone, were shaping a counterattack with a force of unknown strength.

"Feels like a fucking battalion to me," Ilya muttered.

"Sorry, sir?" his RTO said.

"Nothing," Ilya frowned. This felt bad already and worse by the minute.

He heard a shout from below, echoing up the bullet-scarred stairwell.

"Comrades coming in!"

He answered with a shout. "Password?"

"Kamchatka."

"All right! Come in."

Moments later, he heard their footsteps. Ilya waited to see who would appear. Perhaps it was Captain *Pizda*. When the man arrived on Ilya's hastily fortified tower level, he recognized a regimental staff major but couldn't recall his name. He thought he might be the S-3, the intelligence chief.

Ilya stood.

"Sir. I await orders."

The major nodded, Kalashnikov in hand and blood on his boots. He looked around, assessing the room before he spoke.

"You have done well here, Comrade Senior Lieutenant."

"Thank you, sir, but I am only one comrade among twenty."

"Just hold this tower. At all costs."

Ilya simply stared at him. This major had assumed command of the entire operation? Really? He had a few questions.

The S3 made a face.

"Do you understand what that means, Comrade Senior Lieutenant?

Something in his voice jolted Ilya out of his reverie.

"To the death, Comrade Major."

"Hopefully theirs, but yes. You either walk out of here tomorrow to receive the thanks of a grateful proletariat, or somebody carries your body out and dumps it in a pit. Your mission is to hold this tower."

Ilya nodded. Strangely, the order had filled him with new resolve.

"Yes, sir. Do we know who is attacking and in what strength?"

The major shrugged and tried to look untroubled, but Ilya recognized the shadows behind his eyes. He could have been looking into a mirror.

"They are Americans," the S3 said. "This we know. Probably a regiment of elite light infantry. Perhaps the 173rd Airborne. But we are unsure. The fog of war, yes?"

Shit, thought Ilya.

But he answered, "We shall kill them in this fog."

The major seemed happy with that.

"Good. I don't have much time, but I had to stop by. Your position is the key; you command the approaches between the forces attacking in the north and the enemy in the south. You will hold, Lieutenant. You will not leave this tower for any reason, not until the red flag flies over it and over all of this airfield. Is that clear?"

"Yes, sir."

"Do you have any important questions or requests?"

"I hold, no questions. Requests, yes. I need more men, ammunition, and weapons."

"I will send you what I can."

Ilya schooled his face to remain neutral. This man wasn't sending him shit.

"Yes, sir," he answered.

The major's RTO tapped him and spoke.

"Sir, First Battalion."

The major held out his hand.

"This is Vampire."

Ilya watched as the major's shoulders slumped, just for a second. He pressed his lips together and keyed the mic.

"You tell fucking Shevchenko to hold, or he will face the People's Justice. Is that clear to you?"

Ilya, of course, couldn't hear the response. He shifted from one foot to the other. The major handed the mic back. He made a tight fist and jabbed it in Ilya's direction.

"Comrade Lieutenant, I leave; you stay. This fucking dog's breakfast...." He sighed before turning and leaving.

Ilya listened to the men's footsteps stomping away.

Bozhe moi, he thought. This was fucked. A full-strength regiment of American Airborne attacking against what must be a half-strength regiment of surviving Soviets scattered to the four winds? Holy shit, this was bad.

He pressed his lips together and took a very deep breath. Held it. Let it out slowly. Yes, it was a bad situation. But he wore the blue beret, and so did his men. What the fuck did he imagine that meant? Would they be assigned to collect ice cream cones for old ladies on warm summer days? Bad situations were their fucking reason for being.

They would prevail or die, and their deaths would mean nothing because the forces of history worked for the triumph of the people, not the oligarchs and their mercenaries.

At least, that's what Senior Lieutenant Ilya Egorov told himself as the uproar outside grew louder. From any window he cared to look through, he saw muzzle flashes and small explosions. Running figures and the unmoving dead. Streams of tracer fire whipped through the grey light before dawn. He spoke to his AGS gunner.

"Have you spotted the enemy yet?"

"Yes, Comrade."

"How far are they?"

"Perhaps four hundred meters."

A hot wave of anger lapped at the back of Ilya's mind.

"Then why didn't you fire?"

"They weren't attacking us, and I only have three drums of rounds. I wish to kill Americans, not just scratch the tarmac."

Ilya's temper subsided. It was a good answer. He spoke again.

"When they come, do not wait on my order. Smash them down. You hold the trigger, comrade; you make the choice."

The gunner nodded, his eyes on the chaos in the terminal. It looked like a fireworks show in there. Brilliant colours and lights of every hue.

Ilya moved on. He toured all the positions, stopping and saying a few words at each.

"Are you clear with what you must do, Private?"

"Yes, Comrade. Shoot anyone who comes from across the runway."

"Not anyone. Do not shoot our boys."

The young trooper stared for a moment. Ilya raised his brows. The kid stammered.

"N-no, of course not, Comrade Senior Lieutenant."

"I joke, comrade. I do not think you to be that stupid. But when it starts, things get confused. Think, choose, aim, shoot. Kill them all."

Ilya moved on to his second most important post, the machine gun nest. A sergeant lay prone with the stock of the foreign weapon against his cheek. He smoked a hand-rolled cigarette with the reek of *makhorka*. Ilya could see printing on the improvised cigarette. It was probably made from a piece of paper torn from *The Red Star*, the Army's newspaper. Perhaps *Pravda*. He shrugged. Who knew? Ilya spoke.

"What do you see, Sergeant?"

"Big fight on the other side of the runway, sir."

"Yes. Has anyone crossed from there in our direction?"

The gunner's eyes never left his sights. "No, or I would kill them."

Ilya did not think he had to remind a sergeant of the Airborne not to shoot at his own men. This old lag looked like he'd fought every battle from the Oder to Pyongyang.

"Good," Ilya said. "Will you be able to use this gun when things get hot?"

The man nodded and even smiled. He patted the dark plastic stock. Or at least Ilya assumed it was plastic. It certainly wasn't hardwood, like the PK.

"It's different from a PK," the sergeant said. "But not so different.

You see, the belt feeds from the wrong direction and disintegrates when you fire. It is good design. I still haven't figured out how to change barrels quickly, so this one must do." He patted the machine, but his bloodshot eyes stayed steady over the sights. A blue plume curled up lazily from the gunner's cigarette. "I will have Alexei piss on it to cool it down if I need."

He jerked a thumb at the man beside him.

"I have been drinking pisswater from Italian coffee pot for just such a reason," Alexei confirmed.

"Good man," Ilya snorted. "And have you test-fired it?"

The sergeant laughed drily. "Yes. Do you see the imperialist running dog out there? No longer running. Now lying down forever. Three hundred meters, one o'clock." He paused while Ilya searched for the body. Sure enough, there was a corpse. The gunner spoke again. "This thing is accurate. Heavy, but very accurate."

"Good. We don't have much ammo for you."

"I will not need much. One bullet. One kill."

"You know what to do, sergeant. There is no retreat for us. Only victory."

For the first time, the man really looked at him. He drew on the last of his tiny cigarette, then let the stub fall from his mouth to the floor.

"Yes, Comrade Lieutenant. I know what to do."

Ilya nodded and left. They were as ready as could be, and they would hold.

For fucking Stalin, his life.

Ilya sat on a desk and pulled out his own cigarette, a *Belomorkanal*, his first in Italy.

It was delicious.

"Is this Two Six Actual?"

A woman's voice replied. So he knew it wasn't Dave Prezwalksi.

"No. Two Six Actual is a kilo. This is his exec. Major Margie Zimmerman."

Shit.

Lonesome closed his eyes. Prezwalski had been a good guy, for a squid.

He opened his eyes again. Everywhere he looked, there were craters from explosions.

"All right. How many effectives you got, Major?"

"Approximately six hundred, sir."

Six hundred clerks, cooks, and truck drivers.

They would have to do, Lonesome thought.

"Hold tight for instructions," he said.

Jones paused and keyed the mic. "One Six, this is Hammer Six."

"Go ahead, Six," Colonel Perkins replied.

“One-six, how many effectives do you have?"

"Four hundred and thirty-two, Hammer Six."

Jones was impressed. A precise number. But he'd expect nothing less from Perkins. He'd been old school Army before '39.

It helped with the plan he had been cooking for the past five minutes. Jones spoke again.

"Listen up, Perkins, Zimmerman. I want your two battalions to clear out whatever's left on your side of the runway. You figure out how to make that happen with what you got. Your LOA is the end of the runway. Be sure to watch your asses. Ivan will try and ass-fuck you. It's just his nature. When the northern side is in our hands, Second will turn southeast, cross the runway, then attack to the southwest toward Third Battalion and my element. First will stay behind, secure the northern flank, and kill any squirters. We are going to catch these fuckers in a pincer. A fucking nutcracker." He paused. "Is my intent clear? Sound off."

Perkins was first. "Roger, Hammer Six. Clear out what's left, stay behind and secure the northern flank."

Second Battalion's Exec spoke next. He couldn't picture Zimmerman's face, and it annoyed him. Her voice crackled back through the radio.

"We continue to attack northeast, battalions roughly abreast. When we reach the fence, I split off, cross the runway, then attack in your direction. What about friendly fire?"

They understand, Jones thought. Cool. But Zimmerman raised a fair point.

"That's a live problem, Two Five. All I can say is control your people, keep low, and stay in contact with Three Six when the moment comes." He paused. "Three Six, you copy, O'Donnell?"

He heard a roar of gunfire when she keyed the mic. "Yeah, I got it."

O'Donnell was having a rough morning, Jones thought. But who wasn't? He keyed the mic.

"I'll help out where I'm most needed. Acknowledge."

They all came back at him to confirm.

Jones handed the mic back to his RTO. The Lance Corporal was looking a little peaked. He'd been lugging that damn SINCGARS and a full combat load all morning. Jones spoke just as someone fired a long burst from a machine gun.

The Lance Corporal shouted back. "What was that, sir? Sorry sir. Kinda noisy."

"I said, why don't you hand me your radio bag, son? Take a rest? Just for a minute."

"No, sir!"

"You sure? That thing is a chunky sonofabitch."

Jones remembered the old Charlie model from his early service in the twenty-first. This downtime model was a close copy, heavy-ass batteries and all.

"I'm good to go, sir."

"Suit yourself, Lance Corporal."

Jones's XO, Colonel Brennerman, made his way over.

"General, we've swept the whole terminal building. We pushed some people toward the main control tower, and they took us under fire with a grenade launcher."

"One of those shitty 203 copies on their AKs?" Jones asked impatiently. "Don't put up with that crap, Colonel. Just fucking kill them."

His Exec closed his eyes and breathed in. "No, sir. An automatic grenade launcher."

Shit.

Jones had heard that thing earlier, but he'd forgotten about it.

Exhaustion. Chaos. They were catching up with him. He'd be making mistakes soon enough.

He stifled a sigh.

"You got anyone you can flex to take out that thing, Brennerman? It needs killing, or they'll keep chewing our flank to bloody rags."

"All of our officers are committed. But we still have the mess section standing around cupping their balls."

"How many effectives?"

"Sixty-one."

"They'll do."

"All right. Have the Sergeant Major take them?"

"No. I'll deal with this myself. You know the plan. Keep driving everyone while I crack this nut. Clear?"

"As mud, sir." Brennerman paused. "If I may. Sir, let me take this. Generals don't lead assaults."

"They do when shit gets real enough, Colonel. And shit's pretty real right now, don't you think? Besides, if I get zapped, you'll finally have that brigade command you always wanted. I'll get on the net and let everyone know what's happening. You go give the mess section their warning order. They need to be ready in five."

"I'll let Master Sergeant Peterson know."

Lonesome grunted. His favourite pastry cook was going to be thrilled. *C'est la guerre*, he thought. Perhaps summoned by the French phrase, his long-lost wife's face returned to him with urgent clarity. *Monique*, he thought.

I miss you.

He wanted to hold on to the memory, which was stronger than it had been in years.

But he couldn't. Not now.

"Good work and good luck, Colonel Brennerman," he said.

"Good luck to you, too, sir."

Brennerman held out one hand, and Jones took it without thinking. They shook.

Jones gestured at his faithful RTO. The young Marine handed him the headset again.

"All stations this net," Jones announced. "Be advised. There's a chore I have to do. Hammer Five will run the show in my absence. Do you copy?"

All of his commanders came back with their acknowledgments. Jones patted his RTO on the shoulder.

"You ready, son?"

"For another glorious day in the Corps? You bet I am, sir."

Lonesome laughed. This kid was so getting his NAVCOM. "Then let's see what this day brings, Lance Corporal."

They moved to where Master Sergeant Peterson had assembled his potato peelers and chicken stranglers. Jones didn't see a lot of smiles. Not so much enthusiasm for a glorious day in the Corps here. Their faces were grim, set. Some had their eyes closed. One man's lips moved in silent prayer. Jones could easily make out the words. He'd recited them often enough.

"Yea, though I walk through the valley...." he muttered. Then he cranked on his command voice.

"Listen up." All eyes were suddenly on him.

The mad drumbeat of the clearing operation thundered in the background.

"Our mission is to assault the control tower to the north. The enemy has a platoon strength element within, and they are packing heat. An auto launcher like our Mark Nineteen. At least one heavy machine gun."

From close by, there came a series of explosions. The AGS, Jones was sure.

Thump-thump-thump.

"Hear that? That's the motherfuckers we're going to take out."

He paused for effect, then went on.

"Here's how."

Jones kept it as simple as possible. These guys were not fighters. But they would have to fight now. Jones had the Master Sergeant get them ready.

"Drop your packs, dick-weasels," Peterson shouted. "You don't need the weight. Guns and ammo. Knives if you got 'em. You know how to use a knife, dontcha, ladies?"

A minute later, they moved, some actual ladies among them.

Jones led the small force through the ruined terminal, keeping them deep inside, sheltered from the tower's direct line of sight. Sections of the ceiling had collapsed. Ash and debris covered every inch of ground, and rubble littered corridors that once bustled with life. They passed from the baggage claim area to check-in to a relatively undamaged section where a few cafes and gift stores stood open but unattended.

He pulled up outside a Swiss chocolate shop.

"I need my 240 gunners," he called out.

Four soldiers came forward, loaded down with gear. They looked competent. Peterson had chosen well.

Jones pointed at one team, then knife-handed toward a cranny in the wall.

"You. Get set there when I say."

He pointed at the other team, then at a spot on the other side of the hall. "You. Right in there. See it?"

"Yes, sir."

Jones addressed the rest of his troops.

"Listen up. After these guys get set, we wait on that asshole over there to open up. When he does, I'll blow my whistle...." He held up his whistle, "... and our heavy machine guns will open up while we move."

He addressed the gunners again.

"Make the guns talk to each other, link belts. I want continuous fire on those fucks while we cross that open ground. Shoot right over our heads, hose those Russian fucks with fire, and don't stop until I pop red smoke from a window. Understood?"

An Army sergeant spoke up, "Fire at the whistle. Suppress the gun. Ceasefire at red smoke."

Probably not a career pastry chef, Jones thought. Good.

"You got it, sergeant. Now go get set."

As the machine gunners scrambled into position, Jones called out.

"Give me the first ten, Master Sergeant. After we assault, every twenty seconds, send ten more. You come across with the last group. Everyone spread out. Do not bunch up. Do not make yourself a juicy fucking target for them. All those fun runs I made you do? In full battle rattle? They weren't much fucking fun, I know. But this is where they pay off. This is where they save your fucking life, and this is where you take theirs."

He pointed out towards the tower.

Someone yelled, "Hooah!"

And a dozen more yelled back, "Fuck yeah."

Jones cupped one hand to his ear.

"What's that."

Sergeant Peterson led them in the reply.

"Fuck yeah!"

When the shouting died down, he counted off ten cooks. They all stepped forward without hesitation.

General J. Lonesome Jones spoke directly to them.

"Follow me, gentlemen."

13

Joe McCarthy examined his cock. *It still looked pretty good*, he thought. But it was giving him all sorts of trouble. Burning at the tip and leaking like a sonofabitch. He would take it to a doctor, see if he needed a pill or something for the clap, but he'd heard some terrible rumours in the war about what the cock doctors would do to a fella, and on general principles, McCarthy thought it best just to keep an eye on the thing for now.

If the burning at the business end got real bad or if, God forbid, it started leaking anything but God's honest piss, he would definitely get it seen to.

But for the moment, he tucked it away, flushed the toilet in the private bathroom of his Senate office, and washed his hands.

It was late, and he had been drinking. Just a couple-two-three beers. And some brandy. And a few more brewskis, too.

But you couldn't blame a man for that, not with the shit he'd had to put up with. It was a holy miracle he hadn't drunk himself into an early grave, was what it was. The fucking things those uptime bastards said about him. The lies they put in their so-called history books. The lies they'd put into the press about him being killed in the war. Why would you even do that to a fella unless you wanted to mess with his head? And as for history, that hadn't even happened here! But those assholes were still as likely to chip a fella for it as not.

The office was quiet when he emerged. All of his staff gone for the night.

He didn't care about that.

Meant he could get a few more brewskis. And he knew from long experience that the big three-seat office couch was comfortable enough for government work. Weren't like nobody could chip a fella for working so late he had to sleep over at the office.

Joe McCarthy fetched himself another can of Old Milwaukee from the little Frigidaire and dropped onto the couch with a solid grunt. It shook up the beer some, and he cursed when the froths spurted out of the ring-pull hole, but a quick suck took care of the spillage.

The quick suck turned into a long pull, and he finished half the damn can before he even knew about it.

You couldn't blame a fella for that, though.

He didn't even know what he was doing here these days.

It was a miracle of sorts, is what it was. But a mystery, too.

He'd been training as a Marine when those Kolhammer bastards came, though. They said he was only ever gonna be a damn pogue, but even their lying fake history books said he flew twelve missions in the Pacific as a tail gunner.

A helluva thing that woulda been, Joe thought, taking another deep drink from the red and white tube of Old Milwaukee. Tail Gunner Joe!

Wasn't his fault the Corps kept him home when everything went sideways after the Transition.

Just thinking about it gave him agitations, and he was all set to murder the second half of the beer he'd just fetched, but that woulda meant having to get up from the couch to fetch himself another, and now that he was sat down, he wasn't in much of a mood for getting up. With admirable forbearance, he slowed his drinking to a stately sip every now and then. Gave himself time to think on some things.

Not that there was much worth thinking about. The Senate was dark and quiet. He might as well have been the only soul in residence tonight, and he was here for the free beer. It was an accident his being here at all, he knew. Or maybe the accident was his still being here when the guy who got him in through the door was gone.

J Edgar Hoover of sainted memory, that was.

Dead these many years, and by his own hand, it was whispered. Couldn't face the shame of the vicious whispers those Kolhammer bastards started up against him. About him being a sissy and all.

J Edgar, if you could imagine it. Toughest G-man on the beat.

Joe McCarthy wouldn't have a word said against him or his memory. Especially not after J Edgar's friends reached all the ways into that dusty basement office in San Diego where the Corps had figured to hide him away as an embarrassment. They reached in there, and they pulled him out into the light of day and told him he was going home to Wisconsin. He was going to fulfil his destiny. His ass was going into that damned Senate seat, no matter what those bastards from the way up when said about him.

Joe swung his feet up on the couch and got comfy. He would have this one last beer and a little nap, and maybe when he woke up, he'd call the driver to take him to the hotel where he liked to stay.

It was a helluva race he'd run, and here at what felt like the end of it, he was tired. It'd even been fun those first couple of years, brawling —straight-up brawling—with the fools and nincompoops who fell so hard for all that rubbish the uptimers went on with. He'd had some pretty damn good wins too. Was a helluva day, the day they took away all the special privileges and protections those assholes claimed for themselves over in California. No more open celebrations by the perverts and subversives and un-American know-it-alls. No more uppity negroes getting around, not knowing a negro's place.

And then the damned sedition caucus took the state house and the governorship, and the next thing you knew, they had turned the whole damn state of California into a goddamned Sodom and Gomorrah of socialism.

Joe McCarthy drained the last of the beer and tossed the empty can across the room. It clattered away into the shadows.

He got so angry when he thought on it. Got even angrier when he thought there was nothing he could do about it. He was popular out on the streets. Lots of people said so. But here in the gentlemen's club of the Senate, he couldn't get a damn committee slot for love or money, and every day it seemed the country slipped further away from what it had been and what it was meant to be.

So Tail Gunner Joe might just rest here a little while.

He'd done his bit. Him and J Edgar and the good fellows on the Patriots Commission. They'd all done their bit to roll back the false promises of an unwanted future. But that future was coming faster every day.

Everywhere you looked, you could see it. Dozens of states with the universal Medibank. Faggots and blacks as uppity as you please, everywhere you looked, and they were even creeping onto the floor of the House across the way.

And the women! Do not get Joe McCarthy started on the women and the ideas they had inside their pretty little heads these days. The women were absolutely the worst.

But what could he do about it? Business was booming; all the damned charts said the economy was rocketing off the charts, and Ike had a lock on the party.

The Commission had spoken in private about running candidates in a primary, and when they had those conversations, it was always Joe McCarthy's name they whispered.

But Joe was no fool. He knew that was never going to happen. He could probably see out his days here in the Senate if he kept his nose clean. J Edgar was gone, but the other patriots would ensure the bulwark held. They'd told him so more than enough times. Assured him of it.

But what was the damn point, really?

What was even...

His maudlin line of thought came to an abrupt halt, cut off by his senior aide crashing through the front door to the office.

"God dammit, Joe, where the hell have you been?" Roy Cohn shouted.

McCarthy bolted upright on the couch, glad he'd just been to the head for a piss, no matter how painfully uncomfortable it was. Cohn had given him such a shock. He'd a been a laydown certainty to wet his pants otherwise.

"I been here, damn you," Joe barked back at him. "On my own, as usual. Where the hell have you been?"

Ha. That'd show him, Joe thought. Turn the tables right around.

The lawyer stared at him, those big googly Jewish eyes all but popping out of his ugly turtle head.

"You don't even know, do you?" Cohn said. He stood there with his hands on his hips. "Abso-fucking-lutely typical. Get up. Get up now, Joe," he snapped.

Nobody talked to Joe McCarthy like that. Unless it was Roy Cohn. He had more front than Bloomingdales. They said all sorts of things about him, too. Some of them even worse than the stuff they said about Joe, but the pushy little kike seemed to love it. He ate that shit all up, like a big hot meal. Like he was hungry for it or something.

Joe could tell something had happened. And it had to be something real bad for somebody else. Cohn had that grin he got. Like a hammerhead shark sniffing blood in the water.

The junior senator from Wisconsin swung his legs back out and let his stockinged feet drop to the floor.

"This better be good," he said.

The hammerhead smile grew wider, hungrier.

"Oh, it's good, Joe. You're gonna love it."

Joe McCarthy had less than no idea what this little weasel was talking about.

"It's Eisenhower," he said. "He's gone."

McCarthy shook his head, beer-bleary and struggling to comprehend.

"What do you mean he's gone?"

"I mean what I say, Joe. Eisenhower is gone. Dead. He is no longer on the ticket."

Cohn turned left and right, looking for the TV remote.

"Where's the fuckin' TV stick, Joe?"

"You wanna watch TV? Now?"

"I want to fucking show you that Ike is dead. I want you to wake the fuck up. This is our shot."

McCarthy shifted his buttocks to the side. He'd been lying on the remote.

He thumbed on the power to the TV, one of those big new colour ones that GE made.

It always surprised him how quickly it came to life.

And there it was. The fucking White House burning on the news. Or something burning on the lawn out front of the White House. A helicopter.

Eisenhower's, he guessed.

Joe McCarthy's mouth fell open. Wide open. His look of stunned incomprehension was queered somewhat by the colossal burp that suddenly erupted from deep in his guts, and he shifted uncomfortably as a few drops of acidic urine leaked from the end of his manfellow and stung like a son of a bitch.

"Dead for real?"

"Yeah. They're saying it's the fucking Russians," Cohn laughed. "We're gonna nuke those sons of bitches back to the Stone Age, and you are going to be the next fucking president of the United States of America."

"But... Kolhammer's the Veep."

Cohn sneered.

"That fucking putz. Let me take care of that."

14

"You've all met, so we'll skip the pleasantries," McGregor said.

Making a liar of him, Charlotte performed a theatrical curtsy with the hint of a smirk. The whole thing made even more risible by the black combat coveralls and sizeable cache of personal weaponry she wore.

"Your very Highness," she said.

"Or not then," the Scotsman added, rolling his eyes.

The Russian, Ivanov, wearing the same clothes he'd had on back at the hospital in Cairo, nodded at Harry. A minimal gesture with no readable expression behind it.

They stood in the hot shade of the aircraft hangar, with the two mercenaries all but silhouetted by the bright, fierce light of the desert sun.

"Miss François, I did not expect to see you again," Harry said before acknowledging Ivanov. "Tovarisch."

"Your Highness," the Russian deadpanned.

"You can both stop calling me that," Harry said. "Like, five fucking minutes ago. And you," he went on, pointing a finger at McGregor, "Can tell me what the shady fuck is happening here."

"Follow me then," McGregor said, leading them out of the

massive hangar and away from the medevac plane onto which the medical staff were loading Julia. Harry looked over his shoulder, suddenly sure that if he did not run to her, he would never see his fiancée again. He turned just in time to catch the doctor who had escorted Jules from the hospital, disappearing up the loading ramp and into the belly of the aircraft. Harry wanted to call out, to break away and run after her, but McGregor and the others were already out of the building and hastening off to God only knew where. Feeling as if he was about to do something terribly wrong and fatally stupid, Harry bit down on his misgivings and hurried out after them.

He emerged into the scourging heat and light of the North African summer. Here he recognised the unmistakable focus and rigour of a military machine stirring to full power. Nobody moved slowly or without apparent purpose. Squads of soldiers and airmen double-timed to their duties as officers issued orders with performative detachment, and NCOs translated them into a harsher, louder, altogether more urgent torrent of personal abuse and colourful obscenity. Still fretting about Jules, it took all of Harry's will to let her go and commit to his duty, whatever that might be.

Ivanov appeared to be leading them through the gridwork of the massive air base, which was unexpected, but Harry did not dwell on it. He increased his pace, ignoring the pain and discomfort from the fight on the Russian freighter. He caught up with McGregor as they passed a group of pilots running in the opposite direction towards a flight line of helicopter gunships. The Nomex flight suits of the aircrew, their mixed race and gender, and the stars and stripes insignia on the Huey Cobra variants marked them as USAF personnel.

"Where's he taking us?" Harry asked McGregor as Ivanov turned left to skirt around a machine shop that roared with the clatter and clang of urgent work being done.

"I misspoke about travelling cattle class before, your Highness... sorry, I mean Harry. Yon Russian friend has borrowed a rather swish little runabout from his employer, the resourceful Mister Davidson. It'll get you where you're going a helluva lot quicker than anything we could rustle up here," he answered.

They made a few turns left and right before passing through a checkpoint and into a quieter part of the base. Harry noted the presence of a couple of civilian aircraft, including the Davidson Aerospace Learjet knockoff towards which Ivanov and Charlotte headed. A pilot and co-pilot performed final checks on the airframe as a third man waved Harry's party over. Something about him seemed familiar, and Harry recognised him a couple of steps later. Another displaced uptimer. Vincente Rogas. A Navy Seal turned private contractor. He had been with Ivanov at the hospital.

"Hey, Harry," the American said, earning points for the lack of any feigned royal deference.

"Vince," Harry said, shaking his hand. "Are you coming along on this teddy bear's picnic?"

"Part of the way, yeah. I've got the briefing packet," he said, holding up a courier's satchel. "And some goodies for you from Jimbo's medical boffins."

Rogas passed him a packet of wound dressings, or at least they looked like dressings.

"Peptide patches," he explained. Heard you got banged up a little on that Russian freighter. Slap these things on anywhere it hurts."

"What's in them?" Harry asked, turning the packet over and squinting at the print, which was too small for his eyes.

"A real cocktail," Rogas explained. "Some BPC 157, a dash of Ipamorelin, Sermorelin, some Epithalon and Semax, I think. Straight outta the labs. It works."

Harry thanked him and stashed the dressings in a pocket, planning to apply them later.

The pilot told them they were good to get on board and pulled open the cabin door, deploying the small fold-down steps. Charlotte boarded first. Rogas brought up the rear.

Harry hadn't attended to how hot and miserable he'd been, hurrying through the base until he stepped onto the air-conditioned plane.

It was deliciously, almost sinfully cool inside, and goosebumps quickly spread out and down from his sunburned neck in a full-body shiver at the sudden change. He doubted the peptides could make him feel as good. Behind him, Ivanov, the giant Russian, stood slightly bent over to avoid hitting his head on the cabin roof. McGregor waved them to their seats without taking one himself.

"I'll make this quick because we're already running behind time," he said. "You, Colonel Windsor, have been reactivated for service by your regiment but loaned back to MI6 for the duration of hostilities. Miss François here, who was already working on contract with Her Majesty's Government, has agreed to extend that contract to secure the return of Professor Bremmer from Soviet captivity. You will need to regularise any further involvement beyond that, Miss François. But Mister Rogas can explain all that palaver when you're on your way. Mister Ivanov has the support of the Davidson Corporation to carry out any such activities as he deems necessary to support Miss François in pursuing her primary mission."

The Scotsman turned back to Harry.

"And you, Colonel, have orders from the Circus to accompany them to Sardinia. There you will either extract Professor Bremmer or neutralise him. From then on, you will proceed with Mister Ivanov and possibly Miss François to Marseille where..."

"Steady on," Harry said. He was sweating freely as he struggled to cope with the sudden fall in temperature and humidity. "Did you just tell me to kill Ernst Bremmer if we can't get him away from the Sovs?"

"Aye, if you want to be precious about it. You either get him back or make sure he never gets to Moscow. At this point, the boss could'nae give a toss which. Stalin's already dropped the hammer. Sorting out Bremmer is really just tidying up the footnotes. Getting on to Marseille is a larger priority. You are to make contact there with an officer of the French Secret Service, Marcel Ronsard. I believe you've worked together before."

They had.

Harry's head was reeling, but he grabbed onto the mention of Ronsard as an anchor. They had fought together in the raid on the Nazis' missile base at Donzenac and later in Paris.

While Harry put aside the sudden rush of memory and emotion, McGregor continued with his briefing.

"Ronsard will put you together with the top people in the city's

Corsican mafia, and you will determine what material aid we can offer them to completely bugger up the Soviets' operations in that port. It is their major fleet base in the Mediterranean, and the Corsicans are holding the only stick we have to poke them. You both worked with the Mob in Rome," McGregor said, gesturing at Ivanov to bring him into this part of the conversation. "Just do that again. But different this time."

"Different?" Harry said.

"Yeah," Charlotte put in. "Don't fuck it up."

THEY TOOK flight a couple of minutes after McGregor left them. Nobody said anything until the plane levelled off on a track to the northeast. Harry stared out of the window, lost in his thoughts. Parts of Cairo were burning as they banked away. He did not know whether Julia's flight had taken off before him or whether she was still trapped down in that septic, bloody mess of a city. At this point, he could only trust that McGregor would make good on his promise. He seemed a solid sort of bloke in that regard, at least.

They passed over the coast and sped north at low altitude. The Mediterranean rippled, blue-green and quiet, mere hundreds of feet below. There was no escort. If they ran into a couple of Russian MiGs, they'd probably be dead before they hit the water, and they'd hit the water super fucking hard, and very fucking fast. Flying time to Cagliari was nearly four hours. Half an hour into the flight, Rogas called a meeting, which meant Harry and Ivanov spinning their seats around to make a nest of four at the front of the cabin. Harry was quietly impressed with just how closely the engineers and designers at Davidson had remade the experience of flying in an uptime business jet. The seats were even more comfortable than any he remembered from back up when, each clad in hand-stitched, buttery leather. He imagined that there would be a full bar and meal service on a regular flight, and knowing what he did of Slim Jim, the Reprobate-in-Chief, there'd probably be pole dancing and hot tub mudwrestling, too.

Instead, on this flight, four special operators leaned forward to converse over the noise of the turbo jets.

"We've got some assets in place in the local government structure on Sardinia," Rogas said.

Slim Jim has been paying off a bunch of cops and bureaucrats, Harry translated for himself.

"We got a good, hard target hit on Bremmer at Cagliari, leaving the cargo terminal of the main port with a big potato-headed motherfucker..."

"This will be Skarov," said Pavel Ivanov. "They will drive north and attempt to cross to Corsica by boat at night."

"So they could be gone by now," Charlotte pointed out.

"No," Ivanov said. "The roads to the north are not good. The coastal road is better, but they would be more exposed."

Rogas nodded as the plane shook off a couple of seconds of turbulence.

"We got some guys who look out for us. Local cops. They're looking out for Bremmer and Skarov now, too. So, yeah, they'll go up through the mountains in the middle of the island. It's shit country, full of bandits. But no cops. If our boy Skarov has his own boat, he'll probably leave from Capo Testa in the northeast. It's a tiny village. A couple of fishermen's shacks around a sheltered bay. If they're sneaking across on a trawler or something, they'll go from Santa Teresa, the working port a coupla miles west. There's lots of fishing boats coming and going from there every day. Even now. People still gotta eat."

"Then that is where they will go," Ivanov pronounced. "More cover. More movement options. It is procedure."

The way he said it, with such finality, was obviously meant to end the discussion.

"Is there any way we can keep an eye on this Capo Testa place?" Harry asked. "I mean, if we don't expect him to be there, isn't that where the sneaky fuck is likely to be?"

"Is not procedure," Ivanov said, shaking his head.

Harry raised one eyebrow at Rogas.

The American shrugged. "We have no overwatch. We are the agents responsible. We're the final action authority. It's our call."

Charlotte spoke up from across the cabin. She was twirling from side to side in her chair, drinking a Coke through a bright pink straw. Jules had called her Commando Barbie, and she very much looked the part at that moment.

"Sounds like we should go straight to Santa Teresa," she said. "He's not gonna get to Corsica from the ass end of the island, is he?"

Nobody answered, which was an answer in itself.

"So, let's deep-six the idea of wasting our time in Cagliari and head for where we know this douchebag will turn up. Fuck chasing him through the boonies. Let's find a nicely set up little bar on the waterfront at Santa Teresa, enjoy a salty snack and a local beverage, and we can pop a cap in this mofo as soon as he rolls up. I want to be the one to pull the trigger. For old Viv."

"No," Ivanov insisted. "The trigger pulling is for me to do. You have lost something to this man, da. But I have lost more."

Harry stared at Charlotte as she sucked the dregs of the Coca-Cola from her bottle with a loud snorkelling noise.

"You're talking about Skarov, right, Charlotte?" he said. "Because through all your sub-Tarantino dialogue just then, you did sound like you might be talking about Bremmer, and I spent a lot of time keeping him alive at the end of the last war and trying to get him back from the Smedlovs at the start of this one. So I really would rather not see him murdered because you're a little bored and ready to move on."

Charlotte smiled back sweetly.

"It's nice that they let you out of the retirement home, Harry, but whatever you thought you were doing with Bremmer and Skarov, the long story short of it was that my governor, your old mate Viv, and all of my friends on Viv's crew, are dead. And if I hadn't come aboard the *Bulgakov*, you and Duffy would've joined them. So, I dunno, maybe have a nap, change your gentleman's diaper, and get back to us when you're not so tired and cranky. And old. So very, very old."

Harry's mouth dropped open and snapped shut with a slight clicking sound as his teeth came together.

"You fucking what?" He started to say before Rogas cut them both off.

"Extracting Bremmer remains our primary mission," he said, frowning at Charlotte. But he turned to Harry and Ivanov. "Killing Skarov is also a priority. He's too dangerous to have tear-assing around this side of the curtain."

Pavel Ivanov nodded, satisfied.

"If it proves impossible to extract Professor Bremmer, however," Rogas went on, talking directly to Harry, "Your orders from London are explicit. Bremmer dies."

Harry felt a dizzying wave of exhaustion and fever that would have set him on his arse was it not already firmly planted in the soft leather cushions of Slim Jim's bespoke airline seat.

"I'm not new to this," he said, "as Miss François has so kindly pointed out. But I'm not a bloody hitman either. We will do our best to get Professor Bremmer back."

Charlotte smiled again as though the exchange had never occurred, as though she had not subtly knifed him with that comment about Viv.

"Sure," she said. "And then we go to Marseille."

Rogas nodded.

"And then maybe you go to Marseille," he said. He stood up and retrieved a packet of documents from the satchel he'd dropped at the front of the cabin, handing out separate folders to each of them.

"The job in Marseille is not part of your standing contract with Davidson," he explained to Ivanov. "But the boss has offered to support the war effort in any way possible, and as one of his favoured contractors, you are invited to bid on this job. All the hazard pay and bonus details, with the usual performance bumps, are in the file I just gave you."

Ivanov opened the packet, gestured for a pen, and signed the papers without reading them.

"Nothing good will happen in Russia until the Bolsheviks are all dead," he said.

"Okay," Rogas said. "As for you, Miss François, you were a salaried employee of Mister St Clair's business, which Her Majesty's government has nationalised. You are also, of course, an American citizen, so you can tell Whitehall to get fucked if you like. The pay and conditions are not nearly as generous as you would get in the private sector. For instance, if you signed on with Kinetic Solutions, Mister Davidson's private military contracting operation, for which I…"

Charlotte did not open her packet of documents. She handed them back to Rogas.

"Yeah, that sounds more like me," she said. "I want whatever he's getting."

She pointed her empty Coke bottle at Ivanov.

Rogas grinned.

"Good call," he said. "It's a generous offer. You have good references."

He produced another set of documents and passed them across. Charlotte took a few minutes to read them while Harry quietly looked out the window.

"Whatever happened to Queen and country?" he asked himself.

"We kicked your asses to the kerb back in 1770," Charlotte replied, signing her new contract with a flourish. "Don't you remember? I thought you were old enough to be there."

15

"Comrade Senior Lieutenant, I think they're up to something."

"Why do you say that?"

"I don't think we hold the terminal across from us anymore. The firing went that way." The AGS gunner pointed to the left, the northeast. "I don't like this."

"Neither do I, Comrade Sergeant."

Ilya thought, and he thought hard. They had only half a belt of the linked 30mm grenades feeding the launcher, plus one more drum of twenty-nine rounds. He didn't have ammo to waste. He could order the crew to hose down the terminal across from them, but at what cost and for what advantage? If he knew the Americans and their lackeys were massing for an assault on his tower, that would be different.

But he didn't know.

He had been unable to raise the battalion or regimental command on the radio net. So they were in deep shit. That much, at least, was clear. The fucking US Airborne troopers were tearing them up all over this cursed drop site. Anyone could see that.

Ilya made a decision.

"Sergeant, I want you to fire just one round in front of that hall, and we'll see what happens. If they shoot back, we have a problem. We've lost the terminal. If so, unload the rest of your belt into the building. They will be massing for an attack." He smiled grimly. "But we spoil their plans, yes."

"Alright, Comrade Senior Lieutenant. One round. Here goes."

The sergeant tapped the trigger, and his weapon fired once. The round exploded in front of the terminal building, shattering what little remained of the bog glass windows behind the blast.

It was the last thing the man ever did.

A burst of automatic fire struck the sergeant in the face and shoulders, disintegrating everything. A thick cloud of hot blood and heavy gore splashed over Ilya, blinding him. A storm of machine gun fire erupted from the terminal, but by then, Ilya had already dropped to the floor. There was nothing conscious in the evasive move. His knees might have begun to buckle and fold before the first round struck the comrade sergeant. The body just knew, sometimes, before the mind perceived. That's how it was in battle. Until the body and the mind were no more.

Pressing himself into the filthy, blood-smeared floor tiles, Senior Lieutenant Ilya Egorov tried to take some solace from the undeniable fact his question had been answered. But there was no solace to be had. He'd just lost one of his best men and needed to get the AGS running right now, or they would all die in the next few minutes.

JONES WAS ready when the teaser round detonated in front of the Arrivals hall. His whistle was pressed to his lips, and he blew it for all he was worth. A sudden roar of heavy machine-gun fire from his 240 crew almost drowned out the shrill single note, but he was already moving.

Jones charged toward the shattered doors, not bothering to look back. He knew his troops would be right on his heels. They'd be scared, like him, but fear in battle can feel like a killing rage. The trick was to act and not dwell on the difference.

He didn't bother with any fancy movement techniques. They

were all dead if they got caught under fire on the concrete. So he sprinted, his weapon swinging and pumping in front of him. The tower seemed so damn far away, an impossible distance, forever away, and there was zero cover.

Jones ran.

He could cover one hundred meters in less than twelve seconds. He knew that. So he was in for half a minute or so of terror. More than enough time for the defenders to act and cut them down.

As Jones ran, he heard the steady beat of covering fire from his gunners and crouched ever so slightly under the murderous river of tracer fire they poured into the tower's upper levels.

Jones ran.

He heard the guns talking to each other. A long burst from one. A split second of silence, barely there, and the second crew would take up the fight. Alternating streams of bright golden fire and industrial noise, lighting up the concrete fortress, chewing away at cement and steel, atomising any trace of humanity.

Jones felt himself accelerate into that weird flow state where the boundary between subject and object collapses, and he became what he willed. He was speed. He was fury.

He became death, and death flew on the dark wings of fallen angels.

A bullet snapped by. Another.

From behind him, '*oof*,' and the clattering thump of deadweight dropping to the tarmac.

Jones's weapon pumped in his hand, and he prepared a door-knocker as the tower loomed ever closer and larger.

An explosion peppered his body armour and stung his leg, but still, he ran. The door was ahead; he levelled his weapon, still running.

Ilya swore mightily as a ricochet stuck his helmet from behind, knocking him flat as he crawled toward the grenade launcher. His nose crunched on the hard floor, and he tasted blood and pure hatred.

He had to fire the launcher. They would be attacking right now, and the easiest way to die was not to shoot back. Of course, his sergeant would tell him it would be easy to die behind that gun, too. But the sergeant was silent.

Was the gun even operational?

Ilya was about to find out.

He crawled and crouched, extra careful not to expose himself in any way. A round pinged from the weapon and whizzed off to bounce around behind him. The best he could do was to grab the spade handles from below, roughly point the muzzle towards these shitheels, and pull the trigger.

Ilya let out a long, blind burst, holding on for dear life. The AGS bucked and swung, trying to get away from him.

A bullet stuck his left hand, breaking his wrist and destroying two fingers. Worse, though, it shattered the spade handle.

Senior Lieutenant Ilya Egorov howled and writhed in wild pain.

LONESOME STOPPED dead in his tracks and levelled his assault rifle. His finger went to the trigger of the underslung grenade launcher. His guys streaked past him on the left and right. He only had one chance to get this right, but he had a lifetime of practice and a feel for where the High Explosive/Dual Purpose round would fall. He pulled the trigger.

The tower's main door blew apart, and he dashed forward again. His injured leg ached, but he forced it to move and refused to look down. If it was moving, it was good enough for government work. Five guys had run before him in the two seconds he took to fire, and he watched as they rushed inside.

There was gunfire inside, lots of it. Jones didn't pause in the "fatal funnel" of the doorway; he plunged straight through it and into a scene of churning chaos.

An Airman plugged a moving target. Some Russian shithead. A

baker's apprentice struggled with two enemy soldiers, swinging his rifle like a caveman with a club. Jones drilled one of the Russians with a three-round burst, evening the odds for his man. He clocked a hallway. A staircase. A ruined elevator. Someone screamed, "Friendly coming in!" A high-pitched female voice.

Lonesome didn't look back. His baker boy was losing that fight with the Sov - some jacked fucking monster in the striped tee shirt of the VDV. Jones let his carbine drop onto the lanyard that secured it to his body armour. He pulled his pistol, walked over to where the pair were locked in a death match, leaned over, and shot the Russian in the temple.

A flood of his people entered the room. *Must be the second wave*, he thought. He grabbed his RTO. The kid had made it.

Time to get this shitshow under control.

"Comrade! The Americans are in the tower!"

Ilya moaned as he used his teeth to tighten a combat tourniquet around his broken wrist. He nearly blacked out with the pain. It came in waves of dark, red agony. He grunted, squeezed tears and sweat from his eyes, then answered.

"No fucking shit. Help me up. We'll defend this place and drive them out."

Fat fucking chance, he thought. But if he was going to die, he wouldn't go quietly. The paratrooper helped him to his feet, and they left the room with the dead men and the ruined gun.

Ilya didn't bother to recover his carbine. It was useless to him now. He drew his service pistol with his off hand and spoke.

"Do you have grenades?"

They were by the stairwell.

"No. They are all gone."

"Then take mine. I can't use them anymore." The trooper rifled through his load-bearing equipment and removed the explosives.

"I have them, Comrade Lieutenant."

The man, Ilya noted, seemed without fear now. His voice was

steady. His breathing natural. It was because he knew he would die and had accepted that.

Like Ilya.

"When you hear them come up the steps, throw the grenades. Both of them. Then we wait. We hold here."

Gunfire built to a crescendo below. His men were dying, and these fucking pigs would pay for it.

They heard foreign voices down below. Someone clearly giving orders. Even in that gutter tongue, Ilya recognised the firm accent of command. He heard so much chatter, so much loose talk, that he wondered if it was the American Airborne. They were supposed to have discipline. *Had his regiment not been scattered to the four points, the Guards Airborne would have danced on the guts of these blabbermouth bitches*, he thought.

He looked over at the trooper. The man was holding a grenade with the pin pulled and the next one ready to hand.

The chatter downstairs ceased. The gunfire dwindled, and they heard footsteps. Ilya looked at the man and nodded. The trooper lobbed the first grenade down the stairwell, then pulled the pin on the second and threw it, too.

Screams. Ilya smiled. *THUMP.* More screams. *THUMP.* Acrid smoke drifted up the stairwell, with animal screams and shouting.

"They will be coming, Comrade. Be ready for them." He paused. "We shoot the first ones, then retreat and do this again on the next floor. We will bleed them and pick up reinforcements as we fight upwards. We hold at the top until our soldiers arrive, and we take back the tower."

Ilya said this with such eerie calm that the other man looked at him as though he were insane.

"The forces of history, soldier," Ilya assured him, knowing what he said was the purest madness.

The man looked away and shouldered his rifle. Ilya pointed his pistol downwards.

"They will be coming if they are not fools," his companion said. "Or cowards."

"Not cowards," Ilya said. "Just dead men climbing over the bodies of their friends."

JONES LOOKED at the human ruin in the stairwell. *Some sonofabitch*, he thought, *was not selling himself cheap*. Another group pounded through the door, followed by a panting Master Sergeant Peterson. With everyone inside, it was time for the guns to cease fire.

Jones picked his way through bodies and wreckage to a shattered window, taking care not to stand directly in front. He pulled the cylindrical red smoke grenade from his assault harness, yanked the pin, and watched the spoon fly off. Then he tossed it underhand through the window.

Rich red smoke billowed from the grenade, and the chatter of his gunners' weapons ceased.

Jones turned and pulled some people out.

"You need to assault up the stairs. Do you know how to attack up a set of steps?"

Most of them shook their heads. Jones resisted the urge to close his eyes. They had done miracles so far, these cooks and cleaners, but they would need more than a miracle for what came next.

Tag, you're it, he thought.

He pointed at a Marine and an Army corporal who had affirmed they could take a stairwell.

"All right, you two. You take the lead, and you two," Jones pointed at a random pair, "Follow close behind." He paused and pointed at the carnage. "You can see, some asshole is waiting up there. Watch out for grenades and throw a couple yourself. Move quickly. As soon as they explode. Speed is your friend. Speed and violence. Call back once you get a toehold, and I'll send more people up. Clear?"

They nodded.

"Make it happen."

The unlikely Army and Marine Corps duo took the lead, grenades in hand. Their helpers were close behind, maybe too close.

They darted into the stairwell. One tripped over a corpse, crying out as he banged his shin on the concrete step. His buddy helped him up.

Jones turned to Peterson. "You need to set up a CCP, recover the wounded from out on the tarmac, and give me an idea of how many made it over. Capice?"

He nodded.

Jones heard someone scream out, "Grenade!"

Incoming or outgoing?

There was a thump from above, followed by wild shooting. Someone screamed. More firing.

Jones pointed at a squad-sized element.

"You lucky fuckers on me." He paused. "We're going to go clear the second floor, and we are going to set a fucking land speed record doing it."

He stepped off, followed closely by his RTO.

Ilya blinked as a hand appeared around the corner. He shot at it but missed. The hand flung a grenade.

"Fuck your mother!" Ilya shouted.

He swivelled back behind the brick entrance to the stairwell and waited for what seemed an eternity. With an almighty *WHUMP,* the grenade detonated on the staircase. Shrapnel pinged against the opposite wall; stone chips flew off, and dust billowed. He immediately swung through the doorway, his weapon leading the way.

A surprised US Army soldier ran into his pistol, and Ilya shot him in the chest. The soldier's wingman shot back with a carbine not a meter away. He missed. Ilya shot him, too. Or was it a her? He had seen dead females in uniform. Combat fatigues, too. These stupid imperialists.

More of them came up the stairs, shooting wildly.

It was too unhealthy to remain. One unaimed round or ricochet would surely catch him in the next few seconds. He grabbed his trooper, who was firing back.

"Come! We retreat and sting them as they come!"

They formed a rolling line, firing in turn as they moved backward.

At the end of the hall, he had a surprise, the machine gun crew on the other side of the building. And surprise in war was half the game. Ilya would reach him and use that gun to hold out as long as possible. They had started with 700 rounds. And they had used but a fraction of that so far.

The machine gun would form a barrier no one could cross.

They reached the end of the hallway and turned the corner. Ilya grabbed his companion and forced him downward.

"Stay here and sting them. I am going for the machine gun."

The man looked at him, nodded, and then looked back along the hallway leading to the staircase, where they could both hear shouts and commands in English. Ilya needed to move fast. He hastened to the gunner's position. To his surprise, the man was sitting there and smoking a cigarette as if he had not a care in the world.

"Move. I need your gun."

"You are wounded, Comrade."

"No time. Come."

"The Americans have taken the staircase?"

"Yes."

"Then we are fucked. They are crawling like ants outside."

"So? We will kill them like ants. Move."

"Fuck you, Comrade."

The man said *tovarish* like something he scraped off his shoe. Ilya had a bad feeling about this.

He levelled his service pistol at the *refusenik*. "You will come, and you will bring your machine gun."

"Die now, or die in a minute, then?"

"Yes."

The man shrugged. "*Nichevo*."

He lifted the machine gun with its long, shiny belt of bullets dangling from the side. His hand went to the pistol grip, and the barrel slowly swept Ilya's way.

Ilya was about to tell him to lead off so he couldn't be shot in the back, but the man moved fast. Not fast enough, though. The machine gun was heavy, and the belt of bullets tangled on his arm.

Ilya shot him in the face, and the slide racked back on his pistol.

The last round. He was out of ammo on the one weapon he could still operate.

"Fuck!"

Master Sergeant Peterson reported to Lonesome.

"Sir, we've taken the stairwell to the top of the tower, and we're working on some holdouts."

"Not bad for slingers of the Marine Corps' finest slop, Master Sergeant."

"Every Marine a rifleman, sir."

"And every baker a badass," Jones smiled, exhausted. This fight was more or less done. He gestured at his RTO, who passed him the handset. Jones took it and keyed the mic.

"Hammer Five, this is Six."

"Go ahead, Six."

"Be advised; the tower is no longer a threat. I'm gonna have a look around and head back to your position. How do you copy?"

"Good copy, Six. The Third has linked up with the Second inside the terminal, and we are still clearing, but it's just yard work now."

All over but the crying, Jones thought.

"Roger. When I get to you, I'll contact higher and tell them the airport belongs to us."

"They already know. By the way, there's a driver here for you. Says you have to get back to Jordan ASAP. I almost had to restrain her to keep her from locating you. She's on a mission."

Probably that asshole Cronauer, looking to court-martial him for messing up a perfectly good Sustainment Brigade. Lonesome snorted. Fuck that guy. He was going to go look around.

"Let the driver know I'll be at your position in fifteen mikes. I need to wrap up here. Then I'll take a walk. Hammer Six out."

Damn, Jones thought. Just when he'd started to love the 571st, they might be taking that from him, too. A sudden bone-deep weariness struck him. But there was still a job to do. He handed the mic back to his RTO.

"Walk with me, Lance Corporal."

From above came the distinctive jackhammer of a 240.

It wasn't one of his.

What the fuck?

HE COULD HEAR the imperialists talking. Even celebrating. The arrogant bastards. Ilya lugged the FN MAG along the contested hallway with his good hand, the long belt dragging out behind him. He would be lucky if he didn't trip over it. He was so fucking tired.

He rounded the last corner and saw his rifleman shooting at something. For all he knew, they were the final resistance in the building. Ilya shouted out to him.

"Coming up behind you!"

"Fucking finally, Comrade. Where's the gunner?"

"Dead."

"Oh."

Ilya set the weapon down. "Here. Take this and fire it. I'll try to use your carbine."

"An FN MAG. I don't know how to use it."

"Oh, fucking come on. It works the same, except the safety is different. See the button by the hand grip? Push it in, and it's ready to fire."

The man looked unsure. Ilya was just about done with this shit.

"Just pull the trigger. They'll be here any minute."

They exchanged weapons. Ilya lay on the floor, and the other man took care to unkink the belt. Ilya took his carbine and faced the rear. He hefted the gun with his uninjured right arm and supported it with his mangled left. They would hold this corner against all fucking comers. His companion fired a long burst.

"Comrade! They are coming!" He fired. Then, in a panicked tone, "Grenade!"

This was it, thought Ilya. *This is how I die.*

"Sir, someone up there round a corner is giving us a hard time. We don't have any grenades left."

Jones thought about it for all of a second.

"Check it out. I'll throw this," he pulled out a flashbang, "And we assault. How's that?"

The woman, who wore the yellow and green cactus shoulder patch of the 103rd Sustainment Command, nodded. "Sounds great, sir. Whenever you're ready."

Jones nodded slowly. She seemed remarkably detached. "The question is, are you ready, Specialist?"

"Cooking with gas, sir."

He looked over her team. They were stacked on the door, tight up against one another. The lead man tapped the soldier behind him, and the hard taps went backward. Jones knew that he would send it forward again when the last man got a pat. When the lead Marine or whoever felt the tap, he or she would spring into action immediately.

That's how he'd trained them.

Every fucking cook, a rifleman.

Or woman.

When he saw the last troop get tapped, he pulled the pin from his flashbang and tossed it down the hall.

As it cooked off, the taps came back forward. The flashbang went off a second before the lead man got the tap.

In a rush, the soldiers ran through the door. Lonesome heard a shot.

Scratch one 240 gunner, he thought. He charged through in their wake but pulled up quickly. He saw the dead gunner in a spreading pool of blood. Another Sov lay still beside him. Lonesome frowned. Something was wrong with this picture. He covered the man with his rifle.

"Sir! A call for you. Five insists you come back. He says Jordan is getting pretty vocal about you going with that driver."

Lonesome turned to look at her, and something slammed into his chest. It knocked him off balance for a moment.

It was the Sov on the floor, who wasn't on the floor anymore.

ILYA WATCHED the black American through stunned and slitted eyes. He waited. He couldn't hear anything but a high-pitched humming. And that was deep inside his head. He was pretty sure the grenade had shredded his eardrums. The Americans had run past, and they were so fucking stupid they had not thought to shoot him in passing. How had these fools prevailed? Greater numbers and human waves, he assumed.

But this new Yankee, the black one, had his very own radio operator, so he must be an officer. If he got the chance, Ilya would take him down.

Take him with me, he corrected.

A soldier spoke. A woman. Ilya watched as the officer turned his head. He saw his chance. Springing to his feet, only somewhat unsteadily, Ilya raced forward and covered the two meters that separated him from the duo in a flash. He stuck the officer with his bayonet, which jarred out of his grip, cutting his good hand. Still, he had knocked the American off-balance.

He's wearing armour plates, you stupid fuck!

Ilya turned quickly and punched the RTO in the face with his bleeding hand. He fell away, out of the fight. Ilya spun back toward the officer, who had definitely regained his balance.

The man butt-stroked Ilya in his face, and he felt teeth fly from his mouth as his head whipped around. The room spun, and then the American head-butted Ilya with his helmet.

It was enough.

Ilya's fight was over.

Now they would kill him, he thought, as he dropped into darkness.

"YOU OKAY, SON?"

The young Marine came to his feet. He was short a tooth, and blood streamed down his face.

"Not really, sir."

"Peppy motherfucker, this one," Jones gestured at the maimed paratrooper.

Some of his troops approached. "Get some flexicuffs on this asshole. Make sure he don't try and bite you, though. He's got some junkyard dog in him, for sure. Take him to the cage and make sure he gets there," Jones added with a growl. "He's a lieutenant. Might be one of the most senior officers left alive, so intel will want to give his nuts a squeeze."

"Yes, sir."

The soldiers trussed up the unconscious Senior Lieutenant before dragging him away. Jones turned his attention back to his RTO.

"Let's get you back to HQ and patched up. You look like shit, Lance Corporal. They pretty girls are gonna love it."

"Thank you, sir," the kid said, his reply a little mushy through his swollen lips and broken teeth. "By the way, they really need you back."

"Yeah. Let's go."

In ten minutes, they were back in the terminal with the scattered survivors of his staff. He called out to his Executive Officer.

"Looks like you get to run the show, Mister Brennerman. Where's this driver?"

A woman's voice called out, "Here, sir!" Jones turned towards her. A young black woman.

"I was told to get you back to Camp Jordan immediately, sir. I am in for an epic ass-whopping."

Jones snorted.

"I'm in charge of ass-whopping around these parts, private. Stand easy."

She did not, but Jones spoke to his Exec, anyway. "A fine job, Colonel. Tell the 571st I am proud as hell of all of them. Mop up and stand fast here until relieved, all right?"

"Yes, sir."

"A couple more things." He pointed at his RTO. "Make him your RTO. He looks like ninety pounds of misery, dripping wet, but he's good. Got a solid steel pair of balls on him. If he doesn't get a

NAVCOM-V, I'll come back from where they're about to exile me and shit down your throat. Understood?"

Brennerman grinned.

"Fair enough."

"Last item. Write up the 571st for a PUC. If it's the last thing I do in the Marine Corps, I'll sign that fucker. Clear? Your people have done the job. And then some." He paused. "I've been proud to lead you, spread the word. The show is yours, Colonel like it always should have been."

"Godspeed, sir."

"See you on the other side." Jones turned and nodded to his driver, who was so clean and spit-polished she looked...unreal.

"Lead on, Marine."

General J. Lonesome Jones left the field of battle, perhaps for the final time.

16

The dawn sky over London was salmon pink and baroque with the contrails of duelling fighters. Twice the convoy had to detour around ancient boroughs of the British capital set ablaze by Soviet missiles. The Russians were still trying to break out of southern France and eastern Europe, but from the chaos on the streets of London, you might have thought the Red Army had already crossed the Channel. Air raid sirens howled. Traffic crawled slowly when it wasn't grid-locked. Londoners flinched and looked to the skies, where ash and dust billowed from impact craters and burning buildings. The motor-cade had not even crossed the Thames before the Secret Service directed Kolhammer's driver to pull off the designated route and make for a new location outside the city. The agent slid open the little window between the front seat and the passengers.

"I'm sorry, Mister President," he said. "We've got intelligence of a threat to the meeting with Mister Churchill from a Soviet deep field unit. We're diverting to an alpha site. ETA three hours. The Prime Minister will meet you there, sir."

His message delivered, the window slid shut again.

Kolhammer knew it was pointless to argue. The decision had been made. Lieutenant General Andy Porter cursed volubly and colourfully while the British diplomat, Farru-Hill, knitted his brows in a theatrical show of concern. The SAS six-wheelers ahead of them in convoy were already swinging off the arterial road, bordered on both sides with dark, brick tenements. The Rolls-Royce followed them.

Kolhammer leaned forward and rapped on the window.

The agent slid it aside.

"Yes, sir?"

"If we'll be in transit for the rest of the morning, I'll need secure comms. It'll cause havoc if I go dark."

The agent was nodding before he finished.

"Yes, sir. We're already on it. There's a US Army signals unit joining us at Wimbledon. They'll get you plugged in. Thirty minutes, sir."

Satisfied with that because he had to be, Kolhammer sat back.

They made good time through the city after a police detachment joined their SAS escort. A comms van, painted in forest green camouflage pattern, was waiting as promised at Wimbledon, but nowhere near the famous tennis club. The vehicle was parked at the edge of a large open field, which Farru-Hill identified as the Common. The only way for Kolhammer to get a securely encrypted channel was to ride along in the van. After overruling the objections of the diplomats, he transferred with his security detail chief to the Army vehicle.

The green-painted van was a rougher ride, a weird hybrid of augmented technology and retro-futurist design. The two Army comms specialists made space for him and his detail chief between the racks of heavy, ruggedised radio equipment and a rack of beige boxes stamped with the Hewlett-Packard logo. These were the computers that would encrypt and decrypt any traffic, they told him.

Kolhammer thanked them and asked the senior NCO, a sergeant, to hook him up with the Joint Chiefs back in Washington.

The sergeant gulped visibly but set to the task as they motored through London's southern reaches. The van had no windows, leaving Kolhammer blind as to his location. The road surface was uneven, and they progressed in fits and starts, nearly unseating him at one point.

"I have Admiral Tisevich for you, Mister President," the comms sergeant said after a minute, handing him a heavy, old-fashioned telephone receiver.

"Thank you, son," Kolhammer said as he took it. "Admiral, this is...President Kolhammer."

He almost stumbled over his title, and there was a half-second delay before he heard the familiar voice of Paul Tisevich come crackling out of the headset, compressed and tinny sounding from the primitive encryption tools but instantly recognisable as the Chairman of the Joint Chiefs.

Initially, another navy man, Admiral Arthur Radford, would have sat in the chair at this point in history, but he had been killed by a missile strike on the light aircraft carrier USS *Independence* in early 1944.

"Mister President," Tisevich said. "I am relieved to hear from you, sir. We were beginning to worry. There's been a lot of confusion the last few hours."

"Understood, Admiral, and you better keep Sam Rayburn tucked away somewhere safe for the next couple of days, anyway. You might yet need him to step up into my job."

A pause.

"The Speaker of the House has already been moved to a secure and secret location, Mister President."

"Good to hear," Kolhammer said. "Now, this is gonna be a hard row to hoe with me stuck over here, but one thing I can do is order you to commence Operation Reforger immediately."

"I anticipated the order, Mister President. We have already taken all necessary measures to prepare the way. I'll order that Reforger be executed in full now."

"Excellent," Kolhammer said. "Item Two. I am ordering General Jones from Naples to Paris. Lonesome should be there in a few hours. He will be the new boss of Allied forces in Europe. Whatever he needs, Admiral, you make that happen. Before he even knows that he needs it."

"Yes, sir."

Kolhammer cut the connection to Tisevich and asked the sergeant to find General J. Lonesome Jones.

"Last heard of in Naples, son. Try Camp Jordan."

The sergeant, who had looked a little nervous at being ordered to run down the Chairman of the Joint Chiefs, nodded as though finding a footloose Marine Corps general from the back of a van speeding through the bomb-damaged streets of London was something he did every day.

While waiting for the connection, Kolhammer wondered what was happening with Lonesome in Naples. It'd been way too long since they had spoken.

THE CONVOY PULLED INTO CHEQUERS, the country residence of the British Prime Minister, some three hours later. He still hadn't spoken to Jones, but he now knew Naples was under attack from a significant Soviet Airborne force, so if Lonesome was still drawing breath, his old friend would be busy breaking things and hurting people. Kolhammer tried to sit with the frustration of not knowing as the Rolls crunched to a halt on the gravel driveway.

The red brick manor house of Chequers nestled gracefully on the gentle slopes of the Chiltern Hills, creating a striking contrast with the vibrant summer foliage of oak trees and the meticulously manicured lawns. An infantry company secured the perimeter, but Kolhammer knew they'd be useless against Soviet airstrikes. Andy Porter started muttering darkly as soon as it became apparent where they were heading.

"So what, we bailed on one crazy fucking obvious target to hang out at another?" Porter grunted as they rolled through the front gates of the sixteenth-century estate.

Kolhammer was no happier with the choice of venue, but he was determined to finish this meeting as quickly as possible and move on to a secure location where he could get down to work.

A flock of blackbirds lifted off from the lawn in front of the main building, where army engineers were building up sandbag revetments around the ancient masonry walls.

"Jesus fucking Christ," Porter growled. "Is anybody here paying attention?"

"Before you go flopping it out on the table, remember we're the ones who just lost a whole army group," Kolhammer cautioned.

Porter fell into a grizzly, ill-tempered silence. Deputy Minister Farru-Hill attempted to explain away the obvious inconsistencies in abandoning Downing Street for the even less fortified country residence.

"There's a whole air wing devoted to protecting the PM, you know. Anti-rocket batteries and such-like dug into the hills behind the manor. I know it all seems a bit...thingy, but this location is quite safe, and the sneaky beakies will have bamboozled old Ivan with a flood of disinformation about the PM's comings and goings."

"I'd still flatten the place on general principles if I were Stalin," Porter growled.

A butler appeared at the top of the steps. An honest-to-goddamned butler in a penguin suit and white gloves. Kolhammer almost laughed. But the amusement died in his throat as the British Prime Minister appeared from within the deeply shaded portico of the main entry hall.

Churchill was wearing a blue silk bathrobe, which flapped open in the light morning breeze, allowing everyone to see that underneath the thin robe, he wore nothing else. Smoke curled up from a long cigar in his left hand, and he held a thick ceramic mug in the other. The old statesman looked surprisingly fit.

"The PM has been, what do you call it, working out," Farru-Hill informed them. "Lifting lots of weights, they tell me."

Kolhammer stared at Churchill's drink, but he was pretty sure the mug wasn't full of rum or whisky, if only because the old devil was more than capable of necking a bottle in front of them all and damning the eyes of anybody who dared look sideways at him.

"Welcome, welcome, Mister President," the Prime Minister called out.

The famously thick, meat and gravy-bone voice was not the power it had once been, but Kolhammer still marvelled to hear it.

He had been trapped in the past for a long time, and much of the novelty had faded for him.

But hearing Winston Churchill welcome him as President to the Prime Minister's country seat was still a hell of a thing.

CHURCHILL INSISTED they all sit down for breakfast.

"The full English fry-up," he promised, as though they were not under imminent threat of a Soviet missile barrage. Or maybe because they were. "One never knows when one might have the chance of kippers again," the PM explained. "Although I don't imagine this outbreak of belligerency will go on anywhere near as long as the last."

Up and down the length of the dining table, a small swarm of liveried staff got everyone seated and ushered in more guests, more than half of them in military uniform, the rest in the dark, heavy suits still favoured by Britain's governing class. Kolhammer could hear Porter cursing under his breath about what a high-value target they would all make, and for once, he did not tap the brakes on the general's runaway mouth.

This meeting was epic foolishness, and his feet danced under the table, wanting to be done and gone.

But there would be no rushing Winston Churchill's breakfast. While Charles Farru-Hill was set to making introductions up and down the room, more staff arrived, this time bearing cast iron omelette pans, silver chafing dishes, crock pots and bread baskets. By the time the diplomat had done the rounds of the long table, it was fairly groaning under the weight of the feast piled upon it.

Churchill wasn't waiting for anyone. He had already started forking a pile of foul-smelling brown fish onto his plate, slapping away the hand of a waiter who attempted to do it for him.

"Let's not stand on ceremony, gentlemen," the PM said. "We have not the luxury of time."

Kolhammer looked around the assembled group. Churchill was not being a sexist oaf. There really were no women in the room. He had the sensation, increasingly rare these days, of sudden displacement, as though he had only just fallen through Manning Pope's wormhole and eight decades of history.

Kolhammer took a small, fresh-baked loaf, tore it lengthwise, and laid in a couple of bacon strips before spooning scrambled eggs over them.

"No crumpets for you, Sir John," Churchill rumbled at a man in army fatigues. "You're the warm-up act, I'm afraid. Let's have it."

The butler in the penguin suit who had fussed over Churchill stood at the end of the room and announced in a finely modulated bellow, "Field Marshall Sir John Harding, 1st Baron of Petherton, Chief of the Imperial General Staff."

"Fuck me," Andy Porter said quietly, genuinely taken aback by the bizarrely medieval performance. "It's like Game of fucking Thrones."

"You know nothing, Jon Snow," Kolhammer muttered. "So shut the hell up."

Harding had no feudal or chivalric air as he climbed to his feet, nodding in acknowledgment of the Prime Minister and the American President. He was clad in battle dress uniform and wore a pistol at his hip.

"At zero hundred and twenty-three hours this morning, the Soviet Union launched a pre-emptive strike on NATO forces throughout the European theatre. The initial attack originated from several orbital platforms and took the form of space-launched impactors. Giant tungsten spears, we believe, the size of telegraph poles," he explained to a few confused-looking civil servants. "They drop them down on our heads from way up there," he waved at the sky outside. "And the bloody things go off like atom bombs when they land. But without the radioactive effects. The attack was disrupted—"

Harding nodded to Kolhammer.

"By our American friends working with..." he paused and frowned. "Private aerospace interests."

"Davidson Aerospace," Kolhammer supplied, causing a murmur

to run up and down the table. "But I'll explain later. Please continue, Field Marshal."

Harding thanked him and went on.

"On our best intelligence, it seems that the bulk of Stalin's orbital forces were neutralised, but I'm afraid those that did get through have done great damage. The Fifth Army, our main bulwark against any Soviet advance, has been annihilated, and Germany lies open to the Red Army."

More muttering, louder and more urgent this time.

"Carry on, Sir John," Churchill said, raising his voice over the buzz. It quietened things down.

Harding acknowledged the PM and consulted a small notebook, which he had taken from his pocket.

"The Soviet Eighth Guards are massed at the Oder. In southern Europe, the Second and Third Shock Armies are driving north to encircle our surviving forces. There are a hundred brushfires here and there, but those two axes of attack constitute an existential threat to the Atlantic alliance."

Harding resumed his seat.

Churchill spoke around a mouthful of egg and sausage.

"Mister President, for the sake of my curiosity, sir. Your fellow countryman, Mister Davidson? How did he come to play such a vital role?"

Kolhammer answered carefully.

There were so many pitfalls and traps on this path.

"Davidson Aerospace has many contracts with the US government," he began. "But their commercial space program is even larger again. Mister Davidson is something of a...a frontier character, I suppose. And on the frontier, the prudent man looks to secure his interests against predators and those with hostile intent. Davidson's satellite network was always going to be among the first targets of any Eastern Bloc attack. They could not afford to cede the high ground to us. So, he prepared."

The room was deathly quiet. The only sound was the scraping of Churchill's cutlery on his plate.

"I see, and what form did that preparation take? In this instance?"

"His satellites were fitted out with dual-use technologies. In this instance," Kolhammer said, "they were able to launch a volley of anti-missile and anti-satellite munitions against the Soviet platforms that were moving into alignment for an orbital bombardment. He should probably get a medal or a tax cut."

Churchill snorted.

"I very much doubt your Mister Davidson pays tax anywhere but Bermuda, and there only at a penny on the dollar. But," he went on, "it would be churlish were we not to acknowledge our debt to him. Mister Colville, make a note, if you would, to find some suitable bauble for an American carpetbagger who has saved the realm in quite spectacular fashion. The Birthday Honours list would be appropriate, I think."

A younger man in a dark, pin-striped suit spoke up from well down the room.

"As you wish, Prime Minister."

As Colville made his note, a British naval officer, a Lieutenant Commander, Kolhammer thought, appeared at the door, his face flushed.

He spoke to the head butler, who waved him over to Churchill, but he kept glancing at Kolhammer the whole time.

The President did not have a good feeling about this.

Seeing the look on Churchill's face as the Royal Navy commander whispered some dire report in his ear, Kolhammer felt his balls trying to retract.

Churchill thanked the man and dismissed him.

"I'm afraid, Mister President," he said gravely, "I have more bad news."

17

This war was unlike those which came before it. In the past, when tribes, cities, or nation states made war upon each other, the fighting could be savage and the horror vast. But the violence was rarely immediate. Before the God-King Xerxes could throw his boundless host upon the spear tips of three hundred Spartans at the Hot Gates, his million-strong army had first to tramp across the Hellespont from the furthest reaches of Eurasia. When mighty Rome set covetous eyes upon the green fields of Albion, years passed before the sandal of the first Legionnaire trod upon the wet grey shoreline of Kent. Even the fearsome German blitzkrieg of 1940 had been preceded by the eight-month languor of the Phoney War as both sides feinted, manoeuvred, and felt each other out.

No interregnum separated the last hours of unquiet peace from the ferocity of total war in June 1955.

Had Josef Stalin's orbital strike not been parried by the shield of anti-satellite weapons developed in the dark labs at Davidson Aerospace, the Third World War would likely have ended abruptly, in one decisive moment of violence, executed at a planetary scale. Even with that scheme neutralised and the ensuing conflict reduced to a conventional struggle of arms, war took dominion everywhere and all at once.

As Lonesome Jones fought through the ruined terminal of Naples airport and Philip Kolhammer crawled through the smoking boroughs of London, a behemoth came awake a hundred feet below the Atlantic. The Novgorod Class submarine *Alexey Schastny* launched a 'dolphin' from weapons tube number six, just back from the bow of the 594-foot-long monster. The remotely piloted sensor pod drove for the surface, where conditions were excellent – a light cross-chop on a gentle swell of less than a foot. The pre-dawn sky was turning pink with a hint of sunrise.

The dolphin's operator, Senior Lieutenant Aksel Kunikov, adjusted the heavy cups of his earphones and leaned into the bank of CRT screens at his station. Behind him in the Combat Operations Centre, the senior staff of the enormous missile boat worked in the deathly quiet and blood-red glow of general quarters.

Technicians sat in seats of steel mesh bolted to the deck, their pale faces sweating in the dim red lights of the consoles around them, their eyes flickering back and forth between screens, alert to the slightest change in the tactical situation. The Operations Centre smelled of ozone, hot electronics, and sour sweat. The drive system hummed, and the air filters hissed quietly, struggling to scrub clean the recycled atmosphere, which was already hot and moist but not yet uncomfortable.

The dolphin broke surface, and Lieutenant Kunikov got to work.

For the first minute, he did nothing, letting the robot submersible gently drift as its scanners took in the data from the sea around it.

The sensor pod was packed with the most advanced arrays of passive sensors the Functional Projects Bureau had ever designed and built. The blue-grey dolphin, its radar-absorbent, rubberised skin all but invisible to detection, waited on the fateful kiss of an enemy radar sweep or radio transmission. Lieutenant Kunikov listened intently for the telltale crackle and static of contact but heard only the soft hiss of clean spectrum. The thick, curved glass of the monitors in front of him displayed dense columns of data.

With a few deft strokes of his fingers on the control panel,

Kunikov activated all the drone's active systems. Its cameras scanned the horizon, mapping out a fifteen-mile radius of ocean and sky in perfect detail. The sonar suite immediately began searching for any ships or submarines within range. The magnetic anomaly detector began sniffing for any large metallic objects.

A few moments later, Kunikov detected a ship about ten miles north of their position, travelling west toward the continental US.

"Comrade Captain," he whispered. "I have contact. Possible twin-screwed surface vessel. Moving fast. No pings."

Captain of the First Rank Ludomir Kirillovich stood just behind him. Tall and broad-shouldered for a submariner, with pale skin and a closely trimmed, salt-and-pepper beard, the captain of the *Alexey Schastny* spoke quietly.

"Attend and evaluate," he said.

Kunikov adjusted his headset and listened closely, watching his data feeds simultaneously. After five years of honing his skills in the harsh environment of the Arctic Operational Area, he was used to pressure. His mind raced to make sense of the data, and he could feel the tension rising as the bridge crew waited for him to report.

The ship was running hard. He could tell from the sound of its propellers—a deep reverberation like a giant mechanical heartbeat. The vessel's engine roared over a high-pitched whining as the blades spun at...

Kunikov checked his data.

"Approximately seven hundred revolutions per minute," he informed the captain. "Twin screws, four blades. Standard commercial configuration."

"Continue with your assessment," Kirillovich said.

The water was alive with the other vessel's energy. Kunikov was confident it was fleeing to its home port, or at least to safe harbour on the American coast. He thought it would make a fat prize if their target for the day were not so much more rewarding.

Another minute and Kunikov was certain.

"A merchant vessel, Comrade Captain. A heavy tanker, I would say. Making full steam for the coast. No variation in heading. No sensors deployed."

"We shall wait on them to depart," Kirillovich said.

Ten minutes later, the ship had vanished, unaware of ever being watched. Aksel Kunikov allowed himself the merest sigh of relief.

They had arrived on station undetected. He craned his head and rolled his shoulders to work out the hot cramp that settled in his neck.

“Permission to resume active scanning, Comrade Captain?”

“Permission granted, Lieutenant,” the boat’s commander replied. “All sensors to active.”

Kunikov’s fingers flew across his keyboard, a heavy, ruggedised analogue of the units salvaged from the British ship HMS *Vanguard*. The keys were thick and quiet. The *Alexey Schastny* was the most advanced submarine in the Soviet fleet. Better in some ways than the enemy boats which would be searching for her, especially after this morning. Lieutenant Kunikov was confident they were alone.

Under his instruction, signals pulsed up the thin, insulated line to the pod bobbing around on the surface a hundred feet above them. Sensor bay doors slid open on the dolphin, and small, bristling antennae deployed.

Kunikov completed the start-up sequence and pressed three buttons on his console, turning their status lights from red to green.

The Vurdalak-4 fire control system pulsed with a short but massive surge of energy, reaching out across thousands of square miles to connect with pre-sited positional beacons. The simple, robust units woke from their brief slumber. One was affixed to a small rocky outcrop forty miles off the coast of south-eastern Virginia; the other sat atop an isolated hill on the Knotts Island waterfowl refuge, planted there by agents of the Main Directorate for State Security.

With their position fixed and the targeting lock on the American naval station at Norfolk confirmed, Lieutenant Kunikov’s work was almost done. Years of training and preparation for just these few minutes of action.

“Targets confirmed and solutions plotted, Comrade Captain,” he announced.

“Weapons,” Captain Kirillovich said.

Another young officer on the far side of the Op Centre confirmed that all weapons were ready.

Without preamble or ceremony, Kirillovich ordered the launch.

Sixty-four launch bay doors rumbled open along the upper length of the submarine's hull, and the entire load volley-fired over the next minute and a half.

The cruise missiles, all land attack variations of the Raduga state corporation's venerable Styx design, shot away from the sub in watertight sabot casings, which split open and dropped back to the wavetops a couple of seconds after breaking surface. Powerful rocket engines ignited, driving the 6000-pound main vehicles high into the early morning sky on hot, bright spears of fire. The advanced analogue rockets, christened Banshees by their designers, did not stay at those higher altitudes long. Triangulated onto their objective by location data streaming from the dolphin, they dove for the deck, roaring in towards the coast of Norfolk, Virginia, at one-and-a-half times the speed of sound. Four of the Banshees broke away from the pack.

The attack wave quickly synchronised into formation, slaved now to the code written into their guidance systems.

US Navy coastal defence installations had been at the highest levels of alert since the attacks on NATO and quickly detected the flight of incoming cruise missiles. Air defence units initiated rapid countermeasures. Surface-to-air missile batteries loaded with High Explosive, Dual Purpose warheads lit up their search radars, burning up spectrum looking for targets. Jet fighters scrambled, and helicopter gunships lifted off while naval destroyers deployed smoke screens offshore in a futile attempt to obscure the naval base.

But not all the rockets screaming towards Norfolk were armed with high explosive warheads. Four of them carried electronic warfare packages, which now duelled with the air defence radars of their American foes, convincing the imperialists that many hundreds of warheads were inbound from multiple vectors.

Anti-missile systems launched interceptors. Radar jammers throbbed out megawatts of confounding electronic countermeasures, and some defences worked precisely as advertised.

Nine Banshees were destroyed over open water.

Six more were harvested by point-defence auto-cannons seconds after the bluffs around Norfolk Naval Station erupted, sending bright red rivers of high-velocity munitions into the sky.

But thirty-three of the massive cruise missiles punched through the multilayered defences and fell upon the home port of the US Atlantic Fleet in a monstrously destructive tempest of fire and fury.

Two hundred and thirty nautical miles away, Lieutenant Kunikov studied the readouts on his bank of monitors, nodding slightly as the data confirmed a successful attack. Finally, when he was sure, he turned and reported to his commander.

"All links are now dark, Comrade Captain," he said. "Initial data return indicates nearly seventy-five per cent delivery on target."

Captain of the First Rank, Ludomir Kirillovich, nodded. Once.

They had just destroyed American naval power in the Atlantic.

"Secure from general quarters," he said quietly. "Scuttle the dolphin. Prepare to dive."

No cheering. No applause. No celebration of any kind followed.

They would be the hunted now.

18

Geert Veenstra smiled at his wife, Aukje, who was nursing a cup of coffee. Her other hand rested on her swelling midsection. The Veenstras were a growing family. The blue light of early dawn was just starting to seep through the narrow gap in the dark brown curtains, the first glimpse of a new day in their lives together. The dark green Technivorm coffee machine gurgled happily as two more slices of Aukje's favourite black bread toasted silently in their new Morely-Davidson. The twins were asleep in their room but would be up and tearing around soon enough. This then was the golden hour for the family Veenstra, when Geert and his wife could sit quietly in each other's company. He did not even have the radio on. That, too, was a small indulgence. He would need to hear the weather report eventually, what with the job he had going over on the Julianaweg this week.

Geert spent his days making sure the residents of Utrecht had clean water whenever they turned on the tap. He was proud of his job. Happy with the direction fate had taken him in. He took the last bite of his cheese bread, smiled at Aukje, and reached for his pouch of Van Nelle. As he pinched out a wad of rich black tobacco and rolled it up into a thin Rizla paper, Geert recalled seeing Aukje for the first time, all the way back when he was attending the

Middle Technical School. They had made eye contact on the train, and he had blushed fiercely, but he simply could not look away from the loose lock of blonde hair that had fallen between her lively eyes. It was so comical, and yet captivating too. The next day, Geert got her name. She was Aukje Bijlsma, the girl with the runaway hair.

By the time he finished his engineering study and left for two years in the Army, they were a proper couple. They wrote faithfully while he was off tending howitzers in Germany. Old-fashioned letters, of course. They were as poor as church mice, and neither had any money for the new-fangled gizmos coming out of America. No walking phones or electric mail for them. They married as soon as Geert was done with his service. The twins arrived nine months later.

Geert licked the glue strip on the edge of the cigarette paper and rolled the leaf into the flared shape one saw so often in Holland. He lit up and inhaled. God, but he loved the spicy smell of fresh tobacco, no matter what the doctors and the future folk said about it. Why deny himself such a small pleasure when the Red Army might roll in and take all the pleasures from them anyway? Aukje lifted her mug and sipped again. One delicate, blonde eyebrow quirked at him through the curling steam.

"Aren't you going out on the balcony to smoke that?"

"Ah, of course, schat," Geert said. "Sorry."

He did accept what the scientists said about smoking. It was obviously bad for you and even worse for the little ones. Geert was not in denial about such things, unlike his father, who thought all the 'grim tales from the future' were stuff and nonsense. He had reduced his habit, going from two pouches weekly to one every two weeks.

He grabbed his tobacco and a box of Swedish matches from the kitchen counter and squeezed onto the tiny balcony. They were not just lucky to have this apartment; they were blessed in a land with a million people looking for a roof over their heads. He had snagged the top-floor rooms from an older engineer in the city's water department, a supervisor who owned a little bit of property in the medieval town centre, and even more in the newer suburbs being built on the far side of the motorway to the South. Klaas wanted someone reliable in the apartment, and Veenstra met his exacting needs. A trustworthy man, tamed by wife and children, with a secure income.

Utrecht slept beneath him in the pre-dawn gloom. Geert thought he'd heard distant thunder late last night but woke to clear skies and fresh air. The gentle curve of the old canal, the Oudegracht, shaped itself around their little neighbourhood, and it was light enough now to enjoy the colourful spray of flowers planted in beds all along the bank.

He heard the radio come on inside and checked his watch. The weather report should be any time now. The toast popped up, and he turned around with some care on the tiny balcony as Aukje played with the dial to find their station.

There was a lot of static this morning.

Abruptly, he heard a wailing tone, and his happiness died.

A man announced an official bulletin from the ANP and called for attention three times.

His voice crackled out of the speakers as Geert stumbled over the small lip of the balcony doors.

"Military members are directed to report to their duty stations immediately. All leave is cancelled. All active reservists are to report to their units immediately with equipment. This is not a drill. A massive attack by Soviet forces on Germany is confirmed. More information will follow as it becomes available. Attention, attention, attention. Military members are directed to report to their duty stations immediately..."

The message, obviously recorded, started to repeat itself.

Geert was rooted in place. Had he heard correctly? Was this even real? He shook his hand at a sudden burning pain. He had forgotten about his cigarette. The butt fell to the wooden floor, and he crushed it under the heel of his slipper. As if to answer a hundred unspoken questions, jets suddenly screamed in from the west.

They would be NATO aircraft from that direction, but he still flinched and moved instinctively to protect his wife.

Aukje stood by the little breakfast bench, her toast wholly forgotten. The colour had drained from her face, and she held one hand to her mouth.

"You have to report, don't you, Geert," Aukje said. Her voice quivered.

He gathered her into a hug.

"Yes, I do. Verdomme."

Aukje pushed herself out of his arms and walked unsteadily to their little table. She sat down heavily and rubbed her forehead. "Alright. Alright. You get ready, and I'll make you some food to take."

The couple stared at each other. Neither of them moved. Everyone had feared this day would come, and they had prepared as best they could. The Veenstras had laid up a modest supply of canned food and other things that had been rationed in the last war. Laundry detergent, simple medicines, extra linens. But now the day was here, and all their carefully laid plans had gone directly to the *kloten*.

Shit, thought Geert. Shit. He felt a ringing excitement, along with a terrible, draining trepidation. He walked to their tiny bedroom on legs that suddenly did not feel like his own. What he needed was in his wardrobe.

One combat uniform hung there, but he would have to get his green duffel bag out of the storage cellar downstairs. It was packed according to regulations.

He could hear Aukje rattling around in the kitchen as he started to strip out of his pyjamas. It was going to be a long day.

CAPTAIN JOACHIM BOOSFELD waited on the edge of battle. A thick morning mist clung to his skin like a cold sweat as he mechanically smoked his fifth or sixth cigarette with yet another cup of scalding black coffee. He had an Iron Cross but not an iron bladder, and it irked him to keep sneaking inside to relieve himself. He yearned to get moving and into action where he could happily fill his boots with his own piss, and nobody would look twice at him. It would not be long now. As his men raced about their new machines, lashed by the curses and shouts of the non-coms, Boosfeld listened to the God-like grumble of the big guns at Fulda echoing through his skull.

His company boasted fifteen main battle tanks and a support element of wheeled vehicles. His tank, number fifty-nine, was parked at the end of the first row in the open field west of the battalion's HQ. The numbers stood out in red on the turrets, just behind the new Bundeswehr insignia, a stylized black cross. His crew swarmed over the tank, cracking the hatches, and readying her to move.

Boosfeld inhaled deeply from his cigarette and ignored the twitching of his fingers—*he simply itched to move on*, he thought. If he were Ivan, he'd punch through NATO's paper-thin air defences to get at the Fatherland's surviving armour before it could move into the field to commence the iron harvest of old Joe's clanking, primitive tank fleets. Every muscle in his body clenched when a flight of A-10 tank busters screeched over their heads, angling west towards the Gap. He first noticed their approach as an ominous whine, groaning to a heavy metal banshee's howl. It caused a sudden ripple of anxiety and whispered fear among his men, conscripts mostly, and an answering roar from First Sergeant Stark, who bellowed at them to keep working.

"It is just the Americans," he shouted. "Do not shit yourself for nothing. There will be plenty of time for shitting later."

Both men watched the lads swarm the tanks again. It was not so long ago for Joachim that the sound of US Air Force planes meant doom.

He ran a cold eye over the tank directly in front of him.

No. 59.

His gaze traced over the new gleaming armour, its hard exterior lines an exquisite mix of brushed steel and riveted black plating. He allowed himself to imagine what it would be like to drive her into battle, using the advanced sensors and weapons systems of this so-called 'augmented design'. He had pored over the specs and manuals. Practised endlessly with simulators. But now was his first time to feel her true power. Nothing could match the real thing. He ran his hand along her cool metal contours and felt the thrill of anticipation deep in his gut.

He wanted, even needed, to get inside her. But boyish exuberance would not do for a commander. Not even for a lowly company commander in the toy soldier make-believe army of the modern Bundeswehr. There weren't a lot of veterans in this company; most of his boys were draftees who had barely touched a tank—at least to his way of thinking. A smile ghosted across his face. *These young men would learn to hate these iron bitches soon enough*, he thought. Hate them and love them about equally if they lived to understand the paradox. He otherwise kept his face blank, eventually stubbing out his cigarette on the heel of his boot and rolling up the remnants to keep in his pocket, where they joined the tailings and scrap of a dozen previous cigarettes. The habits of an old soldier died hard. Joachim Boosfeld swirled his coffee and looked over at Stark.

"We could have used these in the last war, First Sergeant."

Stark grunted. "I don't think the Americans would have loaned them to us."

Boosfeld snorted.

"No. I suppose not."

"Although," the First Sergeant pondered out loud, "Perhaps Patton might have. He hated the communists more than he hated us."

"Patton hated everyone. But your point is well made. He was a man ahead of his time."

"And we are men out of ours," Stark said before taking a moment to indulge himself in roaring through a private who was dragging a length of rubber hose through the muddy gravel.

First Sergeant Stark had ended that last, strange war fighting rear-guard actions against the Soviets in a Panther; he was fortunate to be standing here in this field. So too, was Joachim.

He raised the final dregs of his cooling coffee to his lips and drank without savouring the taste. He motioned towards tank fifty-nine with the empty cup.

"Let us have a closer look, First Sergeant. I think the lads are ready for us."

"These fools aren't even ready for toilet training," Stark muttered.

Nonetheless, they moved. The old man felt his boots sink into gravel, picking up pebbles as they crunched along. The smell of the diesel and fresh camouflage paint grew stronger until it blotted out the pine scent of the nearby forest.

The driver, young Hoffman, saw their approach and jumped a little. He slid off the tank's deck, hit the gravel and braced to attention, rendering a precise salute.

Boosfeld returned it, but Stark spoke first. "Private Hoffman, tell me something about this tank."

Hoffman gulped, took a second, and recovered. "First Sergeant, this is the Panzer M-60. It weighs 48.9 metric tons, has a range of 480 kilometres, a top speed of 48 kph, and a maximum engagement distance of four kilometres."

Stark nodded. "Go on, Private."

"Its main gun is 120mm. The coaxial is a 7.62mm M240, and the commander controls a 12.7mm Browning. This Panzer is fully night operations capable, with standard NVGs for me, the driver, and a thermal sight shared between the gunner and commander."

The First Sergeant waved him away. "Alright, Hoffman, good enough for now. Return to your duties, and this tank better be spotless the next time I see it."

He pointed at some mud in the treads. Boosfeld struggled to keep a straight face.

Hoffman scurried to clean the tracks as another wave of man-made thunder rolled over them from a great distance. Or maybe not so great now.

The two old soldiers looked at each other.

"I think we are just about done with parade ground foolishness, First Sergeant," Boosfeld said.

"I will be done when they bury me," Stark grinned and gestured toward the tank. "Or hose me out. After you, sir."

Joachim placed his boot on the top of a bogie wheel, grabbed a handhold and heaved himself up. Had life not taken this unfortunate detour into calamity, he might have been hauling himself into a rail carriage to make his way to a long day's drinking with old comrades around about now. He'd planned to catch the bus into Munster today and spend all day getting good and shit-faced drunk with old comrades in the beer garden at the Ratskeller St Georg. There weren't many of them left, and fewer still who were not so shamed by their service that they would deny it. He started to wonder what might become of his old comrades, but he pushed these thoughts away—it was no use thinking about such things any longer.

Nothing mattered more than what he needed to do within the next five minutes.

Sticking his head into the open hatch, he peered around. Everything was painted white, and the blue-green interior lights were on. This tank was as new as he had ever seen and smelled as if it had just come off the assembly line in America.

Probably had, he thought. Boosfeld pulled his head out of the hatch and climbed inside, swinging his legs into the open circle and sliding into the commander's seat. For a green-covered canvas seat, it was as comfortable as any he had ever known. *Gelform cushions*, he thought. The breechblock was to his left; his thermal sight was directly in front. It was different but the same.

For an instant, in his mind's eye, he no longer saw himself dressed in his Bundeswehr olive green Nomex. He wore the black wool tanker's coverall of a Waffen-SS Panzer commander, the twin lightning bolts of the Siegrunen standing out on the collar. It was only a moment but very disorienting, and Boosfeld was glad to be hidden inside the tank. Back here in the present, he knew that Himmler's flashy collar runes had cost him this battalion. He sighed a little raggedly. But at least he had his company and this magnificent Panzer! If it could do only half of what he had been told...

He laid his hand, shaking a little, on the commander's gunner override. *Half-promises*, he thought, *like all the lies he had been told in the last war*. That war, so odd and uncanny in many ways, was never far from his thoughts. So many close calls, both with the enemy and his own SS.

Joachim Boosfeld had nearly been shot when the Gestapo had discovered in the uptime archives that he had retired from a future Bundeswehr as a full colonel. He had fallen under suspicion of treason immediately. They had torn off his Siegrunen, demoted him, and transferred him to a third-tier Wehrmacht unit full of wastrels and criminals.

He cursed.

The past was gone. It was dead. Let it lie.

Boosfeld swivelled his chair and tried to get a feel for his spacious new home. Instead, he remembered being sent out to die in suicide attacks. He went, knowing his own people meant to kill him. He survived to spite them.

He held off dozens of Soviet attacks in those final days of the war before the Americans vaporized Berlin with one of their atomic super weapons. Feverish with exhaustion, stinking with month-old sweat, a general had appeared from somewhere one day in a kubelwagon and had draped a Knight's Cross around Joachim Boosfeld's neck. Ordered personally by Himmler, as Fuhrer.

Himmler, who was but drifting ashes by then. It was like receiving a final curse from the wretched imp.

Joachim stuck his head up through the hatch and called out to Hoffman. "Driver, can you start this beast? I want to hear her run."

"Yes, sir. Just a second, sir."

"Just for this morning, Private Hoffman," Boosfeld replied. "A lazy second will get you killed when we leave here. And we leave very soon."

The hell of it was that damned Iron Cross from Himmler had been the final nail in his coffin as far as the Bundeswehr was concerned. Former SS man and personally awarded Germany's highest decoration by the final Fuhrer? By Himmler? They said they would take him because he was a veteran tanker.

But a lowly captain Joachim Boosfeld was, and a lowly captain he'd remain.

He saw Hoffman drop through the driver's hatch.

A buzz sounded throughout the crew compartment, and the lights flickered for a second. With a clattering roar, Panzer 59 came to life.

Boosfeld couldn't help it. He grinned at last.

19

The Jeep was an older model. Legit World War Two vintage. In this world, as in all others, the Marine Corps sat at the bottom of the procurement food chain.

"General," the young African-American woman said. "We gotta roll, sir. You're really needed at Building H, back at Camp Jordan. Immediately, sir."

What the suffering fuck was next, Jones thought?

'H' was less a building than a bunker; an underground facility, the command centre for Camp Jordan, buried deep. Jones didn't question the marine—she was just the messenger—but he couldn't help the glower that darkened his expression. This was going to be another fucking snipe hunt, for sure.

The driver, whose name tag on the breast pocket of her desert pattern camouflage read Williamson, hurried to explain her orders.

"It's the President, sir. They sent me to get you because the President needs to speak to you. They sent a chopper first, but it got shot down. And you don't have a secure line out here."

Jones couldn't help himself.

"Is this some sort of joke?"

Private Williamson shook her head in mortified denial. Her eyes looked comically wide.

"No, sir. I...Colonel Grieve sent me to fetch you, sir. And Colonel Grieve doesn't have a sense of humour."

Jones snorted softly as a helicopter thundered low overhead as they motored away from the airfield, leaving a trail of dust in their wake. The sky was filled with an orange light from fires in the distance, which glowed with greater power than the first rays of dawn then creeping over the horizon. The sweet stink of gasoline wafted through the air, mixed with heavy smoke and hints of exhaust fumes. As they moved further away from the aftermath of the battle, Jones also tasted a few draughts of fresh, clean air.

Williamson drove well. She was aggressive, but she had good control, working the stick shift and the clutch like a rally driver, never stopping, no matter how thick the tangle of traffic became.

"No, Colonel Grieve does not have a sense of humour," he agreed when the rotor noise trailed off. "But I wouldn't share that observation so freely if I were you, Private. You might end up exiled to Nutritional Studies."

Williamson was at a loss for how to respond, and she fell back on the old reliable, "Sir, yes sir."

After a moment, she added, "They need you in the SCIF, not on a radio, sir."

The road network wasn't gridlocked but slow and clotted with vehicle movement and foot traffic. Williamson threw their antique off-roader into a series of slewing, radical turns to avoid one major stoppage where a broken-down LAV had blocked an intersection. She cleared the obstruction and stomped on the gas when they hit open road on the other side.

Jones wondered if she'd learned to drive in the Corps. No fucking doubt about it, he decided. Her accent placed her origins in the deep South, where few women of her age and background had access to a private motor vehicle.

Williamson weaved a swift path through the structured chaos of mobilization and civilian panic, delivering Jones to the bunker entrance of Building H in less than forty-five minutes. He was grateful. It would have taken hours to make the journey on foot.

"Should I wait here for you, sir?" she asked.

"Might be best, private," Jones conceded. "If you have no other tasking."

"I do not, sir."

"Well, now you do, Private Williamson. Stand ready."

Williamson acknowledged the order with a salute. She seemed glad to have some certainty about what she, at least, was supposed to do next.

Jones left her with the Jeep and strode purposefully into the fortified concrete blockhouse. Two sentries scanned his identity chip and checked his biometrics against an access list. The data slate they used was augmented tech. Much thicker than a flexipad but ruggedized, too.

"Level Three, sir, you're good to go," the corporal said, printing off a barcode sticker for Jones to fix onto a breast pocket. "Colonel Grieve is waiting on you."

Jones thanked the man and took the stairs down three flights. More sentries in full battle rattle checked him in at L3. It had been a few weeks since Jones had been in the command centre and another month before that since he'd had reason to visit the comms section. It had been busy then. Camp Jordan was the Marine Corps' main base in southern Europe, a giant facility home to half a dozen Expeditionary Units tasked with controlling the Mediterranean and North African battle space. It was frenetic now, even though the MEUs were largely deployed. Hundreds of personnel hurried in all directions with the grim focus he recognized from a long career of stepping into the shit all over the world.

"If you'll follow me, General," one of the guards said as soon as he confirmed Jones's ID and access. He didn't wait for Jones to answer; instead, he headed off toward the primary SCIF—the camp's Sensitive Compartmented Information Facility. Jones hastened to keep up.

Another security check at the SCIF entrance delayed him a few seconds, and he soon found himself inside the inner chamber where the technology had a recognizably uptime appearance. The concrete walls were painted a dull grey, with metal vents scattered across the ceiling, blowing cold air down onto uniformed personnel hunched over consoles and keyboards as data streams filled multiple screens in ever-shifting patterns.

Colonel Robert Grieve, a dour but competent man who had never been anything but completely proper with Jones, waited with an expression of grim apprehension that was striking even for him. The air was stale, with a faint hint of ozone from the electronics and the occasional sharp whiff of cleaning supplies. Grieve looked like he'd been breathing it for twenty years.

On seeing Jones, the colonel saluted before giving a systems operator a quiet order to "put the call through." The comms specialist, another young woman, adjusted her headset and started working a keyboard and screen that had obviously been salvaged from one of the ships of the original Multinational Force. It was Apple tech, just about the only uptime IT that still worked. Grieve stepped forward, his eyebrows furrowed.

"I apologize for the delay, General Jones," he muttered. "The President only touched down in London a few hours ago, and the Reds have been interfering with our satellites and cables, and it's been a hell of a mess to sort out the secure lines."

Jones stared at him for a second.

"London?" he said. "What the hell's Ike doing in London?"

The Colonel blinked.

"Oh shit," he grunted. Grieve shook his head as if waking from a bad dream.

"General Jones. President Eisenhower is dead. The Vice President has been sworn into office in transit from Paris to London."

"What?" Jones said, feeling like an idiot. None of this made any sense.

Colonel Grieve looked almost as confused.

"Again, my apologies, sir. You should've been briefed. The fault is mine. An uptime missile took down Marine One as it departed the White House, killing President Eisenhower and all on board. The Russian kill teams have all been captured or killed. President

Kolhammer took the oath on a flight evacuating him from Paris, where he'd been on a state visit and..."

"I know," Jones said, cutting him off, his head reeling with the new information. "I know that Phil...I mean...the President was in Paris."

He had not spoken with Kolhammer in months. Not since Cronauer had fucked him in the neck. Jones didn't doubt for a second Kolhammer would have made things right had he asked, but Jones could not do that. It would only inflame the septic mess of a culture war that leaked from the twenty-first century into the mid-1950s.

"I have London, sir," the sysop announced.

Jones took a wired headset from Grieve and fitted the rig over his shaved skull. He heard a compressed voice through the crackle and hiss of encryption software running on augmented comm channels.

"Stand by for the president, please, General Jones."

And before Jones could answer, he heard the familiar voice of his friend and comrade through the earpiece.

"Lonesome, you there?"

THE BRITS HAD HURRIED Churchill to another site soon after he told Kolhammer what had happened at Norfolk. The President would have followed immediately, but Chequers had a secure comms facility buried deep under the manor, and Kolhammer judged that the risk of exposure for another quarter hour was worth being able to make the calls he now needed to make.

The last was to Jones, who had resurfaced after fending off a Russian air assault on Naples.

Kolhammer sat at a cheap particle board desk in the centre of the room with a half-dozen chairs scattered haphazardly around it. The concrete walls were covered in lead sheeting, a crude but effective defence against EMP strikes.

A musty odour of old sweat told of a place where none but soldiers had spent any time, and a thick rubberized cable ran from the room into a diesel generator next door.

The British Signals Corps squaddie patched him through to Jones before excusing himself.

"I'll be outside if you need me, sir."

"I'll try not to, son," Kolhammer said.

"MISTER PRESIDENT," Jones said, feeling like some trickster god had reached into his head and turned his mind inside out, like an old sock. "I'm here and receiving you."

"Good to hear," Kolhammer said. "And good job at the airport. They just briefed me on that. No time for catchups, though. You're not gonna be there much longer. I want you on a flight to Paris five minutes ago. Report to Fort Mont-Valérien and start kicking ass for me. You're the new Supreme Allied Commander in Europe."

The connection was clear, and Jones had no trouble hearing what Kolhammer said, but he could not quite believe what he had just heard.

"Say again?"

"Cronauer's dead, Lonesome. He was visiting the 5th Army in Germany when the Soviets attacked. I need someone who understands joint operations and someone I trust. That's you. I've issued the order to the Joint Chiefs. Confirmation should be there in minutes if it's not there already. You can't transit directly from Naples to Paris. You'll have to go via Gibraltar. The Air Force has assets in transit to you. Go dark. We'll talk when you're boots down. Good luck."

Jones barely had time to reply, "Yes, sir," before Kolhammer cut in over him.

"That's not all, Lonesome. I'm afraid the Sovs hit the fleet base at Norfolk. Looks like a massive JDAM strike, almost certainly launched from the *Schastny*."

"Damn," Jones grunted, feeling as though he'd been gut punched. "What's the damage?"

"Bad, but it could have been worse," Kolhammer said. "Admiral

Ringo ordered the fleet to put out as soon as he got word of the strike on Germany, but not all of them made it."

"I understand," Jones nodded. You didn't just turn the key on a nuclear-powered aircraft carrier or a heavy cruiser and motor out through the heads for a spot of fishing.

"You'll get the full brief when you land in Paris, but I can tell you now, we've lost the *Midway* and the *Forrestal*. Half of their escorts, too."

"Yes, sir," Jones said. There didn't seem much more he could say. That was forty per cent of the navy's combat strength in the North Atlantic gone.

"I've ordered the Joint Chiefs to activate Reforger, but without those carrier groups, you should plan on doing more with less."

A helluva lot more with a hell of a lot less, Jones thought.

But what he said was, "I've had some recent experience doing just that, Mister President."

He heard Kolhammer's familiar chortle, compressed by distance and encryption software.

"So I heard. Good job again, Lonesome. If they'd taken that airport, we'd be double-plus fucked. Just keep doing what you're doing. And good luck."

"You too, sir," Jones said.

Kolhammer cut the connection, and Jones removed his headset in a daze, blinking slowly at Colonel Grieve. He stared vacantly for a second. A dozen personnel were in the SCIF, most of them enlisted operators working on salvaged technology. It had been super-advanced, almost magical equipment when the Multinational Force fell through Manning Pope's wormhole in 2021. Nowadays, it was hand-me-down kit.

"Damn," he said, forcing his wits to catch up with the moment. "Colonel Grieve, I should have a new tasking through from the Pentagon any moment now. Can you please confirm that ASAP?"

"Of course, sir. Can I ask..."

"Cronauer's dead," Jones said. "The President has appointed me Supreme Allied Commander in Europe. The Sovs took out a huge chunk of Norfolk. I need to haul ass to Paris, and I'm gonna need a chief of staff. So you're coming with me. Pack a toothbrush."

It was Grieve's turn to stare blankly for a second.

"Er...yes sir," he said at last before turning to the sysop. "Corporal, there's flash traffic from the Pentagon coming in. A re-tasking for General Jones. I need to know the moment it arrives. Please find Lieutenant-Colonel Smoler and tell him he's running the shop now. I've been reassigned to SACEUR."

Grieve appeared to question the reality of his own words. He looked to Jones for reassurance.

"We'll need a secure travel plan," Jones said. "Air force is inbound. Assets unknown. I'll leave that to you, Colonel. We can't overfly southern Europe anymore. "I'll also need a driver. Private Williamson impresses with her Nascar mojo. I'll take her."

The systems operator checked a notification onscreen.

Jones watched her double-click an attachment. He recognized the letterhead of the Joint Chiefs on the PDF, which unpacked itself on screen.

"Colonel Grieve," she said. "General Jones's documentation has arrived, sir."

Grieve leaned in to read the pages, sub-vocalizing the highlights.

"By order of President Kolhammer...General J. Lonesome Jones... immediate promotion...Supreme Allied Commander...Europe..."

Grieve stood up. His face was flushed.

"You have your orders from the President," he said. His voice was slightly croaky.

"Then it's hammer time," Jones growled. "Let's roll."

20

Hamilton Manor was a 400-year-old pile of National Trust-listed masonry and stained glass set within twenty-five acres of manicured gardens, ancient forest, and two meandering trout streams. The previous owner, Lord Talbot Willoughby, had sold the entire estate and several titles to Davidson Enterprises before skipping out to Buenos Aires just ahead of Her Majesty's tax collectors. Slim Jim didn't know it until they were driving up the mile-long gravel driveway to his newly acquired ancestral home, but he was not just the owner of the Manor and the nearby village of Little Willoughby, but he was also entitled to style himself as Viscount James, Sheriff, and March Lord of the Three Fens.

"What's a fen?" Slim Jim asked Maria as they swept past a croquet field. Or maybe it was a cricket pitch. How the fuck was he supposed to know?

"I think it's a kind of swamp," she said. "Except boggier."

"Awesome," he said.

Their ride, a Rolls-Royce Platinum Ghost with a long list of uptime amenities and augments, crunched to a stop in front of the main steps where at least twelve butlers and maids awaited them.

"Jesus Christ," Slim Jim said, peering out the window. "How many guys I got running around this penguin farm?"

Maria smiled.

"This is the main household stuff. Another shift looks after you when you're in your Slim-Jim-jams at night and about the same number again toiling in the fields. But apparently, those ones don't smell very nice, so they're not allowed to line up for the big hello with their lord and master. That's you, by the way. Try not to be a massive jerk about it."

Slim Jim gave her one raised eyebrow.

"And why are we really here?"

"This is the alpha site for your European operations. After we paid off Talbot's whisky tab at the Lord Taverners Bar and gave him a big bag of the folding stuff for this place, we had it gutted and redone with the best tech we could find or invent ourselves. Some of that was even original uptime gear off the *Clinton* when she was gutted for salvage. The balance came out of your own skunkworks back in the Valley. There's almost as much fibre-optic cable and satellite dish capacity here as in central London. If we do get stuck here, you can still run the business everywhere else. And there's all the defensive infrastructure too. But you can't see that from here."

"Okay, that sounds cool," Slim Jim said. "It's like my supervillain lair."

"Sure, but like every good supervillain lair, it's a secret. We did the upgrades quietly. Your actual European headquarters is still in the city. This place is off the books. So it's less likely to draw unwanted attention."

"Like the Revenue?'

"No, like Soviet missile strikes."

"Oh right, those. But we've got like anti-missile shit, right."

"Right. But Stalin has a lot of fucking missiles, Jimbo."

"What about bunkers? They fucking love bunkers in this country."

"Renovated dungeons, but a nuke or one of those orbital strike packages will dig it out anyway. Best not to think about it."

"Okay," Slim Jim agreed. "I won't. Let's go meet my party peeps."

He climbed out of the Roller, throwing his arms wide.

"Where my bitches at!"

Maria shook her head.

THREE HOURS later and Slim Jim was going out of his mind. There was nothing to do at Hamilton Manor. Nothing.

Like, sure, he could go trout fishing if he wanted to sleep standing up holding a fucking stick with a string tied to it. Or horse riding, if he knew how to ride a horse. There were pheasants to shoot and foxes to hunt, but to be honest, he'd rather be standing in a freezing cold stream, hoping one of his ancestral fucking trout decided to have a nibble.

There was a kick-ass drinking parlour, but Robert, the maximum butler, told him it wasn't open until the last note of the final hymn of evensong at chapel.

"But it's my fucking bar, Bob," he protested.

"Then I am sure sir will understand," Bob sniffed.

He would have just served himself, but everything was locked away in heavy wooden cabinets that looked like King Arthur might have hidden the good booze there, and he wasn't quite ready to take a sledgehammer to the joinery.

Give it a day or two.

"Maria, there's nothing to do here," he complained. "I'm going down to the pub. Bob the Butler says I own the pub. They have to serve me there."

Maria O'Brien had set up in the main library—there were three—and was back to split-screening and ultra-tasking, and whatever it was he paid her a million bucks a year to do. Whenever he saw her working like this, he knew he was getting the better end of the deal. O'Brien seemed to have five, no seven, conferences on the go. Five were on screen. Another came in through her headset. And occasionally, she would pick up a flexipad and fire off a string of instructions.

Three staffers from London had arrived via helicopter and were tending to their own screen farms and comm channels. Slim Jim could occasionally pick out individual conversation threads and extract meaning from them, but most of it was a hurricane of militarised business jargon. O'Brien held up a hand as soon as he entered the command centre. She showed him the hand every time he tried to speak.

It was only when she was down to three conferences that he was able to get some of her attention.

"I said I'm going to the pub, toots."

She shook her head.

"No, you're not."

She held up the hand again and talked to a screen.

"No, I didn't mean you, Alistair. I was talking to Slim Jim. I know you're not going to the pub."

She tapped the screen again, looked up and said, "Neither are you. Sorry, you can't leave the grounds. Nobody can. Nobody knows we're here. If the Sovs find out we're here, it'll take about twenty minutes for the first Kalibr cruise missiles to come in through that window."

She pointed to a large, medieval-looking portal looking out onto that croquet field. Or cricket pitch.

"Oh, come on, man," Slim Jim whined. "They don't care that much. They're not gonna waste any cruise missiles on me. They still got like Churchill and the Queen and all those other guys to waste first."

"It's not you," Maria said. "It's Kolhammer. He'll be here in half an hour."

MORE BUTLERS.

"Jesus Christ, all you ever hear about in this country are shortages, but they're not going short of butlers, I'll tell you that," Andy Porter snorted.

Kolhammer didn't reply. His stomach was churning with acid reflux, and his head felt like he'd gone a few rounds with Connor McGregor. The stress, the lack of sleep, the sudden crushing weight of it all was bearing down on him as they bumped along in the back of a nondescript Army Humvee, the fourth in a line of six identical vehicles. The Secret Service was still with him, but a Ranger platoon had taken on the escort duties, relieving the SAS. High overhead, USAF Phantoms flew Combat Air Patrol, on constant alert for incoming threats, while an AWACS bird pushed out a 500-mile sensor bubble scanning for any sign of danger.

Despite all this, security at the gate on the edge of the private estate looked comically British. Some old timer in a cloth cap with a duck hunter's shotgun broken over the crook of his arm waved them on through.

"So that guy is what stands between us and the barbarians at the gate?" Porter said.

"Agent Byers says the defences layered around this place are just as dense and hard as anything the military could throw up," Kolhammer explained. "They've even got some of the original Metal-Storm close-in systems from the *Clinton* here. Bought them for research when she was decommissioned."

"Huh. You ever meet this guy?" General Porter asked as they motored through a small forest. Twice, Kolhammer saw air-defence systems hidden back under the canopy.

"Davidson, you mean?" he said. "No. He has a pretty extensive lobbying shop in Washington, as you'd imagine. But he never works the circuit himself. I only know what I've read about him in the press. He fell ass backwards into a pile of money after stealing a couple of flexipads from the *Leyte Gulf*. Cleaned up on some big sports bets before the local bookies realized he had access to cached Wikipedia data."

Andy Porter laughed.

"Yeah, that's what I heard too. And he grabbed up Elvis. He was just a grifter, wasn't he? Before the war?"

"Yeah," Kolhammer agreed. "And not especially good at it. He'd already done time on a chain gang when they caught him bouncing bad checks or something. The judge gave him a choice. The jug or the Navy. That's how he came to be on the *Astoria* and fetched up here."

Both men fell silent for a moment. The *Astoria*, an old US Navy battlewagon, had had the misfortune to be steaming through the exact spacetime coordinates at which the USS *Leyte Gulf*, a 21st-century guided-missile cruiser, had emerged from the wormhole back in 1942. The two ships merged like the blades of an open pair of scissors, and hundreds of sailors died when they were fused into the newly entangled metalwork.

Slim Jim Davidson had dodged that fate and the brief but savage firefight that followed in the chaos.

Hell of a thing, the way the shattering of history had destroyed some people and lifted others to fortune and glory, Kolhammer thought.

He wasn't entirely sure where he stood in that equation.

"The Navy or the jug. Is that why you like him?" Porter said at last. "Because you both followed the same path into uniform."

Kohlhammer paid that one off with a snort of laughter. He even felt his mood lift slightly.

It was late afternoon as their convoy circled the burbling marble fountain at the head of a circular driveway in front of the main building. Kolhammer recognised two of the three people waiting for them. Slim Jim Davidson he knew from press photographs and occasional television news reports. Usually about a scandal involving the billionaire tycoon and some Hollywood starlet. The woman beside Davidson, however, he knew very well.

Maria O'Brien. A former Marine Corps lawyer and one of the founding operators of the Quiet Room. Kolhammer was not entirely truthful with Porter when he implied a lack of interest or knowledge about Davidson's affairs. Maria had identified the former conman and petty criminal as a potential agent of influence for QR. That didn't make him special. The Quiet Room ran hundreds of influence operations over the decade after the Transition, but none of them paid off quite so well as the early investment in the success of James Davidson's rapidly expanding business operations.

An army sergeant held open the door and saluted as Kohlhammer climbed out. He returned the salute and strolled the short distance up the driveway to greet his hosts.

"The President of the United States of America, Mister Philip Kohlhammer," a dark-suited butler announced. He was the third member of the trio waiting on Kohlhammer's arrival. Slim Jim Davidson was nervously shuffling from foot to foot, looking like he would rather be elsewhere. Maria was beaming.

"Mister President," she said. "It is a pleasure to welcome you here, despite the tragic circumstances."

"Yeah, I kinda liked Ike," Davidson said. "He kept my taxes down. But Joe Stalin, eh. Fuck that guy in the neck."

21

The lights of Cagliari twinkled in the long summer twilight as the Learjet analogue popped chaff and flares on its final approach to the landing strip north of the city. With the cabin lights dimmed, Harry was able to pick out quite fine detail on the ground, from the pinprick campfire lights of shepherds and goatherds in the hills east and west of the harbour to the thick snarl of traffic around the port, the gaudy rainbow colours of the waterfront's 'entertainment' district, and the squalling clouds of seagulls and scavengers following a small flotilla of fishing boats as they beat out against the tide. Cagliari was seething with spies, mobsters, and refugees from Soviet-occupied southern Europe. If anything, the opening of hostilities in the hot war seemed to have supercharged the animal spirits of the place. Harry had passed through once before, about three years earlier, with Julia on one of her tax-deductible travel-writing junkets. They had only stayed a few hours while en route to a new Hilton resort in Beirut, and he recalled the capital of Sardinia as a seedy but relatively sleepy backwater. It looked nothing of the sort now.

"Wheels down in two minutes," the pilot announced.

If they were going to be shot out of the sky by some crude heat-seeking missile, fired from a forested ridge by bandits seeking ransom from the local authorities, or Soviet special operators tasked with introducing a little friction into the operations of Allied forces on the island, it would be in the next minute or so.

There was nothing for him to do about it, and so he did nothing. Ivanov and Rogas seemed supremely unconcerned by the prospect, either because they had flown in and out of a thousand places like this over the years or because they knew the Davidson Aerospace jet was kitted out with the best countermeasures and defensive technologies. *Most likely*, Harry thought, *a little from column A and a little from column B.*

They dropped to just a few hundred feet, speeding in over the rooftops of the waterfront district, close enough for Harry to make out individuals down there. He could see patrons spilling out of cafés and taverns, hundreds of bicycles and mopeds cluttering up the narrow cobblestone streets, horse-drawn carts competing with luxury cars and popping flashes of light that might've been fireworks or perhaps even a minor gun battle. They were moving so quickly at a hundred feet off the deck that it all passed below him as an Impressionist blur.

The city dropped away as the aircraft banked left and levelled out. Peering forward through the window, Harry could make out a single line of landing lights, looking very much like somebody had dropped a couple of dozen oil pots into a paddock and set them to burn as the sun dropped below the horizon. He braced himself for a rough landing and was pleasantly surprised when the jet touched down smoothly.

"Welcome to Cagliari," the pilot said through the intercom. "The local time is nineteen hundred and forty-three hours. The weather forecast is for a fine, warm evening, and you can't trust a single human being you meet on this godforsaken island, so keep your wallets close and your weapons closer."

Charlotte François was out of her seat and pulling her kit together before they finished taxiing to the hangar. The aerodrome boasted three old-fashioned corrugated iron structures like giant tin cans cut lengthways and laid next to each other. One was painted in the blue and white livery of Davidson Aerospace. It was busy inside, with groundcrew working on three different aircraft, all cargo planes. Harry noted four armed guards securing the entrance to the facility. They were dressed in black tactical coveralls and equipped with some impressively heavy weapons.

"Are they your people?" he asked Vincente Rogas. "Davidson's, I suppose?"

The American peered out through the window in front of Harry's and nodded.

"Kinetic Solutions," Rogas said. "Slim Jim does business in some pretty rugged places. He's got something like two regiments of full-time operators and about half as many again on retainer. Dilettantes and reprobates like these two," he grinned, jerking a thumb back over his shoulder at Ivanov and François. "You know the sort. Can't hold down a steady job."

Ivanov ignored him. Charlotte smiled sweetly as she gave him the finger. The lights came up in the cabin, and the crew disarmed and opened the doors. Harry had no baggage. He had gone straight from the hospital in Cairo to the RAF camp, to here. The two freelancers carried heavy black duffel bags down the foldout stairs, but like him, Rogas travelled light.

"Don't worry about kitting up," the American said, apparently reading his mind. "Slim Jim's got you covered."

As Harry stepped onto the concrete apron, he saw a vehicle waiting for them, one of the Humvee analogues that had replaced the venerable Jeep. This one was a civilian model, painted black but boasting a load-out to make an old SAS quartermaster envious.

"That's our ride?" Charlotte asked.

"If you can hold onto it through bandit country, yes," Rogas said.

"Bitchin'."

One of the uniformed guards ambled over and waved to Rogas.

"Evening, sir," he said. "I hope this fits the bill. I took it from our own pool. Added a few mods for you. Went with a 50 Cal on the ring mount because you're more likely to get parts and ammo once you get out into the boonies."

"All good," Rogas said, taking a clipboard from the man and quickly running his finger down it. "Five days' worth of food and fuel.

Good. Weapons, check. Ammo, check. Did you get the stuff for Harry that I asked for?"

The man nodded.

"Personal kit in the bag on the front passenger side seat." The man turned to Harry. "It's all civilian gear, sir. You don't want to be going around in battle dress uniform once you get up into bandit country. Those guys up in the mountains, they'll shoot anybody in uniform. Just a matter of pride to them." He turned to Charlotte. "I'd change out of the coveralls if I was you, Miss. We got a kit for you in the back as well."

"Coolio," Charlotte said, breaking away to collect her gear. "Can I change in the hangar?"

"Knock yourself out, ma'am. There is a change room for aircrew just off to the left as you go through."

"This is all very nice," Harry said. "I've been in these clothes for two days now. But isn't that motor going to stand out like tits on a bull if we're going through the mountains? It's pretty bloody primitive up there, isn't it? I can't imagine any local bandit chief worth his salt missing an opportunity to grab a shiny piece of gear like that."

He nodded at the expensive-looking Humvee.

"Fair point," Rogas conceded. "But we have contacts. We've negotiated your passage. You'll find a bunch of trade goods in the back to pay the tolls along the way."

"And if the tolls go up?"

Ivanov shook his head.

"This is not a problem. I have dealt with these people before. They are honourable men. Do not lie to them. Do not try to cheat them. They will not kill you."

Harry snorted. "That's a pretty basic code of honour. But I suppose we can work with it. Do you want to handle any negotiations, Vince?"

The American shook his head.

"I'm not coming with," he said. "I'm going to Marseille to smooth the way there for you."

Harry did not like driving off into the unknown but kept his counsel. Ivanov seemed to have more than a passing familiarity with the arse end of Sardinia and the bandit culture of the mountains.

"I will do all negotiations," the Russian said. "And I will kill Skarov."

He wasn't looking at Harry when he spoke. He was staring after Charlotte François.

Harry followed Charlotte into the hangar, and after a hot shower in the aircrew facilities, he changed into a clean set of clothes. Khaki drill pants, a dark blue denim shirt, and hiking boots. There was a fleece-lined jacket in his duffel bag, but he left it there for the moment. The night was balmy, and although it would be cooler at higher altitudes, he didn't think he would need the extra layers.

Davidson's people provided maps marked up with rendezvous points and briefing packets on each of the clans they would encounter as they passed through the mountains. Charlotte insisted on driving, and Harry was fatigued enough after Cairo to let it be. He was grateful to stretch out on the back seat and doze off as they moved away from the aerodrome. Not just grateful. Amazed. This civilian copy of the uptime Humvee was way more considerate of its passengers' comfort.

"Bugger me," he blurted. "Is there a bar fridge too?"

No bar fridge, but space enough to rack out. He slept for a few hours, waking when Ivanov reached back and punched him in the leg. He woke quickly, a habit he retained from many years in the field, but he was groggy.

"We will be at the first rendezvous point in fifteen minutes," the Russian said. He passed back a thermos. Harry was pleasantly surprised to discover it was full of hot, sweet tea.

"God bless Mother Russia," he said, pouring himself a half cup and throwing it back in a couple of long gulps after a brief sip to ensure he wouldn't burn himself.

"Nice brew," he said.

"Superior to coffee," Ivanov said.

"You pair of old women wouldn't know a decent cup of coffee if it jumped up and bit you on the ass," Charlotte said from behind the wheel. But she still took a cup for herself.

Harry was impressed by the road, a smooth ribbon of blacktop, two lanes wide. It was almost certainly a NATO project. Charlotte was driving without headlights, her face hidden behind a pair of night vision goggles. Harry couldn't tell whether they were original uptime tech or a contemporary design. He could see reasonably well out of the windows of the vehicle. A waxing silver moon shone down from a cloudless sky where millions of stars twinkled hard and bright. *A pleasant night for a stroll*, he thought. But Charlotte was driving at speed through a long, curving stretch of mountain road, with a sickening drop just a few feet off to the left. Harry was glad to have her younger eyes and faster reflexes on the job.

He sat up straight and worked the kinks out of his shoulders and back. The aches and pains of all the damage he'd taken in Cairo were still there, but it felt like the sort of thing he could control with some basic painkillers. He thought he had seen some in his kitbag, but there was no point rummaging around for them in the dark.

"So, who are we meeting up with first?" Harry asked.

Ivanov answered without turning around.

"The Costa clan. They are cattle rustlers and chicken thieves now, but once upon a time, they were feared brigands and kidnappers. The fascists even contemplated using napalm on the valleys where they graze their stolen herds."

"Marvellous," Harry said. "And what are we doing for them?"

"For them, we have cigarettes and whisky. They will escort us to the boundaries of their territory, where we will pass over to the care of the Tolu Clan."

"And what price will Clan Tolu demand for safe passage?"

"Cigarettes and whisky."

"I like these guys already," Charlotte said.

"Are we going to have enough cigarettes and whisky to get all the way to Santa Teresa?" Harry asked.

Ivanov nodded.

"Mr Davidson has no business with the clans. They have nothing to offer him. But he has interests in Cagliari, and the authorities there have business with the clans."

"I see," Harry said. "What sort of business? Something adjacent to cattle rustling and chicken thievery, I imagine."

"Something like that, yes. But also kidnapping and ransom. That was the main business of the mountain clans. Now, they simply extract payment for not kidnapping and ransoming. It is much more...what is the word...streamlined operation."

"Why doesn't someone just stop them, you know, kidnapping peeps, and then like, not pay them anything?" Charlotte asked.

Ivanov laughed out loud.

"You are a very naïve young lady. When there is no business, nobody gets paid. Not the clans, not the police, not the mayor, not the governor. Nobody."

Charlotte shook her head, but it was a discreet movement as she leaned forward, peering over the steering wheel through the twin lenses of her night vision goggles. Heavily forested slopes climbed away towards the stars on the right. Out of the left-hand side of the vehicle, Harry could see fields and pastures far below, bathed in the icy blue light of the moon and stars.

In the front seat, Ivanov unfolded and refolded a paper map and somehow reckoned their location by peering out into the darkness. He marked an X on the map and checked his watch, an old-fashioned but expensive-looking analogue model.

"Charlotte, you should be slowing down now. We will have passed the first of their sentries. They know we are coming."

The young woman did as she was told. Harry was pleased to see it. He had no doubt she was very good at her job. He'd seen her work on the *Bulgakov*, and Viv was a good judge of character. Or had been. But Harry had no idea how François and Ivanov would work together, and she had both the cockiness and perhaps the need to prove herself that was so common at her age. She'd certainly given him enough grief after saving his arse on that Russian freighter.

He sat up a little in the back, leaning forward to see if he could spot anything ahead of them. There wasn't much to see. Just steep, heavily wooded slopes climbing away on one side and that dizzying sheer drop towards certain death on the other.

Ivanov pointed to something in the dark ahead of them.

"That clearing up there," he said. "That is where we are to pull over."

Again, Charlotte did not push back. She just did as he instructed.

Harry instinctively reached for the gun at his hip to check it was there. But it wasn't. He wasn't wearing a side arm because they had been told not to. There was a large cache of weapons in the rear tray of the Humvee, but they were not easily accessed from where they all sat. He understood the need for it. This was not their manor. They were not even guests here. They were intruders, bringing the sorrows and dangers of the world with them.

Charlotte pulled off the road and into the little clearing. She cut the engine, and it seemed that silence flooded in, but Harry quickly attuned to the night sounds. The cry of birds, the whisper of a breeze through the forest canopy, the gurgle of a nearby stream. Ivanov opened the passenger side door.

"We get out and wait," he said.

Harry and Charlotte followed him out. Harry shivered in the cool mountain air. He regretted not unpacking that fleecy jacket.

"Over there, look," Ivanov said, nodding at the forest's edge.

At first, Harry strained to make anything out of the shifting background of shadow and deeper darkness, but slowly, a number of figures emerged into the moonlight. He felt the old familiar creep of fear through his body, and just as quickly, he detached himself from all such feelings and let his training and experience take over. These were not the first bandits he had met by the side of the road under the stars.

They were, however, the first to come with their own Spetsnaz detachment.

Ivanov was quickest to recognise the enemy uniforms.

Charlotte François was quicker on the trigger.

22

Julia recalled only the vaguest details of the flight to London. Hell, she barely remembered anything after the fight on the Russian freighter. Fragments of conversations with Harry, sitting by her hospital bed, holding her hand. A doctor who told her she was lucky to be alive.

Dan Black.

She did not so much come awake then, as topple headfirst into bright consciousness.

She had seen Dan. She was sure of it. He had been standing at the foot of her bed in Cairo. He'd apologised and then disappeared. It wasn't a fever dream or a near-death hallucination.

It had been Dan, as real as the stitches tugging at her skin. As unsettling as the memory of those children she had...

She had killed because they had tried to kill her.

After a week of hovering in a semi-conscious delirium, Julia Duffy seemed to flow back into the world through the hole punched into the heavy rubber sheet separating her from waking reality.

She tried to sit up too quickly and cried out in pain. So much pain flooded into so many parts of her body that she was no longer herself for a few seconds. She was just a shell into which demons poured all the pain and sorrow of the world.

She fell back onto a pillow, shuddering and dry retching as a nurse hurried in.

Alarms blared distantly, and the nurse, a black woman, raced over to her.

Julia's vision blurred and darkened at the edges.

Then it went dark everywhere.

SHE AWOKE. Hours or minutes later, she couldn't say.

"Nurse..." she gasped.

"I'm Doctor Collins," she said. Her accent was cultured. English.

Julia squeezed her eyes shut and opened them again. The woman came into focus. She wore a small nameplate on her white coat.

DR YAZMEEN COLLINS.

Julia could have sworn the doctor was a nurse before, but the woman leaning over her wore a smartly tailored business suit under her white lab coat and a stethoscope around her neck. The universally recognised symbol of a practising MD.

"I'm sorry. Doctor," Julia croaked. Her throat was so dry she almost gagged.

"Here, sip a little water," Collins said. "We had you intubated for a day. Your lungs collapsed, and we had to put you on a respirator. You've been unconscious for two days under our care. And longer, I think, before that."

Julia tried to drink too much, too quickly, and her throat closed up in protest. She coughed and dribbled cold water down her chin.

"Easy there," Doctor Collins said. "Don't be in such a rush. Just lie back and let me examine you first."

Collins took Julia's pulse, listened to her breathing, and ran through a series of external checks that took a few minutes.

"You've got some weeping from the stitches where we had to go in to repair your lung."

"My what?" Julia asked weakly. "I don't smoke anymore."

Collins smiled.

"Good for you. Now give up the knife fighting, and I'll be even happier. You had a small puncture of your right inferior lobe. Not surprising they didn't catch it when they stitched you back together. You had a lot of stitches."

"Oh god," Jules muttered, and then, remembering herself, "Harry! Where's Harry? He was with me in Cairo, and I remember he was... we were at an airbase..."

"It's okay, calm down. His Highness, as I understand it, has been reactivated by his regiment, but there is somebody here from the government to discuss that with you when you feel up to it."

Julia was having trouble keeping up.

"His regiment? And he's not a highness anymore. He gave that up. We were... working...in Cairo. He was working."

Doctor Collins held up a hand. "I'm sorry, Miss Duffy, but I can't talk to you about that. The man from Whitehall was adamant," she frowned. "Are you able to talk to him now? Because he said it was a security matter, what you were doing in Cairo. I could bring him through, but honestly, I would prefer you to rest."

Jules took another sip of water. Now that she was fully conscious, her memory of Dan seemed less concrete. More diffuse and likely to have been a dream.

"I'm okay," she said, sounding anything but. "If there's somebody here from Harry's office, I should talk to them. I guess."

Collins favoured her with a crooked smile.

"You probably should. Poor chap's been camped out in our waiting room overnight. I will send him through, but first, you need your dressings changed and that seeping wound seen to."

Two nurses appeared, both of them younger than Collins and white. They looked like temps to Julia. She could still tell contemporaries from uptimers, even though many younger people aped the aesthetics and attitudes of the far future. The two nurses who tended to her had to have been born here. They were too young to have come through the Transition. Collins, on the other hand, was definitely Twenty-First.

"Which ship?" Julia asked her as she lay awkwardly on one side, enduring a sponge bath of her problematic wound.

"*Trident*," Collins answered. "I was a second-year Surgeon Lieutenant. You were embedded with the Marines, weren't you?"

"On the *Clinton*, with the Navy," Jules corrected her. "But I embedded with the MEU later."

She tried to ignore the discomfort of her wounds by more closely attending to her surroundings for the first time. She was in a private room in a small hospital. A fair assumption given the view out of the window where patients in wheelchairs enjoyed the fresh air. She was on the ground floor of a small modern annexe to what looked like a Victorian-era building. Perhaps a school or a stately home in the past, it had been converted in the last couple of years to its current use. It was a head fuck. She had been in Cairo. They had been in the fight on the *Bulgakov*. And now Harry was God only knew where. She was laid up in Downton Abbey. And Dan Black was... What? Haunting her? Dan was dead, long ago dead.

"Where am I?" she asked, feeling like it was all too much.

"St Andrews, a private facility, about an hour's drive outside London," Collins said. "A medical flight dropped you to the helipad, and we had you in theatre three minutes later."

"Private? Not some government place?"

She was having trouble holding onto her thoughts.

"The Foreign Ministry is picking up the tab. But yes, this is a private facility. I'm one of the directors."

"Oh," Jules said. "Congratulations, I guess. It looks...nice."

Collins responded with a dry chuckle.

"It does now. It was a wreck when we took over in '46. The army had requisitioned the estate for the duration of the war. They were breeding horses here, if you can imagine that."

Collins shook her head in lingering disbelief.

"Anyway, we had some seed funding to adapt and accelerate uptime medical technologies, and honestly, I couldn't get a job as a doctor anywhere else."

Julia didn't need to ask why. Yazmeen Collins, a black woman, would not have been welcome in the clubby world of the British medical profession of 1946.

She winced as the nurses finished cleaning the largest wound on her back and eased her down onto her pillows. Julia let go of a long-held breath in a silent whistle.

"Pain relief?" Collins asked.

"Yes, please."

The doctor instructed her assistants, who hurried away to fulfil the order.

"What is it you do here, Yazmeen?" Julia asked, the embers of her old reporter's instincts flaring up. "Besides looking after rich people?"

She had a thousand questions, mainly about Harry and what had gone wrong in Cairo, but she wasn't ready for that yet.

Collins took a moment to answer and almost seemed as though she might not. But after a pause and walking to the window to gaze out over the bright green lawns and colourful rose gardens, she said, "Women's health is my speciality. I have a personal interest in reproductive issues, and endometriosis in particular. It's not something that would've been on anyone's radar for decades. But I can make a real difference here."

She turned around.

"But that's me. We started out developing and marketing diagnostic technologies. Captain Halabi, Karen, helped with the seed funding when she was with Hewlett-Packard just after the war before she had her start-up and sold it to Boeing. She still has a piece of equity here. So does Boeing, to answer your question. That's how we make payroll. Adapting uptime medical tech and knowledge, pushing it as far as we can, given current constraints. And then a little further."

"Well, thank you," Julia said, feeling weak and quite vulnerable. "I gotta say it feels good, you know, having somebody from up when looking after me."

"I understand," Collins said. "If you're feeling up to it, I'll go fetch your minder before he eats all the good biscuits in the tea room. Or cookies, I mean cookies."

"It's okay. Harry loves to dunk a nice biscuit in his tea."

Julia thanked the doctor again and almost apologised for calling her "nurse" when she first came to. She wasn't sure the other woman had noticed or cared, but she felt awkward. She'd seen a woman of colour and assumed she was the hired help, not the boss. Julia Duffy would bet good folding money Doctor Collins would have had a hell of a time of it after she left her safe space on the *Trident*. Halabi herself had fled to the US for the same reason.

Easing further back into her pillows, Julia tried to escape her embarrassment by wondering what Harry was doing. Something big must have happened for him to have been recalled to service. After all, he was already in service, but with MI6, not his regiment. Instinctively, she looked for a TV set, but there was none. Flatscreens were not rare these days, especially in the US, but they weren't yet ubiquitous the way they had been at home. There was a small radio on her bedside table, however, and she was reaching for it when her visitor knocked on the door.

She saw a surprisingly handsome young man with striking blond curls and a twinkly-eyed, almost baby-faced smile.

"Good morning," he said. "My name is Plunkett, David Plunkett. I work with Harry."

Julia sketched out a thin smile. She was still waiting on her pain meds.

"I understand," she said. "I had to undergo vetting as well."

"Excellent," Plunkett replied. "I won't keep you long. I've come out from the city to get you up to speed. I'm afraid we're all at sixes and sevens with everything that's going on, and your fiancé is rather in the thick of it."

"I'm sorry," Julia said. "Everything that's going on? I've been out of it for a while, Agent Plunkett."

"David, please."

"David, sure. You'll have to excuse me. The last thing I remember is..."

She trailed off. Plunkett waited on her with pronounced interest.

The second last thing she remembered, like really remembered, was a couple of homicidal Russian children coming at her with blades. That last thing was...worse. Much worse.

"Look..." Plunkett said, oblivious to her distress. "I'm not sure how much you know, so I'll just jump in. You understand what Harry was doing in Cairo?"

Plunkett closed the door to her room and turned back.

Julia winced at a flare of pain.

"He was to make contact with Professor Bremmer," she said, searching her memory for the answer. It wasn't easy. "And...and he was supposed to find out whether the Russians were leaning on him. On Bremmer, I mean. And that all went a bit pear-shaped."

"Rather, yes."

"So, the last thing I remember, we were shooting at a bunch of Russians on some freighter, and they were shooting back and..."

She trailed off again.

"That's it. Except I..."

Julia found she could not bring herself to tell him what had happened.

It didn't matter. He knew.

"You were attacked by a couple of Beria's *padshiye angely*," Plunket said softly. "Fallen angels. Orphans, street urchins, whatever. The NKVD takes them very young and turns them to the dark side, as you chaps would say. Often, the turning required is not that great. Life in the rubble of Stalingrad is not so easy, after all."

The wound where the older boy had stabbed her was throbbing.

"They were just children," Julia said, tears filling her eyes. She had seen that they were not. Not really. But she was the one who had made sure they would never grow into adults.

"Do you mind?" Plunkett asked, indicating a chair by her bed.

She shook her head. "No, please. Sit down."

He did so. The sun outside turned his blond curls into a soft, glowing crown. It was a disarming effect. Julia was well aware of what sort of character this man was.

"That pair who tried to do for you on the *Bulgakov* were planted on Bremmer as subs for his children. His wife, too, for that matter. An absolutely horrid fellow called Skarov took the real Mrs Bremmer and her children as leverage over the professor. Those two on the *Bulgakov*? We know of three missions they've carried out. On one of them, they murdered the target in his sleep. They'll not be missed, I can assure you."

"They were children," Jules said again, her throat tight.

"Maybe, once upon a time," Plunkett admitted. "But weren't we all? Now, to Harry," he said, clapping his hands together as though that ended the matter of infanticide. "I cannot, of course, give you any succour as to his whereabouts or what shenanigans he might be up to, but he is on active duty. Who isn't these days?"

"I'm sorry?" Julia said, shaking her head.

She was so tired and in so much pain that nothing made much sense.

"Oh! Of course. My apologies. You have been rather out of touch, haven't you," he grinned ruefully. "Yes, well, unfortunately, the Red Army has launched a pre-emptive strike on NATO, and it's all a bit of a bloody mess. Another war, I'm afraid. And Harry's in the thick of it. We ask that you keep mum about your adventures on the Nile, and we will do what we can to inform you of his welfare. You'll be safe here," he said, waving a hand around, but his voice faded away for Julia.

She was lost, free-falling through her shock at what the British spy had just told her. The world was at war again, and Harry was already gone, thrown into the maw of the hungry beast.

Her vision started to blur and go dark at the edges, and she realised that she had not taken a breath for many long seconds.

She gasped as Plunkett explained that there were all sorts of 'top people' receiving treatment 'in this place' and that she should simply let Doctor Collins see her mended properly.

"Harry will feel better knowing you're being cared for," he finished.

"How would he know?" Julia asked. Her voice was flat and a little breathy.

Plunkett did not seem at all bothered by her stunned and affectless response.

She supposed he thought her adrift on a sea of painkillers and trauma.

"Right now, admittedly, he wouldn't," Plunkett said. "But he'll be back in touch soon enough, and I promise to let him know then, as long as you're still here."

Julia couldn't help but feel she was being treated like a child. But she also felt like she had been stabbed, shot at, and blown up by people who knew exactly what they were doing.

There was little to no chance of her leaving this room, let alone the hospital, any time in the next few days. She was full of holes and tubes running into and out of those holes.

"Okay," she said weakly. "The doctor told me someone was picking up my bill here. Is that you guys? Harry's new outfit?"

"After a fashion, yes," Plunkett smiled.

"Tell them...thank you," Julia said quietly, her voice little more than a croak.

"Thank you, Miss Duffy, for your understanding and cooperation. Now, if you'll excuse me?"

"Yeah. Sure."

Plunkett stood up, inclined his head, and left the room just as the nurse arrived with Julia's meds.

23

It was amazing what a tonic it could be, having a bunch of murderous Smedlovs shooting at you. Harry had been quietly grizzling about his discomforts and injuries since leaving Cairo. Some of it, he admitted, was simply age. He was 36 when he fell through Manning Pope's wormhole, and that was more than ten years ago. He'd kept himself in trim, thanks to Julia, as much as anything. But the years did pile on, and he'd crawled out of that shitshow in Cairo like a bloke getting out from under a rugby scrum. Even dozing in the back seat of the disgracefully comfortable civilian-model Hummer they'd blagged from the Davidson mercs back in Cagliari had occasioned some stiffness and hurt in his lower back.

Now though, with a dozen lines of tracer fire zipping in at them and cracking around his head, Harry found that he had boundless reserves of energy, and his myriad niggles and minor bothers had vanished like a cold fog burned off by the morning sun. Unlike him, Charlotte and Ivanov seemed to have ignored the demands of the Costa clan that they present themselves unarmed at the rendezvous point. Charlotte, who broke left, diving for the cover of a limestone boulder glowing pearly white in the moonlight, was dual wielding a pair of handguns. Ivanov, diving to the right and burrowing into a small, dried-out water course that cut diagonally across the little clearing, had whipped out a machine pistol, possibly an Uzi, and was throwing short angry bursts of fire back at their attackers.

Harry found himself at the rear of the vehicle, with no real memory of how he'd got there, crouching, and flinching as weapons fire crashed into the hummer. He thought about getting to the big 50-cal mount, but the enemy fire was murderous. Instead, he dragged out a heavy plastic container, tore off a fingernail opening it, and took one of the three assault rifles stored inside. He slammed the eighteen-round magazine into place and took up position at the taillights.

He had no idea who was coming at them, other than some Russians, and not much of a clue about where they were. He fired short, nearly random volleys at first, sweeping the darkness with tight arcs of three-round bursts. He heard Charlotte call out his name, shouting for cover.

"Wait for it," Harry yelled, quickly swapping over his mag.

Flipping the selector to automatic, he poured more fire into the cool night, but with more discretion this time. He had noted the muzzle flashes of some attackers and put rounds onto their positions. Ivanov, too, it seemed to Harry, increased his rate of fire. A second or two later, Charlotte dropped to the ground beside him.

"Thanks," she said breathlessly as she pulled another rifle out of the hard plastic lock box. Between barking salvos, he heard Charlotte loading and prepping the weapon, a shortened version of the uptime C4 carbine. Probably another Slim Jim special, given that the businessman's own mercenaries had supplied the guns. Davidson Enterprises hadn't grown to be the largest company in the world by respecting uptime patents and IP.

Charlotte leaned into the opposite corner of the Humvee and worked the tactical problem with fire.

Harry thought they might even have a chance until the RPGs started flying.

The first grenade whooshed past and struck a rocky outcropping somewhere behind them, exploding with enough force to buffet him with the shock wave and a stinging hail of limestone scree. The next rocket flew wide on the other side of the vehicle, disappearing into the void over the edge of the mountaintop road and exploding with muffled thunder a few seconds later. Harry wasn't sure just how good the Sovs' techno-plagiarism game was these days, but he had to assume that knocking up a decent analogue of an RPG 7 or 8 wouldn't stretch the resources of the Red Army.

The volume of gunfire aimed at them didn't seem any lighter. If anything, it was worse, as though Harry and Charlotte's return of fire had somehow offended and enraged their attackers, who now poured on with renewed determination. The Uzi fell silent, and Harry worried that Ivanov had been hit, but a stream of curses rising from the dried-out watercourse told him the Russian had run out of ammo.

"To us," Harry hissed. "We'll cover you."

But the volume of incoming fire seemed to double and then triple.

"Shit," Charlotte cursed. "There's more of them."

Harry swapped out another load and snap-fired from cover. He got a sight picture of absolute chaos. Criss-crossing tracer fire. An RPG shooting almost vertically into the midnight blue sky. Conventional grenades and the pyrotechnic shower of sparks from a big-bore shotgun. The snaking, spiderweb filaments of red and yellow tracer fire swung around madly, indiscriminately, and he heard loud cursing in a new language. Not Italian, but something close to it.

"Charlotte, cease-fire," he barked, almost choking on his dry throat.

"Are you fucking crazy?" she hissed, cracking off single shots.

Harry lurched over, grabbed her collar, and pulled her back.

"Stop firing," he said again. "It's over."

"What?"

"It's over."

And it was.

As suddenly as the uproar had begun, it died away, leaving only the whisper of a cool mountain breeze through the forest.

A single shotgun blast roared out, cutting off the low moans of a wounded man.

A man's voice rang out, strong and heavily accented.

"Prince Harry of Windsor. Come forward if you still live. Costa is here. The traitors and Bolsheviks are dead. All of them."

"What the fuck?" Charlotte said, but Harry was already getting to his feet.

He did not raise his hands in surrender, but he didn't level his weapon at the man who had called out to him either. A short distance away, he saw Ivanov carefully standing up, too. Ivanov did raise his hands as if in surrender.

"It's safe, I think," Harry told Charlotte.

"Oh, I'm glad you think so," she snarked back at him. But nor did she resume the battle.

The almost-Italian voice called out again.

"Pavel Ivanov, is that you? Are you still with us?"

Harry saw the Russian walk carefully towards a group of men, some of whom were only now emerging from the edge of the nearby forest. He slowly lowered his hands.

"Unfortunately for you, Andreas Costa, yes. I am still with you, and you still owe me two hundred lira and your fattest daughter."

A rough, hard-edged laugh answered him.

"You are too late. All of my daughters are betrothed. You will have to make do with my comeliest goat."

"Keep the goat. I will take the money you owe me," Ivanov replied.

Harry edged out from around the arse end of the Hummer.

"Ha! It is you who owes me for saving your miserable life. Again," this Andreas Costa said.

"No. It is you who owes me for your losses at Mariglia, fool," Ivanov declared a second before the two men embraced in the dark. Harry heard more laughing and the heavy thud of old friends back-slapping each other.

"Come on," he told Charlotte. "I think we're good here."

"Sorgono scum," the clan leader spat, putting his heavy boot into the ribcage of the dead man with such force that Harry heard bones crack. He winced. In the next second, however, Andreas Costa turned the light of his brigand's smile and outlaw charm on Harry and Charlotte.

"My apologies, your Highness," he said. "And to you, my lovely. Costa is ashamed that your first experience of my house should taste of betrayal and infamy. But what is to be done with scum like this?"

Another kick crunched into the corpse of the dead peasant at Costa's feet.

"Well, I guess you could just keep kicking him," Charlotte muttered, but low enough that only Harry heard.

The rendezvous point now swarmed with Costa's men, perhaps two dozen of them, methodically stripping the bodies of the Soviet commandos for anything useful. Eventually, the pale white corpses, punctured and torn by their various wounds, lay all but naked under the starlight. Apparently, the only thing Costa's men would not take was the Russians' underwear.

"I knew as soon as we were delayed that a trap awaited you," Andreas explained. "A tree was felled across the road. I suspected ambush, and I was right, but the ambush was up here."

He was thickset and short, with the cast-iron belly of a man who ate well but who had worked at hard labour every day of his life. His clansmen were drawn from the same stock. They looked as tough and dangerous as thorn weeds woven into human form.

Standing in the cone of the Hummer's one surviving headlight, the three outsiders listened to Costa's tale of perfidy and woe. The dead peasants were men from the village of Sorgono, with whom the House of Costa had long nurtured a sanguinary blood feud.

"This," Costa said, gesturing around the scene of murder and chaos, "This will not go unanswered. But first, we must see you to your destination. Your ends and purposes are now Costa's, too."

He spat.

"This the scum of Sorgono have ensured if nothing else."

"We'll need a ride," Harry said.

The Hummer was wrecked, the engine block ruined by dozens, maybe hundreds of impacts. The windscreen was shattered, too, with three of the tyres flat, but they could have coped with that. The engine was a different matter.

"Do you ride, my lovely?" Costa said, addressing Charlotte.

"Horses? Yeah. I can do that."

Costa clapped his hands together, producing a report as loud as any gunshot.

"Excellent. Then we shall ride north together. My cousin, Bautista, will see you to the end of your quest, and my men…"

His eyes narrowed as he took in the aftermath of the battle.

"My men will see Frantziscu Murtas answers for his treachery here."

Harry noted that Costas did not bother to ask whether he or Ivanov knew how to ride. He assumed from the Russian's acceptance of the plan that a lack of horsemanship would not be a problem for him.

Nor for Harry, either, of course. He had been given to the saddle from his earliest days. But he did worry that picking their way on horseback through central Sardinia's famously rugged mountains would see Skarov escape many weeks before they finally made it to Santa Teresa.

"We were supposed to meet with the Tolu Clan," Harry pointed out, addressing Ivanov but intending for Costa to hear him too.

"Plans change," Ivanov shrugged.

"I know Arroccu Tolu," Costa said. "I have had dealings with him. He is a man of honour. He will understand what happened here and the need for new plans because of it."

Harry nodded slowly.

"We had trade goods for him. Will he understand missing out on those?"

Costa smiled like a shark coming upon a school of tasty little fish.

"I will see that Arroccu Tolu does not go uncompensated for any trouble he has gone to on your behalf."

Ivanov nodded, "And I will see that Arroccu Tolu gets his whisky and cigarettes before I collect my lira and your fattest goat."

Costa's men had moved from stripping the dead to stripping the Hummer.

They seemed to know which items to set aside as belonging to the three outsiders and what they could claim as the spoils of war. Pretty much everything except the personal weapons and luggage. Two of the men were excitedly dismantling the 50-cal.

"Come, your Highness, meet my cousin, Bautista," Andreas Costa said, leading them away from the vehicle, which was rapidly being reduced to spare parts and salvage.

Harry half-expected to meet some primitive avatar of the uptime movie star, a great hulking mountain giant swaddled in wolf hide and chain mail. But cousin Bautista was as thin and sinewy as Andreas Costa was paunchy and bearlike.

He carried a shotgun, and Harry recognised him as the man who had gone through the surviving ranks of Russians and Sorgono bandits, doling out the mercy shot.

"Your Highness," Bautista said quietly. "You fought well tonight. Your woman and your kulak servant, too."

The hairs on Harry's neck stood up, expecting Ivanov to lash out at the insult.

But the Russian only snorted.

"*Zasranets*, Bautista."

To Harry's surprise, Charlotte did not object to being described as his woman.

"We have horses coming up from the valley," Bautista explained. "But we will have to meet them further down. We cannot follow the highway. We must use the old tracks."

"How long will it take to get to Santa Teresa?" Ivanov asked.

"There is some urgency?" Bautista asked. "Someone you must kill?"

"Yes. Someone we must kill."

The Sardinian considered the question. He was a few seconds thinking it over. Harry shivered in the cool mountain air. It was after midnight, and they were high enough that none of the day's heat remained.

"If we ride without stopping and do not encounter treachery, I can get you to Nuoro in two days. I have a cousin there. He will find you a vehicle, and we will take the coast road. You will be in Santa Teresa a day after that."

"But we came through the mountains to avoid the coast road," Harry said.

Bautista shrugged.

"And that did not go so well, eh?"

Ivanov frowned.

"This is too long," he said. "Skarov will escape."

"The man you must kill?" Costa asked.

"Yes," Ivanov confirmed.

The clan leader considered the problem for a moment or two before nodding gravely.

"Tell me everything you know of this man and his plans. I have family in the north. They will ensure he does not escape."

Harry spoke up.

"He is travelling with a German. A scientist," he said. "Professor Bremmer"

"An ally?" Costa asked.

"No. A prisoner. I do not want him hurt."

"Unless we have to do it ourselves," Charlotte reminded him.

Costa shrugged.

"This is good for us," he said. "A prisoner will slow your quarry down. It will make it harder for him to find passage off the island. Especially now. Tell me about this German, too. I must know everything."

Of course, they didn't share everything they knew of Skarov and Bremmer. But they told Costa a good deal. It was striking to Harry how quickly things had changed. A day ago, keeping such information secret would have been worth killing for. Now, they traded it freely with these bandits to secure a chance at a small win. And just a chance.

24

The village seemed drained of colour and life. Ossendrecht, a small market town between a patchwork of tilled fields and the wilds of a nature reserve spilling across the Belgian-Dutch border, also played host to a small depot of the Royal Netherlands Army. Geert Veenstra knew the town well from training weekends and was surprised at how quickly the war, or just the threat of war, had turned it from a bustling agricultural hub into something like a movie set. The watery grey light of dawn threw a flat, lifeless pall over the scenery, flattening depth and emphasising the contingent nature of everything now. It felt as though Ossendrecht was waiting to be destroyed.

The garage sliding door rumbled up as Geert and his squad mates jumped down from the truck that had driven them the last two miles to the depot. His butt was already numb from bouncing around on the hardwood bench in the back of the big American truck, and he almost lost his footing and tumbled over as he dropped down from the tray.

"Great work, Geert," he muttered as he staggered awkwardly. "Way to inspire confidence in your fellows and fear in Joe Stalin."

"There's our girl," Heero Bloemsma called out. Geert's eyes followed where the young carpenter pointed.

And there she was: all fifty tons of her.

Officially, she was designated as an M-99 self-propelled howitzer, but almost everyone in NATO called her "the mutt". This particular 99 was lovingly known to Geert and his comrades as "Bernadette". A one-five-five calibre gun on a reworked M-60 tank chassis, her standardised parts had come from all over the Alliance. The hull was built in the US with her driver station switched to the left and the engine (made in Britain by Leyland) at the right in the front of the vehicle. The turret was Swiss, and the gun was forged by Bofors in Sweden with a French autoloader. Assembly had also been completed in Sweden by Landsverk, with a German-made gearbox and optics, Dutch radio equipment and wiring and Portuguese seats.

She was indeed a mutt, but she had a hell of a bite.

"Okay then, dump your stuff and let's wake her up," Geert said. "Bernie's had enough beauty sleep."

"Didn't help much," his deputy, ter Velde, deadpanned.

It took all four men to get the covers off. The waxed canvas tarps were dusty, but she was just as they had left her after their last weekend together three months ago.

Corporal Heero Bloemsma, their driver, dug out the inventory folder. It was not unknown for other units to 'borrow' an item or two from the depot.

Wachtmeester ter Velde, gunner and deputy commander, stood out on the slightly damp concrete tarmac, rolling a cigarette.

"Well, Opper, at least item one is here."

Item one was the vehicle itself.

"Small mercies, Peet," Geert nodded. "Let's mount up and run a check."

He climbed aboard carefully. The pins and needles he'd suffered after the truck ride had nearly gone, but he wasn't a young boy anymore and climbing on board the armoured behemoth was not a jaunt to be lightly undertaken. It would be embarrassing to be sent home to Aukje and the twins with a broken leg before he even saw a Russian.

Embarrassing, but maybe not so bad, Geert thought to himself. He missed his family with a physical pain that surprised him. It was like heartburn all the time.

Half an hour later, the vehicle checklist was done. They were good to go, as the Americans said. Or was that just the uptimers? Sometimes, it was hard to tell how these things had all folded together since those mad days of the time-travellers' arrival.

"You in there, Veenstra?" a voice called from behind the vehicle. It was Lieutenant Eikelboom, their platoon commander. A regular officer, this one, a full-timer, but not a bad fellow for it. He seemed to understand and accept that he was stuck with a bunch of carpenters, journalists, and bookkeepers.

"Yes, sir. One moment, please," Geert called back, cleaning his grease-covered hands with an Army green towel, which was now an oil-stained rag. He crawled out of the Mutt's steel innards, jumped down, and saluted his CO.

"What's the status, Opper?" Eikelboom inquired.

"The engine battery was dead, sir. One of the three camouflage nets and the Fifty we got for the commander's station were damaged, and the thermometer for the powder has gone missing."

"Damned ordnance monkeys," Lieutenant Eikelboom muttered. "Okay, make me a list, and I will get it sorted. You and your men had coffee yet?"

"No, sir," Geert said hopefully.

Eikelboom waved to his driver, a corporal idling the jeep they'd driven out here. The noncom sketched a half-salute and hurried around to fetch a big thermos and a bag of steel cups. To Geert's surprise, he also conjured up a box of powdered milk, sugar cubes and, for a wonder, a dozen packets of *gevulde koeken*—the almond-paste cookies on which the Dutch army could run in the absence of fuel or ammunition. Geert was caught between desperate gratitude and a sinking sense of doom. His wife made the best *gevulde koeken* he had ever tasted, and there was an excellent chance he might never taste them again. Geert almost lost himself in self-pity before a meaty hand smacking his shoulder brought him back to the world of real things.

"There'll be no cookies and coffee once we get Bernie rolling," Peter ter Velde grinned.

The journalist and deputy gun commander was right, of course. And more than that.

If they did not stop the Sovs, Aukje might never make cookies for Geert and the children again.

The lieutenant drove off fifteen minutes later, his face fixed in a mask of dour intent. He had a long list of equipment to shake free of their lords and masters in logistics, the true, beating heart of the military. Half an hour after Eikelboom departed, their next ride turned up—a convoy of heavy lowboys to haul the gun platforms. The trucks were all civilian rigs, pressed into service under emergency war powers, but the trailers were uniformly olive drab. American-made and stamped with unit numbers marking them as survivors of the 5th Army. Geert had no idea how they'd ended up this far north or survived the Russians' orbital bombardment, but he was glad to have them. The heavy steel tracks of the M-99s would chew up the autobahns and burn through most of their diesel before they got anywhere near the enemy. The semis would get them there that much faster, too. A mixed blessing, he supposed.

The June sun burned high and fierce in clear skies when the convoy pulled out with the prodigal Lieutenant Eikelboom leading the way in his jeep. He'd mainly been successful in filling the blanks of his platoon's equipment list. However, Bernadette was still short a couple of camouflage nets, and all the other guns were short of this or that, none of it enough to justify waiting in place for resupply.

Usually, the men would ride separately from the equipment, but peacetime safety regulations had given way to the imperatives of war. Without separate motor transport for the personnel, Geert and the others sat in their machines while the machines rode piggyback on the mix-and-match hauliers. He imagined it was such an obviously urgent and chaotic kludge-together that any Russian aircraft that attacked them might hesitate to gawp at the evidence of Allied desperation and deprivation – right before they shot the convoy to pieces.

To think that a week ago, he had been worried about the roots of an ancient elm that had choked and eventually cracked open the water pipes to the university's chancellery. They said the elm was historically significant, and there could be no cutting it down or harming it in any way. But the Chancellor of Utrecht University needed to flush his toilet, too, and there could be no denying him his amenity.

Fix it, Veenstra. See to it, they said.

It had been such a big deal. Now, it meant nothing to him.

Hours later, the convoy pulled up outside a roadhouse, and Lieutenant Eikelboom reached out on the radio.

"I need some cooks. The roadhouse restaurant is fully stocked, but they have no cooking staff. Everyone has fled west. So, I need a dozen of you with kitchen experience—including peeling taters—to step forward. The rest of you see that the trucks are topped up on diesel. Fuel detail report to the battalion sergeant, food detail form on me."

The sun was dropping towards the west. Geert had stayed with Bernadette, sending Private Aukema and Peter ter Velde with the lieutenant. Aukema had flipped burgers at a Slim Jim's in The Hague when studying his bookkeeping, and before ter Velde had picked up the journalist's quill, he'd been an apprentice baker in Amsterdam.

Somebody had to guard Bernadette, and Geert could man the 50-cal from the commander's hatch in the turret. Heero Bloemsma had rigged up one of those portable transistor radios at his driver's seat, and Veenstra had him search for a radio station with the latest news. A moment or two of scratching around the dial turned up the BBC's World Service.

The American president was on, giving a speech.

But it wasn't Ike. It was the new fellow, this Kolhammer, who had come through the wormhole from the future.

God, what a world.

Ter Velde and Aukema returned with steaming bowls of sauerkraut stew and bratwurst, a carton of German cigarettes and a couple of bottles of Fanta, the local orange-flavoured fizzy drink. It was said you could get it anywhere in the world now that Coca-Cola had bought the recipe.

"How's the war, Geert?" the reporter asked as he handed him the meal. Dutch custom put everybody on a first-name basis, apart from the officers. But off duty, they called Lieutenant Eikelboom Jan anyway. He didn't mind, which was good for a regular soldier. Geert found that some of them could be terrible martinets.

"It is grim, Peet," Geert answered. "They are putting a brave face on it, but down south we are getting one hell of a beating. The Swiss repulsed an attack from Northern Italy near Locarno. Monty is leading a fighting retreat up here in the north. And the Russians did a Pearl Harbor on the US Atlantic Fleet after murdering Eisenhower."

"That is grim," ter Velde agreed.

They ate their meal in silence. In the distance, a helicopter fluttered overhead. It was headed south.

Boosfeld looked intently into the Major's face.

"Are you a German soldier or a fool?" Boosfeld growled.

The other man, already nervous, started gibbering.

"How c-can you speak to me like that, Herr Hauptmann?"

The supply officer, a Major Bidermann, undoubtedly meant to use Jochen's lower rank as a put-down, but instead, he sounded whiny and vulnerable.

Boosfeld said nothing. He did not take his eyes off the man. He did not need to. He was intimately familiar with their surroundings. He stood outside a vast warehouse complex of the Hindenburg Barracks at the edge of Würzburg.

The city beyond was a wreck, its neat buildings and clean lines shattered by Soviet bombing, the avenues strewn with wreckage and debris. Greasy fires polluted the morning sunshine with their foul miasma. A few Red Army aircraft had come calling as a company of local troops was being marshalled there. The screaming, shaking, wounded men had been taken to the barracks' military hospital, but the bodies of dead German soldiers lay everywhere around them. Boosfeld would have policed up this abysmal scene hours ago. Bidermann appeared to have done nothing. Sirens wailed on, even though the skies above Würzburg were clear of immediate threats.

That caterwauling howl was the last thing anyone here needed. What they craved, Jochen knew, was a firm hand and the stern, clear voice of command. And by God, he would provide it if Bidermann could not. Battalion had sent Jochen Boosfeld to this Ammunition Supply Point at Hindenburg Kaserne. It tasked him with ensuring the facility was ready to receive the long line of tanks that were even now piling up on Weissenbergstrasse behind him. What a feast the Reds would make of them all while they waited on this idiot Bidermann, this carpet shuffler, who had misplaced his keys.

On hearing that, Boosfeld had immediately detailed First Sergeant Stark onto locating Bidermann's non-commissioned officers. They would surely know what they were doing.

They undoubtedly would have, Stark reported, were they not smeared all over the walls of a barracks courtyard.

Boosfeld ground his teeth and swallowed a small mouthful of bile.

Ugly things, cluster munitions. A stick had come down on the heads of the ordnance company while they held morning formation, waiting on this *arschloch* of a major—delayed, as he helpfully informed them, by an untimely bout of diarrhoea.

Shitting his pants with terror, for sure. Boosfeld shook his head. Still, it was a left-handed gift, was it not? If the stupid Reds had bombed the actual ammo store...

Mein Gott, what a mess he would now confront.

"So, Herr Major, there is no way into the warehouse without your keys?"

Bidermann looked sick. "No. And I need more than verbal authorisation from the Division Commander if you want to remove the ammunition. There are forms, ...procedures—"

Boosfeld cut him off. "Really. So, an order from Division via me is not good enough for you? You would perhaps prefer a piece of paper signed in triplicate?"

The staff officer's rubbery grin was almost grotesque, surrounded as they were by so much carnage.

"Well, I...I don't know about triplicate being strictly necessary, but..."

Boosfeld understood that hundreds of soldiers were staring at them. Tank commanders, the infantry units assigned to advance with them, and the surviving personnel of the Ammunition Supply Point. And just behind him at the entrance to a small brick office, one step down, Kompaniefeldwebel Stark.

He didn't care.

"First Sergeant," Boosfeld said quietly, not taking his eyes off Bidermann.

"Yes, sir," Stark answered.

"Do you see that severed arm on the ground, not so far away?"

"Which one, sir? There's a few."

"The nearest one. It belonged to a fellow sergeant, I believe."

"Ah, yes, Herr Hauptmann."

"Fetch it for me, would you?"

"Of course."

Major Bidermann's already sallow face paled even further.

"What...what are you...?"

Boosfeld shook his head and made a shushing sound.

Bidermann stammered to a halt, but his eyes went wide as he watched First Sergeant Stark pick up the severed limb and return with it to the steps. Boosfeld watched as Bidermann tried and failed to swallow several times. His throat made a strange gulping sound.

Stark handed Boosfeld the severed arm.

As always, it felt heavier than he would have imagined had he not had so much experience of such horrors.

He took the arm quietly...

Then started roaring as he used it to whip Bidermann in the face.

"You fool! You fucking fool! Here is your authorisation. We are at war. The Reds are pouring through the Gap, and if we do not counterattack right now, they will roll over all of the Fatherland and be pissing in the Atlantic by week's end."

Major Bidermann cried out at the first, muffled slap of the dead man's hand on his face. He kept crying as Boosfeld raged at him.

"Impossible," he whimpered. "Impossible."

Boosfeld finally gave up, throwing the arm aside.

"Very well then," he said, nodding curtly. He saluted sharply and returned to his tank.

He could see the effect his display had had. Hundreds of tankers and foot soldiers stared at him.

He heard the Major behind him. "I didn't dismiss you, Captain! Captain..."

Bidermann collapsed to the ground with a muffled thud.

Boosfeld glanced back over his shoulder. The staffer was sitting on the ground with his head in his hands, rocking back and forth, moaning quietly.

Boosfeld ignored him. He climbed onto the idling Panzer 59 with the agility of a young boy. He slid into the Commander's seat and buckled in before placing a radio call.

"Volga Six, this is Lehr Two-Six."

"Send it."

"Volga Six, we can't access ASP by conventional means."

A pause.

"Define conventional, Lehr Two-Six."

No pause.

"There is an idiot in charge here, Volga Six."

An element of real heat came back in his commander's next transmission. "Lehr Two-Six, I authorise any means necessary to access my ammunition. We don't have time for this."

Boosfeld smiled. "No, sir. We do not. I log your instructions. We will have access in one minute. Lehr Two-Six out."

He called down to his driver, "Corporal Hänke, drive this tank through those doors."

"The big steel sliding ones, sir?"

"Yes. What is your point, Hänke?"

"None, sir. Moving, sir."

The diesel revved up, and Panzer 59 lurched forward, its gun oriented toward the rear, protecting the barrel.

"Hold on," Corporal Hänke warned. "There's going to be a bump."

They hit the sliding doors at about 25 kph, and with a horrible screech and a gigantic BOOM, Jochen Boosfeld gained access to the Ammunition Supply Point. His tank rolled over the remains of the door, and Boosfeld ordered the driver to stop.

The tank halted smoothly. Boosfeld undid his restraints, opened the hatch, and climbed outside. He spotted Major Bidermann staring from the steps. The man's mouth gaped open like a fish. He shook his head, seemingly regaining some control over himself.

"Are you a madman?" Bidermann croaked. "Look what you did to my doors. You'll go to jail. I'll have your rank for this."

The major climbed back to his feet and limped toward Boosfeld's panzer.

Boosfeld shook his head.

"No, you won't, Herr Major. I had direct orders from Volga Six."

He had learned that much, at least in the last war. Always cover your ass.

His voice was casual, conversational as he went on.

"So, Major. We are done with games. All I need is a little help finding things, like tank and small arms ammunition," he said, craning his head around to take in the vast spaces of the warehouse. "Surely you know where those items are stored?"

Bidermann said nothing. Jochen stared at the wet spot that had darkened his crotch.

"Herr Major, we don't have all day."

He saw the man's morale collapse, finally and utterly.

Bidermann nodded and turned to trudge into his warehouse.

"Through here," he said.

"This would have been easier if you knew where the keys were, Herr Major," Boosfeld replied, but mostly under his breath. "One of those little Bluetooth keyrings the Americans have nowadays."

He did not have one for his keyring, but he had heard they were handy. Funny to think that some titanic battle might turn on such a trifle.

Like the horseshoe nail of the old folk saying.

25

He took the oath, he did the work, and increasingly, he was surrounded by the architecture of state power, but Philip Kolhammer did not feel he was the President of the United States. The setting didn't help, even if it was temporary. Jim Davidson's country estate felt like a weird reboot of that old TV show his wife had loved so much. Downton Park or something. It was crawling with butlers in penguin suits and housemaids in pinafores, but also with increasing numbers of staff from the embassy in London and all three branches of the armed forces. Davidson's younger corporate team, dressed in expensive uptime business wear, arrived earlier to build their own C3 facilities, led by Maria O'Brien. He watched with fascination and some surprise as they installed racks of computer hardware and communications equipment that looked so modern and bleeding edge that he wondered if O'Brien had popped open another wormhole somewhere to resupply directly from the twenty-first.

The bandwidth between the two teams—officials of the US government and the agents of a private corporation—was substantial, but not inexplicable—not to Kolhammer. He'd put O'Brien onto an intercept path with Slim Jim many years ago, and it'd paid off massively when she'd thwarted Stalin's pre-emptive strike with Davidson's weaponised communication satellites.

"Mister President?"

"Huh?"

It still caught him by surprise.

Kolhammer turned all the way around in the swivel chair at the desk he'd been given in a library on the ground floor. It was a massive oaken slab of a thing, that desk. Constructed of timbers taken from a Spanish Man-O'-War captured by some lord and master of the estate hundreds of years earlier. The office chair was a striking contrast. A contemporary 'interpretation' of a Herman Miller Aeron, whereby interpretation meant a straight-up copy of the famous dot-com throne of a thousand failed start-ups from the late 1990s.

"Mister President," the young Air Force aide said. He stood just inside the library door, his eyes shadowed by the deep hollows of fatigue and perhaps something worse. "I have the latest casualties and damage estimates from the Soviet strike on Norfolk, sir. And an update from Langley. Eyes only for you."

"I'll take them," Kolhammer replied in a steady voice, waving the young man forward.

At least he was familiar with this part of the job.

He scanned the top-line figures from Norfolk, and Jesus Christ, it was worse than Pearl Harbor. Much worse. More than six thousand dead, half of them civilians, and heavy losses to the Atlantic Fleet. Two aircraft carriers gone, one of them a nuke. One of the new helicopter assault ships sunk. And a dozen escort ships destroyed or too heavily damaged for immediate repair.

On the plus side, Admiral Ringo had surged most of his fleet into open water hours before the Soviets struck. So, they weren't utterly defenceless in the North Atlantic, but the overwhelming superiority the US and her allies had enjoyed was gone.

Kolhammer didn't need a stack of briefing papers to confirm what he already knew. The Allied navies were about even with Stalin's now, and a fair fight was not the sort he wanted. He'd learned that from Colin Powell, who'd learned it from the Vietnam War, which wouldn't happen in this world because Kolhammer had made sure Ike backed Ho Chi Minh over De Gaulle.

What a fucking mess, even so.

He tore open the sealed envelope containing the hard copy briefing from the CIA.

An update on the search for Bremmer, the missing rocket scientist.

Harry Windsor was on the ground in Sardinia with Ivanov and a third operator on Davidson's payroll. They had a lead on Bremmer and were pursuing it with all despatch.

The Agency was preparing options to intervene if needed.

"Much appreciated, son," Kolhammer muttered, trying to hide his exhaustion. He had barely slept for two days, but despite his fatigue, he could feel the familiarity with this kind of hard work settling deep into his bones. It felt like a sort of torment he knew all too well.

"Can I get you anything, sir?"

"Another coffee and a ham sandwich."

The aide frowned anxiously.

"Are we out of coffee?" Kolhammer asked.

"No, sir, it's just that..."

"It's just that I told this kid on pain of castration that you were not to have any more caffeine because you are hitting the rack and stacking some zzz's. Right the fuck now, Mister President."

The intruder who pushed her way past the Air Force lieutenant and into the tiny medieval study was a short, wiry Asian-American woman, fierce, flint-eyed, and utterly un-fuck-with-able. Her close-cropped black hair was streaked with grey.

Kolhammer's smile was tired but genuine.

"Lia. I am so glad to see you."

Lia Pao, his Chief of Staff, or perhaps his former Chief, did not return the smile. She wore a dark, well-cut business suit and stood with her hands crossed low before her as if concealing a weapon. Kolhammer wasn't sure whether his staff automatically followed him from the VP's office into Oval. There would doubtless be rules. Protocols. But he was the boss now, so fuck it. That was his call. Or Lia's.

"You won't be so fucking glad when I finish with you. Have you taken your meds today? I know for a damn fact you haven't slept, so I guess we can assume all self-care has gone down the crapper along with protocol and orderly process," she said, pointing at him with hands too thin, the bones just a bit too prominent, her skin as dry and smooth as brown parchment. "And what the hell is that fucking douchenozzle Jimbo Davidson still doing here?" Lia went on. "We don't need him, just his machine, and we got O'Brien to run that."

"Mister President?"

The Air Force aide had been joined by two secret service agents, drawn to the room by the harsh tone of Pao's voice.

Kolhammer offered a soothing gesture, calming everyone down.

"It's fine. We're good here. Agent Bowen, Miss Pao will need a detail upgrade. She's the White House Chief of Staff now. Lia, who else you got with you?"

Lia Pao narrowed her eyes as though suspecting she was being gamed. She skated forward into the library like a hockey puck on the ice, then caromed off an invisible barrier at the room's centre. She started talking, slowly at first, but building up a head of steam.

"I brought Josh Ovenden and Serge Lazarevski on a chopper with me. We all flew out of Paris together. Seth Parker and Zach Spadoni are in transit from London. They hitched a ride on a military transport. One of the daily scheduled super-lifters out of Andrews. We can upgrade them all from lowly Veep minions when they get here. I dunno how many of Ike's people survived, and we don't want to look like vultures, but it's a shitshow back home right now. Nobody knows nothing about anything. I put out a couple of boilerplate statements for you, and the Speaker's been good. But it would be best to address the nation first thing in the morning. Zach's already drafted up a couple of speeches for you to check. Just highlight the bits you like. We can cut-n-paste between them as needed. But you," she jabbed a small, bony finger at him, "You are done for the day. Get your butt out of that fake-ass tech-bro chair and into whatever medieval four-poster bed isn't already full of Davidson's fucking Playboy bunnies. You can't run the country on black coffee and stim shots."

The three other men in the room stared at her, but Kolhammer smiled and nodded, raising his hands in mock surrender.

Lia had been with him since he'd announced his candidacy in '51.

A helluva thing that'd been.

But Lia had backed him from the get-go.

"I still need a sandwich," he said, retaining some dignity in the face of this Minnesota twister. "I haven't eaten since breakfast."

The woman's eyes narrowed, and her head turned on the Secret Service agents like a gun turret.

"It's not their fault," Kolhammer said quickly. "They're busy, too. I've only got a skeleton crew with me. And I'm literally trying to run a world war here."

"Kitchen. Now," Lia Pao ordered, and the three men parted to let her through, with the President of the United States trailing along obediently behind.

SLIM JIM THOUGHT it'd be cool having the president stay over, but it turned out it sucked ass. That wasn't Kolhammer's fault. He seemed a decent sonofabitch from all reports, some of them in newspapers Slim Jim owned. He was sure the guy would be hell on a keg if he got rolling. But he never let up. A quick howdy-fucking-do when he arrived, just before he disappeared into some drawing room or secret chamber or something. And then he was gone, while Slim Jim's manor filled up with a small army of government nerds and more of his own minions. Sharp-suited, bizoid wolverines and long-legged honey-badgers who were all perfectly polite to their boss. To him. He was their boss.

But they all answered to Maria.

He wasn't cutting up rough about it or nothing.

He knew she had a hell of a job saving the fucking furniture with the Reds pouring into Western Europe. He owned lots of nice things there, castles and factories and literal fucking antique furniture and shit, and Maria had put pedal to the fucking metal extracting what value she could. *Stranded assets*, she called them, like it was funny. But it wasn't funny to Slim Jim. Some of that stuff, like the new compact disc factory in Germany, was already lost behind the Russian advance.

So he wasn't gonna get in her way neither.

But it didn't leave him much to do.

They wouldn't let him go down to the little village that he owned to visit the old English pub that he also owned, to drink a couple of lousy beers which he would have totally fucking paid for even though he must have owned the kegs and the beer inside them too.

Instead, the Lord and Master of Hamilton Manor was sitting in his stupid old-timey kitchen—seriously, it looked like Robin Hood and Friar Tuck could have spit-roasted a wild boar in the gigantic hearth—where he sipped at a sad, lonely guy beer, ate potato chips, and plotted to get his ass back to the States as quickly as he could. Things would be a bit fucked up there for sure because of the whole world war thing and Ike getting assassinated and stuff, but he could take himself out to the west coast. A party was always kicking off somewhere out there.

He entertained these maudlin thoughts as a couple of those humourless torpedoes Kolhammer kept as bodyguards suddenly appeared from the hallway leading back to the main part of the house. They gave him a once-over, nodded, and waved their boss through.

"Whoa," Slim Jim grunted, sitting up straight as President Kolhammer strode into the kitchen, attended by some stringy little Suzy Wong character and a couple more guys in ties. These guys didn't look like the first guys, the Secret Service goombahs. They had to be DC weenies. One of them looked way too young to be an uptimer. Everyone knew the Hammer preferred the company of his own kind. But the other one had that look about him. He was tall and rangy, with that weird fucking sculpted look they all had from spending too much time in the gym. And his sleeves were rolled up, and Slim Jim could see tattoos on his forearms.

Nothing like the honest ink and needlework you saw all the time in the Navy. Ships and anchors and hearts with 'Mom'.

No, this character was painted with something like elf runes or fucking goblin hexes that made no sense at all. Very 21C. And he worked for the fucking president? Jeez, this world.

They seemed surprised to see him there, drinking his flat beer and munching his bag of chips, or crisps as the locals called them. And Slim Jim got a red-hot feeling that the old Asian biddy was gonna straight-up order the Secret Service guys to throw his ass out of his own kitchen. He got ready to give them the bad news about that. But before anyone could say a word, President fucking Sledgehammer laid on a big old politician's smile and came forward with his hand stretched out in greeting.

Slim Jim, a little startled, stood up so quickly he knocked his chair over with a clattering bang, started to reach out to take Kolhammer's hand, remembered his fingers were covered in salty potato chip fixings, wiped them on his pants, almost licked his fingers clean, thought better of it, and finally just gave up.

"Sorry, man," he said, throwing his hands up and punching Kolhammer lightly on the shoulder. "You got my vote. Seriously, O'Brien said I had to."

The Asian chick glared at him; the two DC weenies stared like he'd grown enormous leathery wings from his back, and those Secret Service goons were maybe about half a second away from putting a couple of rounds in his melon.

But Kolhammer snorted and punched him back.

"Good to see you, Slim Jim."

Ouch.

The bastard had a hell of a punch. And fists like fucking cinder blocks.

"You think I could get a beer, too?" Kolhammer went on. "A cold one?"

The mamasan rolled her eyes and headed for the ice chest, asking if anybody else wanted a brew. Still struggling to catch up, Slim Jim blinked at her accent, the same close-mouthed, stiff-jawed vowel-straining yawl he'd had such a hard time training out of his shipmate Moose Molloy back on the old *Astoria*.

It was so familiar but utterly strange coming out of that profoundly fucking alien face.

So she was an uptimer too, then. And weirder looking than most of them. There was something about her that just didn't set.

There was a lot of them like her in the future, they reckoned. A lot of foreigners calling themselves Americans. And a lot of Americans who thought otherwise.

Or that's what they reckoned.

One of the bodyguards fetched his chair from the hard stone floor, and Slim Jim, overwhelmed and unsure of himself, sat down to supper with President Philip Kolhammer.

"SEE, right there, Phil. That's where you're wrong."

Davidson jabbed a finger at him, sloshing a few glugs of beer from the can he was holding, his third since Kolhammer and the others had intruded on his late-night supper.

The boss hog of Davidson Enterprises had taken Kolhammer up on the invite to "Just call me Phil," probably to the annoyance of everyone else who persisted with Mister President. Not that Slim Jim gave a fuck. That was the thing about being a billionaire. Every billion dollars was like a billion fucks you didn't have to give about anything.

"Enlighten me," Kolhammer said, pausing with a ham sandwich halfway to his mouth.

Davidson snorted.

"I didn't start building all those windmills and solar farms to save the future. I leaned into that shit because that asshole Getty came the high hat with me at his stupid club in New York. I could buy and sell that asshole with my goddamn pocket change. And he's giving me the snake eye? Fuck him. But yeah, it'd be nice if the oceans didn't catch fire, too. So that's a bonus. I like the beach."

The manor house kitchen was large and dimly lit, the windows all covered by blackout curtains—not that it would make any difference to the guidance system in a Soviet cruise missile. But you had to lead by example. Kolhammer was tired, and Lia Pao was correct; he would have to catch some rack time soon. But he found Jim Davidson's oafish honesty such a refreshing change from the circles in which he had moved the last few years that it was hard to drag himself away from the conversation.

He saw Maria O'Brien regarding him with a half-smile from the shadows over by the cold kitchen hearth. She'd been wrangling this massive grifter for nearly a decade now, nudging and coaxing and occasionally straight-up dragging him and his growing fortune into the future. Or, to be honest, into the closest approximation of a future he could live with.

"Well, whatever your motivation, you did good for the world," Kolhammer said after washing down a bite of his sandwich with a mouthful of English Lager. "The Chinese got a hell of a head start on us in renewables back upwhen. We wasted a lot of time and made things a lot worse than they should have been. Lots of people died, Jim. Wars. Droughts. Megafires. Famine."

"Plagues that came out of the big Arctic defrost," Maria put in from the fringe. "Don't forget them. They sucked."

"Sucked ass worse than Covid," Lia Pao confirmed.

Davidson nodded and shrugged at the same time. He'd heard of the so-called spicy cough, versions one through a gazillion.

"Happy to help out," he said. "Since there was a buck in it for me. And some shit-eating for Getty."

"Mister President," Pao interrupted. "It's getting very late. And you do have to give that speech in the morning."

"Yeah, I know, Lia," Kolhammer said. "I'll be in my hammock soon enough. And remember, we got the time difference on our side. Five hours up our sleeve. But I don't get to sit much with regular folk anymore."

"Mister Davidson is not regular folk," Pao pushed back. "He's a billionaire."

"A robber baron," Serge Lazarevski muttered. Lazarevski was Kolhammer's national security advisor, a Ukrainian who'd come to America as a child shortly after the fall of the Wall.

"Nah, he's like Bruce Wayne and Tony Stark," Josh Ovenden said. Josh was staring at Davidson with something close to awe. He was Kolhammer's technology and innovation guy. And Davidson Enterprises was a warp engine pushing technology and innovation further, deeper, and faster into the future than any other company in the world.

Maria O'Brien snorted from the shadows.

"I think I like the kid's take best," Davidson said, raising his beer to Josh, who blushed. He took another long pull on his beer, not bothered by the slightly hostile energy coming off Pao and Lazarevski. "But I don't make the calls anymore. I got people for that."

He waved a hand around, slurring his words a little.

"You seen 'em. All the suits rolled in here from fuck knows where. Maybe they beamed in. I dunno. We built one of those yet, Maria? A transporter beam? Wasn't that what went wrong and dumped you guys here in the first place?"

Pao and O'Brien exchanged a look.

"Something like that," Kolhammer said. "An experiment that went wrong, entangling quantum instances across space, not time. Professor Einstein has written a book about it."

Davidson let go a short bark of laughter.

"Yeah, well, I got a bunch of Einsteins on the payroll. Way smarter than me, all of them. But I..."

He trailed off, and his eyes lost focus or maybe shifted their focus to a point out in the darkness beyond the thick stone walls of Hamilton Manor.

"...I just moved first, I guess," he said. "Man. The Honolulu Mob never really forgave me for that, you know. They even sent some guys after me. But by then, I had the advantage...what do you call it? The first mover thing."

They knew. They all knew. Slim Jim Davidson's life story had been told in dozens of books and at least two movies. James Dean's version was the better one, in Kolhammer's opinion. Tyrone Powers didn't have the grit.

"I think you're too hard on yourself," Kolhammer said. "Thousands of devices came through that wormhole with us. And all the servers on Fleetnet. And the information cached on them, of course. But you were the first person who took that information and turned it into something real."

"You signed up Elvis and secured his IP before he was even seven years old," Josh marvelled.

"And you might have just saved the world," Kolhammer added. "With those dual-use satellites."

Davidson came back from wherever he'd been. He stared at Kolhammer.

"If I don't go to jail," he said. "And you don't get impeached."

"The hell you say," Lia Pao growled.

Maria O'Brien pushed herself off the wall and directly into the group gathered around the table.

"Slim Jim, we discussed this."

"After the fact, Maria," he retorted. "After the damn fact, which is that I didn't even know I'd built those fucking things. That was something y'all schemed up."

He twirled a finger around, taking in the rest of the group.

"I don't know one-tenth of one per cent of fuck all that goes on in my own company. We discussed that, too, you might recall. But I got your boss, your real boss, here now." He pointed at Kolhammer. "And I figure it might be time for some straight talk."

The room fell quiet.

"Okay," Kolhammer nodded at last. "It might be."

Davidson started to lift the beer to his lips, realised it was empty and gestured at Josh Ovenden for a refill. The young advisor quickly hopped up and fetched a can from the fridge—a modern unit with double doors clad in brushed stainless steel. An incongruous sight in the four-hundred-year-old kitchen.

"I look around this table, and I see something real familiar to me," Davidson said. "Y'all might think of it as a partnership. Judge Gamble, though, he sent me to the chain gang down in Mississippi, and I reckon he might call it a conspiracy."

He threw his hands up before anyone could object.

"Hey. I'm not judging. I'm just saying is all. You people arrived here in '42, and you did not get the warm welcome you might have expected. Wasn't just the Japs and the Nazis, either. I remember that old faggot Hoover putting his G-men onto you."

A few of them shifted uncomfortably at the homophobic slur,

even though Kohlammer knew O'Brien and the Quiet Room had been responsible for Hoover's fall and outing him had been their weapon of choice.

Davidson didn't care if he'd upset anyone. He just kept on talking.

"And I remember there was lots of fellas with big loud voices on the radio and big, long columns in the press, and they all had plenty to say about how you folks might be helpful seeing off Hitler and Tojo, but what would happen when you wanted to raise the black man above his station? Or let women out of the kitchen?"

He looked directly at O'Brien before turning to Pao.

"Or you wanted to let all the lesser races come pouring in over the border. There'd be fags walking down the street holding hands and kissing each other. Men cutting their dicks off and calling themselves women. Women doing Christ knows what down there and calling themselves men. God-fearing folks afraid of saying boo about it all, in case they're the ones who ended up on the chain gang. Again," he went on quickly because that old Asian chick looked about ready to tear his face off, "Not judging. Just saying. I don't care about any of that shit. Never have. But some folks do, and they're not interested in being raised to your way of thinking. They just want to drag everything down to theirs."

Kolhammer's gaze flicked over to Maria.

She had briefed him that Davidson was becoming...dissatisfied. And curious about his role in the grand design.

"It is a free country," Kolhammer said. "People are free to place their bets and take their winnings or to walk away with the ass out of their pants. So yes. Some of us placed a bet on you and what you were doing. I think it paid off. For all of us."

Davidson appeared to think about that for a while.

Nobody spoke while he was mulling on it.

Finally, he said, "Yeah, well, one thing the Mob taught me, you can make your bet, and you can even win, but those assholes can still send the collectors around to settle up with you."

He submitted to the make-up artist because he looked like ten pounds of shit in a five-pound bag. He'd dropped into deep sleep like a rock down a mine shaft, but coming up again had been hard. He hadn't paid Slim Jim's warning much heed when he'd been tired. But as soon as the alarm at his bedside woke him, he found his thoughts returning to the man's words.

They just want to drag everything down to theirs.

"There you go, Mister President," the young woman said. She was American. Kolhammer had no idea where O'Brien had found her, but he assumed she came from one of Davidson's TV networks or movie production houses.

"Thank you," he said, marvelling at her work in the mirror. She'd disappeared the bags under his eyes and somehow reduced the puffiness of his middle-aged jowls.

"You can admire your do-over later," Lia Pao said from behind his shoulder. "Take a selfie if you have to. But I need you in the chair now, making with the happy talk."

Kolhammer stood up and allowed the makeup artist to remove the paper bib she'd tucked in to protect his shirt and suit jacket. He thanked her again and moved to the chair behind the desk in the library from where he would give the speech.

It was already light outside, but the heavy curtains were drawn—partly to deny Soviet intelligence any geolocation clues, partly to let the blue screen behind his Aeron chair work its magic.

Nearly a dozen people were in the room, half of them media guys supplied by Davidson. The equipment they used was augmented tech. It looked like camcorders and sound gear from the early 2000s, all new. A big, old-fashioned microphone sat on the leather-topped desk, but he also wore a lapel mic that ran a wire into a hard drive, just off-camera.

"Belt and braces," Lia said. "Just in case."

There was no teleprompter, but Kolhammer didn't care about that. He was happier reading off his notes in front of him. Lia had offered two versions of the same speech, but he'd gone with his idea. She didn't fight him. They'd campaigned together enough to know each other's strengths and weaknesses.

He glanced around the room as the production crew backed off, taking up their places. The oak-panelled walls and floor-to-ceiling bookcases were filled with old, rare volumes he knew for a fact Davidson had never read and likely never would.

But the books were here, and they were important. Some of the wisdom of humanity and the ages was undoubtedly folded away between their pages. And some rare foolishness and even ugliness, too. But it was that freedom for ideas to form, to rise and fall on their own merits, that mattered. Those books had been written and collected over four centuries, and hopefully, they'd be here four hundred years hence—if he did his job properly. And his job in the next few minutes was to speak to his fellow Americans and the world beyond them. To reassure them, to ease their fears, and to rally them for the hard days ahead.

"Three seconds," a producer called out.

Lights went green on the recorders.

Lia Pao nodded at him.

"My fellow Americans," he said, directly down the barrel of the camcorder in front of him. He didn't say good evening or good morning because this wasn't a live broadcast, and he wasn't entirely sure when it would go out. "I am Philip Kolhammer, and it is my grave and solemn duty to confirm that President Dwight D. Eisenhower is dead, and I have been sworn in as the thirty-fifth president of the United States of America. I will keep my remarks short because time is short, and there is much to do. I will properly address Congress and you, my fellow citizens, as soon as possible."

Kolhammer paused for a breath, thankful he didn't have to reckon with the deranged media circus they'd left behind back in the twenty-first. At least the newspapers and TV and radio networks here could be trusted not to shit the bed or set their fucking hair on fire because he wasn't in Washington at this very moment.

"You will have heard by now," he continued, "that President Eisenhower was murdered at the White House by the agents of Joseph Stalin and that the Soviet Union has launched massive attacks on Europe. The Red Army is rolling on Germany, and Russian missiles have fallen, without warning or provocation, on American soil, taking thousands of lives at Norfolk Naval Station. Due to these grave crimes, not just against America, but against all of humanity, Congress has declared war on the USSR."

Kolhammer paused for another second.

"These things, you know already," he went on. "But let me assure you of one more thing. Our enemies have made a grave mistake. We have suffered losses, terrible losses, but that is the nature of war. It is sorrow and loss, and I am afraid more will come. But it is also courage and boldness, and I can report to you that the enemy's plans have already faltered thanks to the courage and boldness of our military and our allies. They are already losing."

He allowed himself the merest ghost of a smile at this, a message not for the people watching at home but for the dictator Stalin, who would undoubtedly see it and lose his fucking shit. He might even execute a few generals and field marshals, saving Kolhammer the trouble of authorising a bunch of decapitation strikes on Red Army field headquarters.

He resumed.

"A sneak Russian attack on Naples Airport, with overwhelming numbers of elite paratroopers, has been defeated by a small band of cooks, cleaners, and office clerks. They were simply the Americans nearest to the airport. They stood, they fought, and they won, securing the southern flank of Europe with just a few hours of hard fighting against a numerically superior foe. I promise you will hear more about these ordinary heroes and their extraordinary feats in the coming hours and days. But I also promise that you will hear more stories like this, and very soon, because we will stand, we will fight, and we will prevail. Be not afraid, my friends. Hold your children close, but let them know everything will be all right. God bless you all, and God bless the United States of America."

26

It took nearly two hours to get to Piney Fork. Jack Edmonstone drove through the hills along winding, unpaved roads and didn't unpucker his ass even once the whole time. Not until he had the kids and Alice unloaded at her parent's place, and that was well after midnight.

Piney Fork wasn't much more than a flyspeck on the road map, but he'd made the drive often enough that he didn't need a map anyway, paper, or electronic. Not that they could afford one of those fancy new map gadgets you could get now. Jack needed to get his kin as far as possible from Pittsburgh and, more importantly, from the steel plant at Mingo Junction, where he worked.

They didn't talk much on the way, not at first, with the children wide awake in the back seat. But eventually, the sandman caught up with Louise and Henry, and they dozed off under a blanket. Alice asked Jack about a dozen different ways if everything would be all right, and he found a dozen ways of lying to her that they would be fine. He tried the radio several times, looking for a lighter music station to break the dark mood, but it was all news bulletins and war talk. He turned it off, wishing he'd invested in a cassette tape player. It was like having a jukebox in the car, they said. But, of course, then you'd be on the hook to buy a bunch of tapes too. That's how they got you.

About a quarter of one in the morning, Jack pulled into his in-laws' small farm up on Briar Ridge. He steered up the gravel driveway, careful not to put the wheels into the deep drainage ditches on either side. He parked out front of the house. A light came on inside as Blackie the dog barked like a hellhound from the front porch. Jack got out, walked around to the other side of the car, and opened the door for his wife, telling Blackie to be quiet. The dog finally recognised them but had some trouble coming down off the sudden jag. He kept barking, happier now but with the hackles on his back still raised.

"Blackie, quiet; you'll wake up the whole ridge," Alice said as she gentled the children from the back seat. Louise blinked slowly awake, but Henry looked like he might sleepwalk into his grandparents' house.

Jack breathed a ragged sigh of relief, surprised to find himself shaking a little. He'd made it out before the Russian missiles. Maybe he was crazy or yellow, but his family was here, and they were safe now. A voice called out.

"Who the hell is out there?"

It was Alice's dad, Bob, and he would surely have his shotgun to hand.

"It's Jack, Dad," he called back, not caring if he woke the kids. "I brought the family. Alice and the kids. We're all here."

The porch light came on, an old yellow globe that took a full second to warm up and never entirely stopped flickering. The soft glow instantly drew a cloud of bugs like they'd been waiting all along.

Bob Bishop, a short, thick fireplug of a man, peered out of the light into the dark. Croaky and dishevelled, he'd stepped out in his nightgown, thick, white, hairless legs peeking out from under the hem.

"Jack? What the hell are you doing up here at this hour?"

Sure enough, thought Jack, Bob had that old Remington loaded and cocked, but he made the weapon safe as soon as he saw who had come.

"Better come on then," Bob grunted, not waiting for an answer. "Must be trouble, this time of night. We'll talk inside."

The kids shuffled up the steps first, greeting their granddad with sleepy hugs. He sent them on through to where their grandmother Mildred was already fussing over a pot of hot chocolate on the stove. It was a wood burner, but they kept it going year-round. Farmers needed an early breakfast, a big one too, and Bob did not have the hours to wait around for a cold stove to catch up with his need.

"Hi, Mom," Alice said, "we're so sorry about this, but, you know, the news."

Mildred did not know, and nor did her husband.

"What news is that," Bob asked. "Trouble at the plant? Or something else?"

He had a hard eye for any threat to his daughter, and he'd turned it on Jack more than once, especially over his drinking and his moods.

The two younger parents exchanged a glance.

"Mom, can I put the kids to bed?" Alice asked. "We can take them some cocoa if needed, but they're tired."

"Sure, darling," Mildred said, tilting her head slightly. Alice chivvied the kids towards the upstairs rooms without answering her mother's unspoken question.

They went without protest.

Bob returned his shotgun to the rack on the wall. The kitchen was the biggest room in the house, easily twice the size of the sitting room, and when they visited, everyone tended to fetch up out here. *It never changed*, thought Jack. This room looked exactly as it had the first time he'd driven out here, way back in '42. Nothing of the last strange, momentous decade intruded. Not even one of the cheap little transistor radios everyone had in the kitchen these days.

"So what's all the hoo-ha, Jack? You in some kinda trouble, boy?"

Robert Bishop was barrel-chested and thick-armed from a life of heavy, physical labour. He was an intimidating figure, even standing there in his faintly ridiculous nightshirt. Or he would have been had Jack Edmonstone not seen much worse in the war.

"We're all in trouble," Jack said quietly. "Guessing you haven't heard the news. The Russians have attacked. They even killed President Eisenhower. Assassins, they reckon, armed with shoulder rockets or something."

His father-in-law went very still. Mildred Bishop's hands flew to her mouth, and she gasped.

"The President?"

"Yeah, that's what they say. That Kolhammer's in charge now. If they can find him. I brought the kids and Alice out here because I don't want them sittin' on ground zero. This isn't gonna be like last time. The Russians can reach all the way over here and..."

He almost said, "fuck with our shit", but he caught himself. He tended to fall back into his old barrack-room ways when stressed out. Working the smelters down the plant hadn't improved his ability to keep a civil tongue either.

"Can they really? Can they reach us here, Jack?" Mildred's voice quivered. She had completely forgotten about the hot chocolate bubbling on the stovetop.

Her husband answered the question.

"Yes, they can, dear. And I'll wager Jack here's figured out that one of the biggest steel mills in the country ain't a healthy place to be right now."

Jack moved past Mildred, who seemed to be nailed to the floor. He wrapped an old tea towel around one hand and took the chocolate pot from the hob.

"Couldn't have put it better myself, Bob," he said as he carefully poured the thick mix of fresh milk and drinking cocoa into four mugs. "So I'd like Alice and the kids to stay here until things settle down."

Bob slapped the table with his hand, a declarative gesture that had scared the hell out of a younger Jack Edmonstone back in 1942. "Y'ain't gotta ask, Jack. We'll keep 'em as long as we have to—for the whole war, maybe."

Jack smiled a little grimly.

"Yeah, well, that might only be until tomorrow, the bombs they got now," he said. "Heard Ed Murrow on the wireless say the commies dropped rockets on us from space. Dropped 'em all over Europe. Might even have got the Vice President as well as Eisenhower."

Bob grunted noncommittally. He'd never been a fan of Phillip Kolhammer or his so-called modernising schemes.

Mildred gasped and even flinched a little away from the pine board roof of the kitchen as though a commie rocket might be spearing down towards them right now.

"No space rockets dropped on us yet," Jack hurried on. "Not here."

"But they might," Bob Bishop cautioned.

"On Pittsburgh, for sure. Probably not on Piney Fork, though," Jack assured them as he heard Alice coming down from upstairs. The old wooden staircase creaked under her feet.

"What are you gonna do, son?" Bob asked. "It's too far for you to get to the mill from here every day."

Mildred finally got moving again, throwing herself into a flurry to make up for her previous inaction. She put another pot on to boil and fetched an old-fashioned coffee can from the main kitchen cupboard. Jack smelled the beans as soon as she unscrewed the tin lid.

Jack passed Alice a mug of hot chocolate.

She wasn't going to like what he had to say. He had decided on the car ride up here but hadn't spoken to her about it once on the two-hour trip. Jack blew out a breath.

"Not going back to the mill, Ma."

Alice stopped with the mug halfway to her lips.

"Then what are you going to do?" she asked.

The quiet dread in her voice was unmistakable.

"I'm subject to recall until my forty-second birthday," Jack said. "And there's no way I'm gonna get called up as a replacement. Ain't nobody comes out of the repple-depple lasts more than a few days on the front lines. Nobody cares about them. No one looks out for them. I'm headed back to the armoury and re-enlisting."

Silence.

After all that had happened so far today, Alice now stood there and regarded him, dry-eyed. Ominously, she said nothing.

Bob sighed. "Well, I guess you'd know more about that stuff than any of us."

Jack nodded. "I would. And as soon as we get the car unloaded, I'm driving back into town. Hopefully, I get a chance to come back and say goodbye. If not, I'll call, and someone will have to pick up the Chevy. Don't stay in town any longer than you have to."

He reached into a shirt pocket and took out his smokes.

He tapped one out; Bob lit it from the oven taper.

Still, nobody said much. If Jack had been expecting resistance, he'd been looking for it in the wrong place.

What did that mean? Did nobody care if he stayed or he went?

"Nothin' really to say," Bob declared at last. "We'll pray for you."

Those who were drinking cocoa did so. Jack took a strong black coffee when Mildred offered it.

Alice carried two small cups of cocoa upstairs to the children.

Maybe Louise and Henry might have protested Jack's plan, but he would never know.

He and Bob unloaded the car. When it was empty, Jack shook hands with the old farmer and pecked Alice on the cheek. He got a hug from Mildred Bishop, got into the car, and drove away. He saw Alice standing alone in his rear-view mirror. She didn't move from the spot out front of her parents' place even as he rounded the bend and disappeared into the night.

JACK LISTENED to the radio on the trip back, flipping the channels, chasing the news at first, but finally settling on a station that seemed to play only gospel music. It was just something to fill the car. After an hour and a half, he drove without interruption to the choir.

He was happy.

It was an unusual feeling for him. Uncanny almost.

He had done what he could to protect his kin. His own life had been forfeit long ago in Calais. And now that he was returning to the war, it was as though he'd never left.

Approaching the junction and Pittsburgh beyond it, the traffic grew heavier—but all of it headed away from the city. He passed a burning wreck on the verge of the inbound lane but didn't slow down.

Rolling up McAlister Avenue towards his home, he pulled into the garage where he'd been working and drinking hours earlier. In another world, it seemed.

Jack retrieved the pistol from where he'd left it. He unloaded it, clicked the safety off and dropped the hammer. He rummaged in a drawer and found the old leather holster in the back.

He'd need that. He'd once vowed never to fight house to house again without a handgun. He figured it'd come to that with the Reds unless they blew up the whole world.

Ordinary dog soldiers like him didn't get pistols.

Or at least they didn't back then. Those uptimers had all seemed to carry them, even some of the reporters. So who knew? Maybe that'd changed too; arrived here early, along with colour television. Little radios. And that internet thing.

Jack Edmonston had acquired his pistol the old-fashioned way. He'd stolen it from a dead lieutenant.

He grabbed his duffel bag out of the closet and dumped in some underwear, the Colt, a towel, and a toiletries bag. He gathered every packet of cigarettes he could find. He didn't have his fatigues anymore. He'd trashed those, working around the house. He did have his Class A duds, however. And his discharge paperwork. As the dawn started to show through the window, he put on the old uniform. The pants were a little tight, the jacket too, especially over his belly. But the dress uniform, with its bold 1st Cavalry Division patch on the right shoulder, would do.

Jack left the house with the sun well up. He threw his duffel in the car and took off, headed north to Steubenville. As he rolled through downtown, he saw many people out in the streets, some gesticulating wildly. It wasn't six in the morning yet, and already, people were lining up at the stores. He wondered when the first person would get the idea to throw a brick through a window and take what they needed. That dam would burst for sure. The squat, brick armoury sat up the hill a ways. When he arrived, he found soldiers milling about and the parking lot full of the traffic chaos he'd expected. With the paperwork in hand, he made a beeline for the admin building. Only a few guys glanced at him. They were too busy going through their own shit.

A Sergeant First Class in combat fatigues sat behind the desk, smoking a Pall Mall and sifting through paperwork. Jack knocked on the doorframe. The admin pogue looked up.

"Can I help you..." he glanced at Jack's sleeve. "...Sergeant?"

"Yeah, Sarge. You got an empty slot for an E-5? A 745?"

"Ha," the noncom laughed. "You ain't been around for a while, eh? That MOS is 11B now, not 745. But yeah, maybe. Hold on."

The desk jockey turned his head toward an adjoining office.

"Hey, First Sergeant! You got a minute?"

"No! What do you want, Schultz?"

"We need a sergeant? Infantry?"

"Shit yeah. If he's qualified, take his clothing sizes and swear him in."

Schultz looked back at Jack. "You got any paperwork for that uniform?"

Jack grinned and handed over his discharge papers.

Schultz read aloud for a few seconds. "CIB, Europe-Africa Campaign Medal. Arrowhead device, one star. Seventh Cav. France, '44. Occupation duty. Two years in the Guard, got out as an E-5 in '47." He looked up. "OK, looking good. Raise your right hand and repeat after me..."

Jack Edmonston left the office five minutes later with a bundle of forms and instructions to be back no later than seventeen hundred hours with the paperwork completed, or he'd start the next leg of his service short a stripe.

There was just something so right about it, even the chickenshit administrivia. Or perhaps especially that. Jack couldn't keep the grin off his face. A few guys noticed and stared at him. The only happy man in America this morning.

Jack jumped in his car and pointed it back towards Piney Fork.

Driving along Main, he saw lines at the gas stations and a big fight outside the Trader Joe's. He glanced at his fuel gauge, better than half a tank. More than enough, and the five o'clock deadline fixed one problem at least.

Jack hated long goodbyes.

27

Eighteen hours after leaving Italy, Jones's flight touched down at a decommissioned military airfield about thirty miles south of Paris. The small passenger jet, escorted by a flight of F-5s and two original F-35s off the *Kandahar*, had refuelled in flight and on the ground at Gibraltar. It was late in the afternoon when he disembarked with his staff, which at that point numbered two. Private Williamson, his driver, and Colonel Grieve, his chief of staff. The airfield, which had once hosted the squadron of Luftwaffe ace Adolf Galland, was nestled in a quiet bend of the river Seine at the edge of the Forêt de Rougeau.

Private Williamson, with the air of a young woman who could not quite believe the path upon which fate had set her, had spent that last hour of their journey with her face pressed up against the window of the jet, her mouth open slightly as the setting sun cast a golden shimmer over the sinuous course of the river. She craned around to glimpse Paris away to the north, but Jones knew there was no point. The angle was all wrong. He glanced out his window just once when the pilot announced their final approach. The deep green wilderness of the ancient Rougeau forest stood out starkly among the tilled fields of the rural commune. It was a pleasant, almost idyllic scene for a country at war.

On the ground, the pressurised doors opened with a hiss and reality flooded in. The screaming whine of jet turbines powering down, the stink of av-gas, and the shouts of ground crew rushing to refuel the fighters and send them to where they were most needed. The airfield had not been in regular use since the end of the war, and there was a noticeably makeshift feeling to the operation here.

Jones wondered if any of the planes or their pilots would survive the week, let alone the war.

The late afternoon air was warm and surprisingly humid.

"Oh, it's like back home," Williamson said.

She was talking to herself, but Jones replied, "Not so much for me, Private. Where's home for you?"

"Georgia, sir. My daddy has a barber shop in Marietta."

"Your father's a wise man," Jones said. "There's always somebody in need of a good trim and a close shave. They never did invent an AI to replace the neighbourhood barbershop."

He stepped off the jet's small folding staircase onto the tarmac. No official welcoming party awaited their arrival. Just the ground crew, who ignored them, instead hustling to refuel and check over the escort fighters.

"Private, you might need to scrounge us up some wheels," Jones said, scanning the otherwise deserted facility.

Frowning at the lack of formal reception, Colonel Grieve eased himself past Jones and Williamson.

"I'll find out what's happening, sir," he said.

"Do your worst, Bob. But what's happening is almost nobody knows we're here. That was the plan. Plus, I don't give a shit about red carpets and marching bands. We need to get to Mont-Valérien five minutes ago. Go make that happen."

His driver and his chief of staff answered in unison.

"Yes, sir."

Williamson and Grieve each hurried away. Williamson ran towards a small hut surrounded by an assortment of vehicles. Jeeps.

Military trucks. And a black Citroën sedan polished to a high sheen. Grieve pulled aside an Air Force sergeant supervising the ground crew tending to the F-35s. Jones's driver disappeared into the hut while Grieve stood talking with the Air Force noncom, hands on hips, chin jutting out. Jones had seen Bob Grieve adopt this attitude before. It was not his happy face.

He returned, frowning.

"Well, I guess OpSec's good. They had no idea who you were, sir. They got orders to refuel the escorts. But there's no ground transport for us to Paris."

"I see plenty of wheels, Bob. What about that shiny old clunker over there?"

Grieve snorted.

"That's the mayor's ride. A dairy farmer, as it happens. He's been grazing his cows on the airfield for years and came over to complain and demand recompense when the ground crew chased his herd away."

"Recompense?" Jones said.

Grieve looked embarrassed.

"There...ah, there may have been some shooting, and there may have been some casualties among the er, bovine population. Apparently, they were not inclined to move along."

Jones scanned the field again, noting the singular remains of a black and white milker about two hundred yards away, its legs pointing to the sky. As he shook his head, a portly man in wine-coloured robes and an ornamental chain of office emerged from the small fieldstone building.

The mayor, he guessed.

The fellow stomped across the grass toward Jones and Grieve, throwing caustic glares at the USAF ground crew, who busily ignored him. The mayor announced himself with a loud burst of colourful French abuse directed with a wagging finger at Colonel Grieve.

"I think he thinks I'm the boss," Grieve said out of the side of his mouth.

"He does," Jones confirmed before cutting in on the official with his own less colourful but just as firmly delivered speech in passably coherent French.

"Monsieur Maire," Jones said, *"I am General J. Lonesome Jones, the senior officer here, and thus responsible for approving any claims you have against the United States of America for damage done by our forces to your property or trade goods. Please draw up a bill of goods and present it to my aide-de-camp, Colonel Grieve, and I shall see it expedited."*

Both the colonel and the mayor of Morsang-sur-Seine gaped at him.

Jones quickly explained to Grieve.

"I was stationed in Brussels for three years before the Transition. Did another two years there a while back. And I deployed to Africa a bunch of times back upwhen. Having French as a second language was useful. It's like a goddamn multitool. Never know when you're gonna need it. Just that you will."

The mayor was suddenly babbling and enthusing about any support he might be able to offer Washington, for a reasonable consideration, of course.

"So I see," Grieve muttered. "Are we really paying this guy for his cows?"

"And his car. We need to get moving, right the hell now."

Jones let the mayor talk himself out before offering a frankly ridiculous sum for the Citroen.

The mayor immediately offered to double the price.

They eventually settled on something close to one and a half times Jones' initial offer.

"It won't matter if we lose," he told Grieve, who was already thinking about the paperwork he'd have to submit. "Or if we win," Jones added with a shrug. "And I don't want to take a vehicle from the ground crew. They have real work to do."

Private Williamson returned and declared herself confident of her abilities to pilot the antique French sedan north to Paris. "I drove stuff way older and weirder than this back home," she said. Grieve suggested travelling in convoy with the Air Force crew, who were also heading back north, but who wouldn't be leaving for another half-hour. *It would be more secure*, he thought.

"No," Jones said. "We're already behind schedule, and a convoy is more likely to be targeted than a single civilian vehicle. As long as Private Williamson isn't telling us a tale about her mad driving skills, we'd be better off going now and on our own."

"Ready to roll, General," Williamson snapped back with a grin. She seemed to be enjoying the adventure.

Grieve took a few minutes to confirm the mayor's contact details and write out two copies of the basic compensation agreement Jones had negotiated. The mayor of Morsang-sur-Seine did look somewhat anxious as they loaded their baggage into his official car and made ready to leave, but Jones took a moment with him.

"The United States of America came back in the last war to do what needed to be done, Mister Mayor," he said in French. *"And the United States of America will be back when we finish this war to pay you properly for your cows and car. My condolences about the cows, by the way. A tragedy."*

Yes, yes it was, the mayor agreed. But he waved them off anyway, clutching at the folded piece of paper Colonel Grieve had written out for him.

THEY MADE good time for three-quarters of an hour until they reached the southern outskirts of Paris, where traffic thickened up, and the chaos of a city under threat reduced their progress to a crawl. Williamson proved herself equal to the challenge of making headway through the snarls of traffic, even if it meant putting a few scratches and dents into the mayoral limo. She showed an admirable lack of deference to inconvenient road rules and bizarre European practices at places such as roundabouts. Although she could not speak French, she made her feelings about even minor delays well-known to anybody who occasioned them.

While she muscled her way through the strange mix of old and new road transport—at one point, Jones noted a collision between a horse-drawn cart and a battery-powered milk van—her two passengers worked with what little information they had to hand to plan a defence against the Soviet juggernaut.

"It will be three weeks, minimum before the first heavy units get here by sea," Jones said. "Assuming they get here at all."

The Soviets, like the Germans, had prioritised their submarine program to give themselves the best chance of cutting Europe off from its American ally. That missile attack on Norfolk had really fucking hurt the North Atlantic fleet.

"I need you to move fast when we get to the Fort, Bob," Jones said. "I don't even know how many staff officers Cronauer took to Germany with him. We might need to replace the whole slate."

"You might need to replace them even if they didn't go with him," Grieve said carefully.

Jones said nothing in reply, but he did bow his head slightly in acknowledgement of the point. Leaders tended to create organisations in their own image. Good leaders and bad. And he did not think of General Cronauer as a good leader.

"Find out who's still drawing breath," Jones said. "Give me fifty words on each and a simple yes or no at the end. There are two questions you need to answer. Are they any good? Can I work with them? There is only one acceptable answer to both questions. Any vacancies you create, of course, you'll need to fill. I trust you to do that."

Colonel Grieve swallowed as he looked out of the window. They drove quickly through a forest west of the city's main airport. The woods were surprisingly thick, being so close to the capital's ancient heart, but they were also crisscrossed by small secondary roads and tracks, which Williamson used to great effect.

"I have some ideas already," Grieve said.

"Let me have them," Jones said.

His chief of staff suggested several officers who would have to go if the Soviets' orbital strike had not already removed them. He did not explain why he thought them unsuitable, but Jones recognised two of the men and found himself in agreement. One was a drunk. The other, a straight-up bigot. A good soldier and an even better administrator, but not a man who could set aside his personal feelings about answering to Jones. "If the Russians didn't get him already," Grieve said, "there's a fair chance he handed in his resignation as soon as he heard of your promotion."

Of the names Grieve suggested as good hires, Jones recognised three as young "temp" officers he had already worked with and one who had come through the Transition as an ensign on the *Leyte Gulf*. Jones narrowed his eyes.

"This is a surprisingly comprehensive talent-spotting operation you've put together on short notice, Colonel," he said.

Grieve nodded.

"As soon as you asked me to do the job, General, I got to work pulling down personnel files. I reviewed them as we flew to Gibraltar."

Jones smiled. "I knew I made the right decision kidnapping you."

They tracked north, paralleling the course of the river Seine for a couple of miles through the outer suburbs of the city. The landscape was less densely developed than Jones recalled from his uptime visits to Paris, with small farms and patches of remnant forest persisting amid newly built squares of townhouses and apartment blocks. Williamson did an excellent job of routing them around the worst congestion, demonstrating a natural feel for the ebb and flow of the city's disrupted traffic. Once or twice, Jones peered into the sky as he heard the unmistakable roar of jet fighters overhead, but they were French Mirages heading east.

Private Williamson announced she would have to pull over a mile from their destination.

"Roadblock. Sorry, General."

"Don't apologise," Jones said as he peered ahead through the windscreen.

The way forward was blocked by a herringbone arrangement of old jeeps and one armoured fighting vehicle. He could not tell whether the troops were American, French, or some other flavour of NATO.

"You keep the motor running, Williamson," Jones said. "Colonel, you're with me."

The two senior officers alighted from the rear of the Citroen as a couple of soldiers in full battle rattle approached them, signalling with one raised hand and much shouting that they were to stay the fuck where they were.

"Americans," Colonel Grieve said.

He sounded relieved.

28

Mont-Valérien was a star-shaped fortress that had held out for months against German invaders during the Franco-Prussian War of 1870. It had not done so well against Hitler's divisions. The Nazis had pressed the old fort into service as a prison and a site for the mass execution of Resistance fighters during the last war. In Jones's time, back up in the twenty-first, it had been consecrated as a national memorial to the war dead of France and her allies. That had not happened here, and he wasn't sure why. There were infinite ways in which history had diverged from the written record in the years after the Transition. Stories written and unwritten. Lives cut off, and lives come into being. The vagaries of real estate development in one city were not something he bothered much to contemplate. (Although he had been home to Chicago to see if the grim 19th-century tenement in which he had grown up was still there. It was, but Beatniks had moved in and painted it bright yellow).

France remained a NATO member in this reboot of 1955, and the question had not arisen as to whether she might leave at some point in the future. Not with southern Europe occupied by Soviet and Eastern Bloc forces. But French pride being what it was, the Armée de Terre maintained a sovereign organisational structure independent of NATO's org chart. Fort Mont-Valerian hosted its joint operational command centre. After the Soviet strikes, it was the closest thing Jones had to a working headquarters on the continent.

The American soldiers at the roadblock, a National Guard platoon of the 29th Infantry, had checked and doubled-checked Jones's orders and identity with initial scepticism and dawning horror as they realised just who they were fucking around. Lieutenant Ryan Mercer, from Winchester, Virginia, finally apologised in a sort of half-choking babble and insisted on escorting Jones the rest of the way into the fort. Mercer drove himself in a jeep, leading Private Williamson through a dark stone archway under a rusted iron portcullis and into an outer courtyard that looked to Jones as though it might once have stabled the horses for the Three Musketeers.

Lieutenant Mercer dismounted from his vehicle and sprinted inside a gatehouse, emerging with two French officers after a moment, all but dragging them along behind him. Not waiting for an invitation, Jones un-assed himself from the Citroën, with Colonel Grieve immediately behind. Jones could hear the young American officer trying and failing to make himself understood by his French counterparts, who either wilfully or genuinely appeared to misunderstand everything he said. They kept glancing over at Jones, at Williamson, and less often at Grieve, gesticulating that they could not possibly do whatever Mercer wanted of them.

It was late in the afternoon, and Jones was losing patience. He had been in transit for nearly twenty-four hours, out of contact with his chain of command for the last two, and nothing he had seen since arriving in France gave him any confidence that anyone here could find their asses with both hands and a fully functioning GPS. He stalked over to where Mercer was arguing with the French officers, his combat boots crunching across the gravel.

One of the men looked him up and down, started to salute, thought better of it, and went back to arguing with Mercer. The other simply threw his hands in the air, saying, "It is simply not possible," repeatedly.

Jones spoke in French.

"Who the hell are you, Capitan? I know you're not in charge here at the

Fort. But perhaps you are in charge of this gatehouse. If so, check my fucking orders, verify my identity, and take me to the goddamned senior officer of this facility. I have been ordered to assume command of all Allied forces in the European theatre. That includes you. Unless you want to spend the rest of this war with your hand stuck up a horse's ass, polishing its shitter until it shines to my satisfaction, I suggest you do as I say."

Both Frenchmen stared at him with wide-open eyes and expressions not a thousand miles removed from the stunned surprise which had painted the faces of Colonel Grieve and the Mayor of Morsang-sur-Seine earlier that day. The captain started to speak, appeared to choke on his tongue, coughed, blushed, and recovered just enough to demand everybody's papers. He spoke in quite perfect English.

"I will need to see everyone's documents."

"You only need to see mine," Jones replied, defaulting to English. He handed across a printout of his orders from the Joint Chiefs and his laminated ID card.

"I haven't had a chance to get the card updated yet. But you'll see my pretty face smiling at you," he growled.

The captain looked up at him nervously. Jones was neither pretty nor smiling.

"I shall have to check this, of course," he said. "With my superiors, you understand."

"I understand perfectly," Jones growled.

The French captain turned and hurried back into the gatehouse. Lieutenant Mercer tried to apologise, but Jones waved him off.

"You did your job, son. A simple job, for sure, but you did it well enough. These assholes, not so much. If you could find a place for my driver, Private Williamson, to get our vehicle out of the way, I'd appreciate that."

Mercer snapped out a salute.

"Sir, yes sir," he said. He double-timed back to the Citroen, falling into a hushed but urgent exchange with Williamson, who had been staring all around her like a tourist, wide-eyed at her first taste of Paris.

Colonel Grieve leaned over to mutter under his breath.

"Is it gonna be like this all the way through?"

Jones snorted.

"I promise you, it's gonna be like this a hundred years from now."

Grieve looked at him awkwardly.

"But you people..." He suddenly blushed and hurried on. "I mean...uptimers. You dealt with this stuff, didn't you? You moved on?"

Jones snorted. "Some did. Not everyone."

He fixed Colonel Grieve with a cold stare. "This will be one of your many jobs, Colonel. I already have one impossible fight on my hands. I don't need another. As much as you can, you deal with this racist shit before it gets near me. We don't have time for it."

Grieve shook his head.

"No, sir. We do not."

As the French captain returned with a senior officer, the colonel straightened himself up and wiped all evidence of good cheer and fellow feeling from his expression. A Général de corps d'armée to judge from the four black stars on his epaulettes. He was a surprisingly small man with dark hollows under his high cheekbones. The general was frowning, his eyes darting from Grieve to Jones and back again.

Grieve stepped forward and saluted, initiating the exchange of formalities and speaking before anybody else had a chance.

"General Bouchet," he said, reading from the man's name tape and making a fair stab at the French pronunciation. "Allow me to introduce General J. Lonesome Jones. Supreme Allied Commander Europe and Commander of US Forces in the European theatre."

Bouchet's confusion was written in his rapidly blinking eyes.

"But General Cronauer..." he started.

"Is dead," Jones finished before going on in French. "*The President appointed me in his place. I have been in transit from Naples. I need a theatre-level update immediately. You need to thicken the air defences and anti-missile shield over this facility, and whatever secure comms capacity you had in place will need rapid and massive augmentation. I can make all of that happen for you. I can also kick you to the fucking gutter if I don't get my briefing in five minutes. We good to go?*"

"Er...Oui, mon General," Bouchet spluttered. "I mean, yes. Yes, of course," he added in English.

THE THICK WALLS and crenellated battlements of Mont-Valérien promised safety and security, but Jones knew that promise to be false. A single nuke or a flight of bunker-busting cruise missiles could reduce the tremendous hulking mass of stonework and masonry to rubble and dust in a heartbeat. The ramparts would entomb them, not protect them.

As Bouchet and a growing cadre of French officers led the Americans down into the bowels of the fortress, Colonel Grieve took notes from Jones on layering the fort's defences, occasionally offering suggestions, which Jones authorised with immediate effect. Bouchet insisted that the French Army's preparations were more than up to seeing off a Soviet attack, to which the Marine Corps general replied, "I don't doubt that they were, General—when this was a second-tier target. But it is now the Supreme Headquarters for the Allied Powers in Europe. So you just moved up the kill list. If old Joe Stalin still had any orbital weapon capabilities, the hard rain would be falling here already."

As they descended, their boots scraped and crunched on the ancient flagstones. Jones wondered how many narrow tunnels and winding staircases had survived the siege of 1870. The lighting was minimal, caged sodium bulbs connected by insulated cable, the malarial yellow glow giving the other officers a sick, bilious appearance.

They reached a small antechamber guarded by two military police officers, who stood aside at General Bouchet's impatient wave. The doors to the command centre looked medieval. Great cast-iron plates studded with rivets and firing loops, the latter breaches covered over by welded sheet metal. A touchpad sat where a giant lock box once might have been seated. Bouchet keyed in a code and placed his thumb on a fingerprint reader. Thick, metallic clunks echoed in the small stone room, and the great iron doors rumbled open to reveal a modern command and communications centre within.

Jones and Grieve followed the French Army commanders into the facility, where maybe three dozen officers and another half dozen civilians hunched over large-screen workstations. Jones saw immediately that the fit-out was all contemporary technology but as advanced as current materials, science, and IT would allow. A small committee of uniformed personnel hurried to meet them, saluting Bouchet before the Americans.

"Colonel Debrun, are you prepared for your briefing?" General Bouchet asked brusquely—in English, Jones noted. A courtesy to Colonel Grieve, he assumed.

Debrun replied that he was and led the small party through the CIC to a room behind a glass wall at the rear of the chamber. Jones was almost sure it had once been a series of prison cells. He could still see some of the original cast iron grillwork on the floor. But it was now some sort of sensitive information space. A SCIF to use the uptime term. A conference table with writing materials and water glasses looked onto a large, multiscreen display fixed to one wall. When the audience for the briefing had taken their seats, Colonel Debrun closed the door and flicked a switch that impeded the view through the window wall, presumably in both directions.

"General Jones, General Bouchet," the briefer started. "Gentlemen," he went on to the rest of the group. There were no women present. "This is the latest disposition of forces on both sides. The intelligence was current as of thirty minutes ago."

He looked at Jones as if asking whether that would be good enough.

"Go on, Colonel," Jones said.

Colonel Debrun nodded, took a deep breath, and turned on the wall display with a remote. The screens took a few seconds to warm up, but they were bright, clear and fully colourised when he started talking again.

"Thirty-two hours ago, the Red Army Missile Force launched a pre-emptive strike across the European theatre, targeting concentrations of main force Allied ground units and several critical transport nodes. The strikes landed in Germany and destroyed the US Fifth Army, creating a hundred-mile-wide breach on NATO's eastern frontier. Further strikes, most likely targeted deeper into the rear echelon, were interdicted by the deployment of... unknown American space-based assets on the orders of the US President..."

Colonel Debrun frowned at his briefing notes before looking up.

"I apologise, but this information is still being developed."

"Perhaps the General has some insight which we do not," Bouchet suggested, looking at Jones, who shook his head.

"When I know what happened up there, you'll know," he said, aware that he might never learn the truth or if he did, that he might never be authorised to disclose it.

"Continue, Colonel," he went on. "But I need to know what the Sovs have in the field right now and what we have to stop them."

Jones was staring at the digital map board. Western Europe spread across four screens. Here and there, small blue bands of colour stood out brightly on the contoured surface of the continent, representing surviving Allied forces. Bearing down on them from the east and pushing up from Soviet-Occupied Southern France was a vast blood-red tsunami.

29

Lavrentiy Beria breathed out for what felt like the first time in years. Perhaps for the first time. Truly, he had never been able to relax, even as the head of the NKVD, undoubtedly the second most feared man in the Soviet Union. *Perhaps even the most feared*, he thought, as he leaned back in the creaking leather chair from which Stalin had ruled for so long.

For while Joseph Vissarionovich Stalin was undeniably the supreme leader and thus the most powerful man in all the Rodina, that absolute, limitless, frankly insane order of power did leave him somewhat remote from the lives and daily considerations of the workers. Yes, on any given day these last thirty or forty years, the old monster might have decided to liquidate twenty million of them on a whim. Still, their ending would come as a function of mere fate, an individual's death no more meaningful than that of an insect caught in a wildfire.

The countless traitors, subversives, revanchists, and enemies of the state whom Beria had killed these many years had all died knowing that the Minister of Internal Affairs had turned his all-seeing eye on them, and for good reason. When the agents of the Soviet state came for you on the say-so of Lavrentiy Pavlovich Beria, it was because Lavrentiy Pavlovich Beria had taken a personal interest in your affairs.

So perhaps, he thought, as he waited for his tea and supper, perhaps he was and always had been the most feared man in all the Rodina. The personal is always more terrifying than the impersonal, as he well knew. From high ministers to lowly kulaks, all feared the purposeful inquisitor more than they feared the random stroke of ill fortune delivered by, say, a speeding streetcar or a cancer diagnosis.

Lavrentiy Pavlovich breathed in and out again, hardly daring to believe.

But yes, he lived. And he had outlived Stalin.

What a marvel.

Sitting in the dead man's office, alone for now, gloriously alone at the very pinnacle of power, Beria shook himself with relief. He had done it. He had survived. The tremors of his hands were evidence enough of that. Dead men do not tremble.

His eyes flicked over the rather drab, even depressing interior of Stalin's office in the Kremlin.

No.

No, it was Lavrentiy Pavlovich Beria's office now.

And he did not much care for it, as much as he revelled in the happenstance of his being alive to occupy the dread chamber. The room was dark, bounded on all sides by quite plain wooden panelling, all-natural light cut off by the heavy wine-coloured drapery hanging over the windows. What light there was came from a dozen small table lamps, brass-bottomed and green-shaded, a favourite of the long-dead Lenin, who had insisted the green shades were a salve to his tired eyes when he worked late into the evening.

The hell with that, Beria thought.

He would replace them with the new fluorescent tubing that gave off such clinically exact illumination. He had ordered all the old lighting at the Lubyanka to be replaced with the more contemporary style three years ago. Again, how much more frightful to see with clarity where defiance and treachery had led you as the people's protectors dragged you to your cell?

A soft knock on the double doors at the far end of the office.

"Enter," he said, putting some force into his words and resting his hands on his lap, lest anyone see how they still shook ever so slightly after Stalin's sudden death had dramatically reversed his fortunes.

Both doors swung open, and a wooden tea trolley on iron wheels rattled in, pushed along by Comrade Prokofyev. He was not Stalin's orderly, of course. Beria could not have faith in such a man. Prokofyev he brought from Abkhazia, where he had trusted the old Mingrelian Bolshevik for his personal services since their earliest days together in the Cheka.

"Ah, come in, come in, Valery Dmitriyevich," he said, relieved that his tea and supper were finally here. "These have been seen to, yes?"

"Da," Prokofyev grunted.

He meant they had been tasted for poison. Whomever Prokofyev had selected to sample the Provisional General Secretary's blinis, cream cheese, and lox had survived the encounter, and now he could eat.

At last.

He was famished.

It was hard enough running the People's Republic during its titanic struggle with the capitalists. Doing so on an empty stomach would be intolerable.

"The Political Bureau is also here," Prokofyev informed him as he served the meal and poured the tea. "They wait for you in the meeting room."

"Thank you, Comrade," Beria said. "Ensure they have enough refreshments and tell them I will be along presently. I have some work to attend to here first."

"Yes, boss."

Prokofyev shuffled out to convey the message. The only work Beria had in front of him was the plate full of tiny pancakes and smoked salmon, but he was the Vozdh now, and it would do the Politburo good to be reminded of that; those who still lived, at least.

There had, of course, been the necessity of a purge when he returned from Stalin's dacha at Lake Beloye. Eliminating internal threats and potential foes was as much a part of Soviet Russia as the frozen tundra. But Beria had winnowed out his enemies with a deft hand and a sure blade. The military leadership he left alone, for now. It would not do to distract them from the great struggle with the West, and to be honest, he was as yet only the provisional General Secretary of the party's Central Committee. He would need allies to secure himself in that role, and the best allies were those with the most tank divisions.

Beria did not rush his dinner, but neither did he dawdle. A few minutes delay in attending to the Bureau would be enough time to hone their anxieties and put them slightly on edge.

It had been hell waiting for Stalin to arrive, and even worse when he finally arrived. Beria did not intend to ape his methods, nor would he be a pushover. Almost any of the men waiting for him down the hallway would happily consign him to his death. And they all knew that he could end their lives should it suit his designs. That tension, ceaseless and unavoidable, was inherent to the struggle. It was inescapable, like winter. With Stalin, however, dialectical tension had curdled into abject terror, and having known that terror intimately, Beria also knew it to be a fearful drain on men's capacities.

One could not take off the yoke and forswear the whip immediately, not in a land such as he now ruled. But nor could one make crippling fear the organising principle of life in the manner of a Stalin. Beria wiped up a small blob of cream cheese with the last blini and sipped at his tea.

That fear had driven Stalin to launch a sneak attack on the West, and now Beria was left to deal with the consequences of the old fiend's paranoia. A vast conflagration raging on all fronts. The masterstroke—Beria's masterstroke!—of pre-emptively striking from orbit, foiled by the uber-capitalist Davidson's entirely foreseeable intrigues and conspiracies. A criminal and a rogue of the most American sort. A chancer, a grifter.

If only—if only!—the Vozdh had heeded Beria's warning that as decisive as Projekt Tunguska would be, it still needed time to amass overwhelming force.

Force enough that any secret Allied countermeasures would prove impotent under the steel rain.

But, naturally, he had not.

Listening to good sense was not one of Stalin's strong points at the end.

Beria sighed and burped, tasting a little of the smoked fish he had just eaten.

He was the Vozdh now. Responsibility for prosecuting the final struggle with the capitalists fell to him. On the long drive back from the lake, part of him had even wondered whether he could reach a ceasefire agreement with Washington. It would, of course, freeze in place all the gains the Red Army had made so far, even if those gains were not as significant as might have been hoped for.

He indeed had ample reason to seek an accommodation. So much had gone wrong. So many parts of the grand plan unravelled.

Beria burped and grimaced to taste a small squirt of bile at the back of his throat. This was how it had been since his miraculous escape from the clutches of that dread Georgian fiend at the fucking dacha. He had the most terrible indigestion and trouble sleeping.

And why would he not?

His best agent, Skarov, had gone dark after securing the rocket scientist Bremmer in Cairo. Perhaps Alexi was already returning to Moscow with the one man who could finally bring all of Beria's dreams to fruition. The one man who might win this war for him.

Perhaps they were both dead somewhere. Or worse, captured by the enemy.

That was one minor irritant. A known unknown, as the accursed uptimers said.

A much bigger irritant, which Beria knew only too well, was the ruin of the whole Southern European strategy, the airborne attack on Italy, foiled by incompetence and cowardice. Most likely by traitors and turncoats.

How otherwise to explain the defeat of a supposedly elite regiment by the fucking lumpenproles and vatniks of the US Army. The lying capitalist news organs were full of their tales and faked news. *Fucking cooks and clerks*, they said. Beating Soviet paratroopers? *Not likely*, thought Beria. That his troops were defeated was undoubtedly true. NKVD political officers attached to the airborne regiments had reported back during the battle on the many failures of the army commanders.

But failure was one thing.

Treason and betrayal, another.

And Lavrentiy Pavlovich Beria was sure to get to the bottom of that. He had already quietly arrested the family of a Lieutenant Ilya Egorov, who had surrendered control of Naples airport to the enemy. There would be more arrests to come. Many more.

But there was no arresting the shitstorm of bad news from the front. The submarine rocket attack on the Americans' Atlantic Fleet had missed more than half of the ships, which had already snuck out to sea. More criminal betrayal there, for a certainty. Meanwhile, the Red Army had lost at least a thousand tanks to the wretched computerised shoulder rockets of the Americans and British. And the workers of the world, at least in Western Europe, had not immediately risen to welcome their liberators and throw off the yoke of their exploiters as the party's theorists had concluded.

Oh, there would be some satisfying arrests coming of that, Beria vowed.

Admirals and generals he needed for now.

Fucking theorists he could do without.

He pushed away his plate, his appetite gone.

If you are scared of wolves, do not go in the woods, his grandmother had taught him. Well, he was in the woods now, thanks to the dribbling idiot Stalin. And much as he might fancy seeking an accommodation for a war he did not even mean to start—it had all been Stalin's idea—Beria knew it would be impossible to broach the question of a ceasefire.

Stalin had ensured that, if nothing else. The assassins he sent after Eisenhower had completed their mission, but the team hunting for the Jew Kolhammer had missed him completely in Paris. So now Beria faced an entirely different opponent in the White House – the very *zasranets* whose arrival in 1942 had so obviously destroyed the future and inevitable triumph of the worker's revolution. Old Joseph Vissarionovich had been right about that, he conceded.

The party's theorists avowed that the impossibility of the

Kolhammer fleet's arrival in 1942 testified to the impossibility of the future from which it had come. A future in which the Soviet Union had ceased to exist.

Such a thing was against the laws of history. The dialectic could not countenance it. And so, his theorists said that something, some force, had broken history in 1942, and now the USSR must shoulder the burden of repairing this great rift by defeating the Allies.

Beria sighed.

Theorists. What did they know?

He stood up, burped again quietly, tasted smoked fish and cream cheese, and left to meet with the Politburo.

THE MAP ROOM was a much grander salon than the General Secretary's office that Beria had taken over. Two rooms had been joined together by demolishing a wall some two centuries earlier. The resulting chamber was vast and could have easily accommodated more than a hundred guests from the Central Committee. Dozens of maps adorned the walls, but they were aesthetic treasures, works of art from the pre-revolutionary period, and trophies captured from the invading Hun during the Great Patriotic War. Arriving in the early evening, Beria was greeted by just eight men, two of them in military uniform.

The Politburo had grown to a seventeen-strong executive in the last years of Stalin's reign, but Beria had thinned out the numbers in the usual manner upon his return from the lake. The two military men were not officially Bureau members. Still, one could not hold a council of war without Marshall of the Armies, Arseny Gorgachev, and General Commander of the Soviet Ground Forces, Fyodor Ogarov. Not unless one fancied being compressed to pink paste under the steel treads of the Kantemirovskaya Tank Division.

The generals, dressed in green combat coveralls, stood at the centre of a clutch of men as Beria entered. Everyone turned toward him, some more obviously anxious than the others. The soldiers did well to hide whatever feelings they might have harboured, his Political Bureau comrades not so much. As radiant and regenerated as Lavrentiy Pavlovich appeared, the surviving Politburo members, Merkulov, Kobulov, Goglidize, Dekanozov, Meshik, and Vlodzimirskiy presented as walking dead men. Cheeks hollow, eyes sunken, the pallor of the grave already draining what little colour usually illuminated their features.

All but glistening with relish, Beria smiled at them as a father upon his favoured sons.

"Comrades," he said, "Thank you for joining me. Your time is valuable, and I appreciate you giving it so freely."

A few of the bolder sort exchanged glances.

What fresh hell was this that Lavrentiy Beria offered soft words and gratitude?

"Please," he said, gesturing at the long table with an open palm. There, reports and contemporary maps detailed the correlation of forces in the current struggle. No electronic devices were allowed. Beria did not trust them. He had heard stories from the future of spies reaching all around the world to pry and snoop inside the electronical devices of their foes. His spies were fast becoming masters of it. "We have much to do," he said. "Please join me."

Pavel Meshik, newly installed as Minister of Internal Affairs, coughed nervously.

"Comrade Secretary..." the Ukrainian started.

"Comrade Provisional Secretary General," Marshall Gorgachev corrected.

"Yes, yes, of course," Meshik corrected himself. "Comrade... Beria," he improvised, "we wonder when the time might come to inform the people of Comrade Stalin's passing—"

Beria smiled again, and Meshik's voice trailed off.

The one-time repairman, who died by firing squad in the world from which Kolhammer had arrived, moved his lips, but no words came.

Beria showed them his empty palms.

"A difficult question in challenging times, comrades. I would seek your counsel on this and much more."

Meshik blinked rapidly.

Marshall Gorgachev frowned. "Do you not know your own mind, Comrade?"

A door opened somewhere to the left, and everyone flinched a little. Beria knew it to be the same door through which Marshall Zhukov would have charged in to arrest him in that other world on 26 June 1953. The broken world where the USSR had fallen. In this world, however, it was merely Prokofyev leading a charwoman with more sandwiches and boiling water for the urn.

"But of course, Marshall, I know my own mind," Beria said, all fairness and humility. "However, I am but one man, and we know from the doctrine that the triumph of the proletariat is guaranteed only by the collective wisdom and struggle of all right-thinking comrades. So, I would seek your advice."

The silence that greeted this was so complete that the rattle of porcelain as the charwoman served fresh tea seemed the only sound in Moscow.

When it was evident that nobody knew what to say, Beria spoke again.

"I think we have had quite enough of one man thinking and speaking and acting for one hundred million, don't you agree?"

Meshik turned nervously, almost desperately, to Gorgachev as if seeking another singular figure to whom he might defer in his thoughts and actions. Gradually, all of the Politburo members did.

Beria's heart was pounding, and he was sure that the pulse in his neck must be visible to everyone, but he kept his face neutral or perhaps even a little expectant.

At last, Marshall of the Armies Arseny Semyon Gorgachev nodded brusquely.

"Da. It is so."

Beria was not so foolish or unpractised at palace intrigue that he let his relief show, but he did gesture towards the long, polished table again.

"Then, let us proceed, comrades. Marshall, perhaps you might know how the people's fighting spirit would be affected by news of Joseph Vissarionovich's untimely demise?"

Gorgachev snorted as he sat down.

"His children are long dead. No others would mourn him."

The collective gasp sounded genuine to Beria. It was not the sentiment that shocked but the free expression of it. He nodded in sage agreement, never taking his eye off the top-ranking soldier.

"Maybe," Beria said, taking his seat. "But that does not mean the former Secretary General cannot serve the party and the motherland even in death. He did us no great service with his intemperate, preemptive attack. Naturally, the correlation of forces remains in our favour, but we should have been dipping our toes into the Atlantic by now. We need to – what is it the uptimers say?—to reboot."

Gorgachev's expression was questioning but not hostile.

"You have a plan, Comrade Secretary?"

"I do," Beria smiled, noting that for the first time, Gorgachev had not insisted on reminding everybody of his provisional status.

"I would ask your indulgence, Comrade Marshall. You have American prisoners of war here in Moscow, yes?"

"We do," Gorgachev confirmed. "A small number, but valuable prisoners. Members of their so-called special forces, captured in the Polish territories."

Beria's smile, never long absent, returned like the morning sun.

"Excellent," he beamed. "Comrades, I have a cunning plan."

30

Slim Jim Davidson was familiar with the wee hours. He loved them because to find himself awake at 3:30 in the morning usually meant he'd been partying like a motherfucker and was only two or three martinis away from gathering up some motley crew of degenerates and perverts to lay siege to the breakfast buffet at one of his nearby casinos. And all of that, preparatory to climbing into bed in the presidential suite with a couple of Hollywood starlets. There was always a nearby casino and inevitably a giggle of starlets until suddenly there wasn't. Now, hunkered down in Robin Hood country, hidden from the cold, electronic eyes of Soviet satellites and the missile swarms they would call down on him, Slim Jim Davidson might as well have been a thousand fucking miles from his nearest casino and all-day breakfast buffet.

He stood, yawning and blinking the sleep from his eyes in the grand entry hall of his baronial Manor House. His head was spinning; he was so goddamn tired from getting up so goddamn early. Sunrise got its ass into gear at an absurd fucking hour at this time of year, but even so, it was dark outside.

"Pretty fucking dark everywhere, you ask me," Slim Jim croaked.

But nobody had asked him. Nobody had spoken to him since Maria O'Brien had checked that he was good to go ten minutes earlier.

Hamilton Manor seethed with activity as the two parties prepared to depart: his entourage, including Maria, a couple of her lackeys, a small security detachment, and Phil Kolhammer's way bigger posse. That crew had grown to nearly a hundred strong over the past week, and Slim Jim had to wonder at the effort needed to keep their presence here a secret. Although yawning and stretching his legs out as he sat in some uncomfortable, ugly-ass hardwood chair, he didn't have to wonder. They might've gone to the mattresses here, but they weren't completely cut off from the world. He'd watched with sneaking amazement as Kolhammer's people had faked out the whole world, pretending he'd arrived back in the States on a flight three days ago.

Fake news, Maria called it, with a smirk that told him she wasn't being completely serious. *Disinformation*, the whiz-kid Josh Ovenden corrected her, furrowing his brow. *Active measures*, said Serge Lazarevski, in his thick Ukrainian accent. It was like they were doing a well-rehearsed vaudeville bit, the way they riffed off each other.

A hell of a thing is what it was, and he was grateful they'd managed to pull it off. As much as he'd quickly come to hate being cooped up in his little Disney castle, he still didn't like the idea of a bunch of Russian rockets dropping on the place, or maybe even a nuke or one of those big-ass orbital sledgehammers they'd thrown down all over Germany.

"Wheels up in five, Mister Davidson," one of his lackeys announced as she hurried past, carrying a computer monitor.

Slim Jim wondered where she was going with it. As far as he knew, they would still be using the Manor as a backup site for the company's headquarters in London. Slim Jim wondered about many things. He had no idea how Phil Kolhammer was getting home, only that the Prez was leaving today at the same time as him, give or take a quarter-hour. His Secret Service guys were all over the place, talking into their suit cuffs and acting as though they expected a bunch of Russian commandos to jump out of the woodwork at any moment. Slim Jim wondered how he would fare, jetting across the Atlantic, which was probably filthy with communist jets flying off Russian aircraft carriers because there was nobody to stop them. The US Atlantic Fleet had been gutted by a single Russian missile boat, they reckoned. There was a hell of a stink about it back home, with that asshole McCarthy blaming Kolhammer for the whole thing—even though Phil had barely had time to scratch his ass in the top job. Even though he'd been banging the drum about Stalin and the Reds for years.

Slim Jim gently massaged his eyeballs which were hot and scratchy with the lack of sleep. Fucking politics. What a shit show.

He tried to get comfortable in the old wooden chair, which looked like some Viking warlord's throne from about a thousand years ago, but every way he leaned or slouched, there seemed to be some knobbly hardwood fist to bore into his back or his ass. He supposed that if he sat there long enough, his butt cheeks might go numb.

He did not get to sit there long enough. A wedge of dark-suited Secret Service goons suddenly emerged from the grey stone archway to his left, a second before Kolhammer appeared behind them. Dude looked like he had slept for a week, even though Slim Jim knew that for a lie because he'd run into the president and his perma-pissed chief of staff, that little Asian tornado, sometime after midnight. So, less than four hours ago.

With Kolhammer came the storm. A full-court press of bodyguards and advisors suddenly filled the entry hall of Hamilton Manor. Where the space had been simply abuzz with the low voices and hurried scuffle of minions rushing about their last-minute duties before the boss man bugged out, the high vaulted stone ceiling now echoed with the dull roar of dozens of voices, all of them vying to be the loudest, most important voice in the room.

Kolhammer had a cell phone pressed to one ear and a finger jammed into the other to block out the background roar. He finished whatever call he was on, saw Slim Jim, and lifted his phone as if in greeting. But he made no move towards his host. His entire caravan trooped through the oversized vestibule, heading for the entrance, which stood open to the night. Slim Jim started raising a hand to wave goodbye, but Kolhammer had already passed.

He tried not to get cut up about that. The guy was busier than a bricklayer in Berlin, for sure. But it was hard not to feel a little disappointed. They'd smashed a few beers together that first night he was here and made a pretty good session of it, too. He'd only caught ten minutes with the big guy after that. In the kitchen again, as it happened, about two days later. The Hammer was pounding another late-night sandwich and a bottle of lager from the local pub. He'd invited Slim Jim in past the Secret Service cordon, which had thickened up heaps in just forty-eight hours, and they'd talked about their favourite beers and sandwiches, as you do. Turned out Kolhammer, like Slim Jim, was a fool for barbecue. But he preferred his brisket Texas style. Slim Jim was more of a North Carolina whole hog fan. He'd got the taste for it in Greensboro before his chain gang sojourn.

Fond memories of slow pork and red gravy were lost as Maria O'Brien called out to him over the hubbub.

"Let's roll, Jimbo."

He had trouble locating her in the crush of people and had to climb up to stand on his old Viking throne to pick her out of the crowd. He was waving to her over their heads when everyone seemed to stop. That's when he heard the beeping and the ringtones and all the alarms on the electronic devices everybody but him seemed to be carrying. He'd never seen so many people packing so much handheld gadgetry in such a small place. It wasn't just the Washington types. His people were all checking their phones, tablets, and pagers, and Slim Jim felt himself marooned for a second. A single man on the island he had made the antique chair, staring out across a sea of peeps suddenly transfixed by whatever news they'd just received.

"Holy shit," somebody said into the sudden quiet, setting off the swell of voices again.

It took him a few seconds to determine what they were talking about, but one phrase was repeated often enough to break through the uproar.

"Stalin's dead."

Slim Jim blinked and shook his head, searching for confirmation.

"Stalin's dead."

"He's dead."

A dozen different voices chorused again and again.

They sounded almost dreamily hopeful, and a lot of folks were looking to Kolhammer as if to confirm this was his doing. But Slim Jim could see that it was not. The big guy seemed as surprised as anyone. Looked unhappy with it, too, holding out his phone, which looked like an old uptime model, towards Lazarevski, his national security guy.

The tattooed Ukrainian just shook his head as the tumult quickly grew.

Fuck this, Slim Jim thought.

He jumped down from his perch and pushed through the press of the crowd into the drawing room that sat off the entry hall. Or at least it used to be a drawing room. First thing he'd done when he got here, to the complete fucking horror of Bob, his maximum butler, was turn the joint into a personal sports bar. He had four of the most giant screen TVs you could get in there, all plugged into his satellite network. There was a beer fridge and an intercom running through the kitchen so he could order some spicy chicken wings to go with his beer and whatever game he could pull down off his network.

He didn't completely close the door shut behind him, but enough to block out some of the noise from the entry hall. Lined with bookshelves and lavishly carpeted, the room was much quieter than the crowded stone vault outside. The screens were dark, but Slim Jim grabbed a remote and powered up the nearest set. He clicked away from a replay—the Giants and the Dodgers, it looked like—and quickly found the local news channel. There was only one. The BBC.

Some dude in a three-piece suit was reading from a piece of paper.

"...The new premier, Mister Beria, condemned the attack as murder, not war, and vowed that all the Soviet peoples would rise in anger..."

"The fuck he say?"

Slim Jim turned to the familiar voice.

Lia Pao, Kolhammer's Chief of Staff, had pushed into the drawing room and behind her, the boss himself. And behind him, a phalanx of Secret Service guys holding back the crowd.

"What was that?" Kolhammer asked. "What'd he say about Beria?"

"I just turned it on, man," Slim Jim said. "Gimme a second here."

He used the remote again, jacking up the volume until they could hear the announcer.

"...The footage, supplied by the Kremlin, has not been verified by British sources... but it appears to show the scene of a raid on a house, said to be occupied by the former Soviet leader."

They watched a Red Army officer lead the camera through what passed for lavish accommodations in the USSR. It looked like a fucking dump to Slim Jim, even before the place got torn up in a firefight. You could see the damage plain as day. Shattered glass. Bullet holes and scorch marks. Ruined furniture everywhere.

The Russian officer spoke to the camera, but an English voice provided the translation.

"The American gangster forces..."

"What?" Lia Pao said.

"...parachuted into Comrade Stalin's personal retreat, where he had gone to reduce the threat of American missiles targeting him in Moscow and killing many innocents there..."

"Bullshit," Kolhammer said.

"...but traitors and recidivists gave away his location to the enemy, and gangster commandos attacked."

The camera turned to an outside view of the two-storey dacha, showing smoke still pouring from the upper floor.

"American assassins fell upon Comrade Stalin," the translator went on, "and despite the best efforts of the Secretary's General bodyguards, who died to a man to protect the Rodina, we have lost our greatest leader."

The image changed, and Slim Jim asked, "Who's that asshole?" as a doughy-faced man, bald and pouchy but staring at the camera with the black, calculating eyes of a prison shithouse rat, spoke in thick guttural Russian. Translated again by the BBC.

On-screen text identified him as Provisional Secretary General of the Communist Party, Lavrentiy Beria.

"The counter-revolutionary operatives were admitted to the

homeland through the connivance of traitors within the Party," Beria said. "Most of them have been liquidated. But collaborators remain at large, and all loyal citizens must remain vigilant. All traitors and their lackeys will be tried by the people's courts and feel the people's wrath, starting with the American gangster forces and their British henchmen."

Lia Pao and the president swore as the camera cut away to video of Allied servicemen, apparently captured on the grounds of Stalin's dacha, lined up against a wall of the retreat to be executed by firing squad.

31

"These people could sleep through the end of the bloody world," Harry complained.

He peered out through a crack in the wooden shutters, squinting into the piazza, where the fierce light of the afternoon reflected off white stucco walls with dazzling intensity. Nothing moved out there. The last patrol of British commandos had passed through about ten minutes earlier, their hobnailed boots crunching on the cobblestone streets and sending a cloud of seagulls into the cloudless sky. Since then, stillness.

"Is fine," Ivanov said. "We cannot move without being seen. Skarov cannot move without being seen. Soon enough, it will be time, and we will all move together."

The former Spetsnaz operator lay in a hammock on the other side of the small room, drinking tea from a steel cup and nodding to himself as he read a James Bond novel. *From Russia with Love.*

Harry twitched aside a sun-faded curtain and returned to scoping out the town square. A modest church stood at the other end of the open space; its doors open onto a dark interior. A dozen market stalls, ramshackle constructions of sackcloth and driftwood, stood quietly in front of the church, their wares were offered to the world, but the stall owners were asleep behind the counters. Santa Teresa took its daily siesta seriously.

The bars and cafes, which roared with life in the evening, stood shuttered and mute in the heat of day. Seagulls turned lazy circles in the flawless blue sky above the sleeping township. It was hard to believe that a titanic struggle raged somewhere just over the horizon.

"He's not going to just walk past while you're standing there, gazing out the window, you know," Charlotte said. Her voice was loud. She was talking over the music in her ears.

They had been waiting for three days now, after two days of hard travel through the mountains and along the coast and unlike Ivanov, Charlotte was not content to sit quietly reading a book. She had pushed aside what little furniture occupied the room—a wooden table and two chairs, an old moth-eaten sofa—and was putting her downtime to use polishing up a series of kata exercises that Harry thought he recognised. Viv had probably taught them to her. She wore earbuds, which trailed a thin white wire down into some music player or possibly even a cell phone she wore at her hip. There was no cell service in Santa Teresa. There wasn't much coverage outside the larger capital cities surrounding the Mediterranean. But Harry had to admit that she dealt with enforced isolation much better than he.

The worst of his injuries from Cairo were starting to heal. His bruising, a livid purple horror show, was fading to yellow. The various scratches and scrapes had all scabbed over and were itching deep inside—the familiar discomfort of damaged flesh repairing itself. But there was no salve for the frustration and annoyance he felt. The guilt, too. They had gone dark as soon as they had left Cagliari, and he still did not know whether Jules had made it back to England and, if she had, who might be seeing to her care now. MI6, he supposed, or was it just that he hoped they would?

He was about to say something intemperate and probably quite stupid in reply to Charlotte when they all turned towards the sound of the back door scraping opening and banging closed.

Bautista had returned.

Harry let the curtain fall closed. Charlotte pulled the tiny white buds out of her ears and turned off the furious uptime rap music she had been playing. Harry wondered how she'd been able to follow anything with that rubbish pounding away. Ivanov closed his paperback.

Bautista appeared with a string bag containing food and a bottle of wine. He unpacked everything on the small wooden table Charlotte had pushed aside to make room for her exercise.

"I have news," he said as he laid out two breadsticks, a couple of wedges of hard cheese wrapped in waxed paper, salami, and the wine.

The mountain man unwrapped the cheese and cut a small piece for himself, which he ate with a heel of bread torn off one of the baguettes.

"My cousin Pedru, he works on a trawler in Porto Quadro," he said around a mouthful of bread and cheese. "He tells me of a Russian this morning attempting to buy passage to Marseille for himself and one other. This will be your man, I believe."

All three of them came alert at the news.

"No, this could be our man," Ivanov corrected him. "Or it could be someone Skarov has paid to lay a trail away from his true location and intent."

Bautista shrugged off the suggestion.

"Yes, it could be. But if so, this other Russian who treats with Murtas would still have a connection to your Russian. If we take him, we capture the one you seek, or perhaps just one who knows him."

They gathered around the small wooden table and began to pick at the food. Not wanting to alert Skarov to their presence in Santa Teresa, neither Harry, Charlotte, nor Ivanov had been free to wander the little port, searching for the NKVD man or his prisoner, Professor Bremmer. Instead, they had relied on Bautista and his seemingly endless extended family of cousins, second cousins, and in-laws to do the legwork for them.

Harry did not doubt the Sardinian clansman was more than up to the task of quietly tracking down a fugitive communist spy and his captive. However, having had to rely solely on another to do that work had added to his sense of powerlessness and impatience.

Ivanov tossed away the dregs of his black tea, pulled the cork on the bottle of red wine, and poured himself a solid slug. He pushed a handful of dried sausage meat into his mouth, chewed it briefly and washed it down with the cheap plonk.

"Do you know yet where Skarov is hiding?" he asked.

Bautista shook his head.

"No, but we do know he has secured passage with Frantziscu Murtas. Sorgono scum," he added with a fatalistic gesture meant to convey the pointlessness of wondering at the depths to which anybody from the accursed village of Sorgono might sink.

"So we grab them up getting on to the boat," Charlotte suggested. "Or we sink the boat after they get on. I'm good with either."

She was methodically reducing a hunk of bread to tiny, bite-sized pieces, which she ate, one after the other, with the cheese.

Harry poured himself a cup of wine and cut a hunk of salami away with a folding knife. Now that they had some action in prospect, his appetite and motivation had come roaring back.

"We could just snipe Skarov, couldn't we," he said. "Then swoop in to put old mate Prof in the bag and hand him to the garrison to look after. Job done. On to Marseille."

Both Charlotte and Ivanov answered at once, each with an emphatic "No."

Harry blinked, taken aback. Bautista snorted as though amused.

"This for you is work, yes, Highness?" he said. "But for these two, personal, I think."

"You're fucking right it's personal," Charlotte said with real vehemence. "Harry, that Skarov prick murdered Viv and the rest of my crew. Remember Viv, your mate? Did you forget that Skarov shot him down like a wounded dog? He's not getting away with a clean headshot. He needs to know it's over for him and why. He needs to know that one of Viv's people came for him."

Harry stopped with a piece of bread and cheese halfway to his mouth.

"Are you serious? This isn't a bloody game, Charlotte."

But Ivanov growled, "It is the only game. The little girl is correct. I have more reason to settle with this man. We will get your Professor away. But Skarov is for me to finish."

"Hey," Charlotte said, smacking him hard in the chest with a backhander. "Little girl with a legit vendetta here, pal. You're not hogging all the vengeful goodness for yourself."

Ivanov stared at her as if he might put her down simply for complicating things, but then he grunted and nodded once.

"You have good reason. We will do this together. You have earned that."

"We were always doing this together," Harry said, exasperation getting the better of him. "But we are a hostage rescue party, not a bunch of fucking villains and gangsters. We'll kill Skarov if that makes it easier to get Bremmer. But understand now that you won't be carving him up for chum on the docks. It will be a clean kill."

Bautista shook his head at this.

"Nothing here is clean."

They all looked at him.

"My cousin says Frantziscu Murtas is not just paid to transport your men to Marseille. He is paid a great sum to get this professor to the communists if anything happens to the Russian. And to kill the professor if this is not possible. Although, less money for dead professor. More for live one with communists in Marseille."

WITH TWILIGHT, a new world was born in Santa Teresa. The change came gradually as the sun fell towards the horizon and shadows stretched across the town square. Local villagers appeared from late afternoon to take their daily stroll, a ritual practised in towns and cities around the Mediterranean for hundreds, possibly thousands of years. New to Santa Teresa were the outsiders drawn to the little port since the end of the last war.

Less than an hour's ferry ride to the north, Corsica lay divided between Allied and Soviet control, with the line of demarcation straggling through the island's mountainous heart. Protected from the reach of Moscow by the warm waters of the broad channel running between the two islands, Santa Teresa had benefited greatly from a construction boom after the war, building a small constellation of surveillance facilities. The domes and arrays all pointed north, gathering intelligence from occupied France. Harry wondered how long it would be before Russian rockets or fighter bombers sought them out.

The construction workers had gone, but hundreds of spooks, operators, conspirators, and mercenaries still passed through Santa Teresa, moving to and from the frontline in the civilisational divide between the free world and its greatest adversary. Bautista said there were hundreds more here now, most having arrived from Cagliari or the Italian mainland in the last few days. The small British garrison was expected to be reinforced by NATO, but no support had come. Most of the Russians and Eastern Bloc contractors had fled or been rounded up. However, Santa Teresa was a frontier town, and its ancient streets and irregular little neighbourhood blocks were almost certainly still crawling with hostile outsiders.

Back at the window of their little bolt hole, a cottage owned by another of Bautista's relatives, Harry watched the piazza and the streets beyond it come alive again. When they had the cover of sufficient crowds, he and Ivanov would move to a lay-up point in anticipation of grabbing up Skarov. Charlotte, afforded greater freedom of movement by her gender and a simple disguise, could go now.

"How do I look?" she asked.

Harry closed the curtain and turned back to the hot, airless room. Charlotte was dressed in the blue and white habit of a Sister of Charity, an order that maintained a small orphanage a few miles south of town. Rather than Bautista, Ivanov provided the connection; some history with the Mother Superior, which he resolutely would not disclose.

"Like a bride of Christ," the Russian said. "You have equipment?"

Charlotte hiked up her thick skirt to reveal a handgun in a thigh holster. She pulled back her blue coif and the white cotton wimple under it. A wire ran from an earbud down into her collar.

"Channel 5," she said, indicating the small tactical radio on the table where Ivanov was methodically shelling and eating pistachios.

"Now, Charlotte—" Harry started.

"No, Harry," she cut him off. "I don't need the lecture. I'm just going to recon the ex-fil point. If I scope out Skarov or Bremmer, I will call it in and wait for you. Nothing more."

Harry regarded her somewhat sceptically, but there was little he could do. It would help immensely to have eyes on the dock where Murtas's trawler had moored, and the Sisters were known for tending to the souls of the poor fishermen of Santa Teresa. And sometimes to their children if the men did not return from the sea. Charlotte's presence on the waterfront would not draw hostile attention.

"Your cover?" Harry asked. "You know, in case someone gets curious?"

"My French is better than my Italian, so I am Sister Charlotte," she explained, adding a slightly Gallic twist to her accent. "Keeping it simple. Orphaned during the war. Raised by the Sisters in an American-run refugee camp. Took the cloth just last year."

"It will do," Ivanov said, popping another pistachio into his mouth. "I know these nuns well. They have sisters from all over the world. She will pass."

"Best get on with it then," Harry said. "Don't linger. Don't try to get on the boat. Just settle the tactical situation and report back."

"I would say 'yes, sir,' but you're not my fucking boss," Charlotte pushed back. "And you haven't done this work seriously in years. I have. So maybe you could have a little faith and let me do my job. Like on that Russian freighter."

Harry bristled and almost bit back on the taunt. After all, she hadn't saved Julia, and she hadn't captured or killed Skarov. But he knew his irritation was not with Charlotte but with himself. She was right. He had not been seriously challenged by operational demands since the end of the war. That part of his life had been over for a long time. He'd fallen arse backwards into the work for MI6, and nothing about that had gone smoothly. That's why they were all hunkered down in some Sardinian backwater, hoping they might get a chance to clean up the mess he'd made in Cairo.

"I'm sorry," Harry said at last. "You're right, Charlotte. I used to do this work. But I don't anymore. I'm not up to speed. I'm not as sharp as you," he added for Ivanov's benefit.

The Russian shrugged, cracking open another pistachio, but Harry went on.

"I want to get Professor Bremmer back. It's my fault we lost him. It's unfinished work. I want to make good on that, then get on with the job in Marseille. The sooner it's done, the sooner I can get back to my fiancée."

The young woman looked like she was about to cut him down again, but her features softened unexpectedly.

"I'm sorry," she said. "As bad as you feel about Bremmer, I feel worse about Viv and the others. It's not just a loose end I have to tidy up. I have to settle with Skarov for them. All of them. I'm..." she struggled to find the words.

"You're the only one left," Ivanov supplied after she had gone a while without saying anything. "You feel this in here." He made a fist and thumped it into his chest, just under his heart. "I know this pain. This sickness."

"Yeah," Harry sighed. "Viv was my mate, too, Charlotte. He was a good bloke. And he only ever took the best." He smiled almost apologetically at her. "I understand. They were all good people. The best."

"We all have reason to settle with Colonel-General Skarov," Pavel Ivanov growled from across the room. "But he is not such an easy man to kill. Or even to find. We all know this, too. It is for all of us, personal and professional. Let us do this professionally, then, and when it is done, those who live will take what personal satisfaction they can and toast the memories of those who cannot."

"Cheers to that," Harry said.

Charlotte adjusted her costume, tucking a stray hair inside the headdress along with the insulated wire from the radio.

"I better go. It's time."

Ivanov nodded, "The Mother Superior says to take Via Genova and Via del Porto. None of her little sisters will be there today. Collect your coins for the orphans from the sailors at the marina. Do not converse with them. Observe only. And return with the coins to Saint Michael's. We will meet you there."

She did not object to taking instruction from Ivanov, and Harry supposed it was because the Russian, unlike him, was the real deal. He had earned her respect.

She slipped out of the rear door without saying goodbye.

"It is busy out there soon, yes," Ivanov said, raising his eyes to the window through which Harry had been observing the main square.

Harry twitched aside the curtain briefly and scanned the piazza. A few bars were open, and a scattering of the locals and foreign workers occupied tables in front of cafes serving aperitivo. It was as though the war did not exist.

"Getting there," Harry said.

"Bautista will be here soon. Charlotte François will report on what she finds. Then we will go."

32

Hard to believe uptimers thought nuns were so fucking sexy they dressed up in habits at Halloween and shit. But there were plenty of things Charlotte François found hard to believe about the future, even as she desperately wanted to. She slipped out of the cool of the little, white-washed stone cottage and into the baking heat of a narrow laneway behind, trying to put aside such thoughts and any confusion about what she had to do next.

Weirdly, it'd been easier when she was a little girl, a prisoner of the Japanese at Camp 5. Held captive by monsters, her parents dead, life as she remembered it then was a brutally simple struggle to live. In Camp 5, brutality and simplicity were the twin poles around which all revolved.

It was probably why she'd been drawn so strongly to Margie-Mom, her adopted mother, the combat physician who'd marched into camp and straight-up executed the handful of Japanese officers who remained. A righteous kill, in Charlotte François's maturing opinion. And an act of justified retribution recorded for all time by a young embed named Julia Duffy.

These memories were what Charlotte had instead of a happy childhood, at least until Margie François gathered her up.

Thirteen years later, picking her way along the cobblestones, staying close to the shaded side of the alley, her fingertips brushed against the reassuring weight of the pistol under her heavy skirts. She wouldn't be winning any quick-draw competitions in this outfit, but hopefully, she would not need the weapon. Not yet. Even in the shade, the power of the day's heat was staggering. Flies buzzed around small, stinking garbage piles, and a black cat nervously swiped its tail back and forth as she passed by.

Stepping out into the full glare of the late afternoon sun, Charlotte raised one hand to shield her eyes, squinting at the fierce Mediterranean light. She could've used some powered goggles, a nice set of vintage Oakley's, or even an augmented pair of HP Combat Optics, but that would give the game away.

The laneway delivered her to the quietest corner of the piazza, between a small leather goods store and an empty shop that had once sold uptime books and movies, almost certainly pirated, to construction workers and defence contractors. She could hear the leather-worker at his trade, banging rivets into a belt or something. The muffled *tink* of a small hammer striking metal studs was the loudest noise at this end of the square. Most of the cafes and bars were cantoned at the far end, gathered around an old Roman fountain from which the townspeople still drew fresh water. Four cherubs riding bronzed sunfish happily pissed long streams of sparkling spring water into the wide stone bowl of the fountain. Rainbows danced faintly in the spray.

Charlotte slipped out of the piazza at the southeast corner, strolling, nodding, and smiling at everyone who offered her the greetings of La Passeggiata. She kept it simple, returning a quiet "Bona sera" in the local dialect to anybody who wished her a good evening. But she inflected her words with a noticeable French lilt. The townspeople much preferred Sardu, the ancient Romanesque language closer to the oldest forms of Latin than modern Italian. A bit like the Welsh, she imagined, who could speak perfect English but might decide not to if they felt like messing with your head.

The long day's heat had baked deeply into the crumbling stucco walls and riverstone cobbles. After a couple of minutes, sweat started leaking from her armpits. The nun's habit Ivanov had procured for her was a heavy garment of coarse cotton. Within moments of putting it on, Charlotte itched terribly, and that was before her sweat soaked into the fabric, causing it to cling tighter to her skin. *It was baffling*, she thought, the shit women would put up with. Many of the older women of Santa Teresa wore their Sunday best for passeggiata, dark, heavy dresses which must have been as uncomfortable as her Sexy Sister cosplay outfit. The younger women, those of her generation and late adolescence, had not quite embraced the design language of uptime fashion. You couldn't get away with that sort of wanton, libertine display outside of California or some of the larger global hubs like London or Paris. But Charlotte smiled to see some local girls at least edging in that direction. A slightly higher hemline here or a more daring, fitted blouse there. To them, she would look archaic. Medieval retrogression. To her targets as well, she hoped.

The foot traffic thinned out a block from the piazza, and the storefronts started trending more functional and maritime as she drew closer to the waterfront. Machinists, fishnet repairs, and even a sailmaker replaced the cafes and wine bars clustered around the town square. She could hear the squawking of gulls and taste the brine and salt of the morning's catch in the air. War or no, the shrimp trawlers and lobstermen would be heading out soon, beating into the swell as the sun fell away and the stars took dominion in the heavens. Murtas ran a shrimp boat. And on that boat, according to Bautista, he ran cigarettes, whisky, a little dope and smack, and the occasional passenger looking to get off the island without the bother of customs and immigration.

Charlotte kept to the shaded side of the street, where the temperature was at least bearable. She told herself to stop bitching about the uncomfortable disguise. After all, it was nowhere near as bad as the filthy, sweat-stained battledress and weighted pack she had worn during her last evaluation. She knew, being honest, that she mostly felt uncomfortable in the nun's habit because it symbolised the antithesis of everything she thought she wanted to be. Or at least, she had thought so until she'd watched Skarov murder Viv and the others in Cairo.

A vivid and visceral memory of the Russian putting two bullets into Viv's face filled her whole world, blotting out the pleasant little seaside village of Santa Teresa and replacing it wholly with the darkened docks of Port Said. Charlotte staggered and had to lean against a shop-front window to catch her balance and breath. The pavement seemed to tilt slightly beneath her feet, threatening to spill her over.

"Sister? Sister, you right, luv?"

The man spoke in English, with a thick London accent, confusing Charlotte, who imagined she might have passed out and come to, hallucinating a reunion with Viv, her old boss and mentor. She blinked rapidly and took a deep breath, forcing herself not to react when she felt a strong pair of hands take her by the upper arm. She was leaning against a rusted steel gate protecting a small marine engineering shop.

"Sister, come on. You need to sit down, luv, out of the heat," the same voice said.

She saw him now through the swirl of dizzy colours and disorientation. A sergeant, as Viv had once been. But this man was much younger, somewhere in his early twenties, like her. And he was light-skinned, almost painfully so. The harsh Mediterranean sun had recently given him a bad burn. Dead skin flaked and peeled away from his neck. Charlotte was staring, dialled in so tight on the sun damage to his thick, red neck that she couldn't imagine how she might pull out again.

"I am okay now, thank you, Sergeant," she croaked, still affecting that French accent to stay in character. Her training ran deep. Maintain cover, no matter what.

"I walked in from the orphanage because I missed the bus," she said weakly. "It was foolish but...you know...I have to...for the children."

She raised the small cloth bag that she carried. A handful of coins jingled inside it.

Her head had stopped spinning, and her vision was no longer blurred at the edges. She knew what this was. No sense denying it.

PTSD.

One of the soldiers—she saw now there were four of them—fanned her with a folded map. Another offered his canteen.

"It's nice and cold, ma'am," the young squaddie promised. "I filled it from the fridge in the mess hall. Haven't had much more'n a sip and no backwash, promise."

"Don't give her that, Nobby. It's all backwash, and if it's not, she'll get a bloody headache, you keep that stuff so cold."

The canteen was in front of Charlotte's face.

The soldier had scrounged a neoprene cover from somewhere. Not standard issue. But good for keeping his water cold in summer. It was sweating with cool condensation.

They were with the British occupation force on Sardinia. A four-man squad from the company posted to Santa Teresa. *Nice work if you could get it*, she thought, considering what was happening on the continent.

Charlotte took the cold water with sincere thanks. She sipped at the canteen carefully, holding a mouthful for a few seconds before swallowing it. Long enough to let it warm up a little so that she didn't shock herself with the sudden cold spike. She didn't need another neurological episode right now. As she recovered, she took in the details of the men who had stopped to help her. According to the name tag in his breast pocket, the sergeant's name was Chisholm. They were men of the Royal Sussex Regiment. None looked old enough to be veterans of the last war, but they were about to become veterans of this one if they should live through it.

Charlotte took another swig from the canteen, downing this mouthful a little quicker as she hastened to pull herself together. It would be easy to reveal that she was a contractor for a private military corporation recently nationalised by Her Majesty's Government. It would be simple enough to explain that she and her colleagues, including the once-upon-a-time HRH Prince Harry, were in hot pursuit of an NKVD agent and his prisoner, a German rocket scientist. Given how she felt right now, it would be tempting to turn the whole thing over to the commanding officer of the Royal Sussex Regiment and let him figure it out.

The CO would undoubtedly be a 'him'. Hemlines moved up

much faster than women in this world, even as profoundly changed as it was.

But it would also be as dumb a move as she could make. They had discussed this very option, calling on the resident NATO forces to help in the search for Skarov and Bremmer. And all three had agreed the idea was a non-starter. The Sovs' top field agent would have little to no trouble evading any net thrown out by a bunch of ham-fisted squaddies, and the chaos and turmoil that would accompany a door-to-door search by the military would almost certainly provide the cover Skarov needed to make good his escape.

No, they agreed; this job required a stiletto, not a splitting maul.

"I am feeling better now. Thank you, Sergeant," Charlotte said. "It was just the heat and thirst. I did not drink enough water before setting out."

"You need to carry water with you all the time, Sister," the young man who had offered his canteen said.

His name tag read 'Finter'.

"Thank you, Private Finter," she said. "This is true, yes."

"Derek, Sister," he said, grinning madly. "Me name's Derek."

"Well, thank you, Derek," Charlotte said in her soft French accent, causing Private Finter's squad mates to rip him without mercy.

"That'll be enough, Finter," Sergeant Chisholm said over the banter and teasing. "That'll be enough from all of you."

He softened his voice to speak to Charlotte again.

"If you are feeling better, ma'am, we might get on with our patrol. There's not much happening, but the Russians aren't far away. And a few of the buggers were in town before the MPs threw a bag on them. You never know if a few holdouts are lurking around, looking to cause trouble."

"No, Sergeant, you never do," Charlotte agreed. She took in a deep breath, slowly and carefully. The dizziness was gone. Her vision was clear. Viv no longer haunted her. "I will be fine now. I will see to the collection down at the docks and be sure to drink plenty of water. I hope you have a quiet evening. It is terrible what is happening, is it not?"

"It's terrible that we're stuck here," one of the other soldiers said. "Hardly seems fair, Sarge, missing out on the action."

"I'll give you all the action you need, Walsh, if you don't leave it out with that rubbish. Your job's here. Don't fuck it up by letting your head drift off somewhere else. Pardon my French, Sister," he added hurriedly.

Charlotte smiled.

"Your French is just fine, Sergeant Chisholm," she smiled. "And I too, must be on my way. For the orphans," she said, jingling her coin pouch again. It was just for show, but to her surprise, Chisholm pulled out a few coins and offered them to her. Perhaps shamed by their sergeant's generosity or more likely looking to curry favour with a pretty, young woman, even one they could never have, the other men added their contributions.

Charlotte felt oddly embarrassed to take the money.

But she thanked them for it, and they parted ways.

THE SAFE HOUSE was a bunker of grey cement blocks and corrugated iron, starting to rust in the salt air. It sat alone, halfway along a small headland at the end of the empty beach. There was only one road in, and he had reliable men watching it. Aleksandr Dmitry Skarov, Colonel-General of the People's Commissariat for Internal Affairs, scowled at the tiny cove in front of the bunker. The white sand blazed in the late afternoon sun, like a silver scimitar discarded by some long-dead God during the age of heroes. In another time, he knew, it would be full of witless pleasure-seekers and the parasites who lived off them. The headland where his safe house stood alone among the dunes and clumps of seagrass would be crusted thick with the dachas of capitalists and their enablers in global finance. But in the here and the now, at the only possible time and place, it was deserted.

And still, he scowled.

The small lagoon was sheltered from the swells and shifting currents of the ocean by the crooked finger of land on which he stood. Strange, almost eerily organic rock forms made for a complex littoral environment through which he would soon make his escape with the package. But it was also a point of vulnerability, was it not? Others could sneak in if he could get out of Sardinia through that otherworldly playground of smoothly misshapen rocks and treacherous undertows. He was close, so close to completing this mission, and yet he knew from long and sometimes bitter experience that the most disastrous failures often fell upon you at the very end, with victory in sight.

"Boss, he's coming around. You want me to dose him up or let him come to?"

Skarov checked his watch. A brushed-steel timepiece of Swiss design. It was expensive, but he had to fit in.

Two hours to go.

"Let him wake up. Give him the antagonist dose if you have to. I want him compliant when we move."

"Yes, boss," the Romanian replied.

He disappeared inside the blockhouse, and Skarov let him go without further instruction. Petrescu was reliable and intelligent. Not just another Securitate cutthroat.

Skarov went back to staring into the glassy waters of the lagoon as if, through force of will, he might compel Ivanov to reveal himself. The *podonok* son of a bitch was nearby. Skarov could almost smell the stink of corruption and criminality drifting off him. It would have pleased him no end to have seen to the traitorous dog's demise personally, but such an indulgence could not be. He had his mission, and the mission was everything. Especially now.

Glowering darkly at the shoreline, Skarov turned away from the beauty of the outside world, returning to the damp darkness of the bunker.

The safe house, to the best of his knowledge, remained uncompromised. The owner, a grain merchant in the capital of Cagliari, with whom the People's Commissariat had done business before, could not now give them away to the authorities, should an instant of momentary courage or conscience overcome him. He was one of the first loose ends Skarov had tied up after arriving in Sardinia.

No, if the threat were to come, it would come from Ivanov and his lackeys: the parasite Windsor and the American whore, François, who had all but brought him to ruin in Cairo. So dangerous had been her intervention that he had requested an immediate work-up from the *residentura* before leaving Egypt. She was, it seemed, a fascinating creature of a sort one did not often find in the soft materialist culture of the West, a Baba Yaga, a creator-destroyer, deformed and ferocious on the inside but presenting to the world a comely aspect. That one, he knew, would be the deadliest because she would be masked as the least threatening. Windsor, he dismissed as a buffoon.

Inside, the simple two-room structure was pungent with the aroma of cured tobacco. The soft-cocks and girly men of the European governing classes having outlawed all but the mildest cigarettes, a lucrative contraband trade had naturally emerged. The former owner of this small, undeclared outpost had made a modest fortune supplying southern Italy with Turkish tobacco. A business on which he had paid neither customs, excise, nor income tax, an oversight that made him vulnerable to the merest pressure applied at just the right point.

Skarov weaved his way through the hessian bags and tea chests, moving toward the sound of low voices in the backroom where Professor Ernst Bremmer struggled under the heavy hand of addiction. The German's voice was cracked and wheedling as he begged for more medicine—a synthetic opioid developed from a Chinese formula that came through the Emergence on the Indonesian ship, *Sutanto*. Researchers of the Functional Projects Bureau had tweaked the formula even further. It was extremely addictive, so dangerously destructive to all who received it that Comrade Director Beria himself had judged it too hazardous to release into the black markets of the West. He had cautioned that it would be akin to an act of war, and for a wonder, Stalin had agreed.

"Only fools go to war by accident," the old man said.

And what an irony that was.

This great struggle of the workers against their overlords was beset on all sides by accident, miscalculation, and strife.

Skarov nodded to find Petrescu ministering closely to the needs of the dope-sick rocket scientist. He could see from the uncapped syringe lying in the stainless-steel tray on the table next to the bed that Petrescu had not administered the antagonist dose, which would flush all traces of the opioid from Bremmer's body. That was good. It was better to let the man come naturally to what was left of his senses. There was always the risk with a sudden reversal of the subject going into shock. There had been enough missteps and blunders. Skarov had no desire to add to them. Not with everything so unsettled.

He watched Petrescu nursing their captive like the Securitate man was a matron in a newborn ward and Bremmer a delicate, premature child. This part of the operation at least seemed to be in hand. The German would agree to anything to secure the promise of another taste for himself. It hardly mattered his family were being held to guarantee his cooperation. Having watched the man for a week, Skarov was convinced he would give up his wife and children for the simple promise of another shot. Rendering him into the custody of the commissariat at a safe harbour on the mainland would be the least of his challenges from now on.

More difficult was to figure a way forward that did not see him, Skarov, blamed for the failure of the pre-emptive strike in Europe.

It was, of course, insane that he should shoulder any blame. He was not a scientist, he was not a general of the rocket forces, and he had no operational responsibility for any part of the disaster which had unfolded from the moment Stalin had decided to go to war. And yet, of course, he would be blamed. He had not delivered Bremmer before the launch. He had yet to learn what contribution the German would have made. Most likely, none. The man was a pacifist. That was his whole identity. And while identities can be shattered and remade, that transformation takes time. Months in the cells of the Lubyanka for a start. Not weeks or days, which Beria would have had, even on the original timetable.

Petrescu dipped a hand cloth into a water bowl, squeezed it out and dabbed at Bremmer's forehead. The German muttered something, which Skarov missed, but he did see Petrescu pat the man gently on the shoulder and whisper promises of deliverance or salvation or something to him. Another needle full of Chinese narcotics, probably.

He resisted the urge to recheck his watch.

It was but a few minutes after the last time he had checked.

Murtas would be taking on the decoy soon.

Ivanov would surely reveal himself.

And Aleksandr Dmitry Skarov would be rid of the vermin for good.

33

Captain Jochen Boosfeld was briefing his assembled platoon leaders in a small clearing; the front was close. Like some tremendous subterranean beast, it pulsed, roared, and stuttered, shaking the whole earth. Their line was broken in a hundred places. The Red Army was surging, headed west, devouring all in its path. It had taken two precious days to move all the pieces into place on the giant chessboard of western Germany, but the first Dutch Corps was finally ready to strike the Soviet salient on the northern flank. Boosfeld's division, the 3rd Armoured, would lead the assault. *How very different from the last war*, he thought, *when all the Dutch were good for was fucking, one way or another*. He kept the thought to himself, however. These young fellows he now called comrades were not the *Alte Kameraden* of the last war. They were not so comfortable with certain old-fashioned thoughts or words.

Still, they had fought well so far.

"Our initial objective is the town of Baunatal," he said, pointing out the tiny settlement on the map spread before him. His company leadership had clustered around the big square of folded paper, which Boosfeld had laid out on the hood of a jeep and held down with tins of Spam. A dim red light lit all of their faces in the dark. They looked like killer angels.

"We will cut Highway 44 here," he said, drawing on the map with a wax pencil. "Precluding Soviet high-speed movement and resupply along their northern flank."

A platoon leader spoke up.

"Understood, Herr Kapitan. Supporting fire and air?"

Jochen glanced over at the lieutenant, a promising youngster named Strohmeyer. This was his first sip of the old wine. A rich red drop it would be, too.

"There are Dutch 155 batteries out there, Lieutenant. Brigade controls them. Also, we have limited air support from US and British units, but they are heavily engaged. Whether they are available upon contact, who can say? Assume the worst and dare the devil to disappoint you. I can say that your air support is much better than I had in the last war, and here I am, as pretty as ever."

The men laughed, perhaps dutifully, but he did not care. Only dead men and the defeated could not raise a laugh.

Boosfeld paused.

"We are German soldiers," he said. "And the Fatherland demands we do our duty here. To fight. To win. Now, to your vehicles, gentlemen. Good hunting and good luck."

The small group responded with a round of quiet affirmations.

"Jawohl!"

"Okay!"

And even a couple of 'Hooaahs!' which he knew the younger officers had taken directly from their new overlords, the Americans. And not even the real Americans, but those interlopers from the future.

Again, he did not care. Once upon a time, they would have all roared at him, 'Heil Hitler!' and look where that foolishness had got them. Jochen Boosfeld could put up with a few 'Okays' and 'Hooaahs' if it meant beating the Reds.

As the O-Group under the stars broke up, Boosfeld folded the map and returned to his panzer. He had screens in the tank with almost magical battlefield imagery, fed directly to him from tiny, unmanned planes and helicopters buzzing overhead...when

Battalion could spare the cover. And when the Russians didn't shoot them down with giant shotguns or electronic measures that messed around with the surveillance drones' internal wiring. Or something.

"Pah."

Boosfeld waved away the idle thoughts.

He had his map and his pencil. He had his tanks. It was enough.

Panzer 59 rumbled just ahead of him. The machine-tooled growl was loud enough to blot out the more distant thunder of the active front. Boosfeld grabbed a handhold and pulled himself up like a gymnast. A hell of a thing it was. He felt twenty years younger; truly, he did. He walked alongside the main gun to the turret and opened his hatch. A dim blue-green light greeted him, sparing his night vision. He climbed in, amazed as always by the kiss of cooler air, and stood in the hatch as a panzer leader should. He would 'button up' only in heavy contact.

He plugged in his Combat Vehicle Crewman's helmet and found little chatter on the net. His crew was silent and disciplined; they waited on orders. Idly, he ran his hands over his M2 machine gun, the 'big fifty'. Like everything else in his company, it was ready.

A weak and silly impulse to light a cigarette crept up on him. To provide a perfect data point for a Russian sniper, in other words. He suppressed the urge. There would either be time for that later, or he had already smoked his last, and it would not matter.

As the Americans said, this was the urgent interlude, the moment to hurry up and wait. Always with the smart comments, those fellows. Boosfeld had been through so many of these moments as a soldier that he was well-practised at stilling his thoughts and quelling any feelings that might be tempted to run away with his better judgment.

Feelings like anomie or pointlessness.

Such things were for the French.

He would trust in good steel and bold action.

After some indeterminate time, his headset crackled. It was Lehr Six, the battalion commander.

"All Lehr elements, this is Lehr Six. Move to Phase Line Charlie. Respond in sequence."

One by one, the tankers acknowledged, and the 9th Brigade, 3rd

German Armored, moved in the dark toward their first combat assault since the Second World War. Boosfeld rocked back on his heels as the driver fed diesel to the engine, and Panzer 59 leapt forward. Bending his knees a little with the up and down of the terrain, Boosfeld manoeuvred his tank and his company toward the phase line, an imaginary point on the map, a real place in a field outside Baunatal.

Boosfeld's tanks arrayed echelon left as they moved cross country, with each platoon in a rough wedge. His soul sang, knowing contact would come soon. The silver moon cast a ghostly light upon his command, leaching the scene of colour but imbuing it with dread purpose.

Then, a flash to his far-right followed by a crashing boom. Contact.

His headset crackled. "All Lehr elements, 4th Company is in contact. Move to your objectives. Lehr Six out."

Jochen Boosfeld's face seemed calm, unaffected, but if you knew him, you would recognise the grim set of his jaw. This was his first combat in over a decade, and once again, he was fighting the Reds. But this time, he wasn't fighting with the Gestapo at his back. He was supported by airpower. And to be honest, here, the cause was just. He fought for his own soil, not to conquer other men's lands. As Boosfeld rode, he saw flashes from heaven to his far right, the west. The Dutch artillerymen's light show synched perfectly with his thoughts.

As the steel behemoth raced and bounced across the field beneath him, he had to admit that the M-60 made his trusty old Panzer IV look like a clunker. From the right, a flash. To the southwest, a clang and a ball of flame. His headset crackled.

"Contact! Tanks to the south! Engaging now!"

Boosfeld answered his Third Platoon leader, his blood pulsing like a great drumbeat.

"Roger, Lehr Two-Three Six. Call me when you get the situation under control."

He peered into the night, one hand still resting on Ma Deuce, as the Yankees called the M2. Rivers of tracer and great orange fire blooms painted the landscape in demonic relief. It was almost time to button up. His turn was coming very soon now. Boosfeld dropped down into his seat and slammed closed the hatch. His timing was impeccable.

He had barely taken his seat and strapped in when his gunner, Sergeant Pickelhaupt, spoke. His voice was flat, calm, like a day at the range.

"Tanks. Left front, 1300 meters."

Boosfeld peered through his thermal sight. The young fellow had a good eye. The Bolsheviks were hull down, dug in. As he spied on them, one fired. *But not addressed to me*, the Panzer Leader thought. And Ivan was still a lousy shot. Pickelhaupt was not. Boosfeld had personally selected the lad to ride in his tank.

"Gunner, SABOT. Tanks, pick one."

"Left. Identified," the sergeant replied in a clipped but steady voice,

Boosfeld addressed his loader, Korporal Jonathon Heigel.

"Heigel. Load. Armour-piercing."

The young man stood, partly crouched, to slam a SABOT round into the breech, and closed the block. He sat back down, out of the way and called out. "Up!"

The gunner Pickelhaupt called out, "Lasing!" as he painted the Soviet tank with an invisible light beam.

God, but so much had changed. How he could have used such wonders on the road to Moscow.

Boosfeld called out, "Fire!"

The big gun roared and recoiled.

"On the way!" Pickelhaupt confirmed.

Peering through the thermal sight, Boosfeld saw his round impact with the tank on the left of the Soviet line. The fatal blow was spectacular; the turret flew off and landed some distance away as a geyser of flame erupted from within. Less than a second later, all the other tanks in his command fired. Destruction passed over the Soviet position in a terrible, blazing wave.

The comms net was full of terse commands, queries, and orders. His panzers were moving and shooting at great speed now, the heart ripped out of the enemy's position. *It couldn't be this easy*, he thought.

There was no way. But as he scanned his thermals and checked the drone displays, which for once were functional, the enemy tanks burned everywhere. They flared out his black and white viewscreen as they drew near.

But where was the infantry? He wondered. He hadn't seen any soldiers running around.

Then it struck him. They would be dug in. Invisible to thermals and night vision and the cold, glass eyes of the battalion's lingering drone force. And his company was almost within RPG range. He punched out a call across the whole unit.

"2nd Company, this is Lehr Two Six. Beware *panzergrenadiere*! They will be waiting!"

There was nothing for it but to pop his hatch and stand into the enemy's fire. He needed to see. He needed to know. And he would not trust anything but the evidence of his own eyes.

Boosfeld gripped the spade handles of his machine gun and flipped off the safety. He scanned all around, his tanks easy to see with the flames and moonlight. And if his old man's eyes easily saw them, they would make fine targets for the enemy's rocket men.

His platoon was almost on top of the burning tanks when Boosfeld heard a boom followed by an enormous explosion.

RPG, he thought. He was right. The Red infantry had held their fire in an impressive show of discipline. And now they had sprung their trap.

Panzer 59's coaxial gun opened up just a few feet away. At the very same moment, Boosfeld spotted a flash. He did not hesitate; swinging his fifty-calibre machine gun toward the glimmer, he mashed the butterfly triggers with his thumbs. He poured out a long burst, hosing the spot where he thought the hunter-killer team was hiding. Shell casings and links clinked and skittered merrily across the turret roof. Ma Deuce roared, and red tracers ploughed up the earth or bounced wildly toward the heavens.

Phweet.

A bullet snapped by, too close for comfort. He saw a muzzle flash to his right front, about fifty meters away, and pivoted to engage the rifleman. The Russian flew apart. Dead ahead, Boosfeld saw an RPG man stand up. Pickelhaupt mowed him down with the coaxial. Boosfeld, however, was sure there were more men in the slit trench. He called down to Korporal Hänke, the driver.

"Driver, park over that trench and iron it down."

"Sir?"

Boosfeld hadn't taught Hänke that trick in training. It was not the sort of thing of which Major Bidermann would approve.

Well, he thought, *experience is the best teacher*.

"Korporal, park over the trench, hold the brake and spin your treads. Do it now!"

Hanke blinked in horror but did as he was told. The horror would pass, Boosfeld knew. There was nothing like a victory to silence the doubts of the conscience. Panzer 59 slewed left and right as Hanke threw the treads back and forth. Boosfeld, still riding high in the commander's hatch, gunned down a Russian who tried to escape. He was the lucky one. The others died screaming underneath 59 as it dug in. After a few seconds, the awful deed was done. An old quote from an English play came to him as he swivelled the 50-cal back and forth, looking for more targets.

"There are few die well who die in a battle," he muttered.

Boosfeld ordered his tanks forward.

GEERT WISHED DESPERATELY for a cigarette in the creeping dark near Bad Arolsen, Germany. The LT was speaking, his voice raised over the thunder of battle to the southeast. The front pulsed down there. It thudded like a bass drum in a chorus from hell.

"Geert, I need you to lead the advance party to our first firing position," Lieutenant Eikelboom said. He held a small red lamp over a military map spread upon the hood of his jeep. In the background, the battery's self-propelled guns idled, spread out over hundreds of metres of semi-wooded terrain. It was just a little after one-thirty in the morning.

"The minute you have the position prepared," the officer said, "you call me back, and we'll move up to occupy. We need to get this done, Sergeant. The Reds aren't stopping for shit."

Geert, who no longer thought of himself as a municipal engineer for Utrecht city council, ran through all the things he had to do as the platoon gunnery sergeant—organise the security sweep, make an occupation plan, lay out where each of the howitzers would set up, prepare the aiming circle that dictated the fire azimuth, determine the initial deflection, distance and vertical angle of the guns...the list was endless. And it all had to happen so quickly. The pace would be relentless.

"Understood, LT," Geert Veenstra said. "When does the commander want to leave?"

Lieutenant Eikelboom, Jan, pulled back his cuff to check his luminescent watch. "You roll at 0200. You'll have to do a terrain march to get to the position. Any questions?"

Good God, he thought. That was hardly any time at all. Geert had a million questions, but he kept himself to just one.

"What's the security situation on site?"

Eikelboom looked like he had aged ten years in a week. "All we have is a map recon, I'm afraid. But our first position is ten klicks behind the forward line, so it should be all right."

I hope we are not confusing what should be with what is, thought Geert. But aloud, he said, "Okay, sir, I'll give the warning order. We'll have to hustle to make this."

"You will," Lieutenant Eikelboom said sternly.

Fortunately, the battery had trained for the hasty occupation of a firing position repeatedly. Two trucks carried all the necessary equipment, such as guide stakes and field telephones, and every gun guide had a flashlight with a coloured lens. Geert's gun, Bernadette, would head toward the guide with a blue lens. But first, the position had to be prepared. That was the gunnery sergeant's job. His responsibility.

It was so far away from worrying about tree roots and the vice chancellor's toilet plumbing.

He passed command of Gun Number Three down to his deputy, Wachtmeester Peter Ter Velde, and called the men from the rest of the platoon to gather on him. As Geert briefed the assembled troops in the dark, he had to swig from his canteen repeatedly, his throat was so dry. When he mounted in the lead jeep, he felt a terrible need to piss again. He had already relieved himself just a little earlier. When the convoy moved out into the vast darkness of the German night, he could feel every bump in his bladder.

At first, the small convoy travelled slowly along a fire trail while Geert navigated with a map, compass, and a red-lens flashlight. Giant pine trees reached for the stars all around him. When he was sure they were close to the small clearing in the lee of a hill the commander had selected, he directed his driver to leave the road. They smashed through a small wooden fence protecting a field where a dozen or more sheep grazed. The poor, frightened animals scattered as the rest of the convoy followed him through the breach.

Something whipped past Geert's head. He saw winking flashes in the trees about a hundred meters away. He heard a single metallic plink. It sounded like a small rock hitting a tin can. Another *plink*. And then his jeep's gunner let loose with the machine gun, a sudden, terrifying industrial roar. The strobing muzzle flash of the 50-cal destroyed the night's darkness. Red tracers zipped out toward the tree line, and all hell broke loose around Geert.

He heard a boom, a fluttering noise, and then another boom. The windshield shattered, and his driver screamed. The jeep slewed this way and that before crunching to a sudden stop. The momentum threw him forward, and Geert's head hit the flat metal dash with a colossal bang that he felt from his teeth to his balls. He saw stars, tasted blood, and realised that if he hadn't been wearing his helmet, he would've been badly messed up. Probably dead. Of a car accident in a war.

It was darkly amusing, and he giggled like a crazy man as he hit the buckle on his lap belt and rolled out of the jeep. A green flare burst above him, followed by a yellow one. A white-green tracer bounced off a rock somewhere to his right. Suddenly, none of it was funny. Geert hugged the earth and watched another jeep roar toward the tree line, long lines of tracer fire snaking out of the mounted machine gun.

In a rush, Geert realised he was in a kill zone and had no weapon. It was probably still in the jeep if it hadn't been thrown clear.

So, the security situation was a bit crap.

Laying as flat and motionless as possible while gunfire roared around him, he heard shouts, more explosions, and the pounding of boots as someone ran past. Geert finally heaved himself up and looked in the jeep for his personal weapon. The Uzi was lying half under his seat, and he grabbed it. It was wet, sticky. *What is this?* he thought stupidly. And even more stupidly, *I always keep a clean weapon*.

Two rounds hit the driver's body, slumping further across Geert's passenger seat. Now he knew what had soiled his Uzi; he fought the urge to retch and throw the weapon away from him as far as he could. Instead, he wiped his hands furiously on his tunic while checking on the gunner in the back. Geert couldn't see him anywhere but the machine gun, mounted high on a pintle, pointed skyward and silent.

He heard more engines coming closer, the rattle of small arms fire, and then silence. Somebody was shouting, calling his name. Geert recognised the voice. It was his First Sergeant. Geert sagged against the jeep in relief. Someone popped another flare, and Geert saw First Sergeant Schappert hustling toward him.

"You shot, Geert? You good there?"

Geert waved and nodded. He fumbled for a smoke. *Fuck noise and light discipline*, he thought. After a firefight, with all these flares? He stuck the cigarette in his mouth and lit it with trembling hands. He took a drag and answered.

"No. Pim and Rolf have had it, though."

He glanced toward the jeep, paused, and took another drag. "So much for map recon, Top. Who the fuck was that? We're supposed to be ten fucking klicks behind the forward line of troops."

He did not recognise his voice. The coarseness, the harsh and bitter inflection. The fear.

First Sergeant Schappert made an exasperated gesture. "The Brits are checking them now. Perhaps East German pathfinders, and only a squad of them. Probably they were as surprised as us, and now they're dead."

"So are Pim and Rolf," Geert said flatly.

The flares burned out, and he flicked his cigarette butt away. The radiator on his shot-up jeep hissed in the hot darkness.

Schappert spoke again. "Well, we occupied the position all right, verdomme." He shook his head. His tone grew formal. "Sergeant Veenstra, I want the battery in here and firing within the hour."

Geert looked toward his jeep; Pim's body was illuminated by Geert's red-lens flashlight. He pressed his lips together.

"Yes, First Sergeant."

A LITTLE AFTER FOUR, the field telephone buzzed inside the fighting compartment. Geert, who had been dozing, startled awake and picked it up. He heard the Fire Direction Officer's voice on the other end.

"Fire Mission, Platoon adjust, Number Three, one round, shell HE, Lot XY, Charge 4, Fuze Quick, Deflection 2573, Quadrant 247, continuous fire."

Gun Number Three was Bernadette. For a brief moment, Geert's eyebrows went up. He knew the command 'continuous fire' meant their gun would fire at the maximum rate until 'check fire' was given, but he had never heard it. Not even in training. He had expected something such as 'five rounds for effect.'

But all of that training snapped into place. Geert woke the rest of the crew, set the announced deflection on the panoramic telescope, and traversed the tube until he had the correct sight picture on the proper aiming point. He called out, "Deflection 2573."

Bauke Aukema, his gun loader, used a semi-automatic hydraulic ram to press the round into the chamber, followed by 'green bag' propellant. Once everyone was clear, they closed the breech block and installed the primer.

Peter ter Velde, the journalist-turned-gunner, elevated Bernie's tube, centred the quadrant range bubbles and called out, "Quadrant 247, set!" He took the firing lanyard in hand, clipped it to the firing striker and stood as far away from the breech block as possible.

In mere seconds, the enormous howitzer was ready to go; all the platoon's guns would adjust off Geert's gun once the rounds were calibrated down range.

"Fire!" Geert yelled.

Ter Velde made a turn like a matador, lanyard in hand. With a heavy thud, the breech block recoiled a few feet into the fighting compartment. Heero Bloemsma, their driver, now acting as the assistant gunner, levered the block open and blackish powder fumes puffed out. He cleaned the breech and face of the breech block with a swab while Bauke Aukema prepped the ram. Within moments the weapon was ready to fire again.

The night was already warm, and a trickle of sweat stung Geert's eyes. *One good thing about the reek of propellant was that it blocked out the funk of the crew*, he thought. After a week in the field, the boys all reeked like demon poop. He waited on the fire adjustment, and it wasn't long in coming. The field telephone buzzed again.

"Special correction. Number three left three mils."

Geert called out the mod. Peter ter Velde corrected, and with another jerk of the lanyard, the next round headed downrange. The crew went through their carefully choreographed dance once more. Heero Bloemsma swabbing and cleaning. Bauke Aukema loading. Peter ter Velde checking the aim while Geert waited on orders.

The field telephone buzzed for a third time. It was the Fire Direction Officer again.

"Platoon, continuous fire."

Professionally, Geert was pleased. His part-time crew—a carpenter's mate, a journalist, and an insurance clerk—had struck the target with only one correction. (*Human beings,* his quiet inner voice reminded him. They had just killed an unknown number of human beings.) As the lads tended to Bernadette and round after round, left the tube, Geert imagined what it must be like in the Fire Direction Centre, with a hundred cries for help from the heaving front.

How could anyone stand it, listening to the radio and triaging life-saving, life-taking fires?

All Geert could do was his duty, managing the lads while they cranked out death at four rounds a minute. Geert glanced down at his watch; the face easy to read in the man-made lightning storm of the barrage. Surely soon, he would have to dial back the rate of fire to one round per minute? His gun was heating up, and Private Aukema, his loader, was flagging. Geert decided that he would swap Bauke and Heero for the next mission. They were cross trained in each other's jobs, and Heero Bloemsma was the fitter and stronger of the pair from his work on the building sites. Bauke Aukema's desk job with the insurance company had not prepared him well for the physical demands of loading the howitzer in combat.

Bernie roared again, and Geert watched more closely for the signs of real fatigue in his crew. The sort of bone-deep exhaustion that would get them all killed. That was the hell of this business. They could all die out here at any moment. Or they could die weeks from now, having survived through the end. It was so different from everything he was used to—even with his years of reserve training. The worst—the very worst week in his normal life—could not cast a shadow on a simple minute of hell in combat.

The fighting compartment stank of cordite, even with the evacuator fans cranked up and the hatches wide open. Geert could hear the other guns firing, B Battery going flat-out, and he knew he would have to call for a re-supply track soon. The gun was getting hot. And they had yet to hear from the Russians, not since that skirmish on the way to set up this firing site.

After this next shot, thought Geert, *we are reducing our rate*. Aukema was fumbling with a fuze wrench when the field telephone buzzed. Geert picked it up.

A voice crackled out at him.

"Check fire, check fire. End of mission. Be advised we reposition in five mikes. Counter-battery. All guns respond in sequence."

He waited his turn; then, he spoke up. "Three, roger."

He was looking at his loader; even with the help from the semi-auto rammer, sweat was pouring off poor Bauke, and he looked about ready to pass out.

Geert pitched his voice over the uproar. "Check fire. Do not load. We're leaving in five minutes. Bauke, take a break. I will clean the gun, and Heero will load it at the next site, but now, we get the hell gone from here."

They all scrambled out of the vehicle and scattered. Field wire had to be rolled up, aiming stakes pulled; it was organised chaos across the entire position. Geert prepared Bernie for movement while ter Velde hurried to assist the others rolling up their part of the temporary firebase.

Nobody wanted to be around when the Soviet artillery, or worse yet, the Red Air Force, figured out where they were. Geert's armpits oozed as he sat and waited for the lads to return. He wanted to get out and help them, to speed things along, but protocol insisted he stay with the gun. Time stretched like toffee on a hot summer's day, and he realised he was shaking all over.

At last, Aukema, Heero and Pete climbed back aboard and strapped in. Ter Velde confirmed they were good to go. The radio, silent until now to prevent triangulation, clicked through his Combat Vehicle Crewman's headset. Geert recognised the Battery Commander's voice. "All elements, displace, now."

Geert spoke up. "You heard the old man, Bauke. Let's get the fuck out of here!"

He opened the hatch and stood up. He gave the driver minor corrections as they formed a convoy and left hurriedly, following a trail through the forest to their next firing position. Geert smelled diesel, earth, and shattered pine.

As Geert stood in his hatch like a tanker, he heard a new sound, a whooshing roar like freight trains overhead, speeding in the direction of the field where he had been just minutes earlier.

Geert didn't look back as yet another small corner of Germany disintegrated in fire and fury.

34

Julia had always hated rehab, and she hated it even more as she got older. It'd been over a decade since she'd logged significant hospital time—not since she'd been dragged out from under a pile of dead Rangers, murdered by the SS in the Ardennes. She was so much younger then. Even with four broken ribs and masses of internal bruising, her recovery had been faster than this, she was sure.

"You need to go a little slower, ma'am," the nurse said, but with her accent, it sounded like 'mum', which made Jules feel about twenty years older and an old imperial shit-ton worse.

"I'll be fine," she protested, shuffling a few steps closer to the French doors, leaning on the aluminium walking stick with one hand and dragging the wheeled IV stand with all her drains, fluid bags, and monitors. She could see the garden through the doors and was determined to enjoy at least a few minutes in the fresh air.

"You won't be fine if you pop all your stitches and your insides end up on the outside," the nurse cautioned her.

Nurse Radcliffe was a bit of an old battle axe. *Nurse Ratched was more like it*, Jules thought, but she kept her mouth shut and shuffled on. How many people here would get that reference anyway? And there was no intimidating this one. No bullshitting her, either. You had to prove yourself fit and worthy with Radcliffe whenever you wanted something. Jules struggled to keep her cool as the drainage tube they'd punched into her ribcage rubbed up against some poorly placed nerve bundle, sending a bright jagged flare of pain up her left flank and into her neck.

She gritted her teeth. She was leaving this ward, even if only for a few minutes.

The flowers bloomed outside, a riot of colour, all reds and yellows against the impossible green of the manicured lawns. Her room in the recovery ward was pleasant enough—luxurious, she supposed, by the standards of most people's homes. A new flat-screen TV hung from the ceiling on an adjustable arm. A lovely pair of Danish speakers streamed music or live radio from a tuner built right into her bedside table (*probably to hide the bulk of the thing*, she imagined). There was even a little bar fridge where she could keep Ratched-approved treats and snacks. Were it not for all the medical equipment and constant nursing staff surveillance, she might have been in a country resort somewhere. But she wasn't. Julia Duffy remained under watch, if not under guard, at Saint Andrew's.

After a week and a half, it was starting to grind.

"Let me get that for you if you absolutely must," Nurse Radcliffe said in her clipped, disapproving tone. Radcliffe unlatched the French doors, pushing them wide open and securing them with little metal hooks. Warm, sweet-smelling air from the garden wafted into the ward. Julia resumed her slow shuffle towards freedom before the nurse returned to help her.

"Let's not get ahead of ourselves, shall we?" Radcliffe cautioned.

"I don't think there's much chance of that, do you?" Jules said, her frustration getting the better of her.

"I'm just telling you to take it easy," Radcliffe said in a softer tone. "You are recovering from surgery. Carrying some very serious injuries. You are not yourself, Miss Duffy."

Already fatigued by the five minutes it had taken to inch along the corridor, Julia could not be bothered wasting the energy to correct her. She was not a 'miss' and never had been. But she suspected the old biddy knew that. Nurse Radcliffe seemed to know almost everything about her, including the exact location of every button to push and chain to yank.

Still, she did not stop Julia from walking out to the garden, for which she was grateful. The recovery ward was edged by ancient stone cloisters, at least on this side of the building. Jules decided that rather than tempting her balance and injuries trying to negotiate the soft grass, she would take her exercise in the shade of the covered walkway. Worn smooth by centuries of use, the dark grey paving stones were a simple but manageable physical challenge, which Radcliffe helped her negotiate by taking charge of the IV pole.

It was a warm day outside, with only a few strips of cloud marring an otherwise flawless sky. Birds sang pleasantly in the trees scattered through the courtyard, and a gardener pruned a hedge with a small electric trimmer some distance away. It was a restful scene, and Julia was happy to take her ease on a wooden bench not too far from the entrance to the ward.

She needed Radcliffe's assistance to lower herself onto the seat, and the same drainage tube which had pained her so fiercely just a minute ago put her in real discomfort again as she planted ass. But having achieved her goal, she was happy to enjoy the beauty of the gardens. It was also nice to escape the overpowering smell of disinfectant on the ward and the wounds and rot of broken bodies underneath it.

"Thank you," she said, genuinely grateful for the assistance and the escape.

Radcliffe was a moment in replying as if Julia's gratitude had surprised her.

"That's all right, dear," she said at last. "I'm just here to make sure you get better, despite your best efforts to the contrary."

Jules might have pushed back on that if she'd had more energy, but her annoyance was fleeting. It was something in Nurse Radcliffe's voice. She wasn't admonishing Jules. She was giving her some gentle advice. The wooden bench creaked a little as Radcliffe settled onto it, where she could watch the monitors hanging from the stainless-steel IV pole.

"There should be contrails," she said, confusing Julia for a second until she looked over and saw the nurse peering up into the clear blue sky.

"No way," Jules replied. "You don't want that. If you had Russian jets overhead, we'd be fucked. Sorry," she added when the nurse bristled at her language.

"Oh, don't bother," Radcliffe said. "I've heard worse. But I remember those white trails in the sky as very pretty. I know what happened up there wasn't pretty. But I was younger then, and it was marvellous to look up in the sky and see those boys of ours up there."

Julia sketched the faintest of smiles.

"We happy few," she quoted.

"But not such a band of brothers these days, are they?" Nurse Radcliffe said, obviously getting the reference. "I heard on the wireless the other day that over a dozen young ladies are flying fighters for the RAF now. Jets, too. What a time we do live in, Miss Duffy."

This time, Julia's smile was a little brighter.

"That would've happened anyway, you know," she said. "It just would have taken longer."

They sat silently for maybe a minute, each content with their thoughts. For Jules, her thoughts always turned to Harry. Agent Plunkett had returned just once with the vaguest news that her fiancé Harry was well, Plunkett said. MI6 had received word from the field, and Julia had nothing to concern herself with. She had raised one eyebrow at that, and Plunkett was polite enough to look embarrassed. They both understood the nature of Harry's work, and they knew too well the risks involved. Moreover, Plunkett understood that Julia knew his reassurances were not to be trusted. After all, she was lying abed full of tubes and holes because a simple job to make a pass at a German scientist in Cairo had gone all sorts of wrong.

She closed her eyes and breathed carefully, trying to let go of her fears. She steadied her breathing and focused only on those things she could hear. The gritty crunch of the gardener's shovel biting into the soil of the rose beds. The *tick-tick-tick* of a lawn sprinkler. Leaves rustling in a light breeze, and birds twittering to each other from the trees.

But it was no good. It wasn't just Harry. That was bad enough. But she could not let go of the memory of the man who had visited her while in hospital in Cairo. At the time, drifting in and out of her hazy, drug-addled delirium, she had thought herself lost in some long-ago dream. But the further away in time she was from Cairo, the less like a dream it seemed.

Dan had come back; she was sure of it. He had been on that Russian freighter, the *Bulgakov*, and at the hospital later. He was thicker through the waist and chest but not with the soft, slouching weight of middle age. He had always been a big man, but in her dream, he had packed even more muscle around his shoulders and neck. His hair was as thick as ever but cut short and sprinkled with the salt and pepper of middle age.

That's why she could not concentrate on the simple sounds of the garden.

If she had dreamed of Dan, why had he aged?

"Where will it all end? That's what I worry about," Nurse Radcliffe said.

Jules opened her eyes, turning to the older woman a little too quickly. Her stitches pulled, and she winced. Her voice, when she spoke, was more challenging than she intended.

"It'll end with women like Yazmeen Collins running places like St Andrews and doing research that makes life better for women like you and me decades before it would've happened," Julia said, letting her frustrations get the better of her now. "A hundred years earlier."

"Oh, I don't mean that, dear," Radcliffe said. "Doctor Collins is an absolute marvel. Not just as a physician, you know. She's rather an able administrator, too. I've never seen a place run so well as St Andrews after she took over. No, I mean the war. I've seen three of them, although I was just a little girl during the first one. But where does it all end, Miss Duffy? You tell me. You've seen it happen. The future and all that. Does it ever end? People being so utterly beastly to each other?"

Julia almost snorted.

She was about to say something very knowing and cruel but managed to restrain herself.

"It never ends, no," she said with some care for the other woman's feelings. "I'm sorry; I wish I could say that it will. But it doesn't."

"So it made no difference at all then?" Nurse Radcliffe said. "Women like Doctor Collins being in charge? The world ended up in a big mess anyway?"

It almost sounded like an accusation. Jules shrugged.

"I guess some things got better, some stayed the same, and some got worse," she said. Radcliffe seemed to think that was an acceptable answer. She nodded as if the matter were now closed.

"You're looking a bit peaky to me, dear. I think we will sit here just a little while until you get your colour back, and then I'm afraid it's into bed for you for a nice long rest."

Julia didn't resist. The fact was, she did feel tired. The short walk from her room to the garden had exhausted her. But it had also convinced her that she wasn't crazy. She had not been dreaming. She had seen Dan Black in Cairo. She resolved that she would return to her bed and rest and gather her strength. And when she had strength enough to go on, she would search for the man she had once loved and to whom she had done so much wrong. It was not her old reporter's instincts coming back to life. It was not the rekindling of an old flame. She loved Harry, and she would make her life with him. But she remembered keenly the guilt and sorrow she felt lying in the sickbay of the *Trident* after being medevacked from the *Ardennes*.

For a long time, she had blamed herself for Dan's death. She'd given him good reason to leave her. Even to hate her. And if he was alive, and she had a chance to apologise to him now, she didn't feel she could go on with her life until she had made those amends.

She took a deep breath, very carefully, and said to Nurse Radcliffe, "I think I'm ready now."

35

He now had an entourage big enough they couldn't all squeeze into the small USAF commuter jet that carried him from Paris to a secondary RAF field north of London. Colonel Grieve had done outstanding work throwing together a small command team to run the Allied war effort in Europe. Just quietly, old Joe Stalin had done them a solid on that front by killing so many of General Cronauer's staff in Germany. It made the clean-out of the SACEUR org chart that much easier.

His plane, a General Dynamics Gulfstream analogue cribbed from an uptime design by the same company, banked hard to the left and popped chaff as they spiralled down to land. There were no Soviet fighters within the threat bubble, and six USAF fighter escorts flew protective CAP thousands of feet above. But the Russians had salted deep-cover hunter-killer squads throughout Western Europe. *Molniya* or 'thunderbolt' squads, they called them, and you could never be sure some Smedlov with a shoulder-launched missile wasn't hiding in a bush somewhere down below. Half a dozen thunderbolts had sown chaos throughout North America in the last few days simply by hitting a bunch of high-profile transport nodes. Murdering thirty-five commuters at New

York's Grand Central Station with hand grenades and pistols hadn't done a damn thing to sabotage the US military machine, but along with the other *Molniya* attacks on civilian infrastructure, they had thrown a shit-ton of sand into the gearbox of the country's broader mobilisation.

It seemed that rock and rap and microprocessors weren't the only things that'd come back through the wormhole. Beria and Stalin had done their research on twenty-first-century urban terrorism.

Or, more likely, just Beria, Jones thought as he tried to clear his mind by staring out the window at the view. Stalin had been a pretty tired old communist for a few years now. And he was gone anyway.

It was a bright, hot summer's day, and the greenery of the English countryside struck Jones. So different from all the places he'd fought, both uptime and back here. And different again from the grim tenements of Chicago where he had grown up.

"Goddamnit," his Chief of Staff muttered from beside him.

"What's that, Colonel?" Jones asked, turning away from the view.

"I'm sorry, General," Colonel Grieve said, frowning at some text on the screen of his pager. "But I think there's going to be a band and an honour guard waiting for us."

Jones snorted, but his temper didn't flare, even though he'd specifically instructed Grieve that he wanted to go straight from the airfield to the meeting with Kolhammer. Private Williamson was even sitting by the front door to the Gulfstream, ready to book it double time down the foldout stairs to get his Humvee rolling.

"Don't sweat it, Bob," Jones said. "You can't stop some local yokel kicking out the jams if he thinks it's the best shot he's gonna get at polishing his resume today. Believe it; there'll be some half-bird Colonel or baby General down there who decided to ignore you because in their heart of hearts, they knew what I wanted to do when I got off this plane was delay my meeting with the President to inspect the closely shaved ass cracks of some National Guard marching band."

Colonel Grieve, who might once have had a sense of humour before the Army Medical Corps surgically removed it, frowned but said nothing.

"Anyway," Jones continued, "it's a better reception than we got in Paris. So there's that."

"I suppose so," Grieve conceded but with no natural grace. He remained something of a mystery to Jones. A profoundly conservative man, prayerful to a fault, sceptical of so much that the uptimers had brought into his world, Colonel Grieve nonetheless exhibited genuine distress and affront whenever he encountered even a suggestion of disrespect directed at Jones, or for that matter, his driver, Private Williamson.

Jones didn't ponder the matter too deeply. He took the man's offering of loyalty and undeniable competence and thanked the good Lord for having sent him.

The other dozen men and women on the flight, primarily American and British, with a few German and French officers for regional seasoning, remained quiet as the small jet touched down with a gentle bump. Grieve had chosen and vetted them all, and so far, they had meshed well enough into a solid, working team. Jones was still getting to know most of them, except for the German Bundeswehr Major, Majella Hand, who had come through Pope's wormhole on secondment to the Australians as a young lieutenant. It was wrong he should feel so much more comfortable around his kind, an uptimer, but there it was. Majella was a professional military officer, as they all were, but beyond that, she just seemed to see the world differently. Or rather—she saw the world in the same way he did.

The jet taxied off the main landing strip and came to a halt in front of a large hangar where a band was waiting to strike up a tune. Colonel Grieve seemed ready to jump down the stairs and start bending tubas over his knee when his pager buzzed again, distracting him momentarily. Private Williamson was already out the door and hurrying across the apron towards a small convoy, which appeared to be their ground transport. Jones grabbed his document case and travel pack, about to follow her out when Grieve stopped him.

"I'm sorry, sir," he said, "But they're telling me the president has been delayed by an hour and..."

Jones cut him off.

"I don't need the details, Colonel," he said. "Let's get on the road and get our commlinks up. He's the president. Shit happens."

As Jones and his staff deplaned, the band struck up a creditable rendition of Grand Old Flag. There was an eager US Army General and a multinational brace of colonels waiting for him at the foot of the steps, and he took five minutes to inspect the guard with conspicuous graciousness. At the same time, Bob Grieve brought up the rear, playing bad cop, checking his watch every minute. They were on the road, heading north, within ten minutes, and pulled into another airfield a little less than an hour later.

THE RAF BASE had once hosted Spitfires and Hurricanes, but it had been mothballed after the war's end, and the facilities were basic. It was a transit point, not a destination.

"General Jones just arrived on site, Mister President," a young Ranger Lieutenant informed him. "Your chopper's inbound. Wheels down in thirty-six minutes."

"Thank you, son," Kolhammer said before dismissing him with a casual nod towards the door. It wasn't the kid's fault they'd had to divert here. The Secret Service had insisted on the last-minute change after receiving intelligence of a possible hunter-killer squad waiting in ambush on their previous route. *Almost certainly bullshit*, Kolhammer thought. Possibly even misinformation fed to them by the Russians to disrupt and delay—and to test the reaction protocols of Kolhammer's protective detail. Lord knows he'd authorised the US intelligence services to use all necessary means to locate and decapitate the Soviet leadership. This was not a dispute among gentlemen.

"Here he comes," Andy Porter announced from over by the window. They waited on Jones in a dusty, cobwebbed Quonset hut that had been stripped of all its furnishings at some point in the last ten years and left to rot. The old concrete aprons of the airfield were not long enough for modern jet fighters. Although the Brits had enjoyed a faster economic recovery from the war than was the case initially, they did not have unlimited riches to spend on military infrastructure when so much of the country had desperately needed reconstruction.

The old fighter base was a neglected backwater, making it perfect for this meeting.

He heard Jones's convoy pull up outside the hut and resisted the natural urge to hurry outside and greet his old friend. On his own, the Supreme Commander of Allied Forces in Europe would make a tempting target. Together with Kolhammer, they could probably call down whatever remained of the Red Army's missile arsenal on this old airfield.

Kolhammer heard boots marching up the corridor and the mutter of voices. A soft knock sounded at the door, and he said, "Come on in, Lonesome."

General J. Lonesome Jones appeared a moment later, his face arranged in the stern but neutral expression of a military officer about to report to his Commander in Chief, but with an old familiar warmth still lighting his eyes. Jones saluted, and Kolhammer returned the salute.

"Mr President," Jones said. And then, smiling, "Damn, but that sounds good."

"We've had better days," Kolhammer reminded him, but he smiled as he said it before introducing General Porter, who had stayed with him as liaison to the Brits. His other staff were already en route back to the US. Safely en route, he hoped.

Jones introduced Kolhammer and Porter to a colonel called Grieve. His chief of staff. To judge from the buzz of voices just outside the door, Jones had plenty more in reserve.

"Let's just keep it between us for now, shall we, gentlemen?" Kolhammer said. "There's something we must discuss in private before we get to the general briefing."

Jones nodded to Grieve, who locked the door. The four men stood quietly for a moment.

Finally, Kolhammer spoke.

"Can we hold them back without going nuclear?"

Jones shook his head.

"No. We can't. They will break through the German lines in the next couple of days and possibly even punch up out of occupied France at the same time. Although they don't have the same concentration of forces there."

Kolhammer nodded. It was what he'd expected, but his stomach was still filled with ice water to hear it.

"And when they break through and get rolling, can you stop them from reaching the Atlantic?"

Jones answered this question slowly.

"That depends on the losses they're willing to take. We're outnumbered on the ground, but we have a slight advantage in the air for the moment, mostly because of the quality of our electronic systems and drone fleets. It's one of the reasons, probably the only reason, that they haven't been able to prosecute their advance through the breach left by the 5th Army. We're walloping them from the air. That will only get worse for them as our main force and reserve USAF squadrons arrive in theatre, and we surge the drone fleets out of California. Their rocket forces and drone fleets haven't been as effective as we feared. Our air defences have held."

Kolhammer frowned, thinking of the missing rocket scientist Bremmer.

He had yet to receive further updates from the CIA.

"Let me know if you get any indications of that changing," he said. "The Sovs will be looking to improve and adapt on that front. It could make all the difference to them."

Jones nodded.

"Sure, but from what I can tell so far, Red Army tactics haven't advanced much beyond building up overwhelming mass and simply moving forward to crush everything in front of them."

"Makes for a tasty fucking kill box if you're flying a BUFF," Andy Porter said.

Kolhammer did not call out the interruption. Porter had flown prototype B52s at the end of the last war. He knew what he was talking about.

"You're right, General," Jones agreed, nodding to the Air Force man. "We haven't deployed the strategic assets for tactical support yet, but I am loading that sledgehammer. I intend to swing it to full effect if and when they break through the Germans. If we can channel them where I want them, we can achieve atomic-level kinetic effects with conventional smart munitions."

"But will it stop them?" Kolhammer asked.

"It'll kill 'em," Jones said. "A hell of a lot of them. Just depends on how many more Beria is willing to sacrifice. And we will lose aircraft and crew. We will lose them in numbers that would have been impossible to contemplate back up when. But they'll destroy whole Soviet armies before they're lost to us."

Kolhammer frowned.

"Mister Beria has never struck me as a guy who was squeamish about sacrificing other people's lives to pursue his ends."

"True that," Jones said.

Kolhammer stepped away from the small conference for a moment. He looked out of the window across the abandoned airfield. Grass grew knee-high between the cracked and weed-choked runways. A flight of birds took off from a stand of trees in the distance, drawing his eye to a couple of old prop-driven fighters. They looked like Hurricanes to him. Authentic museum pieces now, slowly rusting and rotting away in a field of clover.

He turned around.

"General Jones," he began.

Lonesome stood up a little straighter. The other two men did the same.

"If, in your judgement," Kolhammer went on, "it becomes necessary to employ tactical nuclear weapons, do not delay requesting authorisation from me. I will make the final decision myself. But I need to know as soon as possible if you think it's necessary. Do I make myself clear?"

"Yes, sir," Jones said. "I will not make that call unless I think it is unavoidable."

36

Bautista came for them just after dark. Harry and Ivanov had already changed into the anonymous working man's outfits the clansman had provided. Rough denim pants and rank, sweat-stained shirts. Ivanov hid his face beneath a black fisherman's cap, pulled low. Harry's distinctive red-gold thatch of thick hair disappeared inside a tattered bucket cap.

"You look stupid and disreputable. This will do," Bautista said.

The mountain man had not changed his outfit at all. He was still dressed in dusty black pants and a once fine-looking jacket, now sadly gone to seed and patches.

They all carried weapons, but not heavy arms. Harry tucked a pistol into the small of his back and extra magazines into each of his pockets. Ivanov took two guns and a fighting knife.

"I have transport," Bautista announced. "It is parked just beyond the piazza."

They followed the same route Charlotte had taken an hour earlier, exiting through the back door and tracking along the narrow back alley. It was busier than before, with kitchen hands from the many bars and cafes coming and going as they dumped rubbish or snuck in a quick cigarette break. One or two of them waved to

Bautista, and he returned their greetings with a nod or a raised chin. Harry could hear the buzz of the crowds on the far side of the buildings, in the open air of the piazza. Live guitar music at some older, established place battled with recorded and amplified tracks booming from speakers in the newer cafes and bars. He wondered why the Russians hadn't lobbed a couple of rockets in here on general principles. There'd have to be any number of contractors scattered around the town square and likely some military and intelligence personnel, too. But even muffled by the buildings fronting the square, Santa Teresa sounded to Harry like any other resort town as the sun went down. A place of laughter and forgetting.

"Have there been any attacks at all here?" He asked their guide.

"Not yet," Bautista replied as he led them up the narrow walkway between the leather workshop and the abandoned bookstore. "All of the fighting has been on Corsica."

"This is a third or fourth-order target," Ivanov said, waving his hand at the crowds of drinkers and diners. "If the communists wish to take this island, they will put out the eyes of the NATO forces here. But for now, they have better things to destroy, more important people to kill."

"Let's hope so," Harry said. "I wouldn't want to run into our old mate Skarov with a crew of handy Spetsnaz hoods to back him up. No offence intended, comrade."

"No offence to take," Pavel Ivanov assured him. "For you, this is a war against the old Soviet Union. For me, it is fight to build a new Russia. Better than the others I have known."

"You both shut up now, or no one build anything but caskets for your loud-mouth corpses," Bautista told them. "Remember, you are stupid fisherman. Do not be talking of your high politics in English now. Just shutting up, getting in truck, and grabbing professor of rockets."

"I will be killing Skarov, too," Ivanov reminded them.

Bautista shrugged. "Pah. Somebody is always killed."

When they found Bautista's truck, Harry could not imagine they would all fit in. A small pre-war Renault, it looked like the bastard offspring of an early Beetle and a cashew nut.

"You get in back," Bautista ordered when he saw Ivanov staring sceptically at the tiny passenger seat.

"Maybe we should just walk down to the docks," Harry suggested.

"This is not for getting to Frantziscu Murtas' boat. This is for getting away," Batista explained. "We put rocket professor in back and cover him with old sacks. This is my brother-in-law's cousin's van. The polizia know they are not to stop it."

Ivanov looked at Harry and shrugged, folding himself into the vehicle's rear. Harry sat up front next to the Sardinian, who started the engine by pulling on a small rope, reminding Harry of the starter cord for a lawnmower back in the upwhen. The Renault spluttered into life, the little engine drowning out the sounds of revelry drifting over from the Piazza, and they were off.

It had no headlamps, and the streets were not well-lit away from the town centre, making for a bumpy, slightly hair-raising ride down the steepening cobblestone roads to the waterfront. *On the upside*, Harry thought, *they didn't look like an assault force conducting a tactical insertion*. More like three drunken fishermen had woken up from a bender and realised they were late for the shrimp boat, occasioning the hasty theft of an unguarded clown car.

There was no regularity or predictability to the street map in this part of the town. The narrow winding avenues seemed to follow the lie of the land, affording Harry occasional frustrating glimpses of their destination.

Porto Qaudro looked busy, with the smaller shrimp boats jostling to be first out through the heads while the larger ocean-going trawlers prepared for longer hauls into deeper water.

"That is Murtas' boat," Bautista said, pointing through the wide-open aperture on the driver's side. Harry tried to look in the direction he had indicated, but they suddenly swung around a hairpin turn. He lost sight of the waterfront for a moment as Bautista motored down a pastel-coloured canyon of apartment blocks and shuttered shops. When they turned back a minute later, he looked at a different part of the docks, where most of the berths had only been occupied by the shrimp boats now trailing out to sea in a long, straggling line.

He ignored an urge to call Charlotte for an update. They could not afford to break radio silence, with the near certainty of the Russians monitoring the airwaves for such a call. They would open comms only if something went wrong. Instead, they puttered on, closing the distance to their agreed kick-off point—a tavern owned by an uncle of Andreas Costa. It stood out from the darkened warehouses on either side, a lively spot in blue and white, decked with rainbow strings of party lights.

If everything had gone to plan, Charlotte would be inside the tavern, having shaken down the occupants for any copper coins they might spare to support the Sisters of Charity. She would now be perched on a wooden stool at a window bench overlooking the old stone jetty, enjoying a bowl of soup, compliments of the house, while she maintained surveillance on the trawler that would be Skarov's escape route from the island.

After negotiating a couple more hairpin turns, they settled into a long curving descent to the harbour, letting Harry scope out the objective. He could not see Charlotte but had to assume from the lack of communication that everything had gone well so far. He cursed himself for having forgotten to bring a pair of binoculars. Still, the night was clear, and in contrast to the backstreets of Santa Teresa, the waterfront area was brightly illuminated. The last of the shrimp boat fleet was beating out on a rising tide, and the first of the long-haul trawlers were slipping their anchorage on the other side of the harbour. Great flocks of seabirds, mostly gulls and cormorants, swirled and swooped off the sterns of the boats, passing out into the open channel. He fancied that he could hear their distant calls even over the racket of the Renault's engine. Smaller numbers of petrels and pelicans remained behind on the docks, perhaps hopeful of a favour from the fishermen loading out the larger trawlers. Harry counted at least forty men either on the jetty or working the decks of those boats. As best he could tell, they looked legit.

Or they did until the shooting started.

TURNED out Charlotte was a pretty good hustler for a nun. The small calico bag she carried to collect the offerings for the orphanage was heavy with coins, not just bent and timeworn coppers. Her green eyes and wide smile had shaken free nearly two handfuls of five hundred and thousand lire coins. Those orphans were making out like bandits.

She had enjoyed less success scoping out the objective. None of the men on the Murtas boat, a barnacled tub called the Mirabella, had kicked a single centimo into her beggar's bag, but they had given her something. In lazily sneering at her to *fuck off*, one of the deck-hands had cursed in Romanian until another slapped him into shutting up. Without Bautista to google up for information, Charlotte had waited until she finished her rounds of the dock and settled in at the Costas family tavern, where old Uncle Mariu had filled a wooden bowl with a rich stew of white fish and bright orange mussels and confirmed with a grunt that only local men were supposed to work the boats of Porto Quadro. Five families, including the Murtas clan, had long ago settled the division of the spoils to be taken from the waters around the island. And those spoils were not to be shared outside the clans, certainly not with any filthy Romanians.

"They are not Murtas' men," old Mariu confirmed as he tore a heel of bread off a long stick and added it to her plate. "They are *arrogh'e merda*."

Pieces of shit.

Charlotte dipped the heel of crusty bread into the rich broth and chewed slowly as she contemplated the tactical problem. Two pings on her headset told her that Harry and Ivanov were inbound with Bautista. They would play at making a delivery of food or drink to the tavern before setting up in ambush to watch over the trawler and wait on Skarov's arrival, hopefully with the kidnapped rocket scientist in tow. They had no idea whether Bremmer was coming or what state he would be in. The Sovs still had his family somewhere, so they had leverage over him—enough to complicate any rescue.

She tore off another chunk of bread. Behind her, the tavern had fallen quiet. An hour ago, as she made her rounds of the docks—seeking donations for the orphanage and scoping out the opposition

—the place had been crowded with fishermen enjoying a hot meal and a glass of *mirto,* a local liqueur, often thrown down with a short cup of bitter, black coffee. Now, the main bar was empty save for old Mariu and a couple of his cronies, who quietly played cards at a table in the corner. A younger man, probably one of about a hundred Costas nephews, wiped the bar with a wet rag and watched Charlotte watching the waterfront.

Outside, in the gathering gloom of early evening, the other long-haul trawlers appeared ready to put out to sea. Diesel engines grunted and spewed dark, oily smoke into the burnt orange sky. Deckhands cast off thick mooring ropes while a helmsman spun the wheels and yelled at their rivals to make way. On the Mirabella, however, the thin, sallow-faced Romanian who had cursed at her when she'd approached him for charity was the only crew member she could see up on deck.

Charlotte tore off another piece of bread and dunked it mindlessly into her bowl. Something was wrong. The Romanian stood at the prow of the boat; his hands jammed deep into the pockets of a coat much too heavy for the warm evening. He scowled at something further up the dock, which she could not see from where she was sitting. The man called over his shoulder, and his two crewmates suddenly appeared from below decks. Like him, they were dressed too heavily for the hot summer night. They looked like men rugged up for a voyage to the North Sea, not the Mediterranean. They wore long, heavy coats that concealed everything down to their knees. Or at least they were meant to conceal. To Charlotte, they screamed of hidden weapons. The men made no move to further prepare their boat for departure. Instead, the two who had just appeared from below hurried down the gangway and across the stone quay like men running for cover.

She slipped off the bar stool, hitched up her skirts and drew her weapon, moving toward the tavern door in a shooter's crouch and gesturing to the old men at the back of the bar to seek shelter. Uncle Mariu did nothing of the sort. He barked a few words in Sardu to the boy behind the counter. Three shotguns appeared in short order, and the card players advanced on her like a phalanx of aged gangsters, which, Charlotte supposed, they were.

For one dread moment, she thought they were coming for her. And in a way, they were, but the expression of undeniable hostility which stretched the old men's hawk-like features into even more vulpine hatred settled on the men outside, not her.

"Is not right," Uncle Mariu growled. "Murtas' *arrogh'e merda* will pay for the insult to my blood."

"Wait. Whoa," Charlotte said quickly, throwing up one hand like a traffic cop, but to no effect. The three old hoods advanced implacably.

Charlotte could feel all the pieces of the plan coming apart. It disintegrated completely with the double boom of an ancient shotgun when Mariu discharged both barrels through the front window of his tavern and into the back of the man who had foolishly taken cover behind a thick stone pillar just outside the front door but in full view of anybody inside. He slammed forward and slumped to the ground, leaving an oily red smear down the rough-hewn stone blocks. The trio of ancient devils took up firing positions at the ruined window, smashing what was left of the glazing out of the way with the heavy wooden stocks of their shotguns. The crash of falling glass was loud but not loud enough to drown out the rising storm of gunfire.

Torn between the understandable urge to dive into cover and her need to know what the hell was happening, Charlotte forced herself out through the door but kept her gun hidden in the folds of her skirt, hoping that any shooters would see the nun's habit before they saw what it concealed. Behind her, Mariu and his cronies kept up a drumbeat of booming shotgun fire. It was the only reason she made it out of the tavern alive. Both surviving shooters from the Murtas boat recognised her the second she emerged, and both drew down on her. They had no hesitation. They either knew who she was, or they hated nuns. The Romanian, crouching at the prow, risked standing into the bullet storm to get a better shot at her. He had produced a Kalashnikov assault rifle and squeezed off two poorly aimed bursts before a volley of shotgun blasts from the tavern raked him from the deck.

Knowing she was made, Charlotte gave up all pretence of her cover identity and snapped up her pistol, squeezing off three rounds as poorly aimed as the Romanian's useless burst. She put her shots into a stack of ice chests, behind which the third man from the boat was hiding and shooting from cover. He ducked, and she used the opportunity to dash forward and dive behind an old stone water trough. It was massive and looked to have been carved in place from some ancient granite boulder, probably an artefact of the days when horse-drawn carts clopped up into the town from the waterfront, carrying nets full of fish directly from the trawlers to the wet markets in the piazza.

Hunkered down behind the solid granite obstacle, enjoying the cover offered by Mariu and his wrinkled OG crew, she had time to catch her breath and assess the broader tactical situation.

It looked like shit.

HARRY WAS a moment realising that the gunfire was directed at them. Luckily, Bautista was quicker off the mark. The first shots were heavy booming reports, muffled by distance and the crash of breaking glass. Quickly answered by the crack of small-arms fire, the opening volleys seemed disconnected from their presence. Had the shooting died away, Harry might have put it down to a sudden flare-up in one of the interminable feuds that were part of the rustic charm of places like Sardinia. But Bautista, with his encyclopaedic knowledge and enthusiastic history of participating in such feuds, had no such illusions.

He wrenched the wheel of the little van to the right and stomped on the accelerator, clipping the corner of a wooden cart to send it spinning and crashing into the front of a small shipping office.

"It is trap," he called out as individual rounds began to punch into the brickwork of the buildings around them. Ivanov needed no further encouragement to draw both of his handguns and dive out. He folded into a judo roll, which carried him to cover behind the wreckage of the cart they had just destroyed. The narrow alleyway Bautista had swerved into forced Harry to scramble out through the rear of the vehicle after Ivanov.

As slow as he had been to realise that they were the target of the ambush, Harry had no trouble accelerating now. It was as though the crack of gunfire had swept away his previous confusion and lethargy, stripping back the accumulated weight of injury and years. Without knowing how he got there, he crouched next to the Russian behind the overturned fish cart, grateful for the heavy construction. The stink of day-old seafood was nothing to be glad of, but he appreciated the thick baseboards of thorny oak as round after round of small arms fire crashed into it.

Bautista joined them, snarling and cursing in his native tongue, pausing only to loose off return fire from a sawn-off pump-action shotgun he had brought from the van. Likewise, Ivanov had reverted to his own language and was yelling something indecipherable, but doubtless deeply profane, at the men trying to kill them. So great was the din that Harry didn't notice the chirping of the tactical radio for a moment. His earpiece had come out and dangled from a wire near his chin. A small, tinny voice called out for his attention. Only during a random, half-second lull in the exchange of fire did he realise Charlotte was trying to contact them. He fumbled for the earpiece, found it, and pressed it back into place. It was a good piece of kit. Another toy from one of the many companies devoted to ransacking and recreating future technologies. The soft rubber tip and rudimentary but effective noise cancellation delivered Charlotte to his hearing with enough volume to make him flinch.

"They're not here, Harry, they're not here," she cried. "Harry, can you hear me? Skarov and Bremmer aren't here. It's a trap."

Harry glanced over at Bautista, irrationally confident he and Charlotte had been talking to each other. But, of course, they had not. They had both stated the bleeding obvious. It was a trap, and they had blundered into it.

"Charlotte," Harry sent back. "Charlotte, are you at the meet-up point?"

Her voice came back through the crackle and wash of static.

"...Tavern...Skarov's men...boat...."

Drawing coherent meaning from the patchy transmission was challenging. Harry waited until he knew she had finished speaking before telling her to switch to their secondary channel. After some faffing around, he found her again, coming through with much greater clarity.

The volume of fire hitting the overturned cart was so great that even with clear comms, it was difficult to make out what she was saying, but he concluded that Skarov had never turned up. However, he had set up a welcoming party for the rescue squad he must have known was coming. At least it meant they hadn't been betrayed, like up in the mountains. Knowing he was being pursued, it made simple sense to fake an extraction from the main port, especially as it could be refashioned into an ambush, while he made good his escape from a secondary site.

Capo Testa. They had to be going from Capo Testa.

"There are at least twelve shooters that I can make," Charlotte told him, detailing their locations up and down the waterfront. A fireteam of four men with long arms, working from the decks of a trawler, almost certainly another boat owned by Frantziscu Murtas, had opened up on their van as soon as it arrived at the docks. Probably because Costas' uncle had sprung the trap early by shooting down one of the Romanians on the other boat. The whole bloody thing was a complete dog's breakfast. But what would Skarov care as long as he got away?

"Can you flank them?" Harry asked Charlotte, knowing the answer before it came back. She was just one woman with a single handgun. No, she couldn't fucking flank them.

"Maybe," came the reply.

"Say again," he said, unsure he'd heard correctly.

"If I can get these old bastards out of the tavern and rolling on these motherfuckers in their walking frames, then yeah, maybe," Charlotte replied.

Bautista's shotgun thundered away. Ivanov swapped out the mags in his two handguns while Harry poked his weapon over the top of the cart and squeezed off a few rounds on general principles.

They had to break out of this trap, not just to survive, but because every minute they spent here was time their quarry had to make good his escape.

"I'm going to try something else," Harry told her. "Stay where you are and wait for me."

He signed off before she could argue with him. He knew that Charlotte's natural aggression would not let her stay fixed in one place for long. Especially not once she realised that the Russian was likely to escape.

Harry smacked Ivanov on the shoulder and Bautista on the upper arm to get their attention. He used hand signals to pantomime sneaking back along the alleyway and looping around the block to join Charlotte and the old tavern gangsters at the other end of the dock.

"I will come, too," Bautista insisted.

"I can hold this position," Ivanov said. "It is good cover. But we cannot break out of it."

"Take this", Bautista said, handing him the sawn-off shotgun and a bag of shells. He produced an old revolver from inside his jacket and kissed it. "This one has never let me down," he said.

Ivanov gave them a three count before rising into a crouch to dual wield his guns, cracking off shot after shot.

Harry and Bautista charged back into the alleyway, ducking low and scrambling past the van.

"We need to get to the tavern," Harry said. "Charlotte and Mariu are there, and maybe enough blokes to sweep the dock clean."

"Mariu Costas is too old to sweep a clean floor with a woman's broom," Bautista said. "But he will have guns there. We can use the guns."

Harry let Bautista take the lead, and they covered the ground in less than a minute. It was a nerve-racking passage, but for all that, they made it quickly and in relative safety. Harry could not help his shoulder blades twitching and his scalp itching with anticipation of the fire that might rain down on them should any of Skarov's men be smart enough to claim the high ground by climbing onto the roof of one of the waterfront buildings.

A small yard, enclosed by a high brick wall, stood to the rear of the tap house, and Harry was about to push through the gate when Bautista slapped a hand on his shoulder and pulled him back.

"You will get your head shot off, and I will have to answer to Andreas Costas, which will be even worse," he hissed.

The Sardinian banged on the heavy wooden gate with the butt of his revolver and called out in Sardu to anybody inside that he was coming through with a friend.

Harry blinked to find a young man in a barman's apron waiting for them on the other side with yet another shotgun pointed at the gate. He smiled and lowered the weapon when he saw Bautista.

They exchanged a few words in their language before the barman spoke to Harry.

"My grandfather and your woman are waiting for you in the dining room," he said in slow, careful English.

"She's not my woman," Harry said, causing the barman to brighten.

He spoke to Bautista again, a rush of florid, Latin babble that eventually caused the other man to throw up his hands and slap the boy across the face.

"First, we deal with Romanians, then we worry about your virginity," Bautista scolded. Harry wasn't sure what the young man said next, but he would bet good folding money that it was either protesting his vast experience with women or doubting the necessity of waiting until the Romanians were dealt with before asking Miss Charlotte François on a date.

37

The bartender led them into the tavern and through a confusing series of switchback corridors piled high with stainless steel kegs and wooden boxes filled with produce for the kitchen. Once or twice, Harry was forced to crabwalk sideways, so narrow were the confines. And then, without warning, they emerged into the main dining room. He crouched low, instinctively, his reflexes triggered by the uproar of gunfire. Taking a sight picture of the space, he noted three old men, all armed with shotguns, taking cover at the front of the dining room and firing out onto the waterfront. Shattered glass lay around their feet. More glass had been broken behind the bar, presumably by return fire. Harry smelled strong liquor and fried foods. Probably what he would have smelled coming in here any other day of the week, but it seemed more potent. Feeling Bautista brush past him, he ignored everything but the tactical demands.

Charlotte was nowhere that he could see. He tried to reassure himself that she would try to develop the situation to their advantage. Most likely, she was already outside, scoping out lines of fire and angles of attack.

"Mariu," Bautista called out before going on in Sardu.

One of the old men made a quarter-turn back towards them and waved briefly, summoning both men forward. Before Harry could take another step, he felt a hand on his shoulder. It was the young barman offering him a weapon. A very modern-looking pump action shotgun. Not an uptime weapon, to be sure, but undoubtedly reverse-engineered from a future design. It reminded him of the combat shotguns the marines had carried when they deployed to Indonesia. Harry thanked the young man and took the gun with a box of shells.

"It is already loaded," the barman said in slow, careful English. "Five shots. Then reload."

"Thank you," Harry said and turned to go.

But the young man grabbed him again.

"Your friend, the nun. She is no Sister of Charity, yes?"

Harry found a smile from somewhere.

"Go carefully, my friend," he said. "Pursuing her could be the most dangerous thing you do today."

He hefted the shotgun in thanks and hurried forward to take cover next to Bautista.

As soon as he made it to the front of the tavern, crouching low behind the remains of the window, he saw Charlotte. She was hiding behind a water trough, a great granite slab that looked old enough to have watered the horses of the first Roman legion to have passed through here. She was quite a sight in her long black robes, lying flat on the cobblestoned surface of the roadway, occasionally rolling left or right to fire around the corner of the trough with an assault rifle she had fetched from somewhere. Perhaps from the dead man lying a few feet away, face down, in a spreading pool of dark blood.

Bautista was yammering to his relatives, or perhaps they were somebody else's relatives; Harry had lost track of the maze of familial ties and feuds within which he'd been moving for the past week. All the Sardinians were engaged in a full and frank exchange of views, and he could follow none of it.

But he could tell there was no way Charlotte's suggestion of having these old duffers charge out into the street to flank Skarov's men would fly. They were so bloody old he imagined they'd be heads down for an afternoon nap any moment now.

It was also impossible to tell how many shooters they faced, but the volume of fire was tremendous, and almost all of it was automatic. The familiar metallic rattle and resounding bass thud of the Kalashnikov. Maybe a dozen of them. Harry's balls tried to retract into his body—an unconscious reaction, recalling all the other times men had wanted to kill him with that particular weapon.

He added a couple of shots from his puny handgun to the barrage of outgoing fire, most coming from shotguns and so essentially useless at extended range. He wondered how Ivanov was getting on. He was confident the Russian would be able to look after himself. He had good cover and plenty of weapons. But his ammunition was a finite resource. Eventually, it would run out, and they would overwhelm him.

And, of course, every minute they spent trapped here was a minute Skarov had to get away from wherever he had stashed Professor Bremmer.

Harry risked another look over the lip of the shattered window, out into the free fire zone. Two men lay dead on the upper deck of a trawler, no more than thirty metres away from Charlotte. He supposed she had killed them, then been pinned down before she could make it to the boat. He thought he could see another AK47 near one of the men, dropped into the confusion of equipment on the deck of the fishing boat. There would probably be more guns onboard and ammunition for them. Trying to reach them, however, was an idiot's gamble. Those men had died because they were exposed to the fire from Charlotte's handgun. If Harry tried to get across, he would die under the guns of a dozen NKVD men armed with much heavier weapons.

Shotguns boomed, Bautista's pistol cracked, Harry's handgun added to the uproar, and he could see no way out of the tactical dead end.

He was beginning to concede that it had been a mistake to come down here and to wonder whether he should seek the high ground, clambering up onto the roof, when the density of gunfire seemed to double and redouble again. The Sardinians started swearing at each other. Bautista bobbed up and down like a swarthy ferret, looking left and right for the source of the new danger. And Charlotte suddenly leapt up from cover and dashed out of Harry's line of sight.

In the sudden escalation of the moment, however, there was a corresponding fall in the amount of fire, inaccurate or otherwise, they were taking in the tavern. The Smedlovs had switched their attention to another threat or perhaps to an opportunity.

Harry recognised his opportunity and took it. Standing quickly, he dashed out through the front door, picking a course from one instance of cover to the next until he fetched up at the heavy stone trough where Charlotte had been sheltering just a few moments earlier. From there, he saw she had moved up the pier towards Ivanov's position. She hid behind a fat stone pillar in front of a ship's chandler. She noticed him and raised a hand, redirecting his attention up the curve of the quayside, and there he saw the reason for the sudden change in circumstance. A platoon of British soldiers had assaulted onto the waterfront and taken the Russians under fire. As well-armed as Skarov's men were, they were no match for thirty-plus squaddies from the Royal Sussex Regiment.

Heavy machine-gun fire, the explosive crump of grenades, and the murderous, industrial-scale violence of heavy infantry soon suppressed and silenced all opposition.

Harry was not so foolish as to run immediately into the open, but Charlotte François appeared to have no such qualms. She stepped out of cover and raised her hands to wave to the soldiers, calling out, "Sergeant! Sergeant Chisholm! Private Finter! Derek!"

And all of it in a strangely Gallic accent.

Harry watched as one of the soldiers, and then another, waved to her, calling her forward. She took a few steps, paused, and turned back to him, gesturing for Harry to come out of cover, too. He did so much more cautiously than her, being sure to present himself to the soldiers as unarmed and non-threatening. He lay down his weapons, put up his empty hands and laced his fingers behind his head.

Even so, a couple of the squaddies kept their rifles trained on him as their comrades searched the bodies of the fallen enemy. There appeared to be no survivors. Harry started walking towards Charlotte but paused briefly to wave old Mariu and his friends back inside as they emerged from the tavern with their shotguns in hand. Bautista made sure the old goats didn't get slaughtered for their trouble, arguing with them in Sardu, and prevailed upon them to at least lay down their shotguns.

Harry resumed his progress up the wharf. Once upon a time, it would have been a marvel to him just how much damage you could do to a place with a couple of minutes of unrestrained gunfire, but he had been young a long time ago in another world far, far away. He was not surprised by the shattered windows, the broken woodwork and pummelled masonry. Or even by the small fires which burned here and there. The silence that descended on the waterfront was familiar, too. The shock and paralysis that always poured into the vacuum created by violence.

He took his time walking towards the platoon. Charlotte meanwhile hurried forward at a jog. He could hear the whisper of her heavy black skirts and the muffled clicking of her boot heels on the cobblestones. She reached the soldiers and threw her arms around one of them, and Harry knew instantly that she was playing a role, acting out her cover still. She was not Charlotte François, the mercenary survivor of Viv Richards' private military company. She was play-acting, even now. *She was good at it*, he thought, as he watched her perform for the men. What were their names? Sergeant Chisholm and some bloke called Derek? She had probably encountered them while doing surveillance or walking from the safe house to the waterfront.

It didn't matter. It meant they had a connection to the men, which would make the next few minutes a lot easier. A lot safer for Ivanov, too, Harry hoped. He could not see the Russian anywhere, but he thanked God that Ivanov had the good sense to keep his arse well hidden while the situation remained unsettled.

Charlotte pointed at him and waved him forward again. Harry could see the man she had been talking to, looking at him quizzically. For a moment, he wondered if they had recognised him, which was a thing that happened occasionally back in London, but he rejected the idea. For now, they saw a local fisherman who had been caught up in whatever madness had erupted here. He started to unlace his fingers and lower his hands. Nobody shot or made to shoot him, and he began to relax.

There would be no passing himself off as a Sardinian deckhand, but he knew he had some explaining to do.

38

Jammed into the back of a deuce-and-a-half with his new squad, ass numb from hours of sitting on the hard wooden bench, Jack Edmonston fended off boredom, pondering how much things had changed and how they stayed the same. The roar of the heavy truck's motor drowned out most sound, as it always had. Two squads' worth of duffels occupied the centre aisle. The bench opposite held another twelve men. They could have been his guys from the last go around, except for those three black fellas, of course, who were all but invisible in the darkness.

They were all headed north on Route Eleven for the Ravenna Arsenal, where they would assemble for the first time as a division, the 37th Infantry. The three seven had fought in the Pacific last time, dragging ass the old-fashioned way through the Solomons and Luzon. They were fully mechanised this time and headed for Europe, so they'd have to spend the next couple of days loading armoured vehicles onto rolling stock. When they got where they were going, they'd spend more time training as a Division with all the armour and artillery they'd shed as jungle fighters.

The truck thudded through a huge pothole, reminding Jack that although his ass was numb, the army could always find a way of kicking it some more. He grunted as the bench slammed into his butt cheeks, sending an electric tingle up his spine. They'd all heard tall tales of new equipment modelled on uptime designs, trucks with airline seating and cup holders to deliver a man to his doom in first-class style. Jack didn't believe a word of it, but he could see plenty new to the US Army in just the second week of this latest war.

The M-4 clamped between his legs, all his equipment stuffed into plastic baggies and jammed into a duffel bag somewhere in a pile in front of him. It was all top-shelf gear and smelt of the factory wrap it'd come in. No mix-n-match this time, no making-do with Great War hand-me-downs. It all felt very different from his first days in the previous war. It felt, now, at the start, like it had at the end back then. Like he was part of some massive, superbly tuned machine that served just one purpose: to make war.

In the gloom, Jack looked down at his stiff, new, camouflaged fatigues; the only thing they couldn't produce on short notice was an embroidered name tag, EDMONSTON. So, he'd written his last name with a permanent marker on the narrow rectangular Velcro patch on his right chest. They'd even given him a rank patch and a Combat Infantrymen's pin-on badge in subdued black. Not everybody in the truck had one of those. It marked him out, set him apart and even above those without the totem.

It was all impressive as hell to Jack. A week back, he'd been a millwright. Tonight, riding in the back of a military transport under the stars of Ohio, he was a soldier again. And he knew the machine was turning out millions like him all over the country. Jack recalled his last moments with Alice and the kids. His wife had held him, but they didn't say much. One last kiss and he was gone. Bob had driven him back into town and dropped him off barely before noon. Some chaos along the way had slowed them down. Looters with whatever they could carry, all dispersing like flies at any sign of the cops or the Guard. One man was even laid out dead by the road, a thick pool of red-black blood congealed beneath him.

Old Bob had shaken his hand, wished him the best, turned the car around, and left. Eight hours later, with no ceremony, Jack had hauled his ass into this truck. And here he remained on a highway headed north. Most of the guys were trying to sleep; a few were smoking. One thing that hadn't changed—you couldn't make much conversation in the canvas-covered ass-end of a deuce-and-a-half. Not that Jack felt like talking to anyone. Soon enough, he'd get to know First Squad, Second Platoon, as they would him.

Instead, he reached into the shoulder pocket of his new fatigues and fished out his Luckies. He plucked one and put it between his lips. With practised ease, he flipped open his Zippo and lit up. The tiny yellow flame illuminated the truck bed in a spooky, dancing light, but only briefly. It was enough to spy the wide-open eyes of the man across from him. One of those buffalo soldiers from First Squad. He seemed genuinely terrified to have been caught out looking at Edmonston.

Jack smiled as best he could with an aching back and a numb ass, offering the Luckies across the line of duffel bags.

The other man seemed reluctant to take it.

"Go on," Jack said, adding his Zippo to the offering. This kid looked raw. He might not smoke, but he likely hadn't thought to pack his fixings.

On the second attempt, Jack got through, and the private took a cigarette but not the lighter. Had his own, as it turned out. He lit up, said, "Thank you, Sergeant," and passed the pack of Luckies back over. He drew deeply on the cigarette and leaned back, closing his eyes like a man reprieved from a death sentence.

Jack went back to cataloguing his equipment.

The lighter he had from the last war. The fatigues, like everything else, were brand new. He figured they must have come off a mountain-high stockpile somewhere. Jack put the smokes away and admired the uniform. Not because he was an idiot who got off on playing soldier but because he was a soldier who respected practicality. And this rig was practical-plus. It was covered with pockets, and they were handy as hell. Much better than what he'd been issued last time. There were even pockets down by his calves, one bulging with the 'combat application tourniquet' he'd been given. The other he'd filled with more smokes and candy bars.

Of course, he knew the cigarette makers were intent on killing him; odd, given he was such a good customer. But he also knew they'd be a good long while doing so. Chances were much better that some fucking Russian would pull a trigger on him first. Or some random shell fall would blow him apart. Or maybe a torpedo in the guts of his troopship if that's how they got to the fight. He did not doubt the Surgeon General's warnings on the dangers of smoking. You saw that everywhere these days. There was even talk of putting it right there on the packs of ol' Joe Camel and Mister Lucky Strike themselves, and Jack supposed that made a direct sort of sense. But he did not imagine he would ever live long enough to see the Surgeon General proved correct, at least not in his case.

The pitch of the truck's motor changed, and Jack felt the vehicle make a turn. He jostled along with everyone else. His ass was cold and sore. He took another drag as the truck climbed back through its gears.

A pity about those airline seats and cupholders, though, wasn't it?

He snorted in the dark, amused at himself. Nobody heard him over the engine noise.

Yeah, it was probably true, all the stuff he'd read and seen about how things would have gone in the future. Robot planes and death rays and stuff. Maybe they'd get back there again and even sooner this time around. But that was just stuff. Things.

What Jack wondered about was people.

Those three black fellas from the other squad, invisible in the dark across from him. Were they looking for things to be different in the future? Probably. But were they expecting them to be any different? That was a whole other question. And not just different from now, but from how they'd been upwhen the Kolhammer folks arrived from. Jack Edmonston was not politically minded at all. He liked to keep himself to himself. But he wasn't wilfully ignorant, either. He could see things how they were, he liked to think, and for all the uptime folks talked a big game about equality this and fairness that, you only had to read their histories or watch some of the movies and TV stories from their day to know that was a bunch of sweet-smelling bullshit. Guys like him, working guys, it seemed they got stomped on and ground down just as much up then as back now. Maybe even more so. And as for womenfolk and the black man—jeez, there was more equality and fairness in the back of this damn truck, as best Jack could tell. The private he'd given the cigarette was just as likely to get his ass shot off as Jack, and vice versa. Just as likely to save Jack's life, too.

For the next little while, at least, that made them closer than brothers. Be the same, whatever asshole was sitting over there.

He took another hit and drew hard. The smoke burned down to his knuckles. He could feel the heat of the cherry. With a practised gesture, he flicked it out of the back of the truck. The glowing butt sailed past a trio of sleepers and hit the truck behind them with a tiny shower of sparks. The small orange explosion was brighter than its damned blackout lights. He shrugged. Maybe he'd catch some shit for that later. But who cared?

He was cut off from everything in the back of this truck. Most of all, from his family. And as much as he loved them, that was nothing new. There was a big part of himself that he could never share with them, a chasm he knew for sure just could not be bridged because he did not want them visiting where he now lived. The hell of it was that he had more in common with those Buffalo soldiers than with his own flesh and blood.

Jack closed his eyes, trying not to think about that, and he surprised himself a little later by dozing off.

He woke up when the truck stopped, snorted fumes and smoke, and fell into a deep-throated idle. Blinking the sleep from his eyes, he looked around, bleary and lost. Bright lights and voices. All around him, fellas were coming to with more or less the same crumpled, exhausted and kind of bewildered expressions.

A head popped over the rear gate, wearing a shiny white helmet liner emblazoned with the letters MP.

Huh, Jack thought. So, the Military Police are still wearing those stupid things. That hasn't changed, then. A voice barked out from under the helmet, and the hell of it was, the voice was a woman.

"Second Platoon, Bravo Company, 2/145?"

Someone answered. "Uh, yeah."

"Everyone, hold up your IDs. Lemme see your pretty faces."

Jack reached into his chest pocket and produced his brand-new card, still smelling of the laminator back at the armoury in Steubenville. He held it up as the woman shined her flashlight about.

She nodded. "Alrighty then, good to go. Welcome to Ravenna Arsenal, gentlemen. Hurry up and wait a while right here."

She disappeared. After a few minutes, the truck lurched forward again. Through the rear, he could see soldiers with guard dogs. The truck rolled slowly past a pillbox with a machine gun. And that was just what he could see from his hugely restricted viewpoint. So it looked to him like security was pretty tight.

Finally, the truck stopped again after half a dozen twists and turns. Someone was walking along the convoy, a male voice this time, calling out, "Dismount. Dismount. Take a piss. Formation in fifteen."

The rear gate dropped, and the soldiers started to pile out with care. It was a long way to the ground. Easy enough to turn or even break an ankle. After shuffling for a bit in an uncomfortable bent-over posture, it was Jack's turn. He grabbed his rifle, climbed down, and checked its serial number unconsciously. At the same time, he pulled the charging handle back, ensured the chamber was empty, and double-checked that it was on safe.

A voice behind him.

"It's all coming back to you then, Sergeant?"

Jack turned around. It was his company commander, Captain Pearce.

"Like riding a bicycle, Captain. If the bicycle was liable to blow your head clean off."

The officer smiled wryly and gestured to his surroundings, a well-lit complex of massive metal sheds and railroad tracks. "Been to Ravenna before?"

"Yes, sir. Back in '47, when I got out of Seventh Cav and did my two years in the Guard. This a visit to memory lane for you too, Captain?"

Jack had met his new CO just once before, when Pearce had taken a moment back in Steubenville to welcome him to the unit. He said he'd fought in the Pacific, come home, and decided to make a career of it.

Pearce nodded. "Hasn't changed much. We show up here and do live fires, work on our equipment, or we put our shit on the trains and make a happy trail for somewhere else."

Jack raised an eyebrow and reflexively reached for his smokes. He got them out, put one in his mouth, and lit it without thinking. "Happy trails. That's one way of looking at it."

He inhaled the noxious plume a little deeper than usual.

"The only way if you want to keep your head together," Pearce said lightly.

"You sound like one-a-them shrinks but different, if you don't mind me saying so, Captain."

Pearce smiled and bummed a cigarette off of him.

"We just do what's got to be done, Sergeant. Should be our motto. But in Latin. It's fancier."

Jack grunted. Ten minutes later, all the men stood in neat rows in company formation. The First Sergeant, Tom West, announced that rations were coming from Battalion, and after the meal, work crews would head into the huge green barns and start preparing the unit's vehicles for movement to the railhead. There would be no sleep tonight. Jack heard the first mutters of quiet bitching.

First Sergeant West stopped dead and bellowed. "Shut the fuck up, you knuckleheads! I don't know what you all were doing last week besides squeezing your tiny dicks, but this week those teeny-weeny penises belong to me and your Uncle Sam. Old Sam is a kindly fellow, full of goodwill to all men. But me, I am a fuckin' cast-iron sledgehammer and if I hear any more grumbling about your uncle's grand designs and the place of you miserably insignificant motherfuckers within them, that sledgehammer is gonna swing hard and smash your little micro weenies flat. Do I make myself clear?"

"Yes, First Sergeant," roared one hundred voices.

Including Jack Edmonston's.

But he was smiling.

It was all the same but different.

Like the word motherfucker. That was something you didn't used to hear when first sergeants were tearing you a new one.

39

Lonesome and his guys departed the airfield before Kolhammer, heading south for a bunch of meetups with the British High Command. Kolhammer's convoy of Hummers and armoured trucks prepared for their departure some thirty minutes later, but he would not be riding along with them. Instead, his Secret Service detail led him to an old hanger at the very edge of the airfield. The place appeared authentically haunted, with birds nesting in the gutters, windows obscured by years of dust, and weeds sprouting from cracks in the tarmac before the enormous roller doors.

He couldn't help it. His heart beat faster, and his mouth dried as they slipped into the hangar through a side door. He smelled the tang of rust, the smell of old things, the musty reek of dry dung and wet feathers. It took a moment for his eyes to adjust to the darkness, but once they had, a slight grin stretched at the corners of his mouth. The longer he looked at the scene, the wider his grin became.

"Mister President? You are on a schedule, sir."

He shook his head, emerging from his daydream, properly chastened by the gentle reprimand.

"My apologies, Agent Whitting," he said. "It's not like I haven't flown one recently. I re-certified end of last year in California, but…" He trailed off for a moment. "Things change. The circumstances were different."

"Very different, Mister President," Agent Whitting agreed. "If you'll follow me, sir, we have a small area for you to change."

"Of course, let's go," Kolhammer said.

His detail chief led him across the hangar towards a small screened-off area. A couple of dozen people were inside the old structure, the usual crowd that followed the president of the United States everywhere. He was still getting used to it.

He returned the salutes of the personnel prepping his aircraft for flight. And still, he couldn't help staring.

The F-35 was a naval variant, one of the original fast-movers from the Clinton. A space-grey arrowhead of lethal intent and super-advanced meta-materials, it was one of only thirteen still flying. He stepped up to the nose of the aircraft and ran his calloused fingers over the rough surface of its skin as if to draw out some special force from within. His Secret Service detail stood a respectful distance away, not wanting to interrupt his reverie.

The dozens of 35s scattered throughout the Multinational Force had primarily been reduced to spare parts and test beds in the decade since the end of the war. They were much more valuable as treasure stores of twenty-first-century technology than they were as weapons platforms.

In many ways, they had suffered from a reverse redundancy. Many of the threats they'd evolved to meet no longer existed—or would not exist for decades. And the greater ecosystem in which they had functioned, a hypercomplex architecture of globally distributed sensors, processors, data channels and combat systems, had disappeared the moment the *Clinton* passed through Manning Pope's wormhole. Kolhammer had been surprised, even impressed, by how quickly the temps had moved to accelerate their technology. Still, you couldn't just magic up an F-22 or a massively parallel quantum processing array. Before you could do that, there were many steps and precursor technologies to develop and deploy at scale. It was the difference between building a basic colour television set and rolling out Netflix everywhere, all at once.

If he hadn't been Vice President, there was no way he could have re-certified on the F-35. It was a pure privilege of rank which he had exploited without shame.

He could tell as they wandered around the needlepoint nose of the jet fighter that the ground crew were close to completing their load-out and pre-flight routine.

The crew chief was so busy and intent on double-checking the work of his people that he didn't even notice his Commander-in-Chief marching past. A much younger airman had to gesture frantically before the master chief looked up from his clipboard and was startled a little in surprise. Before Kolhammer could tell him to carry on, he had barked an order, calling all his crew to attention.

Kolhammer returned the salute but indicated that they should get on to it.

"I'll get back to you in a few minutes, Master Chief," he said.

"Through here, Mister President," Agent Whitting said, indicating that he should step behind a flimsy screen that looked like it had come out of a doctor's office. Kolhammer did so, finding himself alone in a small changing room. Flight suit, helmet, flying boots, and kit had been laid on a table for him. His name tag was sewn over the left breast. It was the same flight suit he'd worn for his re-cert. The rank insignia still designated him as an admiral of the US Navy. Somebody had sewn a US Air Force patch on the right sleeve.

He changed out of his civilian clothes—a dark suit and tie, leather brogues—and climbed into the heavier, bulkier armour of a jet fighter pilot; over forty pounds of specialised clothing and equipment designed to keep him alive in the hostile environment at the very edge of the F-35's performance envelope. First, a Nomex liner suit, then the one-piece jumpsuit to protect him against blacking out at high gees. After a couple of minutes of shucking himself into those layers of coveralls, he sat down to pull on boots, gloves, harness, and floatation vest. Agent Whitting was on the other side of the screen with Kolhammer's survival vest, containing a radio and beacon, flares, GPS unit, infrared tape, a strobe light, compass and the various bits and pieces of kit he might need if he had to put down over land.

If he ditched or crashed into the ocean, he'd probably die.

And there was a non-zero chance of that since he would pilot his F-35 across thousands of miles of open ocean.

It was time to go home.

It hadn't mattered much that he'd been in Paris when the Soviets attacked. After all, he was just the Vice President, a role once famously described as less valuable than a bucket of warm piss. It hadn't mattered until Stalin's operatives had reached out and taken the life of President Eisenhower.

Of course, he could never admit it, but Kolhammer had seen an upside to his travelling out of the US when the Sovs struck. For one thing, it put him right in the middle of the action. Meeting with Churchill and Jones, promising de Gaulle that America would pay any cost and meet any burden to defeat the communist aggressors, all of those things had been made possible by the accident of his being away from Washington.

Lia Pao, however, was right when she'd straight-up told him he had to haul ass back to the US. Things felt like they were going sideways without a steady hand on the tiller.

"You gotta kick some ass and take some names," she'd said. "You can't do that here. Ass kicking is an interpersonal skill. Best done up close."

What she hadn't been able to do was suggest a way to get home without the Russians reaching out. He'd dispersed his staff across multiple civilian and military flights and ordered them on ahead of him, judging that Lavrenty Beria would not waste resources tracking and targeting a passenger flight carrying the likes of Josh Ovenden or Seth Parker. But the new communist supremo would definitely spend some of his military capital attacking any route that Kolhammer himself took home. He knew this for a certainty because it was precisely what he would do if he could decapitate the Soviet leadership.

He emerged from behind the screens, took the survival vest from Agent Whitting with a nod of thanks, and strode across the hangar towards his ride. It was Andy Porter who'd suggested he should fly himself home in a fully tricked-out fighter jet.

"You still know how to do that, right, Mister President?" he smirked.

He did, even if his flight suit was a little tighter around the waist now.

The ground crew came to attention again as Kolhammer approached, and he returned their salute as crisply as he would have done thirty years earlier, reporting to his first assignment on the old USS *George Bush*.

"Sir, she's good to go," Command Chief Master Sergeant Chadderton reported.

"Thank you, Master Sergeant," Kolhammer replied. "Thank you all," he added to the rest of the crew.

They each responded in their own way, some embarrassed, others grinning hugely.

"If you'll allow me, Mister President," Chadderton said, "I'll give you the tour."

They walked the complete circuit around the aircraft.

"I see we're rigged for stealth, Master Sergeant," Kolhammer remarked as they stepped off.

There were no drop tanks or missiles fixed to external hard points. The F-35 was naked, or rather, she had concealed her charms entirely.

"Not my call, Mister President," Chadderton said. He glanced back at Agent Whitting. "Wiser heads than mine decided you were flying into a non-permissive environment."

Kolhammer could hear the scare quotes around the words non-permissive. The sergeant was a temp and probably the sort to resist the lure of uptime weasel words.

"So, stealth it is. You got a full tank, 20,000 lbs of jet fuel. That'll easily get you to the first tanker, where you can top off. You'll re-sup five times on the flight."

"That's a lot," Kolhammer said. "We should only need three stops for gas."

"Uh huh," Chadderton said. "Like I said, above my pay grade.

Partly, it's your escorts, I guess. Those Tigers you got on your wing don't have the legs that this old girl's got."

He ran his hand along the leading edge of one wing.

"The internal weapons bays are all carrying AIM 120s and a Hammerhead. Augmented. These are mods, fresh off the line from LA. I think it was the Marines who carried the 120s on the *Kandahar*. Your birds on the *Clinton* had those nice AIM 260s. But we can't replicate them yet. The chips are too hard, and the radar's damn near impossible. The hammerhead came directly from the proving grounds in Nevada. Hope it works."

"We don't need the 260s since we're not going up against Beijing's air defence grid, back up when," Kolhammer said. "But a Hammerhead drone?"

He whistled.

"There is a fair chance you might run into trouble on the way home," Chadderton said. "The Russian northern fleet was out on 'manoeuvres' when Stalin dropped the hammer. They got a flat-top out there somewhere. So we filled your pockets with Am-rams. The F-5s in your escort are getting them, too."

"But..." Kolhammer started.

"Yeah, but," Chadderton confirmed before Kolhammer could ask the question. "They'll be loaded externally. Along with the drop tanks. Now you see what I have to put with, Mister President."

"Yeah, I see," Kolhammer said.

His plane had been stripped of external armaments to decrease its radar profile, but his escort fighters would be lighting up Russian radar sets from hundreds of miles away.

"Well, you've done a great job here, Master Sergeant," Kolhammer said. "My compliments to your crew. I'll look after your old girl as best I can."

A young crew woman came forward with his helmet and face mask.

The helmet was an original.

"The heads-up display still working?" Kolhammer asked.

"Like a charm," Chadderton said. "But you don't have one-tenth of the sensors you need to feed it."

"Have to make do with the Mark 1 eyeball," Kolhammer shrugged.

"I am ordered to suggest the President just punches out of any trouble at maximum power," Chadderton said drily. "You can still outrun anything the Reds can put in the air."

Kolhammer grinned, "Yeah, but where's the fun in that?"

40

Slim Jim was used to dealing with the press. Or at least he thought so. The truth was he was used to softball questions from tame reporters working for the newspapers and TV stations he owned. And they never ambushed him. If Slim Jim Davidson took a question from a girl reporter or some gossip news hottie, it was either because he'd asked to meet them or he had something to sell. The pack of howling wolverines waiting for him outside the transit lounge at Idlewild were not tame. And they were hungry.

"Jesus Christ," he muttered as the storm of flashbulbs exploded in his face, blinding and disorienting him.

"I tried to warn you," Maria O'Brien said, leaning in close so that he could hear her over the uproar. There had to be a coupla dozen of these jackals, not a one of them looking like fans of Slim Jim Davidson, all yelling their questions over the top of each other.

He almost turned around and ran back into the business lounge, but Maria arrested his escape with a firm grip on his elbow. She grabbed him hard enough to hurt, sending small jags of lightning up and down his arm. He sometimes forgot that she had been a marine. This was not one of those times.

"Ouch. Shit," he hissed.

"Just throw the tough questions to me," she urged. Her mouth was so close to his ear that he could feel each word in her warm breath. "You do you. And I'll do the hard part."

He knew what that meant. He could at least manage that.

Stretching that famous party-boy grin across his face, Slim Jim threw up his hands as if in surrender. The press pack surged in. He looked for a friendly and familiar face in the seething crowd, but although he recognised a few of them—mostly the big TV guys like Cronkite and Murrow—they didn't look friendly. They didn't look pissed off either, which was something, he supposed. But there was a frantic, dangerous energy to them as a whole.

"Boys, boys, boys," he called out. "And ladies." He winked at one of the few female reporters in the pack. "Plenty of Jimbo to go around. What can I help y'all with today?"

It had once been his habit, under pressure, to lapse into the southern drawl of his misspent youth—a po'boy affectation that he thought he'd left behind on that chain gang in Georgia.

The terminal echoed to the sudden roar of fifty or sixty voices raised as one, all competing to be heard. It was a new building designed by some fancy-ass Euro-dink architect. All curvy lines and super-hard brushed metal surfaces. *It made the riot of noise so much worse*, Slim Jim thought.

"Okay, ladies first," he called out, pointing at the female reporter who'd pushed her way into the front row. *She wasn't TV pretty, but she was all right*, he thought, and there was no way he was putting his dick on the chopping block for Cronkite or Murrow.

"Mister Davidson," she started in a thick Milwaukee accent, and to Slim Jim's surprise, the small riot calmed down some. "Mister Davidson," she repeated, "did you or anyone in your company conspire with the President to commit criminal violations of the Trotter-McNeil Act?"

"The fuck now?" Slim Jim shot back, speaking much louder in his surprise than he'd intended.

He hadn't intended to curse at the woman, but in the moment's shock, he'd regressed a few years.

The press pack regressed, too, falling back into the rowdy scrum of shouting, bellowing men and one or two women who'd first greeted them as they left the lounge to walk the short distance to the Davidson Airlines gates. A whole DC-10 waited at Gate 23 just for him. He imagined that the little business jet they'd flown back in from the UK had already turned around and disappeared east over the horizon—detailed onto some corporate black op back in Europe. Or maybe North Africa. Maria hadn't told him, and he hadn't bothered asking. He'd just wanted to get back to his mansion in California —about as far away from the murderous hordes of Soviet berserkers as possible. His security guys were still with him but arrayed in a thick-shouldered wedge behind the businessman and his executive assistant. On the orders of that assistant.

A bad look, the third world potentate or sub-Bond villain with his goon squad, Maria said.

And so, he was trapped here, in New York's brand-new airport, surrounded by murderous hordes of reporters.

The flashbulbs were going again, further dazzling and unsettling him. The roar of shouted questions was so wild and raucous as to be completely incoherent, but somehow Maria stepped into it and projected her voice far enough and loud enough to calm that shit down.

She was dressed in her best uptime business bitch style, but she sounded like a drill instructor as she yelled her demand for quiet, calm, and good order.

"We will take three questions today, even though you are delaying us grievously, and Mister Davidson is needed urgently at his headquarters in LA. The first question, from Miss Shostakowksi, is an easy one. No. Neither Mister Davidson nor anybody from Davidson Enterprises conspired with President Kolhammer to commit criminal violations of the Trotter-McNeil Act."

She looked at the young woman who'd set off the minor rampage.

"I would like to thank you for asking such a dumb question, Miss Shostakowksi. It saves time when a simple no will suffice for an answer. Next?"

The familiar roar swelled up, but this time, Slim Jim was ready for it, and Maria seemed almost to relish the challenge.

"Mister de Grazia," she called out. "From the Trib. You're a handsome fellow with good manners. You're next."

The roars turned to groans from dozens of disappointed reporters, but they quieted down. The Tribune wasn't a paper Slim Jim owned, so nobody could complain about Maria playing favourites. Or at least that's how Slim Jim saw it. If it'd been him running this shit show instead of standing gape-mouthed and drooling in front of it, he'd have only taken questions from his people.

"Thank you, ma'am," the Chicago guy said. "Can you provide some details of how Mister Davidson's civilian satellites were able to shoot down a bunch of Russian space weapons?"

Most everyone turned to Slim Jim for the answer, but he just shrugged and grinned. He was starting to recover his balance.

"I'm not a big science guy," he said, holding up his hands, open and honest. "I failed most things but gym class in high school, and I cut that whenever I could."

He got a few grudging laughs for that.

"But I learned street math," he went on, "and I know we spent a heap of money on those satellites to bring y'all the best in uptime and contemporary entertainment."

A few more despairing chuckles at his salesmanship gave him the confidence to continue. He leaned into the performance.

"I also knew I didn't want to lose all that money just cos the commies might try and grab the high ground off of us one day. So I told my science guys to give me some cover. Put some big honking guns and rockets and stuff on my birds. My lawyers told me I could do that cos I got the right to defend my property, no matter where it is. And if defending my property means I can defend the whole world from a bunch of no-good commies—I call that a bonus. Not a goddamn crime."

He sent that last barb directly back at the Shostakowksi bitch.

He had no idea who she was, but he was gonna find out. He was gonna buy that business this very day, and she was gonna find herself out of a job.

The reporters were baying for more answers again, shouting more questions, and Maria stepped up to wrangle them.

"Last question," she warned, "then we must go. You people are delaying our flight and hundreds of other travellers with this nonsense. Normal folks who don't have jet planes to get around in, too. Mister Cronkite, please."

Walter Cronkite identified himself and his network, CBS, which was weird, Slim Jim thought. Because everybody already knew who he was.

"Will Mister Davidson be giving testimony to the Senate Committee on Investigations? Senator McCarthy has announced his intention to subpoena him if he refuses."

"The fucking what committee?" Slim Jim blurted.

He was about to add, 'And fucking who?' when Maria's steel claws dug into his elbow again.

"Mister Davidson, I will remind you, is not just a successful businessman who has brought incredible prosperity to America and hundreds of thousands of good, secure, well-paying jobs to Americans. He is also a veteran of frontline combat and a patriot. He has done more in the last week to secure this country and her friends from the depredations of our enemies than Joe McCarthy has managed in his whole miserable life. Mister Davidson will not respond to any subpoenas because there will be no subpoenas. Mister Davidson stands ready to do anything necessary to help defend this country, even if it is necessary to waste his valuable time explaining himself to some drunken blowhard from Wisconsin. And with that, ladies and gentlemen, we take our leave of you today. We have a war to fight, and the very considerable resources of Mister Davidson's companies will be devoted to ensuring we win that fight. Good day to you all."

His security detail suddenly formed around him, fashioning themselves into a tight wedge of bodyguards moving towards the terminal gates. Slim Jim found himself carried along within their midst or possibly pushed along by Maria, whose hand sat on the small of his back, urging him forward.

The baying pack of pressmen redoubled their efforts, shouting questions and demands for his attention, but his detail had already worked up some speed, and there was no question of them stopping now.

Slim Jim let himself be carried along. He wasn't quite sure what had just happened, and making things worse, he was pretty sure that Maria didn't have much of a clue either. One of the reasons he paid her so much was that she had this uncanny ability to see around corners, but she seemed to have been blindsided just as he had, not so much by the presence of the press but by their focused aggression.

"What the hell was that about?" he asked. "I thought that McCarthy asshole drank himself to death or something."

"Wrong timeline," Maria deadpanned. She had a strange knack for making herself heard over the din without needing to shout at him. "I'm sorry, this is news to me too. We had him tagged as a problem child a long time ago, but because of that, we put him in the naughty corner. I don't know how he escaped, but it looks like he has."

"Probably got something to do with a couple of million commies charging across Germany," Slim Jim suggested.

"Probably," Maria agreed.

His security detail started to bear left, taking them down a long corridor with boarding gates on either side. At least half of the reporters had fallen away, probably to file whatever stories they could spin up out of the conference back at the transit lounge. The big swinging dicks were gone. There was no sign of Murrow or Cronkite anywhere, but that Polack horror pig who'd ambushed him with the question about some bullshit criminal thing kept up with them, still throwing questions at him. Slim Jim resisted the urge to flip her the bird. Flashbulbs were still going off every couple of seconds, and he knew what sort of a picture it would paint. They'd probably use a Frankenstein flash, too. Shoot him from below and darken all the shadows on his face for the full Bela Lugosi effect.

He ignored the woman, looking past the thinning crowd of reporters to see a bright silver Constellation pulled up to an air bridge at the nearest gate. He almost snorted with derision, and it made him feel much better. She was undoubtedly a beautiful-looking aircraft, but the jetliners his factories were turning out at the rate of two or three every month meant the old Connie would be better off in a museum.

Only a few reporters were left when they reached the gate where his DC-10 was waiting. The Polack was one of them, of course. She tried shouting one last question.

"Do you think they'll put you back on the chain gang, Slim Jim?"

He felt Maria's fingers dig into his arm again, painfully. But it wasn't enough. He stopped and turned on her.

"What do you mean by 'they'?" he said.

It seemed to throw a wrench into the machinery which had delivered them to the gate. Maria stumbled to a halt, and the security detail, as well. The few reporters who were left stood quietly by for the first time, seemingly lost for something to say or shout at him.

"Seriously," Slim Jim said. "They, who?"

"The authorities," said the reporter, recovering a little. "If you've committed a crime."

Slim Jim smiled.

"I committed plenty of crimes in my day, lady," he said. "But I ain't like that no more. Good fortune and even better advice from people like Ms O'Brien here," he leaned into the uptime pronunciation of *Ms*, "She done cured me of my wicked ways. I don't need to do no crimes. Crime is for folks who can't work the system, and lady, I own the system now."

He winked at the other reporters.

"I hope you boys are packing Davidson Corporation digital recorders," he said. "Because I want to make sure you get every word of that right."

Maria's hand fell from his arm. The reporters finally backed off. And his aircrew welcomed him to the flight.

As they passed onto the aerobridge, Slim Jim turned to Maria and said, "Find out who she works for."

His assistant started to argue, but he cut her off.

"Yeah, yeah, yeah, I know what you're thinking, but you're wrong. I'm not going to have her sacked. I want to know who she's working for. Because a loser like Joe McCarthy couldn't drag his ass out of the gutter with a tow rope and a tractor. If he's suddenly got juice in DC again, and he's making trouble for us, it's because somebody wants him to make trouble for us. Find out who, Maria. And when we do get to LA, we're going straight to the Death Star, and you're gonna tell me absolutely everything I own that can be turned into a weapon we can use in the next couple of weeks."

"A weapon against who?" she asked.

"Joe McCarthy, Joe Stalin, that crazy fucking toilet brush-looking Lenny Beria motherfucker they got running the clown show in Moscow now," he said. "I don't care. You come at the king, baby; you better not fucking miss. And the fact we're still walking around means that somebody tried and missed."

THE MAN HAD STOOD at the back of the press pack. Unlike the reporters elbowing each other and baying for Davidson's attention, he hadn't made much effort to push himself forward. It was almost as though he was playing at being a reporter.

The man did follow Davidson and his entourage through the airport, however. He didn't rush to keep up with the handful of journalists who stuck with the businessman, but he stayed close enough to keep an eye on them. And on Emily Shostakowksi.

When Davidson finally escaped through the boarding lounge to his jet, the man waited by a newsstand, flicking through a magazine.

"Nice work," he said when Shostakowksi returned to him.

"Thanks for the Trotter-McNeil tip-off," she said, "but he didn't seem bothered by it."

Roy Cohn smiled.

"Not yet," he said. "But Davidson's a criminal. He says so himself. Even boasts about it. You keep the questions coming, Emily. You're gonna get a story worth having."

She made a face.

"What questions? His lawyer straight-up denied everything."

Cohn grinned.

"I'm a lawyer. That's what we do. And Davidson confirmed everything she denied. Keep digging. Start with this guy if you can find him."

Roy Cohn gave her a slip of paper.

It had one name written on it.

Dan Black.

41

Sergeant Chisholm tilted his head to one side, a quizzical expression creeping across his sunburned face as Harry approached. The man didn't even need to say anything. Harry recognised the moment when Chisholm recognised him. The reaction was almost comical, a cartoon double-take, his eyes blinking rapidly as he tried to shake himself free of the ridiculous notion that he had just made the acquaintance of...

"Your Highness!" Chisholm croaked, the words struggling to escape his surprise and disbelief. But he was a sergeant of Her Majesty's Royal Sussex Regiment and knew exactly what to do in this or any other situation. He started roaring through his men.

"Atten-*SHUN*!" Chisholm bellowed in his best parade ground voice, and up and down the docks, surrounded by the aftermath of what they'd done, the squaddies snapped into formal postures of alertness and obedience; all except for one who was still holding onto Sister Charlotte and seemed reluctant to let her go.

Before Harry could say anything, Chisholm noticed the poor devil and turned his surprise and creeping uncertainty into performative, non-commissioned fury. Sergeant Chisholm's nostrils flared. Sergeant Chisholm's jaw muscles bunched. And Sergeant Chisholm sucked in a deep breath of hot Sardinian air before unloading on poor Private Finter.

"Finter, YOU FUCKING HORRIBLE LITTLE MAN—please excuse my language, Sister—YOU LET GO OF THAT NUN AND ATTEND TO HIS ROYAL HIGHNESS BEFORE I PLANT MY BOOT SO FAR UP YOUR FUCKING ARSE YOU'LL NEED A FUCKING BRAIN SURGEON TO UNTIE THE SHOELACES."

Finter was already standing perfectly to attention when Chisholm made his quiet aside to Sister Charlotte. Still, like all good sergeants, Chisholm had a genuine commitment to the bit and carried on with the show until the very last line.

Charlotte, too, remained in character and twittered her apologies to Private Finter as though the whole thing had been her fault. Finter's comrades remained perfectly still, thirty khaki statues sweltering under the high Mediterranean sun, all keeping at least one eye on their exploding NCO.

Harry was sweating from the day's heat and shivering with the adrenaline backwash of combat shock.

"Have your men stand at ease, Sergeant Chisholm," he said. "We are very grateful for the help, but there's no need for any of this."

He couldn't be bothered adding or explaining that he was no longer an actual royal. He had no claim to the throne and had not considered himself a prince of the realm in many years. Only gossip columnists and favour-seeking social crawlers carried on with that rubbish nowadays.

Chisholm put his men back to work, policing up the damage and destruction of the gunfight.

"I don't suppose you could tell me what the hell was happening here, sir?" he asked, almost plaintively. Harry understood the edge of anxiety in his voice. He'd be held responsible if things had turned to custard on his watch.

"Who is your commanding officer, Sergeant?" Harry asked gently.

Chisholm slumped a little as if a great weight had settled upon him.

"That would be Lieutenant Lane, sir."

Harry smiled.

"Then I shall tell Lieutenant Lane that you and your men have done an excellent day's work here."

Chisholm straightened up a little, but the confused expression on his face did not change. His gaze flitted up and down the waterfront, where some of his men fought a small fire that had broken out in the ship's chandlery, and others dragged a dozen or so corpses into a straggling line where they could be searched and later disposed of in better order.

"I'm back with the Regiment," Harry lied, "doing some...unconventional work. These hoodlums are Russian spies," he explained, nodding at the nearest dead man. "Sister Charlotte, myself, a major Pavel Ivanov, and our local guide, Mister Bautista, were tracking an NKVD operator, Alexi Skarov, and the rocket scientist he'd abducted and was trying to smuggle back to Moscow. We had information they might be leaving on a fishing boat from these docks."

Chisholm considered the scope of all the chaos and destruction.

"Pretty good information then, Sir. Is your bloke here, the scientist, I mean? I'm sorry if we shot him."

Harry shook his head.

"Doesn't look like it, no. I think this was a trap to delay or kill us while this man Skarov got away with Professor Bremmer."

Charlotte was staring at him, half pissed off, half disbelieving that he had just vomited up the details of their mission to some dumb grunt. But Harry knew what he was doing. Their cover was blown here, and now, if they were to have any chance of lying hands on Skarov or Bremmer, they would need the help of Chisholm and his superiors.

"But I forget my manners," Harry said. "Sergeant Chisholm, please say hello to Miss Charlotte François, a special operator working with my old mate and regimental sergeant major until Comrade Skarov murdered him and his team back in Cairo. She is now on secondment to the Regiment, too."

"A nun, sir? A lady?"

"Oh, for fucks sake," Charlotte swore in her natural American accent. Both Chisolm and Finter, who were still hanging around, looked even more surprised at that than they had been to recognise Harry.

Charlotte shrugged and shook her head.

"What are you gonna do? A girl's gotta earn a living. And my job is finding and killing assholes like Alexei Skarov."

Private Finter took a whole step backwards away from her, almost tripping over a coil of rope.

"I might go help the lads, Sarge," Finter said. His voice sounded a little choked.

"Yeah, you do that, son," Chisholm said. He looked from Charlotte to Harry and back to Charlotte again.

"And these other blokes you've got with you? The Russian one and your local guide?"

"Major Pavel Ivanov, Russian Federation special forces from, you know, up when," Harry said, jerking his thumb at the sky as though that explained where they had come from. "And Bautista is a local brigand from one of the major clans on the island. He got us up here through bandit country when we ran into another ambush set up in the mountains by our friend Skarov."

"You've been busy, your Highness," Chisholm said, sounding more than a little sceptical.

Harry nodded.

"Not so much the last couple of days, Sergeant. We've been holed up in town waiting for Skarov to show himself. I'm sorry if we've made a right bloody mess on your manor, but you know how it goes. Operational security. Need to know. All that rubbish."

Chisholm nodded slowly.

"Is this really a regimental job, sir?" he asked.

Harry smiled.

"As close enough as makes no difference, Sergeant Chisholm. Rest assured, we are here fighting the good fight, like you. And we should probably get on with it. There's another place he might take his leave from. A little anchorage around the coast called Capo Testa. Do you know it?"

Chisholm nodded, his brow furrowing.

"Not much around there, your Highness," he said. "A couple of old fisherman shacks. And a bit of a lockup for one of the local smugglers. We take a wander through the hills behind the bay occasionally. But on the quiet; we're not supposed to stray down to the beach. I'm not sure who the bloke is what owns that setup, but he's well connected."

"He's dead," Charlotte said.

Harry turned quickly to look at her.

Charlotte waved away any questions.

"Skarov needed a lay-up point, so I'd bet he took it and killed anybody who needed killing to avoid any complications."

"Are you sure about that?" Harry said.

She shrugged.

"I don't know it for a fact, but I'd bet good folding money on it. I've been tracking this prick for weeks, Harry. It's how he operates. He works in the shadows and doesn't leave loose ends behind. If he's exfiltrating via Capo Testa, he's probably gone. Bremmer too. But we should at least go check it out. Should probably let Ivanov out of the naughty corner, too," she added, nodding toward the alleyway where Harry had left the Russian.

"If you've got some Ivan tucked away over there, you should go get him before one of my lads finds him," Chisholm said.

"Yeah, that wouldn't go well for your lads," Charlotte said.

"You two!" Chisholm yelled at a couple of squaddies heading towards Ivanov's hiding place. "Get out of it. Colonel Windsor here and his mates are going to clear that sector."

The two soldiers backed away from the little side street. Harry had no idea whether Ivanov was even there anymore, but keeping him away from the British platoon would be a good idea.

He could see that Chisholm wasn't happy about any of it.

"Sergeant, I meant what I said about your men doing good work here. They saved the day. We didn't get our man, but that wasn't your fault. It was bad intelligence and a piss-poor effort on our part."

"Speak for yourself," Charlotte said.

Chisholm looked at her as if he couldn't believe what he saw.

"Either way," Harry went on. "We'd appreciate a lift to Capo Testa. And maybe a squad of your lads while you're at it."

42

The jeep sped through the hills outside Capo Testa, turning the craggy limestone rockfaces and parched Mediterranean scrub into a blur. The hottest part of the day was behind them, but the sun still hammered down, beating the surface of the blue-green ocean into a rippling sheet of silver sparks. Harry wore a pair of dark sunglasses but still had to squint occasionally as a sharp turn or steep climb put the sun directly into his face. He sat in the rear of the jeep with Ivanov and Charlotte. Sergeant Chisholm and Private Finter rode up front, the enlisted man behind the wheel.

Chisholm's face was an unhappy mask, but Finter appeared to be enjoying himself, pouring on as much speed as he could to get them to the little cove as quickly as possible. Another jeep with a heavy, vehicle-mounted machine gun in its rear tray kept pace with them about twenty yards back. And about a minute behind that, a two-tonne lorry with the rest of Chisholm's squaddies brought up the rear. Harry had a feeling like a cold stone in his stomach. They were already too late. The ambush on the harbour front had almost certainly given Skarov enough time to escape.

He glanced over at Ivanov and Charlotte. Neither looked any happier than Chisholm, but the Russian was less guarded in his gloom. Charlotte merely stared out to sea as though looking for Viv's ghost out there, hoping to ask forgiveness. Ivanov ground his jaw, pressed his lips together, and fought the violent motion of the Jeep as it swerved back and forth through the tight climbing turns. Occasionally, he would mutter something to himself, almost like a prayer, were it not for the Russian profanities Harry could read on his pressed white lips.

"We're almost there," Chisholm called back over the roar of the engine and the wind of their passage. Private Finter wiped off at least half their speed as they approached a craggy ridge line, only lightly shaded by a stand of gnarled and ancient olive trees.

"We don't want to go charging over the top," Chisholm said at a slightly more reasonable volume as Finter brought the jeep to a halt. "One bloke with an old rifle could pick off the lot of us before we got close."

Harry nodded in acknowledgement. Back in the upwhen, he'd choppered into plenty of raids that required his team to walk the last mile. Neither Charlotte nor Ivanov objected either. They dismounted the jeep, checked their weapons, and looked to the ridge line. The gunner in the second vehicle charged his weapon and brought it to bear on the high ground. Harry could hear the truck approaching through the ravine but could not yet see it. He felt an unpleasant, low-grade electrical tingle just under the surface of his skin. This felt like a bad day in Afghanistan.

"Knock it off," he muttered, knowing this was nothing like that. They weren't fighting tribesmen or jihadis whose ancestors had walked these hills for a thousand years. They were chasing after a man who had probably escaped from the island hours earlier.

"You right, guv?" Private Finter asked.

Harry tried to let the tension run out of his shoulders. He smiled and started to answer, but Ivanov spoke up before he could say anything.

"His Royal Highness is remembering the good old days," the Russian said without even the trace of a grin. He, too, was scanning the ridge line and frowning.

"I'm not a Highness anymore," Harry said.

"But a prince among men, yes?" Ivanov deadpanned. It was as close to humour as he was ever likely to get.

"What next, Sergeant?" Charlotte asked. She had let her French accent fall away and now spoke with the soft West Coast lilt she'd picked up in San Diego from her foster mother, Doctor Margie François.

"The boys will know what to do," Chisholm said as the truck grumbled around the final bend.

True to his word, the platoon deployed quickly from the back of the transport, fanning out and moving up the hill in a series of leapfrogging movements, which caused Harry to nod in admiration. It had been a while, a very long while, since he had fought as a trooper, but he could still appreciate a well-practised moment of tactical expertise.

The men floated up the hill silently, ghosting from one patch of cover to the next, fire teams providing overwatch to each other, noncoms and squad leaders effecting slight changes in speed and direction with simple hand signals. Within a minute, they had the high ground.

"Looks like it's time for us to go and claim all the credit," Chisholm grunted.

"Looks like, Sergeant," Harry acknowledged, gesturing for him to lead the way. It was Chisholm's turf and his men.

HARRY MARVELLED AGAIN at the ease with which the squaddies, who would still be getting over the firefight on the docks, appeared to glide up the hill. He was fit and recovering well from his injuries in Cairo, but he found the climb challenging primarily because of the uncertain footing and punishing heat. By the time he reached the military crest, shy of the actual ridgeline, he was sweating profusely and short of breath.

"Looks like somebody skipped cardio," Charlotte quipped. She had danced lightly up the slope well ahead of him.

"Your turn'll come," Harry promised grimly.

Sergeant Chisholm was already standing with a good view of the cove, scanning the little beach and the blockhouse structure at the northern end with binoculars. He passed them to Harry with a grunt and a look of deep dissatisfaction.

"Seems clear," he said, as though every nerve ending was humming to him that it wasn't. He was shorter and broader than Harry and probably massed out much heavier. He was undoubtedly carrying more kit. But Chisholm looked no more discomforted by the climb than Charlotte.

Harry took the glasses from him.

Capo Testa presented an idyllic vision, marred by a single human intrusion, the ugly cinder block bunker sitting in the dunes above the high tide line. It was not a beach shack or a building devoted to leisure or ease. It was a lock-up.

"So, the fellow who built that is a smuggler?" Harry said.

"Was," Charlotte replied. "Dollars to doughnuts, Skarov killed him."

"You ever been down there?" Harry asked Chisholm. "Seen inside?"

The sergeant shook his head.

"No, sir. The higher-ups made it bleeding obvious that anybody who stuck their nose in down there was on a promise to get it cut off. I suppose he had protection."

"What? Even from the Army?" Harry asked.

"From whoever mattered," Ivanov laughed, but it was more of a short, bitter cough than a genuine laugh.

"It doesn't look like there's anyone here now," Harry said. The sun had tracked far enough west to be behind them. It flared on the windows of the blockhouse, which were secured behind thick iron bars.

"You can see where they took the boats out," Charlotte said, pointing down at the small golden crescent of sand. Harry moved the binoculars to scope out where she was pointing. He nodded. He could see the tracks of at least two small boats in the sand. They'd been dragged to the water's edge from higher up on the beach. They were gone now.

"I should send a couple of the boys down to have a look," Chisholm said. He didn't sound at all pleased by the idea.

"You have grenade throwers?" Ivanov asked. "Toss a few down there. See what it sets off. I know this man. He will have booby-trapped everything."

"Can confirm," Charlotte agreed. She was scoping out the structure through her pair of much more advanced field glasses. "I think I can already see some of the tripwires."

Chisholm was about to start barking orders at his men when Harry spoke up again.

"Wait," he said. "What if the professor is down there?"

"Bremmer?" Ivanov said. "He is gone, too. Bremmer was Skarov's mission, and his mission was accomplished. Skarov is gone, and the scientist with him."

Harry looked to Charlotte, hoping for support, but all he found was the blank, dead eyes of the profoundly uninterested. She had come here to kill the man who killed her friend. Harry's friend, too. Everything else was secondary to that.

"Time for a face facts moment, Harry," she said. "We lost. He won. He's in the wind now. That thing down there..." she gestured at the beachfront bunker, "...that'll be rigged to blow in at least half a dozen different ways. Take it as a draw. He tried to kill us in Santa Teresa. He failed. So we get a chance to..."

Whatever she had been about to say died on her lips as the small cement building exploded with a shocking, gut-shaking boom. Instinctively, Harry dropped to the ground. They all did. Half a second later, large chunks of cinder block and twisted rebar flew over them. Debris began to rain down, and he burrowed into the hard ground as best he could, which was not much at all.

A second and a third explosion quickly followed, with more debris flying out of the bomb site. A stainless-steel beer keg crunched into a rocky prominence just a few feet away. He heard men swearing, seagulls screeching, and beneath it all, the sound of small waves breaking on the beach, as they had for thousands of years.

Eventually, Chisholm declared it safe to stand up. Harry was a little shaky getting back to his feet. His vision blurred at the edges, and he realised he'd been holding his breath. He let it go, took in some clean air, let that go, and breathed deeply again.

Down in the dunes, the smuggler's lockup had been demolished by the series of explosions and was burning freely. Harry tried to put aside the sick feeling of shame and failure that had settled into his stomach like a leaden weight.

Charlotte and Ivanov were almost certainly right. Bremmer wasn't there. Extracting the German rocket scientist had been Skarov's primary mission, and he was nothing if not mission-focused. This... was just another middle finger jammed in the face of his enemies.

"Timer switch," Ivanov declared, almost as if satisfied things had turned out exactly as he expected.

"Maybe," Charlotte replied. "Or it could have been a seagull landing on a tripwire."

"Could've been, I suppose," Harry conceded.

He knew he would have to go down and pick through the wreckage anyway. Just to be sure. He returned the binoculars to Chisholm, and the sergeant scanned the burning.

"I'll get the sappers out here," he said. "A bloke what'd go to that much trouble to blow up a perfectly good shed would probably leave a few other nasty surprises lying around, too. You gonna be right with that, sir?" he asked Harry.

Staring down at the beach, Harry shook his head at how quickly the scene was returning to normal. Sort of. Burning wreckage lay everywhere, but it had stopped raining from the sky. Seagulls and pelicans had landed warily on the sand to pick through the plunder. And the waters of the cove had settled back into a languorous rhythm, with small waves breaking on the wet sand with a crash and a hiss as the water retreated from the land.

"I suppose so," Harry said. "I will need them to check for bodies or one body in particular. But..." he trailed off.

"Our work here is done," Ivanov said. "We must move on. To Marseille. We will have another chance to find Skarov and the professor there."

43

Kolhammer had long thought that outside of aerial combat, only a bad weather landing on a carrier or inflight refuelling at night compared for ass-puckering exhilaration. He would not be putting the F-35 down on a flat-top during this trip, but he would have to top up the tanks at least four times, and this, his first refill, was scheduled for oh-two-hundred local, under a full moon some five hundred nautical miles west of Ireland.

Nudging the stick ever so slightly, he took up position underneath and behind the massive right wing of the RAF jumbo tanker. It looked like a giant bird against the star field, its powerful engines glowing at night. In a few moments, he would try to aim the aircraft's bulbous fuel probe into the floating basket at the end of the tanker's hose, like a knight from the Middle Ages demonstrating some obscure but extreme feat of skill with a lance, a wicker basket and a horse galloping through the night sky at six hundred miles an hour.

The last of his escorts, an F-5 Tiger, was finishing. The President was next. Not that the crew of the tanker would know that. For them, he was simply HAWAII 5-0. The other pilots in the flight addressed him by his callsign QUICKY, a handle which had come to him long ago and back upwhen. While doing his primary flight training on

NAS Whiting Field near Pensacola, a young Lieutenant Kolhammer had so often had to leave the station to fix up lodgings for himself and his fiancée that gossip soon started that he was off base for 'a quicky with the missus'. The name stuck. Even after being separated from Marie for so long, he had not felt able to let go of that link to her. It would have been a betrayal.

The nickname remained a secret, protected by some aggressively leaked disinformation that the President's call sign as a young flyer had been the rather unimaginative 'Sledge'.

The tanker's boom operator might get a scare when it came time to chat over the closed-circuit link, but then again, thought Kolhammer, *maybe not*. The tanker was RAF, and the flight crew wouldn't necessarily recognise his voice. There were still a handful of carefully husbanded F-35s flying black ops and few enough tankers to support them, so it wouldn't be all that unusual to service a flight like this.

Cloud tops, silvered by moonlight, lay far below him, a silent landscape of fantastic shapes and sometimes eerie effect. It was a magical sight, these impossible shapes illuminated by the cool moonlight; some like rolling waves of silver, some like fantastic castles. The effect was both enchanting and slightly unnerving. The fighters and their great, lumbering fuel cow flew straight and level over the vast ranges of cirrostratus, staying close enough together that Kolhammer fancied he could make out individual rivets on the fuselage of his nearest escort if he just squinted a little.

He couldn't, of course.

But it was a pleasant enough conceit, aided by the crystal-clear air at this altitude, the combat optics processors in his helmet, and the bright wash of moonlight and the stars.

It was such a fairytale scene, painted in hues of tranquillity and romance that a younger, more naïve observer might have struggled to believe that the world beneath the clouds was ravaged by war. But Kolhammer was no longer young and had never been especially innocent. As he waited his turn at the bowser, he scanned for threats and prepared for the worst.

"You're up, Quicky."

Kolhammer eased forward and up, inching towards a connection between the probe and drogue unit.

The voice of the RAF specialist crackled inside his helmet, guiding him in. He was inches from making the hook-up when both planes flew into a pocket of rough air, buffeting them. It wasn't especially turbulent, but it was enough to throw him out of sync. Kolhammer gripped the stick tighter and tried to steady himself, cursing silently as he missed the connection. He nudged back and prepared to make another attempt, trying to clear his head and sharpen his focus. He could hear the RAF specialist's voice, "Apologies from the captain. We're good to go again if you are, 5-0."

"I'm coming in now," Kolhammer said. "God willing, and the creek don't rise."

He had performed this manoeuvre countless times as a young pilot officer. Dozens of times in the hot zone around Taiwan. But that was a long time ago, in a future far, far away, and the handful of training runs he'd done to maintain his certification could not truly prepare him for the real thing. He took a deep breath, counted a second and let it go slowly. Another breath. Held this one for seconds. Let it go.

Second time lucky, he thought, as the probe settled into the basket and connectors locked into place. He felt his balls had dropped from whatever cave they'd been hiding in. The tanker started pumping while Kolhammer scanned his readouts, received to see his fuel gauge going up.

There were no further problems, and with his tanks filled, HAWAII 5-0 disengaged and quickly cleared the tanker's jetwash. Kolhammer rejoined the four escort jets at 40,000 feet.

A tone in his helmet alerted him to an incoming burst of quantum-encrypted satellite data. He wondered if it was from a USAF bird or one of Davidson's dual-use sats. The audio message played in his earphones as an electronic map popped up in his HUD, a series of bright, vividly coloured dots, lines and symbols that provided a navigational and tactical overview out to five hundred klicks.

"Be advised 5-0, this is Atlantic Command. We have a hard target confirm on a Soviet Carrier Battlegroup three hundred klicks to your north. The main hull is the *Stalingrad*."

"Acknowledged," Kolhammer sent back.

The 35's onboard systems compressed and encrypted the short transmission before squirting it into space in a tight beam transmission back to the satellite.

The *Stalingrad* was the second carrier the Soviets had built to replace the Moskva class carriers, which the Japanese had ripped to pieces in '44. Displacing 67,000 tons, she carried forty-eight jets and bristled with close-in-weapons systems. For sure, the jets were crudely navalized MiG-19s, but the four Raduga air-to-air missiles each carried were not to be fucked with.

A quick check on the data dump told him he was about 400 nautical miles southwest of Keflavik Airbase in Iceland and could get down on the ground there before any of the *Stalingrad*'s fighters could find them. Alternatively, they could just put pedal to the metal and burn hard for home.

The big RAF tanker wobbled its wings and began a long looping turn east, a fragile tin whale trailing a kite tail of vapour.

It hadn't been twenty seconds before the F-35's passive systems had detected the kiss of an E band radar pulse on the plane's EM absorbent skin. The jet's AI instantly matched the signal to an entry in its database and confirmed that a Soviet AEW plane was 200 klicks northeast of them. A Minion, most likely. That far out into the Atlantic, it had to mean that there was a carrier nearby. The Minion didn't have the legs to have flown from Polyarny.

Kolhammer grunted, "Looks like we've got some friends from the *Stalingrad* come to play."

"Engage laser communication system," he told the plane.

"Communication enabled", the system replied.

The F-35 found the escort fighters' laser-receiving pods, a hurried addition to this mission. Communication would be one way.

"Rise and shine, ladies and gentlemen. We have company, 300 klicks north. I'll bet good folding money that it's the Stalingrad Battlegroup. We've just been painted by an active sweeper a hundred klicks southwest of the *Stalingrad*. I'll keep an eye out for unwanted guests and will advise. Stay dark for now."

The escorts all waggled their wingtips in acknowledgment.

He deployed a hunter-killer drone from the stealth fighter's weapons bay and instructed it to take station fifty klicks back east. The scram jets in the fast, wedge-shaped drone fired up, and it raced away to the southeast at speeds no human pilot could endure.

Kolhammer powered up the F-35's suite of threat detection and analysis tools. His Heads Up Display quickly filled with tactical information. None of it was good.

The Russians had already locked onto the RAF tanker and were burning up the airspace around her with electromagnetic effects, searching for whoever she'd been servicing.

The invisible EM cone washed over the Tigers once, twice, and three times before suddenly fixing on them. They'd been seen.

He could imagine the activity on the flight deck of the *Stalingrad* as the CIC relayed the data to her commander. The first MiGs could be roaring down the armoured deck plates if the carrier sailed into the wind.

He checked the enemy's heading against the meteorological data for her position and decided, yes, the Sovs had caught a break.

The RAF tanker increased her speed by seventy knots and adjusted her heading to increase the delta between her track and the enemy. Soft, wispy layers of cirrostratus unfurled beneath her wings, reaching as far as the eye could see. They rolled and curled with gentle grace like fog gliding over a lake.

The tanker did not break radio silence to contact Kolhammer or his escorts as it disappeared inside one of the largest formations.

Brave people, he thought. If the Minion's sensors and processor stacks were advanced enough to identify the tanker by type, the *Stalingrad*'s commander would surge whatever he could spare to bring her down. The flying Avgas barges were not glamorous, but they were massive force multipliers. Losing even one would be a hard blow.

Kolhammer decided before he realized he'd even asked himself the question.

He re-opened the laser link to the Tigers and said, "Good morning, ladies and gentlemen. There will be a temporary disruption to our planned itinerary. Please follow me and prepare to engage the enemy."

THE TUMANSKY TURBOJETS threw Pilot Officer Vladimir Komarov off the ski jump of the *Stalingrad* with five and half thousand pounds of thrust. His nuts, his guts, perhaps his very soul seemed to drop through the metal floor of the fighter as he pulled back on the stick and fed even more power to the engines. The sound of take-off was always shocking. A deep, bellowing roar vibrated through the cockpit and into Pilot Officer Komarov's chest, shaking every cell and nerve ending from his toes to his scalp. His wingman, Shoigu, often joked that it sounded like the screams of two thousand angry brides as he fled the chapel with his nuts intact.

The feeling of sudden freedom was exhilarating.

Komarov took the MiG into a battle climb, spearing her towards heaven to gain vital altitude and fighting space as quickly as possible. Of course, being a good and reliable communist, he did not believe in heaven, but the old archaic word seemed somehow... appropriate. Or perhaps just poetically descriptive of the vast, black, star-dusted universe into which he led his squadron. Calves of soft, creamy clouds drooped over the dark shadow peaks, pushing one massive dome-shaped protrusion up against the moon. Thin, ragged fingers of lightning flickered there, bathing the clouds in brilliant white and electric blue as they slithered from one peak to the other. Komarov fancied he could taste the ozone frying.

All twelve of his men followed him into the night sky, riding hard for the enemy like the old Cossacks. The target was a small flight of American fast jets and a much larger, slower tanker that could be American or British. Both of the fascist air forces flew the KC-25. Bagging her would be the main prize, the strategic payoff for the vigilance of his comrade pilots in the *Stalingrad*'s AEW division. To take down a tanker would mean squeezing the chokehold just that little bit harder around all the fighters she would otherwise have supported.

However, personally, Pilot Officer Vladimir Komarov was most looking forward to finding and killing the little Tigers.

There were four of them, probably heading to Iceland to reinforce the American outpost there, and cutting them out of the sky would immeasurably improve the odds of the *Stalingrad*'s task force seizing the island. On his radar display, they hung suspended as fuzzy little yellow blobs. They appeared so innocent. But this would be a worthy battle. A good kill, even with their numbers unevenly matched. The American planes were, after all, somewhat more advanced than his simple warcraft.

Komarov let the engines scream all the way to the fighter's ceiling, well above the clouds. Punching out of the grey-black fog and into the moonlit sky was a moment of pure joy in a seemingly infinite reach of darkness and mystery. Shimmering stars twinkled against the black canvas with a brilliant white moon.

Far away, to the north, he saw the northern lights. Ribbons of energy twisted and turned across the sky, wrapping the stars in a soft haze of pastel colour. Komarov smiled for the last time in his short life.

THE SMALL WEDGE-SHAPED HAMMERHEAD drone sped away from Kolhammer's F-35 at speeds no human pilot could hope to endure; its exhaust trails a bright blue streak in the sky. Along the great arc of its flight path, it deployed smaller, less capable sub-drones, which held station within a complicated matrix refreshed thousands of times a second by the hammerhead's onboard Combat Intelligence.

Triangulating against the US and Soviet squadrons, the primary UAV pulsed out a signal to its subordinates, lighting them up. Active sensors suddenly flared across hundreds of miles of airspace, bathing the MiGs in a rich electromagnetic radiance that the Russians could barely detect, let alone disrupt.

In the cockpit of his F-35, Kolhammer's helmet displays filled with strike options. The airspace around him crawled with red lines representing enemy planes and flight paths, green lines for friendlies, and a swarm of yellow blips indicating the Hammerhead drones. He heard a light beep whenever a new strike option appeared on his display.

It had been many decades since he had flown in combat, and even then, he had ridden to war in an F-18. He had thousands of hours of stick time on the old Hornets, only a hundred or so in the plane he was currently flying, and no direct experience of fighting with a drone swarm.

But the potency of the F-35 wasn't hidden in its stealth capabilities or the programmable warheads stowed away inside its weapons bay.

The F-35's power came from data.

Kolhammer knew he wasn't seeing even a fraction of the vast rivers of data flowing from the Hammerhead drone and its string of tiny minions. Most of that information was sucked up, processed, analyzed, and actioned somewhere inside the dense carbon nanoweave wafer stack of the jet fighter's Combat Intelligence. If you took the time to think about it, it was disturbing and uncanny how much agency had been ceded to those alien intellects back upwhen. It wouldn't have surprised him to find out an Intelligence had been responsible for creating the wormhole that exiled him back here.

He did not have the time to dwell on such things, however.

The Intelligence observed and acted upon the data feed long before any human would have known what to do. However, it gave him six response options, and Kolhammer chose the first, slaving the much more primitive systems on board the Tigers to his own. His eyes settled on the red hologram, and he toggled a switch on his control stick to create the instant network of supersonic weapons platforms.

A message pulsed out on the laser link, warning the other pilots who were now just along for the ride. There was no sign of the enemy within visual range when the volley rippled away from the Tigers on long, white fingers of rocket exhaust. The small, bright supernovas threw eldritch fans of white light on the grey battlements of cloud below. The coordinated launch of so many missiles cut through his helmet like the hissing roar of a dragon.

Four long-range air-to-air missiles dropped into the void from the concealed missile bays underneath his fuselage, fired up, and shot north towards the enemy.

Kolhammer followed the track of the warshots until they closed with the tiny red triangles of the onrushing MiGs. One after another, the hostiles winked out of existence.

PILOT OFFICER VLADIMIR KOMAROV knew something was wrong a heartbeat before realising he could do nothing about it.

He had formed his squadron into three tactical packets, which he would deploy as soon as he saw how the fascists responded to the attack.

They would respond one way or another. Their technologies were undeniably more advanced than those of his aircraft, but they were outgunned. They would have the disadvantage of needing to manoeuvre to protect the vulnerable, slow-moving tanker. It was such a deliciously promising set-up that Komarov felt his mouth start to water. The very opposite of what he'd been trained to expect.

The wingtips of his planes moved in perfect unison, and the moonlight reflecting off metal made them look like a single, shimmering entity. The People's spearhead, driving towards their foe.

He glanced to his left to nod to Shoigu, wondering when the Americans would discern they were under attack when Komarov realised with a start that he had been targeted.

He almost choked on his spit.

It was not the warning systems of his MiG that alerted him, but rather the keen eye of Junior Lieutenant Piotr Chrulski, who broke radio silence with some babbling torrent about incoming jets on his two o'clock.

Komarov was about to tear him a new one when he saw what Chrulski had seen. One...no, three or more bright, golden flares of starlight, growing larger and...

He had just enough time to call out a warning before the missile swarm intercepted them.

JUST BEFORE THE last hostile track disappeared from his VR projections, Kolhammer searched the far horizon for some indication that he had reached out and touched the world for real. Some flash of light, a flicker of distant fire. He listened for any loud booms echoing across the sky, like thunderclaps and drums. He did so, knowing he could not expect to hear anything.

There was nothing. Just the blue-silver wash of starlight on the clouds.

A pleasing tone in his helmet informed him that the RAF tanker had already flown beyond the known attack radius of the Soviet battle group. He smiled to think of the relief among the crew and was sorry it wasn't impossible to talk to them again.

Kolhammer released the other fighters from his network just as the F-35's Combat Intelligence recommended a single follow-up strike, which he quickly authorised.

One hundred and thirty nautical miles away, the Hammerhead drone received its final order. Tilting over at thirty degrees and diving down through the clouds, it dropped through thousands of feet, picking up speed. Kolhammer watched a feed from the Hammerhead in a small pop-up window on his VR monitor. It raced across the surface of the sea, the blue-back composites of its stealth shielding beginning to glow with the heat of friction, but it stayed on course, accelerating to the edge of its hypersonic envelope until it reached its target.

There was no sign that the enemy even knew they were dead. A second pop-up displayed a super-slow replay of the take from the drone's sensor suite. Kolhammer watched, fascinated and a little horrified. He had once sailed on ships like that one. Hundreds of men hurried about their duties on the deck, where a squadron of fighters was being readied for take-off. The battle pennants of the 7th Soviet

Operational Squadron snapped and fluttered proudly in the freshening breeze.

As it dived and accelerated to a little over six thousand kilometres an hour, algorithms in the Hammerhead's onboard processors evaluated all the data streaming in through its sensors. In a fraction of a second, the drone decided on the location of the carrier's nuclear reactor and adjusted its attack path.

When it struck the *Stalingrad*, the programmable warhead detonated with a sub-nuclear yield powerful enough to cleave the giant carrier in two and destroy a much smaller frigate from her escort group, which took the full force of the blast wave. The detonation lit up the night sky like a miniature sun, and this he did see. They could all see it from hundreds of klicks away.

Video capture from the surviving drones died momentarily inside a brilliant, blinding white light. But optical processors quickly reformatted, and he could see the mammoth fireball that had consumed the thousand-foot-long flat-top. Around its edges flickered tinges of yellow, orange, and red, a ring of fire radiating outwards. As its power weakened, the night sky pushed back in, glowing an eerie green before fading to its natural darkness.

Just lost the Greenpeace vote, Kolhammer thought before opening the radio channel to his escorts.

"My apologies, ladies and gentlemen. I didn't mean to cut in like that, but we didn't have time to stay and party. We need to get gone."

The five aircraft turned south and poured on speed for home.

EPILOGUE

The First Comrade's sleep was unsettled. Lavrenty Beria stirred in his bed, his eyes fluttering open to the dimly lit room. The lights were turned low as if the whole Kremlin was trying to hide from him.

A shiver ran through him as he pushed the light woollen blanket aside and swung his legs over the side of the bed. The summer night was warm, but the tiles under his feet were surprisingly cool. The room smelled of old wax and cigarettes. The air did not move.

His eyes caught the reflection of his face in a mirror, and before he could recognise himself and mentally edit the image into some more pleasing visage, he saw the reality. The mask of a haunted man, the lines etched deeply into his flesh. The room was dead silent, save for the rasp of his breathing.

With a grunt, Beria rose and went to the window, looking out over an internal courtyard. The pale moon cast an eerie glow on the lush grass and flower beds. The Kremlin's towers stood watch like silent sentinels.

He stared out into the night. It was after 2 am, the hour when he would send men to haul the enemies of the state from their beds. His heart quickened for no reason he could think of.

He turned away from the window, his eyes on the pistol by his bed. If his turn came, it would make little or no difference. But it still felt good to have the gun close to hand. And for now, at least, he judged himself more likely to die from some American bomb or long-range rocket than from treachery within the Kremlin walls.

The soft rustle of footsteps outside his chamber broke his reverie, causing his heart to skip another beat. A soft knock at the door, three taps. It was only his trusted aide, Prokofiev.

"Enter," Beria said, almost choking on his dry throat.

He picked up a glass of water from the bedside table and was about to sip when he thought the better of it.

He had not slept well, but he had slept.

He did not know what was in the glass now.

Prokofiev entered the room, bearing a tray with a single steaming cup of tea. The old comrade's face was stoic, as always.

"Comrade, I heard you rise. I thought you might like tea. I have made it myself," Prokofiev spoke quietly. Beria nodded, his hand trembling slightly as he reached for the cup, the porcelain feeling thin and fragile against his fingertips. His fears, he could let this man see. But this man alone.

"There is news," Prokofiev said. "From Comrade Skarov."

As he sipped the sweet, hot brew, Beria felt a sudden sense of hope and dread, the two so closely entwined he could not tell one from the other.

"What news?" Beria asked, his whisper harsh and almost too eager.

"Good news," Prokofiev smiled. “Good news, Comrade.”

ALSO BY JOHN BIRMINGHAM

The *End of Days* series.
Zero Day Code.
Fail State.
American Kill Switch.

The Axis of Time.
Weapons of Choice
Designated Targets
Final Impact
Stalin's Hammer
World War 3.1
(World War 3.2 & 3.3 coming in 2024)

A Girl Time in Time.
A Girl in Time.
The Golden Minute.
The Clockwork Heart (coming in 2024)

The Cruel Stars series.
The Cruel Stars

The Shattered Skies
The Forever Dead (2024)

Dave vs the Monsters series
Emergence.
Resistance.
Ascendance.
A Soul Full of Guns.
A Protocol for Monsters.

CHEESEBURGERGOTHIC

Hi. It's me, JB. If you liked this book and you'd like more of the same, sometimes for free, please join me over at my blog/book club/dive bar on the internet.

At the moment, it's hosted on Substack, but it kind of moves around, and wherever it ends up, it's *always* called CheeseburgerGothic.

Just throw that into el Goog or whatever AI chatbot runs the world now, and I'm sure they'll hook you up. I give away free stories there at least once a month. And my faves—everyone who signs up at the Burger is my favourite—get steep discounts on new releases.

Everyone else? Well, my friends, don't be like them.

I look forward to seeing you there.

John Birmingham

PO Box 437

Bulimba, Queensland 4171

Australia

Created with Vellum

www.ingramcontent.com/pod-product-compliance
Lightning Source LLC
LaVergne TN
LVHW050922080826
845145LV00001B/181